PUSHKIN PRESS
In association with
WALTER PRESENTS

THE SECOND LIFE OF INSPECTOR CANESSA

In a world where we have so much choice, curation is becoming increasingly key. Walter Presents was first set up to champion brilliant drama from around the world and bring it to a wider audience.

Now, in collaboration with Pushkin Press, we're hoping to do the same thing for foreign literature: translating brilliant books into English, introducing them to readers who are hungry for quality fiction.

This book was recommended to me by an Italian friend with impeccable taste. Set in the 1970s, it follows the story of legendary former cop, Annibale Canessa, forced out of his Italian Riviera retirement to investigate the brutal killing of his estranged brother in Milan. The action flicks between Canessa's past and present, weaving a page-turning web of corruption and deception. A quintessential Italian hero is born in this thrilling crime story.

THE
SECOND LIFE
OF INSPECTOR
CANESSA

ROBERTO
PERRONE

TRANSLATED FROM THE ITALIAN
BY HAMISH GOSLOW

PUSHKIN PRESS
In association with
WALTER PRESENTS

Pushkin Press
71–75 Shelton Street
London WC2H 9JQ

The Second Life of Inspector Canessa was first published as
La Seconda Vita di Annibale Canessa by Rizzoli in Milan, 2017

First published by Pushkin Press in 2020

1 3 5 7 9 8 6 4 2

ISBN 13: 978-1-78227-621-0

Designed and typeset by Tetragon, London
Printed and bound by CPI Group (UK) Ltd, Croydon, CRO 4YY

www.pushkinpress.com

THE
SECOND LIFE
OF INSPECTOR
CANESSA

To Gérard de Villiers

TRANSLATOR'S NOTE ON CARABINIERI

Annibale Canessa and Ivan Repetto, the main characters in the novel, belong to the Carabinieri, Italy's national gendarmerie. Carabinieri are one of the four major branches of Italian law enforcement, alongside the Polizia (Police), the Guardia di Finanza (Finance Police), and the Army proper, from which they split in 2001. Their duties overlap with the Polizia, though they are also employed to police the military, and are regularly deployed alongside the latter in missions abroad.

Their ranking system follows its own rules, though names may be similar to other forces, and are divided into four major careers: Officer, Inspector, Superintendent, and Carabiniere. Throughout the text, Canessa follows the Officer path, eventually leaving the force as a Colonel, while Repetto remains in the Inspector bracket, leaving with the role of First Marshal.

Their official motto is *Nei Secoli Fedele* – 'Loyal through the centuries' – which is not dissimilar to the US Marine Corps' *Semper Fidelis*. One of their unofficial sayings, however, can also be found in the text: *Usi Obbedir Tacendo* [*e Tacendo Morir*] (lit. 'used to obey in silence, and in silence die'); this is a quotation from the poem 'La Rassegna di Novara' by Costantino Nigra, in which the poet uses the line to describe the Carabinieri as King of Sardinia Charles Albert looks over the various parts of what will eventually become the Royal Italian Army.

PROLOGUE

Many years earlier, many years later

H E FELT, rather than saw, the gun in his hands. This was no dream, but a vivid memory, with the power to tear apart whatever he was doing at that moment. Once it came over him, it was all there was. And here it was again.

How could an actual memory break into a dream? He was sure this only happened to him. And when it did, he had to sit down or lean against something. Calm down, let the images run their course, wait for them to stop. That's what he did this time too, perching on the edge of the mattress. He could hear soft snoring from the bed above him. He'd given his place to the latest arrival – almost begged him to take it.

He breathed and waited in the darkness.

It started with touch, then moved to sight. Everything was clear in his memory, even though the day was dark and the main colour, grey. He felt the rough stock of the Tokarev TT-33, a Yugoslavian pistol with nine rounds.

Gazing down the barrel of the gun, he saw a man holding two children by the hand, a boy and a girl. He stared at them, knowing full well what was about to happen. He wasn't afraid – not for himself anyway. Looking around, he saw trees, flowerbeds, a crowded street, the road ahead and cars stuck in traffic on this winter's morning. The chaos, crowds, and people – none of this had ever stopped them. But the children were new. They'd chosen to strike before the man dropped them off at school. Why? Wouldn't it have been better *after*? That was the one detail he couldn't see clearly. Maybe because it belonged to the previous days.

He looked at the gun again. Nothing was happening. Everything was on hold. It was all down to him. He was supposed to open fire. He was the leader. In the meantime, the man pushed the girl a few metres away and she looked shocked, almost hurt by his sudden behaviour. He couldn't move the boy, who held on to his hand with improbable strength, sticking stubbornly at his side. That's why he hesitated. He gripped the Tokarev, which was just waiting for his orders: loyal, reliable, a weapon that had never let him down.

The gun sat still in his hand while he watched the boy, who wouldn't let go of his father's. He felt something sharp – a knife in his guts – at the scene. It wasn't just fear in the boy's eyes: there was something deeper, something that went beyond familial affection. This was more than a lifeline chucked to a dinghy from a rescue boat during a storm. But even if it hadn't been, he asked himself: is there anyone I could throw a rope to? He didn't care about the man or the boy. It wasn't pity or emotion he was feeling. He only cared about that question, so violent it stopped him in his tracks.

His thoughts were drowned out by a gunshot. He turned to his accomplice, who had just opened fire and he grimaced as if to say: what are we doing here with our guns in the middle of the road, while people are screaming and fleeing, and somebody's called the police? So he started shooting too, on auto-pilot: one, two, three times. The man, at first hit only in the arm, now collapsed to the ground, dragging the boy with him. The boy started sobbing, but he was unharmed, considering that he was still clinging to his bullet-riddled dad and covered in his blood. The accomplice was moving in to finish the man off, when sirens started blaring close by. He turned back with a nasty grin. 'He's croaked.'

He looked at the boy once more, before someone pulled him away.

A few minutes later, when they'd driven some way from the shooting, the other man growled: 'The fuck were you thinkin', eh, Pino?' That Neapolitan accent grated on him like nothing else in the world.

He didn't reply. He was thinking, like he would nearly every day for the next thirty years, of the small hand gripping the larger one, of the tie that bound them together. Something powerful, something absolute. Something he would start feeling himself only many years later, during his life's second act, on the final downhill slope.

Dedication. Loyalty.

There: that's what it was. Having someone you'd never let go of, someone you'd hold on to tightly. Someone who was special.

Dedication. Loyalty.

For thirty years, that memory had knocked him sideways each time he mentally reran the details. (He added nothing, omitted nothing: if he wanted, he'd have been the perfect witness.)

Yet even though it kept coming back, the memory no longer troubled him.

He'd found the answers he'd been looking for. He could finally make that phone call.

I

The Third Millennium

I

C URSING HER AGE, Maggese's widow struggled out of bed. Climbing out of that sarcophagus was even worse than getting into it. 'I'll get a new one tomorrow,' she kept saying, 'this is the last time I'm sleeping in that.' The following night, of course, she'd be back, and every time she felt like she was jumping from an even greater height. Naturally, it was just an impression: the bed had been the same for the past thirty years. It was an old bed, dating back to the end of the 1900s, already too high to begin with. And then her poor late husband Aristide had put a mattress on it that was so tall it looked like a six-storey building. She'd tried to tell him that it was too high, and he, never domineering, had kindly replied that it was good for their health, and they'd come to love it over time. 'Because it's so far from the city smog?'

Aristide was a big man, and he never had to jump to get off. He just let his feet touch the floor. But she was so small that when they got together, their families said they'd have to use a ladder in order to kiss. In any case, she'd never complained and she never changed the bed out of respect and nostalgia, not even after his passing.

Some of her students said cruelly, 'Yeah, he died because she tested him on the Pythagoras theorem, too.' Maggese's widow had taught maths all her life. She only retired when they wouldn't let her stay any longer. Had it been up to her, she'd still be teaching equations and geometry – pointlessly, for the most part. She was a widow and a grandma four times over, thanks to her sons, who lived in Bologna.

They didn't live too far from her neighbourhood in Reggio Emilia, but she barely even saw them at Easter or Christmas. 'Ah, young people these days,' she thought, 'they don't observe the church festivals, they don't even eat' – and admittedly only her late husband had done justice to her impressive Christmas menu. Her sons, their wives, and her grandchildren just picked at the dishes – 'They don't respect their mothers and fathers.' As a young teacher on the Po delta, she'd endured a hellish bus journey, crossing the whole of Emilia to get to her parents' farm as soon as she could. A woman who often made the same journey once told her, 'It'd be easier to reach America by steamer.'

'Oh well,' she cut herself off. 'I should let it go, these are an old woman's thoughts.' She jumped off the bed, her landing as shaky as ever, and headed to the bathroom. On her way back, passing through what she liked to call the dinette, she shifted the curtain aside to look out, drawn by the light of a full moon. She nearly let out a surprised 'Oh!'

Under the large orange tree that dominated the garden of a semi identical to hers, on a swing he'd built for his daughter, was her neighbour from across the road. Maggese's widow looked at the bright kitchen wall clock. It was almost too bright – she hadn't

14

worked out how to change the settings. Four-thirty a.m. What was he doing there at that hour, pushing himself gently on the swing? Had he and his wife had a domestic? Strange, they were such a kind and loving couple. All three of them very well mannered, the girl too: 'Good morning Mrs Maggese,' she learned to say, right after her first steps.

She stared at him a little longer, trying to make out his expression, but the moonlight made his features hard to read. He didn't look like an adulterer.

'I hope it's nothing too serious,' the widow concluded. She headed back towards her bed and prepared herself yet again for the ascent.

'I was baptised and brought up in the Orthodox Christian faith.'

Whenever he read the opening line of Tolstoy's *A Confession*, he'd see himself a child again in a big church, holding on to a small ivory book. In shorts and long white socks, he frantically directed his thoughts towards the heavens, trying to be pure and close to God, as he'd been taught in Sunday School. Who knows why the only church he really remembered from his childhood was the baroque one in the centre of Genoa. He'd stand under the vault in a grey suit, his shorts barely grazing his knee, hands joined together, the bored uncle behind him playing godfather, and the small prayer book he kept happily turning in his hands because it was shiny and new. He'd always liked books, especially new ones.

Like Tolstoy, he'd also been raised within a faith. It had all ended quickly, not long after his confirmation.

He'd picked up that library book, compelled by an unsettling feeling he'd had ever since he'd grabbed the phone some time before, answering on the third ring. And so, for the four hours' train journey ahead, two there, two back, he'd chosen the reading that had always been, for him, a precursor to change.

It was a small edition, a youthful theft (back then they were called 'proletarian expropriations') from some occupied library: first edition, December 1979. The unsettling feeling got stronger when he read the date and linked it to the phone conversation and the period of his life it had unearthed. But he hadn't been able to say no. He might have been good at omitting facts, but he couldn't tell an out-and-out lie. If it had happened a day earlier, on Thursday, he could've used work as an excuse, blaming the impossibility of asking for leave at such short notice from the public library where he worked as a supervisor. A weird irony, really: he'd spent so many years removing books (illegally, he knew now, but not back then), that now in the second half of his life he looked after and defended them. But not today, not on a Saturday.

Sara would be taking their daughter to Scouts and he'd planned a long lazy day of reading. Then, at dinner, the phone call came and he found himself here, at four-thirty in the morning, swaying gently on the swing he'd built for his daughter under their wild orange tree.

On the other side of the street, a light came on. Maggese's widow pulled her curtain aside.

Napoleone Canessa smiled and lit himself a cigarette. The light from the match flickered for a second in the darkness. He thought about the meeting, the reason the man wanted to see him in Milan just before eight. Why such a rush? as if time were slipping through his fingers. He sat there, thinking, uncertain, asking himself the same question that had been weighing on him for hours, and had kept him from enjoying a nice evening with his wife and daughter. *Why me?* Then he realised. *Maybe I'm just a middleman, a means to get to someone else.*

The potential role of mediator worried him even more than the phone call, the journey ahead, the uncertainties raised by the voice from his past. If his suspicions turned out to be true, he would end up confronting the one person in the world he hoped never to see again, and hadn't seen in thirty years: his brother.

2

Judge Federico Astroni became aware of the woman only when she was directly behind him. If she'd wanted to take him out – as he often imagined it going down: killed by a woman, a *pasionaria*, like Marat with Charlotte Conday in the consul's bathroom – she could've done so at any moment. She was incredibly quiet and, of course, incredibly thorough. Though her world was so different to his she was always ahead of the game, a quality he shared and was glad to have found in her – and in his collaborators more generally – after searching long and hard.

The Filipina help placed the small tray on the desk and said, '*Signor*, your coffee.'

The magistrate smiled at that word. She never said *signore*, only *signor*. He'd once tried to convince her to finish the word, but no joy. Whenever she spoke to a guest, that *signor* would linger and the guests waited in vain for the addition of their name or surname: *Signor… Rossi, Signor… Carlo*. But no. Her *signor* would float in mid-air, and disappear along with her.

Astroni's linguistic musings had been inspired by the work he was doing on that warm, bright morning in Milan. So, he went back to his paperwork and took out the Tippex to remove the adjective *indissoluble*. He really didn't like it. He grabbed the thesaurus and opted for *indivisible*, which was a better fit for the theory he was trying to get across: a real leader exercises power and doesn't manage it; therefore, crucial decisions cannot be shared, or even worse, delegated. They fall on one person; therefore, one person had to be guilty.

Judge Astroni wrote his statements, speeches, and talks on the computer (well, he didn't, his team did), later editing them by hand, polishing them with his enormous, black, phallic Montblanc and its silver tip. It was a precious gift from a Milan aristocrat. He made frequent visits to her salons, and cautious ones to her bed. 'So when you send all those people to the stake,' she'd told him with melodramatic flair, 'I'll be pleased to know I have a part in it.'

She was an attractive fifty-year-old. Back in the 70s she'd taken on the revolutionary aesthetic along with so many others. They'd marched around Italy wearing colourful fake jewellery, shapeless jumpers, long skirts, messy hair. Sworn enemies of cleanliness and tidiness, they now sought the priciest beauty salons. They were worse than the men, more extreme. They took part in assemblies, marches, *okkupations*, convinced that they were history's heroes, instead of realising that it was a phase, a hobby, something they'd drop as they might drop fishing, crochet, restoring old furniture or yoga. Which is exactly what had happened. Admittedly, some of them stayed true to their youthful ideals, some to the clothing or the infrequent showers and baths. But they'd long since left the squats and communes in favour of mansion blocks and flats, the nice comfy houses their families could afford.

He smiled. In those days, Astroni would've pushed her away: he had *actually* tried bringing about the revolution. He hadn't just played a part. He truly wanted to believe that his struggle had not changed – the times had. And with them, above all, the means. He would never have thought back then that the State would be on his side, the same institutions he'd dreamt of overthrowing and was now serving, supported by adoring masses he wholeheartedly despised.

So he'd included her in his invisible harem, which everyone knew about, including the journalists at the courts of law, but no one was brave enough to reveal – one or two out of respect, but most out of fear. Because he was Judge Federico Astroni, the Office's former *enfant prodige*, the protégé of the prosecutor himself. The real leader of the group, the best read, the best prepared, the man who had 'fucked' everyone (horrible phrase, but he did enjoy its crudeness), who broke the law, politicians, business people, small fry and big cheese in public office, political parties and private companies.

Playing both accuser and judge, he'd forgiven a few of those he'd led to his office in handcuffs blubbing, waving photos of their young children, old mothers, widows, and telling him of terminal illnesses in an appeal to his sentimentality. Others he'd simply destroyed, even for the smallest of sins. It depended on his role, the situation, sometimes a spur-of-the-moment thing. But there was one thing above all others that really sparked his cold, determined rage: resistance. That was the reason he had wanted to drag to court – successfully, too – the leader of the biggest opposition party, the only one who hadn't come crawling but had challenged him outright, in public, claiming political persecution, calling him a 'terrorist', setting his journalist friends on him, taking refuge in private TV studios. Maybe Judge Astroni had started his investigation because he saw the remains of the country's toxic politics, an enemy of his own ideas and what he believed he stood for. But later, it was no longer for that reason. Even if he'd never admit as much, it had turned into pure, visceral hatred. It was personal. Me or him. Sure, the wealthy politician had some faults, but nothing that warranted that amount of effort or attention.

Everything in his life had led up to this, and it would destroy him in the end.

He recalled another man he'd hated in the same way, though for different reasons. He dismissed the memory, drank his coffee and headed over to the window.

Because of him, no one could park outside his apartment building, which was located in a square in the city centre. At the height of the corruption investigation, when the names of the presiding magistrates were on everyone's lips and everyone saw them at home thanks to the papers and TV, talk shows, and live court reports, one of his neighbours had practically knelt before him on the street: 'For you, I'd park my car in Beijing, even give you my home.'

That kneeling man was now behind a petition lying on a table at the building's entrance, where the post accumulated. Essentially, they were requesting that life return to normal: no bans (especially the no-parking ban), no security checks, no more heavy police presence. If his safety was truly at stake, why didn't he get out of there? They were tired of the tight security and having to park some blocks away.

He'd have felt disheartened if he had built his beliefs, convictions and work around these people. Serve the masses? Nonsense. Luckily, everything he'd done had been for his own benefit.

Astroni felt good. His reflection in the window showed a tall man with thick, curly hair. Behind golden glasses (used only for reading, since his sight was pretty good otherwise) were the eyes he'd inherited from his father, a royal magistrate removed from his post for refusing to join the fascist party. Happily, the family had enough money for that not to have been a problem.

Downstairs were two parked cars, his own and the escort's. One of the Carabinieri was leaning against the car, his gaze focused, scanning the rooftops. Their eyes met. The judge waved and the Carabiniere replied with a slight nod. Another loyal subject, chosen after many attempts.

But just then, a shadow fell over the bright day, the working weekend ahead of him and his general optimism. That wave had brought back some bad memories, even worse feelings. For some-one who boasted an ability to predict almost anything, seeing that face on the way out of the courts two weeks earlier had been a real surprise. They'd been in the car at a red light – he didn't like using sirens to weave through the streets unless it was actually necessary. 'Impossible,' he'd thought, and looked again. The person he'd glimpsed had vanished: perhaps a mirage, or if it actually had been him, just a coincidence. Milan was a big city. He could've been there for any reason at all. But then, the following Saturday, he'd headed into the office to pick up some missing paperwork, and there he was again, in the same spot: no crowd this time, so he couldn't be wrong. He'd even used binoculars to make sure. There he was, on the paved area in front of the church of San Pietro in Gessate. He was alone, hands in his jacket pockets, thin grey hair, his icy blue eyes staring at the courts – and almost directly at him, even though it wasn't actually possible from so far away. He was unmistakable, despite the years carved into his face. He'd casually looked into his current situation. No, there was no reason for him to be here, reawakening an old nightmare.

So he'd dialled a number with a heavy heart, and spoken with an even heavier heart to another ghost from the past, the legacy of a time he had erased from his life. Reservations had almost held him back: even touching the phone irritated him. But having talked to him and listened to him, he felt better.

3

Rocco finished his third Coke and threw the empty can into a non-recyclable plastic bag at his feet. In any other situation, he wouldn't have hesitated to chuck it out the window, without a care for the city's cleanliness or decorum, or onto the back seat. But he didn't want to risk leaving any traces behind. Coke was his addiction, maybe because he'd always been too poor to buy it as a kid, and the colourful adverts full of happy people and jingles had made it even more of a success symbol. Now he drank litres of it every day.

Rocco had little regard for the police, especially forensics ('We're not on CSI, mate') and he didn't even believe in DNA testing ('Anything can be disproved in this country'). But better not to leave anything lying around. He suddenly belched long and hard, before turning his fierce grin on the man in the driver's seat of the blue Astra. They were parked in via Cappellini, on the corner of Vittor Pisani.

Nando Panattoni looked at Rocco in disgust, pulled out his phone and punched in a number. 'Train here yet?' he asked.

'Two minutes,' chirped the voice of his assistant Carletti. It was drowned out by the announcement of a freight train entering the station. 'The fast train is right on time.'

Panattoni glanced at the silent, empty street, and pulled on his baseball cap.

'Don't lose him. Try to follow those two when they meet up. I want to know what they're saying to each other, so make good use of the mic. And don't get caught.' Nando put away the phone. He wouldn't fail. This was the toughest, most delicate task of his life, his turning point. No more dirty jobs or secret missions. It was risky, but he had made up his mind; he couldn't put up with that shit any more.

'On your marks,' he barked. Rocco looked at him, on the verge of replying to orders with some obnoxious profanity. Instead, he tilted his head slightly and patted the tennis bag on his lap. There weren't any rackets in it – he'd never played that 'game for sissies'. Instead, there was a short-gripped AK-47, loaded, clean, and checked: 40 shiny 7.62 bullets he'd personally modified to hold an explosive charge at their tip.

Nando Panattoni had met Rocco in his previous life, before he'd become a private investigator in a cushy office on via Bergamo in Milan, and was still a retired fascist enforcer, a former Lazio hooligan a little too old to beat up Rome fans (or anyone else, for that matter). He collected debts for a loan shark in Testaccio, a butcher who paid him in steaks and cuts of lamb. This one time, he'd had to pay a visit to a furniture maker in Formia who found himself priced out by the big furniture companies, the ones that were all the rage in the 80s. The 'bastard' – as the loan shark inevitably called all of his customers – had made the mistake of seeking out the butcher, but hadn't paid him by the deadline. Despite repaying more than double the amount he'd borrowed, he hadn't been able to pay the remaining interest, which meant there was no chance his debt would be cancelled.

And so the 'bastard' had called the butcher to say he considered the matter settled. Thanks, see you later. 'Mate, you gotta break his legs,' the butcher had ordered Panattoni, wrapping up a hundred quid's worth of ribs. 'Tasty, need cookin' Milan style, bit o' rocket, coupla tomatoes on top.' Panattoni had taken his third-hand Fiat 128 (a car that struggled with first gear, and outright ignored second) and driven to the outskirts of Formia with some friends who needed the extra cash. When the furniture maker came out in the dark, Panattoni and his friends blocked his path. Just then, a skinny guy jumped out from behind the 'bastard' brandishing a butterfly knife. Twirling it around, up and down, left and right. It was hypnotising.

'Who the fuck are you?' Panattoni had asked.

'My bodyguard,' the furniture man replied. He was small and ugly. Scary, and suddenly smug.

'This punk?' said one of Panattoni's grunts. But his comment stuck in his throat as Rocco plunged the knife into his leg. At the sight of his friend on the ground, his calf oozing blood, the other man fled the scene. Rocco stared at Panattoni, daring him to follow suit, but Panattoni just stood there.

'How much is this bastard paying you?'

The question threw the kid off.

'Why?'

'I'll double it.'

Rocco gave him the first of many hideous grins and immediately switched sides. The furniture maker ended up with broken tibias and femurs.

And so their partnership began. Panattoni would find and plan the jobs, Rocco would execute them. Intimidation, collections, a couple of extortions. Then the hits started, but Panattoni was only the go-between on those. He didn't want to get directly involved in murder: petty crooks, loan shark victims who squealed too loud, nothing too dangerous. It was during the investigation of one of those crimes that he met his current employers. His existence had definitely improved, but over time he'd become increasingly uneasy. He moved to Milan, opened an investigative agency as a front and started working for his new bosses. He dealt with the dirty work as it got progressively dirtier. And it was all the more two-faced since the instigators were hiding behind a façade of respectable luxury. But there was money. Tons of money. Even more money for that last dirty job. At least, he hoped it would be his last.

'This is it,' he'd tell himself. 'We're going our own separate ways after this'. After all, they'd never been friends. Panattoni had stayed in Rome for a while before moving to Milan, and Rocco was still based in Naples. They used public phones, no mobiles, and only for work: rendezvous, timings, type of job. Harmless conversations, on the surface. No mention of their private lives, at least not from Nando.

Rocco was different. He'd confessed everything about himself, starting with his nickname: his legal name was Ciro D'Alletto. 'Rocco' was after Rocco Siffredi, the porn star.

'Is it a size thing?' Panattoni had asked.

'I wish,' was the answer. His awful boorishness somehow hid sparks of humour, even self-deprecation. It was his gigantic collection of porn, initially videotapes, then DVDs that had earned him his nickname. 'Rare stuff,' he'd say. He spoke as a connoisseur, as if he held a selection of ceramics and not hardcore films of a very specific kind: extreme sex, violence, rapes. All fiction, 'Except,' he'd say, lowering his voice, 'for a dozen originals, from

25

the former Yugoslavia and Thailand.' Snuff films, essentially. Though no one had ever seen them and very few of those privy to the fact believed that filth was real.

The only tangible, objective fact was that Ciro D'Alletto, aka Rocco, was a serial offender, and he'd pounce on women as soon as he could. That's why he had to be kept on a short leash, as Nando Panattoni had always explained to his employers, who were convinced that day trips would arouse suspicion. He insisted that Rocco had to arrive in the morning and leave in the evening – or night at the latest, on the sleeper train. Keeping him around for longer or putting him up overnight would create inevitable security breaches. He was a ticking bomb: he might attack a cleaning lady in a hotel, molest a roommate or, perhaps worse, brutalise a prostitute as soon as he was alone.

Panattoni shook the thought away in disgust. The guy was a psychopathic maniac. Efficient, sure, but a psychopath nonetheless.

Rocco lived in Secondigliano with his grandmother: no father to speak of, and his mother would surface every now and then from some brothel where she was working to support her addiction. But she'd only show up to scrounge a meal, a packet of biscuits, a bed.

His first victim had been a twelve-year-old girl. That's what had made him a killer. Or rather, that's what had made him kill the first time. Panattoni was convinced that he'd have become a killer eventually no matter what. The girl lived in the building across from his, and their road was a type of Berlin wall, a border. Fewer than ten metres divided rampant crime and slums from honest, dignified poverty. On one side people lived in awful conditions by choice, on the other they survived with discipline, clean houses, and everyone had a small job somewhere. She was the daughter of an Alfa Romeo employee – a good man and a card-carrying communist, like his wife. They'd go round the neighbourhood on Sundays selling the party newspaper, and Rocco used their absence to get into their house and rape their daughter. Her father lost his mind. Instead of reporting Rocco, he'd waited for him at the front door and gave him such a beating that he landed him in hospital. Rocco was in a terrible condition. He ended up in traction and they removed his spleen. But he never revealed the name of his attacker, nor did the police ask for it. They couldn't care less who'd beaten up that piece of human garbage. In fact, they might've congratulated him if they'd known.

Rocco got out a couple of months later, and it took him three more to walk again. He waited. As soon as he thought he was ready, he stole a scooter and went to wait for the girl's father in the employee car park of the Alfa factory. It was dusk, he was starting the night shift. Rocco approached with his hand out.

'I'm not angry with you. You did what you had to do. In fact, you did the right thing. I deserved much worse.'

The girl's father, who'd been wary as soon as he saw Rocco, lowered his guard and took his hand. Without breaking eye contact, Rocco plunged a bread knife into his chest, twisting as he pushed it into his heart. The man collapsed in front of him without losing a drop of blood. Methodical.

'The only one I ever killed for free,' he'd cackled to Panattoni.

As he thought of the girl and her father, murdered in a car park on a moonless night, Panattoni felt his phone vibrate through his shirt pocket.

27

4

Carla Trovati tossed and turned in her bed with a strange uneasiness. A sliver of light came in from the window on the other side of a wide room that effectively made up her entire flat, cleverly divided by screens and furniture. She looked at the clock: WAKE UP, NYT NEVER SLEEPS. The *New York Times* never sleeps, and tonight, neither did she – not after the evening before, which had ended her promise to herself: never get in bed with your managing editor.

Her anger was keeping her from sleeping, but was it because she'd slept with the legendary Giulio Strozzi – or because she'd kicked him out? Main reporter for the *Corriere della Sera*, lead journalist on the Mani Pulite case that uncovered mass scale political corruption, official biographer, friend and confidant of Judge Federico Astroni. He'd found a perfect match in Astroni at the time of the case that had placed the DA's office in Milan at the centre of the universe. Strozzi had climbed that ladder, and he would climb even higher: he was attractive to both women and men, especially the powerful and the rich. It was no secret at the paper that the higher-ups loved him more than his colleagues.

Carla sat up in bed, going over what had happened. She wasn't a prude or naive, but she wasn't 'easy' either. And she especially didn't want to be seen as 'the reporter who sleeps with her boss'. Maybe a colleague, if she really liked them that much. Which was something she'd always carefully avoided – until now.

Catching sight of herself in the mirror, she saw a face she liked, despite the tangle of brown hair and the bags under her eyes. But what she liked most was what was behind it: her brains, her soul.

Carla Trovati was a beautiful woman, but even more importantly, she was good. She wasn't where she was thanks to her arse – she knew many a mediocre colleague, male and female, who'd used their bodies to get promotions and raises – but because she put effort, sweat, and intelligence into her work. She couldn't ignore the fact that someone like her was bound to receive attention on the main floor of the paper, especially with all the men there. But she had no time for those games. And in any case, she definitely didn't care to join the long list of Giulio Strozzi's lovers. After her law degree – honouring a promise to her father, a famous Milan lawyer – she'd studied journalism and started her internship at the *Corriere*.

Her breakthrough, the one every journalist dreams about, especially early in their career, had come when she'd been sent to the Town Hall for a city council meeting. Nothing special. A regular meeting. A normal, routine, boring reporting gig. During a moment of fatigue during the endless council session, she'd gone to the loo. In the corridor that led to the toilets, she'd found the deputy mayor in tears. He was a quiet, serious man in his forties, a physics teacher at the polytechnic, but politically engaged since youth. 'Is everything okay?' she'd asked him, sincerely worried. And he'd started talking like someone needing to let it all out, as if her formal gesture of politeness had been proof of kindness on planet Earth. He'd needed a shoulder, a confessor, a human being capable of listening. He told her his party was dropping him because he was gay. Of course, none of his colleagues, all parading as politically correct, had or would ever mention it. Too sly. The official reasons were something else entirely, but to him, the reality was plain and clear.

Carla hadn't taken any notes at the time. The first rule her journalism teacher, a retired reporter for the late and venerable

Notte, had taught her was this: 'Only use notepad and pens during press conferences, never when you bump into someone, never when you realise that someone is confiding in you. At that moment, they think you're a good person offering them a shoulder to cry on, and not a stinking bastard, a cynical journalist who will jot down every last word.'

Carla had memorised every single word and as soon as the deputy had left, she pulled out her phone. The story was on the first page for a week, and the director had called her to his office, the 'red office'. He'd made her sit on one of the famous worn leather armchairs while he, solemnly leaning against the bookshelf that housed the *Treccani* encyclopaedia, had told her she was hired.

Two years had passed since then. Carla had put serious effort into her work, staying at the office until the wee hours, standing in for anyone absent or sick, running back and forth in the archives when they needed to find an old cutting that hadn't yet been digitised. 'You know you have nothing to prove, right?' old De Blasi would tell her. He was the established commissioner's office reporter, worn out, scruffy, shrouded in a permanent cloud of smoke (he'd moved his office into the courtyard so he could keep smoking at work), the last of a dying breed of journalists. 'This place is filled with total arseholes who should be licking the ground you walk on…' he'd add, not entirely innocently. But Carla let some of his comments slide, realising he meant nothing by them. With everyone else, she was stony. Especially with Strozzi, though she clearly wasn't immune to his charm.

Now she knew: he had been subtly wooing her, never crossing the line, never pressing for more than friendship. They'd gone for a drink several times after work, but always with other people. Only now was she noticing the trap she'd fallen into.

Giulio had made her feel comfortable, made her feel important as a journalist, special as a woman. He'd calmly waited for
the right moment, and it had come the previous evening. They'd
gone for dinner at the Navigli, this time just the two of them. It
was a lovely night in mid-April when they could eat outside, her
boss's company was pleasant, the conversation stimulating. They
drank together, laughed, joked, and locked hands, but especially
gazes. Then he'd given her a lift home, without saying much more.
When they'd reached corso Garibaldi, Giulio had got out to open
her door, leaving the engine running, giving the impression that –
for him – the evening was over, and they were both going home.
That's when she'd asked if he wanted to come upstairs.

She lived in one of those blocks with communal balconies,
once council housing but now fully renovated and gentrified,
and only for the wealthy. The daughter of Trovati, Esq., prince
of the courtroom, could afford it. Her flat looked like a loft: not
so spacious, but very New York.

'This is a nice place. You've decorated it really well.' Giulio ran
his eyes over the flat, lingering over the brass bed in the corner.

'It's not that big, but it's enough for me.'

He'd smiled mournfully. 'I'd really like to leave via dei Missaglia.
It's too far out, and the area is depressing. But journalists' houses
are lovely and big, comfortable. For those of us with kids, space
is important. Also, my wife hates the city centre.'

Mentioning his kids was part of his wooing, too: it set him
apart from other men looking for an affair, the ones who hid
their families, erased their other ties, played the teenager on a
first date, slipped their wedding rings into their pockets. Not him.
He was sly, kept his ring on display and talked openly about his
family, letting a feeling of sadness come off him, as if staying

married to his wife – whom he'd married in the past, when he'd also been 'just anyone' – was a sacrifice, but careful of playing the husband who felt 'no more spark in the relationship'. Giulio Strozzi was clever. He never cut things off when the subject came round to his family. Oh no, he always let others draw their own conclusions.

While they were having another drink, he'd told her that signing the kids up (a boy and a girl) for a private school had shown him the true joy of the weekend, when you could finally get up late. That was when she'd kissed him. She had no idea what had happened, or what had come over her. She pulled back immediately, regretting it, convinced that it would all end there, but the man who'd just been talking about his children with fatherly love had moved fast, as if he'd been waiting for it the whole time.

Of course, she thought now.

Giulio had followed her retreat, practically sucking her lips and tenderly reigniting the kiss. He'd caressed the back of her head, leaving his hand at the base of her neck – his way of preventing any further escape, something she hadn't even considered, caught as she was in his web. Then, as if for the first time in his life, Giulio had run a finger down her entire spine. And there, as she was lost in the kiss, her mouth fully open, the poetry had ended. He'd grabbed her hips, throwing her onto the couch, and almost ripped her shirt open. Her breasts burst out of her bra and he sucked her nipples as he lifted up her skirt. He'd smiled, aroused, at the sight of her hold-ups. A moment later, he was fully naked. He'd got up from the couch, taken her by hand to the bed, and finished undressing her.

'And then he fucked me, the bastard. Not bad, either. Vanilla, but satisfying.'

32

The thing that had angered her and left her with a sense of nausea had happened that morning, just before she carefully reconstructed every detail of the encounter for herself as a lesson for the future. At some point, half awake, she'd heard Giulio move. She'd opened her eyes, propping herself up on an elbow. She didn't immediately understand what that thing pointing at her face was – and then she realised: it was Giulio Strozzi's 'tool'. He was standing by her side of the bed, watching her tenderly, as if what was happening were entirely natural. He'd touched her face with measured technique, grazing her lips with a finger, circling, letting her mouth open. Suddenly, he'd pushed with his other hand on the back of her head, bringing her to his penis, plunging it into her mouth. Carla, though she felt trapped, hadn't resisted. But when he was coming – 'Yes, good girl!' – she fully realised what was happening and remembered her promise to herself, not to become one of his many conquests. Sure, Giulio would never say anything about them. That fake gentleman had never spilled anything about his affairs. Yet all they needed was a word, a look, a smile, and everyone at the *Corriere* would know that she'd been added to the list. Before she could react, he'd filled her up. Disgusted more by her own weakness than what had happened, she ran to the bathroom. When she came back, Giulio Strozzi was lying on the bed, eyes closed, happily convinced that he'd lounge there until ten and then walk the couple of blocks to via Solferino for their eleven o'clock meeting. She picked up his clothes, including his shoes, and threw them at him in anger.

'Get out. You got what you wanted, now go sleep it off at your own place.'

That was the only moment in the entire encounter when she'd foreseen his next move. Giulio had been quiet and demure, no

33

lashing out, no obvious anger. A *gentleman*. He got dressed quickly. At the door, he poured oil on the fire by saying, 'I'm sorry, I might have let myself go too far, but you're special. In every way.'

An hour later, Carla was still there, staring at the blade of light coming in at the window, and thinking just what an idiot she'd been. She made her decision, pulled open the curtains and stared at the courtyard downstairs. The custodian was watering the flowers in the small communal garden. 'I can't sleep anyway.'

She made herself a coffee as the clock from the *New York Times* read 6.48 a.m. She'd willingly have gone to New York there and then in order to put an ocean between herself and the office.

5

His seat was wide and comfortable, and the service excellent, but lawyer Giannino Salemme was mourning the time when you could even smoke cigars on planes. Almost pre-history now. The legal consultant for a British chemical giant that had 'made a mistake' – some thousand dead in Pakistan from a toxic cloud at a disinfectant factory built in that multinationals' paradise – had asked for help from their partners in the States, and he'd said that you could still smoke absolutely anything on Pakistani airlines. Was it true? He'd never checked, though he'd always been tempted to book a return ticket Milan–London–Islamabad to find out.

He'd spent the entire red-eye flight from Newark thinking about the packets of Partagas in his soft leather bag in the overhead locker: they were tucked in a chic travel humidor he'd found at a famous tobacconist on the Upper East Side. A gift from an American partner who knew his vices and carefully cultivated them: Bacchus? hardly, but tobacco and Venus were pretty hard-core interests.

Salemme wasn't one for whores, meaning he didn't like to pay. He preferred to think of himself as the Latin Lover of forty years earlier, as if those times at the Capannina club and the hot summers in Versilia, when women were more open and less demanding than nowadays, weren't gone for good. His wife, bless her soul, had been the one to introduce him to Forte dei Marmi, before swiftly passing on to a better life for both of them. Bland, shy and awkward, but with plenty of dosh. The daughter of the boomer middle class. Her father had got a gong, and made his money through construction. He'd bought houses everywhere, from Cortina to Montecarlo. Now all those houses belonged to him, Salemme, the Neapolitan lawyer, ex-magistrate. His father-in-law (God, the irony of a southerner like him marrying the daughter of an industrialist!) had looked at him askance until his dying breath, a magnificent sound, for what it meant: the release of all that wealth destined for his daughter. Salemme organised a yearly mass and rosary, two, in fact: one for his wife and one for her entire (late) family. His feelings for her were a mixture of brotherly love and profound gratitude. In life, she'd done two crucial things: she'd given him a son in his image (he'd worried during the pregnancy that the baby would be a girl or turn out to be as bland and insignificant as its mother) and she'd buggered off quickly. Not that she'd taken up much space or been clingy. Poor thing, not at all. But things were better like this. He was free.

And so Salemme – despite several suggestions of a second marriage – had 'remained faithful to the memory of his late wife' (as far as weddings went, anyway) and had been living his

35

second life to the full. At nearly seventy, he was still handsome. Maybe not to women under forty, but he liked them young and didn't want to pay.

So the lawyer for foreign partners of an important American legal firm (even his closest affiliates were mystified about the link) had found him a good-looking girl, set her up in the Village and paid her rent and tuition fees. That way his Italian friend could have fun every time he crossed the pond with a girl young enough to be his granddaughter. 'Matters of productivity,' he'd insist when the board of Harper, Johnson & Meredith of Madison Avenue queried the significant 'rep costs' in the books. However, what the book-cookers and Salemme didn't know was that when the Italian partner wasn't stateside – i.e. most of the year – it was the liaison lawyer who slept with the college student.

Salemme disembarked the Newark–Malpensa Continental flight with a feeling of satisfaction, thinking about his past week in the Big Apple and looking forward to the mossy flavour of the Partagas he'd light as soon as he left the airport.

He was a big man and, though the tight physique of his youth was only a memory, he'd retained some elegance. It wasn't a matter of style. Sure, his grey suit from a famous Milan tailor hung perfectly despite the night spent at 30,000 feet over the Atlantic (bespoke, of course; he'd been a loyal customer since the beginning). But his elegance wasn't a matter of his clothing alone.

He fetched his luggage quickly and used a trolley to wheel it to arrivals, scanning the crowd for Germano, his chauffeur.

Instead, among the dazed and sleepy faces waiting at the break of day, he spotted his son Claudio, waving at him. He felt a pang of worry: something was wrong. Claudio out of bed at dawn? Germano appeared behind his son and took the trolley.

'Morning, sir. How was the flight?'

'Not bad, thanks, Germano. Go to the car and wait there, please. I need a word with my son.'

The chauffeur disappeared discreetly, and the lawyer led his son by the arm towards a semi-deserted area of the airport.

'What's going on?' he asked in front of a still-shuttered flower shop.

'What do you mean? Can't I just come see my good old dad?'

Claudio was tall, smart and handsome, but he'd been born arrogant, and that troubled Salemme. He'd built his power and wealth on silence, invisibility, and working under the radar. 'Hidden power is a sure thing,' he always said. 'Visible power ultimately collapses.'

Claudio was efficient and precise, and presumptuous as well. He was a good student but lacked discipline, convinced anything could be solved by instinct and not by hard work. He tended towards arrogance, at times unpleasantly so, and that was dangerous, for him as well as for others since it led to brash decisions. When he was younger, his father had had to get him out of his fair share of troubles: unwanted pregnancies, beatings outside clubs, drink driving. 'At least no drugs,' Salemme senior sighed. It all slid off a spoiled rich boy who wouldn't grow up.

Claudio was his only child and he'd been terrified of losing him, literally. Surprisingly, after the train wreck of his high-school years – he'd only graduated after hefty donations to private schools – and two years of a law degree, mostly hungover at his desk at university after rowdy nights out, he'd suddenly shifted gears. He'd actually started studying, given up his bad habits, graduated, and joined his father's company.

The reason? He'd walked out of a literal car crash, almost unscathed. But his friends had died in it, a boy and an underage

37

girl. Fortunately, he hadn't been driving, or Giannino Salemme would've had to struggle to get him out of a sentence, despite his past as a magistrate and the contacts he still had almost everywhere. He remembered the police phone call and the nightmare of that evening spent in the Magenta hospital, shrouded in January fog.

When the boy had opened his eyes after surgery and they'd been allowed to have a minute together, Salemme had stared at his son and said: 'Read this, then sign it.' He'd handed him a contract stipulating that he'd graduate within three years, taking the exams for all four years of the programme, and would pass the bar exam. Otherwise he'd be removed from the will – and that meant no pocket money, not even for a coffee. He would hand over receipts for every purchase. Salemme knew, however, that this wasn't what had changed the kid's path: he wasn't afraid of losing money, but of having almost lost his life. Claudio had followed through on the agreement, but since then there'd been a cold light in his eyes that only warmed up when he was feeling arrogant. 'Arrogance is a luxury you can only afford if you have solid foundations,' Salemme often told him.

'Don't be an idiot. Why are you here?'

'I told you about it on the phone.'

'What about it?'

'I'm taking care of it.'

'You should've waited for me to come back… What does "taking care of it" mean, anyway?'

Salemme had been a magistrate before deciding that life would bring him more satisfaction, or just more money, really, if he set up his own firm. Yet he still had an authority that turned all conversations into interrogations. Especially when the other person got lost in small talk.

'It's going to happen in about half an hour. That's why I'm here. We can still stop it.'

The care and attention to detail, so out of character for Claudio, impressed him. 'Give me a quick summary.'

Claudio gave him all the details of the tailing, right up to the phone call. 'I couldn't reach you on your flight, so I had to put something together myself. It's clear that he's looking for a link with his brother, but whatever the case, this sudden visibility is worrying, don't you think? I felt like the situation was getting out of hand and he might say or do something dangerous, so the threat to us might become real. But we still have time to call it off, if you want.' He pulled his phone out of his pocket. 'One call, and nothing happens.'

Giannino looked at his son with sincere affection. He'd been prepared and cautious at the same time: sometimes his cruel efficiency, his heightened level of immorality, scared him – he wasn't like that at Claudio's age. For a brief period of his life, he'd had ideals. Nonetheless, no one could say he made bad decisions, even in his father's absence.

The lawyer ruffled his son's hair and Claudio relaxed. He'd been fearing one of his father's angry outbursts. Instead, he pulled a box of cigars out of his bag: he took one and used a pocket knife to make a hole in the end of the precious Partagas, the beginning of a ritual that never failed to excite him. He wet it with his lips and lit it, savouring it, puffing out a small grey cloud that elicited a glare from a woman in a fur coat standing next to the NO SMOKING sign.

Salemme senior didn't care. In the sudden fog of tobacco, Claudio heard his father's soothing voice: 'No, you did the right thing. Let's head home. I need a proper Italian coffee.'

6

The water was clear, and he could feel its icy grip through the black wetsuit. His lungs full of air, Annibale Canessa gave another push, and using his flippers, he reached the base of the Christ. He held on to it for the length of an Our Father, then let go, grazing the raised arms of the statue as he ascended. He shot out of the water, lungs burning, eyes filled with the blue of the sky and the green of the vegetation surrounding the small bay. He let himself be cradled by the sea, calm, smooth, and cold. Then he picked up his perfect crawl to the beach.

The restaurant was fully booked for lunch and dinner. A group had hired a night boat to reach San Fruttuoso, one of the most beautiful spots on the Ligurian Riviera. 'In the world, even,' he'd say to his old aunt. She was cook and owner of one of the only three restaurants.

His aunt had grumbled about another busy Saturday. She'd told him off, feigning disapproval. 'Before you came, we got along just fine, even at this time of year. Now it's a constant invasion. If you only knew how the other restaurant folks look at me!' She was stereotypically, marvellously Ligurian, frugal even in her social interactions, despite her burgeoning income. She'd always had something to live on and that had been enough, no need for the novelties her nephew had initiated since he'd joined her as her business partner.

Annibale Canessa looked over the peaceful town, his eyes level with the water. He liked that spot, and he liked San Fruttuoso first thing on a spring morning. It was a nice place to live: no traffic, no noise, far removed from everyone and everything.

His aunt was a great cook, but she was satisfied with what she

40

earned during the summer season. It would've been enough for him too, but he'd gradually started offering trips and buffets not just in the spring, but in the autumn and even the winter. He'd fixed up a sort of platform on the beach which he rented from the council, and set up the catering there, while the owners of the other two restaurants grumbled, pitched between laziness and envy. Then he'd started events in the old abbey: book launches, business conferences. People saw prestige, and they saw money. His aunt laughed every time they received bank statements for their business.

'Now what? How am I supposed to spend all this at my age?'

'Go travel! You never go anywhere. I'll look after the bookings.'

She'd mumble something and shake her head, going nowhere, day after day. Her greatest adventure was taking the ferry to Camogli, or if she was feeling more exotic, Rapallo.

Annibale was happy. It had taken him some time to get used to life on the outskirts, to that beautiful, inaccessible village, which could only be reached on foot or by boat, or not at all if the day was stormy. He was still fascinated by the uncertainty of a sailor's life on land, even now, eight years since moving there. He'd moved there at forty-five, after his second degree in philosophy. Back then he'd had a steady income with his consultancy, working with companies, security firms, and private clients with security issues. He was using his experience of fifteen years, and meanwhile he'd read, study, and build his new life brick by brick – though he still wasn't sure what it might actually be.

Zia Mariarosa wasn't actually his aunt but his mother's widowed cousin, with two sons in Genoa who had no interest in the restaurant. And so Annibale, exchanging loneliness for isolation, had decided to buy their shares and take over one floor of the old stone house that hosted his aunt's home and restaurant.

He looked at it as he walked up the beach towards the stairs leading back to town. Two windows: a bedroom, a study-cum-living room, one small bathroom. Those were his earthly possessions – the official ones, anyway. Everything else was stored in a warehouse on the outskirts of Rapallo, behind the San Pietro motorway entrance. A nondescript, industrial warehouse, hidden among the others. He kept books, furniture, and an old but extremely well-maintained Porsche 911 and a modified Fiat Punto, along with what he called the *caveau*, filled with old tools of the trade. There was also a sort of safe-haven where he could live if necessary, complete with kitchenette, a bed (a real one, not a cot), a toilet, an office. The warehouse was owned by a company, in its turn owned by a school friend who was part of the 'Canessa network'. The network was a group of old friends who loved him, warts and all, or people who owed him something, usually their life or that of someone they loved. Once he'd fixed their 'problems', they inevitably uttered the same words: 'If you ever need anything, please let me know.' Canessa always warned them, 'I'll hold you to it. These are not things I take lightly, so I'll understand if you want to back out.' They'd stand there looking vaguely panic-stricken, but no one ever reneged. They helped him as best they could.

The warehouse showed up as a rental for a German entrepreneur who used it for his yacht. And in fact there was a yacht (totally unseaworthy) which filled up the front of the space, shielding the rest from sight.

It was a whim, a sliver of self-defence, cover, a holdover from his obsession with security and safe routes. You just never know.

In the restaurant kitchen he found his aunt fussing with the coffee maker.

'How was your morning swim?'

'Water's wonderful today.'

'Good! We're waiting for the co-op's fish. With any luck they had a good catch. Do you want some coffee?'

'Keep it warm for me. I'm going to take a shower.'

He went through the restaurant – fifty covers – and headed upstairs. He took off his wetsuit and stood under the warm stream. All of a sudden, he felt a pang in his left side. *Weird*, he thought, *that old wound usually pops up on cold, dark, damp days.* This was a Saturday morning in April, and the sun was rising outside. The wound, however, served another function: it acted as a sort of sentinel's call.

Still in his robe, Annibale Canessa moved to the window. The co-op boat was mooring. A man hopped on land and started taking crates of fish from the fisherman still on board. Annibale would usually head down to help, but this time he wanted to stay and listen to the sounds of the small town waking up and take in the scent of the maritime pines bent by the sea breeze.

The pain wasn't subsiding. So it wasn't the weather. It was a portent of something bad to come, though with his new, hard-won equilibrium and in his state of controlled emotion, he couldn't see what it was. He wanted to believe it was just an old bullet wound, a scar tickled by the cold, salty water.

The aroma of his aunt Mariarosa's dense, black coffee rose up from downstairs, drawing him from his observation point. His wristwatch read 7:34.

7

Giuseppe 'Pino' Petri almost felt like a free man. Not because of his sentence, or the parole that was coming to an end, but because he was about to finish his course. This was just one of the steps – the penultimate one, in fact.

He stood under the wide concrete and steel arch of the Centrale train station, taking note of the departures and arrivals. They'd just announced the one he was waiting for: platform 13, a few minutes to go. Pino knew he'd done the right thing. This was the road that would lead him to the end of his own. He'd thought about it a lot in the past year, overcoming the old sense of loyalty that had always held him back and prevented him from talking. The institutions considered him a lost cause, but his refusal to reveal that corner of his life wasn't founded on unwillingness to become a supergrass or some absurd loyalty to the cause. Though he'd probably never handle a weapon or kill anyone else – in fact, he definitely wouldn't, even if they let him start all over again – he wanted to stay true to himself, despite the fact that everything he'd done had been wrong. He'd never sung, and he wouldn't start at his age.

In any case, he'd realised twenty years ago, the State and the institutions had more or less figured everything out. More or less. But there was still one detail niggling at him. He'd had to live with that, but it had become unbearable in the past year. No, he had some loose ends to tie up before starting his new life.

It hadn't been hard to find the phone number of the person he was about to meet. All he had to do was call the phone directory services. Nor had it surprised him that he still lived in the same city where they'd crossed paths the first time – and by chance – several years earlier. Pino had once studied faces as a survival mechanism. He'd scanned them intently, making the people around him uneasy, since they thought he was trying to look through them. No, he was just memorising details. The same face in two different places

44

aroused suspicion. But he'd focused on the boy because someone had told him who he was, his surname.

He suddenly felt he was being followed. Actually, he'd felt it for the past couple of days. He'd tried to work it out, tried to see something, but no luck. Then he figured it might be an age thing. He wasn't used to it. There was no reason for someone to follow him, apart from a cop making sure he wasn't messing up. So he dropped his guard. He looked around once in a while, but he never spotted anyone reminding him of anyone or anything, some other moment, something jarring with the rest of the tableau.

Maybe I'm too old for this game, he said to himself.

Next to him was a family, a mother and her kids. The youngest, in a red dress and red bobble hat, winked at him. She couldn't have been older than three. He winked back and saw himself as a father for a second. Once this was over, maybe he could try having a family after all. He was old, but not too old to find someone, maybe a little younger, and have kids. Who cared if people saw the child as more of a grandchild? Maybe he'd follow up on one of the hundreds of letters he'd received since the news of his parole had come through, get in touch with one of them, try to meet someone. The majority were from women asking him for help, giving their advice, offering love, comfort, friendship. The sheer number of single women out there was impressive, though he suspected that a fair few of those writing were actually married and looking for a daring fling with a famous ex-killer. Chasing novelty and excitement, escaping their anonymous existence. Or maybe they just wanted to venture into the unknown. He smiled. Those women would be very disappointed. He wished he could live their lives and slip into anonymity, instead of the opposite.

Giuseppe Petri yearned for an everyday kind of life: a flat in a block outside the city, a job that paid his bills, the morning commute, two headlights in the fog. Hell, everyone else kept trying to escape from that sort of thing, and here he was hoping to end up like that: one among many, happily forgotten, going through motions. He hadn't done so for forty years. Sometimes, in the early days of his parole, he'd felt clumsy, even fearful. He was afraid of messing up the job they'd found him, of not being welcome. But in fact it had been easy enough to start again, to hope, to feel like everyone else in a world he'd tried desperately to change, to the point of almost destroying it. It *had* changed, enormously, but not in the way he thought. It had taken him months to realise that.

He savoured every moment, every place. Even the rusty smell of the station, the coating on the tracks which invisibly settled over everything within the giant monolith, that barbarian invading the city.

He didn't feel like an old man, though technically he was one. At the moment, he was the kid he'd never been during his short, sharp childhood in the rocky South, poor and hungry. Or in his invisible teenage years in Turin, before the rays of revolution had broken through the clouds. At that moment he was a young boy who liked looking at women. And there was a young woman in the café outside the office who always smiled at him. She could've been his daughter. He'd joke, she'd laugh. Maybe one day he'd ask her out, once he no longer had to head back to prison every night. He'd never been more than average looking, and now he'd lost half his hair too. But Pino had a sort of charm. It used to be mothers who fell for him; now it was their daughters. He never figured out why. Maybe it was his air of mystery, the thought of his secret past, the stories he might tell…

Yes, he would start living again. He just had to sort out this one last thing.

The tinny recorded voice called his train, and he moved closer to watch it pull into the station. He moved back and stopped in the middle of the concourse to avoid missing the man he was supposed to meet. He didn't notice the figure in an oversized coat standing three feet away: through a pair of fake reading glasses he was watching the first passengers get off the train, which was bang on time: 7:43.

8

Napoleone Canessa recognised him as soon as he stepped onto the platform. They'd met once at a radical political meeting. Petri was a fugitive, the terrorism phase was behind them, the troops dispersed. No one had recognised him, no one had paid any attention to him. Petri had shaved off his beard. But when the meeting was over, someone from the committee had spoken to Napoleone.

'Come with me. There's someone who'd like to meet you.'

He'd ended up in a room with this man staring at him, and then he'd recognised him. He noted a flicker of fear. Petri, however, had looked at him with pity rather than anger. 'You're the cop's brother,' he'd said without reproach. Just to categorise him – a fact, pure and simple – but Napoleone had felt ashamed nonetheless. And later he'd regretted that. He still did. 'It's not my fault,' he'd replied, his throat dry. Petri shot him a smile of resignation. 'No, nothing we can do about it. Your brother is one hell of a bastard, but at least he's honest.' With that, he'd left.

Here he was now, thirty years later, standing on the platform with sparse grey hair and a puffer jacket, corduroy trousers, and boots. Just like he used to dress back then: anonymously, simple, the exact opposite of the rest with their parkas and furrowed faces, instantly recognisable to the cops and the Carabinieri. Petri would blend in. He still did. When Napoleone reached him, he held out his hand and Petri shook it. A firm shake, respectful, neither too tight nor too loose. He looked Napoleone in the eyes, and Napoleone felt the need to break the tension. 'It's been a while.'

'Too long,' was the reply, and he knew Petri wasn't talking about him.

After the initial awkwardness, they headed down the escalators towards the station entrance along with a group of army boys on leave from Novara, ready for Saturday night in the city. 'I know a small place close to via Vittor Pisani. Let's get some coffee and talk. There's a train in an hour. You can be home by lunchtime.'

He was planning, like he used to, but no longer out of strategy, just concern.

Napoleone walked beside him as he stepped into the large square in front of the imposing Fascist building. 'This square wasn't here last time I was in Milan,' he said.

'Everything's changed,' Petri replied, walking through a dozen young immigrants of all ethnicities, chatting around a bench.

'How about you, have you changed too?' Canessa suddenly asked as they crossed via Vitruvio and headed towards the centre.

Petri turned towards Napoleone and smiled. 'You have no idea.' He was about to add more, but something caught his attention and he gestured towards the Gallia. 'Do you like football? They used to talk transfers in that hotel.'

And there he was, the man in the overcoat. Petri had spotted him earlier on the platform. It couldn't be a coincidence. 'Keep walking, we're being followed.'

But Napoleone stopped to look behind them. 'What do you—'

Petri grabbed his arm and forced him round again.

'Keep going. Talk naturally.'

'What do you mean, someone's following us?' Napoleone was clearly worried, suddenly realising the absurd irony of the situation.

'I don't know, maybe police. They like keeping tabs on who I see, who I talk to. I can't think who else it could be. It's okay. Relax.'

Petri's words didn't help.

'Look, I don't know why you wanted to see me, though I may be able to guess. And I'm telling you, we both made a mistake: you seeking me out, me agreeing to come here. I don't think I can help you.'

'I actually think you can, and I won't take much of your time. Trust me.'

They came to the crossing on via Boscovich. The road was clear. On Saturday mornings in Milan, the whole business area practically empty. A car pulled over and a smiling face leaned out of the window.

A man with a Southern accent asked, 'Excuse me, can you help?'

'They're coming towards you.'

Nando Panattoni slipped his phone back into his pocket and started the engine. Driving slowly, he circled the block to take via Vittor Pisani towards the station. Beside him, Rocco pulled out the AK-47 and started loading it.

'I don't like this. Can't we wait until they're somewhere else? Plan this out better?'

Panattoni was furious with Rocco's last-minute hesitation. '*Now* you say it, arsehole! Do your job, and do it well.'

Rocco saw them walking. The other guy, the one from the train, suddenly turned round.

'They're onto us. There's no going back now.'

Panattoni pulled over on the corner of via Boscovich, cutting them off. Rocco leaned out the window and beamed his best fake smile. 'Excuse me, can you help? We're headed for viale Fulvio Testi.'

Napoleone Canessa moved closer to answer him and almost didn't hear Petri's scream: 'Run! It's a trap!' A black weapon appeared in the man's hands.

From where he was in the middle of the road, Napoleone saw flashes, but the shots weren't for him. The volley was aimed at Pino Petri, who might have been able to save himself if he hadn't grabbed Napoleone's arm to get him to move. Napoleone heard Petri's body thud as it hit the ground. Then, just like in a syncopated FPS game, the weapon swung towards him. It was the last thing he saw. He collapsed next to Petri, riddled with at least fifteen explosive rounds.

The silencer allowed the killers to leave the scene calmly. Panattoni accelerated only once they crossed the first traffic lights on via Vitruvio, disappearing on the roads leading to corso Buenos Aires. The following day the car, stolen just hours before the crime by Panattoni, was found burning at the Idroscalo. No one connected it to the murders.

While the killers were escaping unnoticed, a guy out for his Saturday morning jog on via Vittor Pisani almost stumbled over the corpses.

He called the emergency services and soon after, a couple of railway police officers hurried over from Centrale station. 'Jesus, what a mess,' the younger one said. His colleague contacted the police station. 'Double murder on the corner of Vittor Pisani and Boscovich. Numerous shots, two dead.' He hung up, looked at the victims and let out a long whistle.

'Hey, have you seen who that is?'

'Which one?'

'The older guy. Don't you recognise him?'

'Should I?'

'It's Giuseppe Petri! Pino, one of the most famous terrorists in Italy. No one actually knows how many victims. What the fuck do they teach you in schools these days – ancient Egyptian history?'

9

Chief Magistrate Calandra was dreaming. A woman was calling him from below. He was somewhere up high but the location of the dream was hazy. A building maybe? or a villa. He pushed the heavy brocade curtains aside and leaned out of a window. The woman was in a pool, gesturing for him to join her. 'Come down, the water's great!' Beyond the pool, he could see a scorched savannah with grassy patches and scattered boulders. Strange place for a villa. Calandra considered going back to his room to put on his swimming costume and join the woman. She did have a gorgeous face. But it was no longer a room – it was an office. His office. Before he could take a single step, the phone on his desk started ringing. He didn't move. The phone kept ringing. But he wouldn't move. Then the place where he was standing vanished, but the phone kept ringing.

He suddenly realised it wasn't part of the dream. He reached out to his bedside table and grabbed the phone.

The display read 8:16 am. Why hadn't his alarm gone off? Oh! it was Saturday, and he slept in as long as he could on Saturdays.

'Yes?'

'Sir, I'm sorry to disturb you…'

The voice, less attractive than the one in his dream, belonged to one of his assistants.

He cleared his throat, assuming his usual curt manner.

'Don't apologise. There must be a reason for your call.'

'There's been a shooting in Milan, and I believe it might have repercussions on the developments we're following.'

'Keep talking.'

1984

T HE FIST that slammed onto the Alfetta's dashboard sent one of the radio dials flying, but the air conditioner gave no sign of life. Not a breath of air filtered out of the useless device.

They'd taken the Serravalle motorway for Milan shortly after dawn. At that hour there'd been almost no traffic and the cool early morning air had blown in through the open windows. Now, on the way back, the unbearable mugginess was starting to suffocate them.

'You fucking idiot, why didn't you make sure it was working before we left?'

But it wasn't the muggy July afternoon or the bugs crashing against the windscreen that were getting to major Annibale Canessa. It was the time he'd wasted, the pointlessness of it all. The trip to Milan for a court hearing, which was immediately adjourned, and then the drive back along a shimmering, hot motorway through flat plains shrouded in haze. It was all wearing on him. It wasn't even tiredness, though he'd slept very little in the past few weeks. It was impatience.

The young Carabiniere in the driver's seat was sweating profusely, and not just from the summer heat. The excitement of

53

being so close to this legend made him more nervous than usual. As he tightened his grip on the steering wheel, he noticed one of the red display lights start to blink.

Canessa saw that something was wrong from his sudden terrified expression. He glanced at the dashboard.

'I can't believe it! We're running out of petrol? Didn't you fill the tank before we left? You're the living inspiration for all those jokes about the Carabinieri!'

The calm voice of Marshal Ivan Repetto came from the back seat. 'Easy, Annibale – the next service station is only a couple of kilometres away. I don't know about you, but I was going to ask to stop anyway for a piss.'

Repetto was Canessa's right hand, his escort, but most of all his conscience. He shadowed him everywhere, spoke with irony and wisdom and watched his back whenever Canessa acted rashly. Repetto was his only confidant, the only dam against the major's impetuous tides.

The young driver overtook a long-haul vehicle and turned on his indicator. The moment they took the exit ramp, the services restaurant materialised from the shimmering summer horizon like a mirage.

'Go and get some petrol, then join us inside for a cold drink,' Canessa told him, calm once more. He jumped out the door with the motor still running, seeking shelter in the cool oasis of the café, and didn't even hear the young man's shy thanks. Giordano, his regular driver, had left a couple of weeks earlier and Canessa was looking for a substitute.

'One thing's for sure: this one's a definite no,' he murmured to Repetto, who mentally crossed another off the list. 'Number five is out.'

Canessa had had a weird feeling ever since they'd left that morning. His bullet wound had started bothering him, as if trying to warn him that things weren't going the right way. Something was wrong.

'It's really late,' he told Repetto as they sipped a cold soft drink, surrounded by holiday makers admiring the small group of uniformed Carabinieri. Only a couple of years earlier, they would have avoided appearing in public in full uniform. Repetto smiled at his friend. He always addressed Canessa informally, even in front of superiors. It was a privilege allowed to him and no one else, not even generals.

'I don't get your hurry. He'll never get away from you now.'

'I don't know. This call feels weird, summoning me for absolutely nothing the night after his arrest. As if they didn't know how important it is to interrogate him immediately.'

'Annibale, what's got into you? You and interrogations... Just because a couple of them talked when you took them down, it doesn't mean they all will. Remember: most of them keep their mouths shut. Petri's one of the toughest. He ain't gonna talk. He's not like Filippi and his posse of young rich kids playing terrorists. They started crying for mummy as soon as we nicked them – they wanted to play at something safer. This one believes in what he does. You could electrocute his dick and he still wouldn't talk.'

Canessa smirked. 'Yes, but *I* haven't interrogated him yet. He might let something slip. Or maybe he's had a change of heart because he wants to go back to his girl on the tomato farm.'

Repetto's humour kept the tension in check for a while. They'd been partners since 1977. Seven years of the same high intensity that had distinguished the career of the young Lieutenant Canessa, fresh out of the academy. He'd forged ahead thanks to his arrests and some impressive operations. They'd got through all those years of terrorism together, somehow surviving a brutal existence and sharing with their enemies the uncertainty of life under the threat of war. And in a way, they too had embarked on a life of secrecy, never sleeping more than one night in the same place, staying away from home for months at a time. The Carabinieri had bulging folders on the terrorists, sure, but the terrorists had equally thick ones on them. They were targets, same as anyone on the front line.

It had been harder for Repetto since he was married and, during the brief respites, had managed to have a family. But he'd never abandoned that kid ten years younger, that uncompromising lieutenant who too often mixed personal with business on duty. The son of a retired general with a medal from Libya in 1940, Annibale Canessa had no romantic ties, only flings that lasted a few dates, a holed-up weekend, or a night. Those that might've lasted longer never did. The major was still a handsome man, with messy hair that had gone prematurely grey. Women liked him and stories had started spreading about his lovers. About how he'd sleep with his colleagues' wives, because he had no time to find anyone outside his circle. He'd 'help himself in the barracks', ran the rumour.

Bollocks. Repetto took it all with a pinch of salt. Canessa's mother had died when he was still young. His father had given him and his brother Napoleone a military education, and got proud results from one, rebellion from the other. His younger son had thrown over his military career for a degree in Bologna on the trendy new Drama, Arts and Music programme. 'A hotbed of extremism,' was the general's response. In the confidential reports Annibale had sent to him, you could trace the 'black sheep' all the way through the radical left. No ties to the armed wing of the party, however; no violence or beatings, only active participation in 'proletarian expropriations'. Clean record. And yet, the grey area his brother operated in was one used by terrorists to recruit not only new soldiers but also sideline supporters, the ones who never joined the ranks but were crucial to operations, providing homes, food and other forms of support. Annibale worried that his brother Napoleone might end up doing something of that sort. He had no proof, only a hunch. He'd had him followed, discreetly of course; if Napoleone ever found out, their already rocky relationship would explode. And Annibale didn't want that, out of respect for their father.

Annibale occasionally met up with his brother, but he never told anyone except Repetto. Napoleone's name was forbidden, and everyone, including his superiors, knew it. It had become like the story of Cyrano's nose: those unfortunate enough to intrude on Major Canessa by mentioning his brother ended up very badly.

Repetto looked around, taking in the crowd in sundresses, shorts, tank tops and flip flops. He set his glass back down on the bar. Seven years. He hadn't had the courage to tell Annibale that this arrest spelled the end of their long breathless chase, at least for him. Enough. He'd already sent in his notice, asking them to hold on to it. He had to tell Annibale first. He'd go and work with his father-in-law, who'd started a security firm: from security doors to alarm systems, all the way through to full surveillance for companies. With his experience and the name he'd made for himself during those dangerous years, Repetto would be marketing and publicising the business. He'd been on the verge of telling Canessa the night before when they'd landed in Genoa on their way back from Cartagena, the Spanish city where they'd finally tracked down

Pino Petri and taken him into custody. He was the last fugitive, a member of the hit squad of the infamous, bloody Red Brigades. But then they'd received the court summons, Annibale's temper had spiked, and he'd decided to wait till things settled down.

Petri was one the most dangerous killers during the Years of Lead. With an alleged record of six murders and sentenced to life a couple of times over in absentia, he'd fled the country two years earlier. Canessa had been hunting him for years, but he'd only really focused on the case for the past few months. He'd tied up loose ends on his list (the legendary 'Canessa List') before going after Petri. He'd tracked him halfway across the world, from France to the US, to Brazil, then back to Europe, and Spain.

'He's the type who'll come back,' he'd once told Repetto. 'We'll catch him close to home. He's not one of those wankers who end up making pizza in some small South American country or being protected by the French and their love for due process. No, he'll be back, sooner or later.'

For the past year Petri had been living between Cartagena and Murcia on a farm in the countryside. He'd met a local woman while in hiding in South America. She'd studied agriculture and was involved with a cooperative project over there. Her father owned a farm, and on his death, she'd gone back to Spain. Petri had followed her and started growing tomatoes, aubergines, cucumbers, peppers, and more on that good soil.

The day they found him, Repetto had tasted one of the tomatoes, plucking it out of a crate while the Guardia Civil searched the house. He'd brushed the soil off it and wolfed it down as the sun set in the hills. He turned to Canessa, his mouth full.

'You should try one. They're amazing! I'd happily take a box. Actually, I might ask that Spanish captain, what's his name…'

Canessa wasn't listening, though. He was staring out towards the Mediterranean – you could see the water thirty kilometres away that evening, even from the farm. Or maybe he was looking deep inside himself.

Repetto knew that expression well.

Canessa was frustrated. First of all, he'd realised when he'd found himself face to face with Petri that the fierce terrorist was no longer the man they knew. He was sitting at the table in a blue vest and dirty work trousers next to the woman he'd let his guard down for. They didn't need weapons or bulletproof vests to cuff him. When they burst through the door, they found him with his partner and the other workers, eating vegetables and jamón, laughing, a dinner like any other interrupted by fully armed men in uniform. They'd found him thanks to her. A tip had taken them to Paraguay. He'd been smart, Petri, heading to a country famous for having given refuge to ex-Nazis. The police informant on the ground had told them that a Spanish woman was having a thing with an Italian, a commie. Had he been the opposite colour, they probably wouldn't have reported him. Using her name, they'd contacted airlines and border control posts to see if any other name regularly appeared with hers. And so they'd followed the intricate route they suspected the terrorist had travelled. It had taken them months, but they'd finally located the woman there, in Spain. A week-long stakeout had confirmed that Petri was at her farm.

At the moment of arrest, all he was holding was a fork. He'd lowered it, slowly, and raised his hands.

On his way back from talking to the Guardia Civil's special unit (they'd blessed his request for a few crates of tomatoes: 'they'll rot anyway, *hombre*') Repetto found the major sitting at the table, finishing up the scraps of food.

Annibale Canessa looked up from his plate.

'You're right, the vegetables are really tasty, but you were going to toss the jamón?'

Repetto shook his head. He'd never really get used to Canessa's mood swings.

Petri had surrendered without a word and didn't open his mouth until the arrival of the special flight in Genoa. Once they got into the armoured van waiting for them at the Cristoforo Colombo airport, packed with a small squad of Carabinieri with assault rifles (Canessa had been clear: 'if you send me a bunch of academy kids, I'll kick them all the way back to you'), he addressed the major as a peer, the captured enemy acknowledging his victorious opponent.

'The woman doesn't know who I am. She did suspect I was a fugitive, but she has no idea why. She has nothing to do with this.'

Canessa looked at him with contempt. 'You'd better worry about what's going to happen to you, you son of a bitch.' But when they reached the barracks he said, 'She's already out of the picture, but she'll be charged with aiding and abetting. She'll get through it.'

That was the major, Repetto mused. He'd explode in anger, crawling all over people in his fury, but then he'd be back, apologising, or showing – like just then – a scrap of humanity towards someone who hadn't demonstrated any to the people they'd massacred. It would've been seen as a weakness in anyone else, but it actually made Annibale a bigger man, fostering respect in those close to him, especially his team. Maybe it was a smile, or just a reflection of the lights from the van, but something glinted on Petri's face as they led him away.

What had really saddened Canessa was the devastating realisation of his farewell to arms. The war was over, the future uncertain.

He'd spent his youth on the front line, turned thirty, and ridden like a Horseman of the Apocalypse during the period of terror. That all-consuming battle had taken it out of him. And now the warrior was left with no enemies. Some wise person would've pointed out to him that a Carabiniere always has enemies, not just terrorists, but Repetto – the only one who knew him closely – knew this was about something else.

The men who'd given that war their all, on either side, knew only how to fight. How to fight *that* war. Find another enemy? Come up with a new way of life? Those were luxuries reserved to people who hadn't lived through those times in the way Annibale and Pino had. They, along with everyone else who'd taken it personally, would always be war veterans.

But for me, it's time to retire. I'm just a public servant who has served his duty, was Repetto's thought on that suffocating July afternoon at the dirty table of a services restaurant. He pondered the best way to take Annibale aside and tell him about his decision. But Canessa kept on acting impatient, as if facing off against Petri in front of the judge were a matter of life and death. Canessa unbuttoned his uniform jacket and stroked his side.

'That hole is hurting.'

'It's the humidity,' Repetto replied.

'No. It's a bad feeling.'

They reached Corso Europa at 6 p.m. They'd run into traffic and when they finally drove into the car park at the barracks, Canessa once again exited the car before it came to a halt. Repetto did his best to reassure the young driver, who had no idea how to deal with the situation. The major ran into the building and plunged down the stairs leading to the cells in the basement. He couldn't see any of the four Carabinieri from the morning shift. The door to Petri's cell was ajar. He kicked it open and proceeded to check the other five. Two were occupied but not by the man he'd arrested. No one. Petri had disappeared. His world collapsed around him. Repetto, now coming downstairs himself, had to move to one side to avoid being trampled by Canessa on his way back up to the entrance and the guards.

'Where is he?'

'Sir?'

'Where the fuck is Petri? What about the men I ordered to guard him?'

The two men looked at him, then at each other, uncertain which one of them should speak.

'Spit it out. Now!'

One of them, a brigadier, plucked up his courage.

'They moved him, sir, at around noon today.'

'I left specific orders. Who made that decision?'

'Sir, we arrived after the fact. They told us the magistrates had come in with high-ranking officers, including a general. He's still here, upstairs with the colonel.'

Canessa stopped listening to them. Repetto couldn't stop the man. Ignoring the lift, he leapt upstairs and burst into the commander's fifth-floor office without knocking.

'Where is Petri?!'

At his heels, a breathless Repetto arrived to witness a scene he'd never forget. Sitting in Colonel Botti's study were three colonels and General Verde, deputy commander general of the force. They sat staring, somewhat baffled by Major Canessa, his shirt untucked and sweat-stained, his tie loose and his jacket unbuttoned. Canessa planted himself in the middle of the room. If not for his tight fists and a complete absence of shame, he might have been standing to attention. One of the colonels, the usual self-important kid who'd never been on the front line (as Canessa would say), put his coffee down on the table and addressed Canessa's direct superior, Colonel Botti, with more than his fair share of attitude.

'You should probably do a bit more to discipline your subordinates.'

Colonel Botti stood up, moving closer to Canessa.

'Major, care to explain?'

'Colonel, *sir*,' he replied, the word dripping with sarcasm. The two had never had such a formal exchange. 'Where is Petri?'

'None of your business.'

'I had an agreement with the prosecutor's office.'

'Enough!'

General Verde stood up, moving Botti aside and pushing his own face into Canessa's.

'Your behaviour is unacceptable, Major. The case is no longer under your jurisdiction.'

'Not my jurisdiction? I hunt him down for years, I snag him, and I can't interrogate him or even witness the interrogation? I demand an explanation.'

'*Demand*? How dare you, Major! I'll have you court-martialled!'

Repetto could see Canessa inching closer. Their faces were almost touching. The marshal was about to intervene to prevent his friend from doing something incredibly stupid, but Canessa held his hands at his sides. It would've been better if he'd hit the general. But his words, spoken softly and straight into Verde's ear, were worse than a punch to the gut followed by a hook to the chin. Fortunately, Repetto was the only one who heard them, or the situation would've spiralled out of control.

'Yes, General, demand, because your ass is mine. Because if you're able to fuck your wife once a year, it's thanks to me; because if you've been able to walk your daughter to the altar for a "good marriage" to that fancy boy from the Guardia di Finanza, it's thanks to me; because if one of these cologne-drenched fuckers you've surrounded yourself with had been on the Appia Antica at the time, you'd be court-martialling worms today.'

Everyone knew the story. Verde had been targeted by a hit squad from the Rome chapter of the Red Brigades. Unfortunately for them, they hadn't counted on Annibale Canessa's involvement. Their car cut him off, but he'd already spotted them. He'd noticed someone following them, and when the trap was sprung, he was ready. He left the car and opened fire first, using the guns he always carried: a standard issue Beretta and a Walther PKK his father had given him. His subordinates called him 'Tex Willer', 'dual wielder'; his superiors sent him reproachful memos about the use of non-authorised weapons. Canessa didn't care and, after 13 July 1978, no one had had anything more to say about his guns. Two terrorists had fallen; one had managed to survive but ended up in prison in a wheelchair. So Verde owed him his life. True, a Carabiniere doesn't say what he'd just said to a general, but there was truth in every word. Including the bit about his superior officer's son-in-law, an official dimwit from a good family.

Nonetheless, Repetto broke out in a cold sweat. It felt as though someone had wheeled a humongous iceberg into the room.

No one breathed a word. Canessa and Verde stood locked in a staring match.

It was the general who broke the silence, not once lowering his gaze.

'Gentlemen, could you leave us alone for a minute?' Repetto vanished, followed by the other officers. Botti closed the door behind him.

'You're mad, Annibale,' Verde exclaimed. He threw himself into an armchair and undid a few buttons on his shirt. 'I have to report you now. Do you realise what kind of scene you just made?'

'Bollocks. Those officers are worthless, just like all the rest of them you surround yourself with, you and the commander general. They'll keep grovelling. You just need to bark at them. Where's Petri?'

General Verde brought his hands to his face. 'Annibale, Annibale… Calm down a minute. Come here, sit down.'

'I'll stand, thanks.'

Verde shook his head. He couldn't bring himself to be angry, and not just because Canessa had saved his life.

He remembered it well. The difficult period after Aldo Moro's kidnapping. The State was still unprepared in the face of armed threats. It acted slowly and predictably; it was muddled. Despite the increase in attacks, Carabinieri, police, and magistrates inhabited a sort of limbo, with a suicidal self-confidence: it won't happen to me. With Annibale Canessa, it was a different story. He was born suspicious – it was in his DNA – and wherever he went he was on high-alert, trusting no one. Day or night, his Beretta was in its holster and the Walther behind his back, with its stock to the left. Even the way he stored them had become legend.

Verde and young Lieutenant Canessa had ended up in an ambush in Rome. There was never any traffic then, which is why

Canessa had noticed two cars appearing from side streets. The first one had overtaken them but the second had not, and that was suspicious. The driver had died immediately. Canessa had told him to stay down, but he'd hesitated, and ended up riddled by the hit squad's bullets. Canessa, on the other hand, had saved Verde's life and his own. When the car in front of them had screeched to a halt – almost a rerun of the attack on Moro and his escort – gun-wielding terrorists had appeared from behind the cars parked nearby. Canessa had already thrown open the car door. He pushed Verde out and started shooting in every direction, convinced that they were surrounded. Witnesses described him standing against the car, the Beretta in his right hand aimed at the men who'd cut them off, while he discharged the Walther at the men behind them with his left. He reloaded and kept firing from behind a bench, where he was sheltering with Verde. Of the five people involved in the ambush, only two escaped. But they were identified, and ended up on Canessa's list; he hunted them down for three years and finally caught them. It was one their rare failures before the raid in via Gaeta, an event that changed the history of Italian terrorism.

'Look, Annibale,' Verde continued. 'The magistrates in charge of Petri's case came from Turin today and took him away. That's it.'

'I'll catch up with them.'

'No, you won't. That's an order. The Petri chapter is closed as far as you're concerned.'

'What's your game, General?'

'There is no game, Major. It's over. You're the only one still playing. The war is over. This country has had enough of terrorism, the Years of Lead. Look around. Can't you see what the people want? They want to forget. They want to go shopping in town on Saturday mornings. The season of direct conflict is over. The State won. The other side – not all of them mind you – are in prison. We let some off, and some escaped. Look at the stuff on TV, the adverts, and you'll see which way the wind is blowing. No one wants to see guns and rifles! They want swimming costumes in the summer and ski suits in the winter. Pretty girls with their tits out. You were the only mad dog left, and with Petri's arrest, your mission is over.'

Canessa went quiet for a moment, letting the general's words sink in before he said wearily, 'The victims' families don't want to forget.'

'Bollocks, as you'd say. They're a minority, a sideline. This has been a war and there have been deaths, most of them innocent. Some will pay, many will not. But this country is focused on other things now. We won the World Cup, we have a new Prime Minister, a socialist. It's a new season, who's to say if it'll be better or worse, but it's a new one.'

Annibale was pacing.

'You're making me feel like an old tool, General.'

'You are, even if you're only just past thirty. You're still chasing fugitives when we have special departments for the task. You have no friends, except for that marshal who's about to retire.'

Canessa stopped in his tracks. He looked at his superior in disbelief, his arms limp at his sides.

Verde spread his arms, shook his head.

'He hasn't told you? I'm sorry. He hasn't officially sent in his notice. Maybe he wanted to talk to you first. He has a family and it's time you got one too. I like you, Annibale, but I can't protect you any longer. You're a hero, but your temper, your behaviour, your crusades… they belong to wartime, not today. History repeats

67

itself. It's happened to others before you, in other circumstances. The city needed a gunslinger – and then they didn't. I'll come clean with you: we've had some pressure from above. They wanted to stop you sooner, but I convinced them to keep you on because you were this close to catching one of the worst terrorists in Italian history. You got him! Applause, speeches, another medal. You must have lost count by now. You want more? You want another war? Go to Sicily. There's a great group of *mafiosi* there who can't wait to meet you.'

'You think I haven't considered it? My transfer request for Palermo is in my desk drawer. But I'll decide when. First I need to—'

'—tie up loose ends. Sure, Canessa tying something up. Good. You're done.'

Annibale headed for the door without looking back.

'I'm going to find those magistrates.'

'You won't. You're on paid leave, effective immediately.'

The words sent him reeling. He turned around, but before he could say anything, General Verde explained.

'I'm sorry, but this morning your brother was arrested in Reggio Emilia, in an alleged hideout. I said "alleged". We still don't know how involved he is in criminal deeds, but these are the rules, and you know it. You'll have to stay benched until the situation has been cleared up. That's the reason I'm here. I came for you, not Petri. No one's questioning your integrity, but with a brother accused of terrorism you can't waltz around like a vigilante. While you're waiting for your next duty, go and have a nice holiday. You've got years of unspent leave. Go see your father, hit the beach, run after women without the risk of being shot by a jealous colleague. Come back once this thing with your brother has blown over. I'll say it again: if you still want to be a soldier, they're waiting for you with open arms in Sicily. Their war is still raging. It'll be raging when you get back, and unfortunately it will still be going once you leave.'

It had been a difficult trip, with dense fog from Busalla to Bologna, dead slow traffic. There were only a few days left to Christmas and Lieutenant Colonel Annibale Canessa (his new title – Verde had called him to Rome for his promotion, first time for someone that young) had put his uniform back on after three months. It was the second time since the day they'd taken Pino Petri away from him and given him a tower and two stars on his epaulette instead. To be honest, he'd also worn his uniform a month earlier, in November, when he'd buried his father in the Staglieno cemetery. It had been a short, emotional service, especially for the handful of old soldiers, veterans of actual wars – great ones, but almost all of them lost. They'd come to say their goodbyes to a friend, with ribbons, medals and flags as proud and threadbare as they were themselves. The old Genoese military chaplain had spoken a few words at Annibale's mother's grave. She'd belonged to one of the city's historic families. The Bisagno Valley knew how to be cruel to humans, and on winter days the north wind would whistle down the mountains. On that bitterly cold Thursday, the sky over Genoa – dark, grey – matched the Carabiniere's own mood.

Verde had come especially from Rome, but they hadn't spoken. He stood to one side, surrounded by his escort and only paid his respects with a handshake after the service, queueing up with the other fifty or so people attending.

The old man died one morning in the cool hours of dawn.

'A fighter, your father, a real soldier. Anyone else would've surrendered much sooner,' the doctor had said, trying in vain to console him.

Annibale Canessa was now taking a leisurely drive in his Porsche 911. He'd bought the car on a whim a couple of years earlier, in a flurry of regret for the youth he never had, and there was something sentimental about this trip. He was setting out to burn bridges with his past, and he wanted to exert control by doing the driving, rather than trusting a pilot or a train conductor. His first stop was the restaurant in the train station in Modena. There, in that foggy, anonymous, distracted place, his brother Napoleone sat waiting for him.

He smiled at the thought of their names. An officer obsessed by military history had given his sons the names of two great leaders, both remarkable strategists.

'Both beaten, in the end,' Annibale had said, during one of his rare rebellions with the general.

His father didn't get angry at his impertinence. 'True, but no one won battles the way they did. Everybody knows their names, but not those of the victors. And anyway, everyone loses at some point.'

His father wasn't militaristic, or a warmonger. He didn't look like one either. He looked more like an academic than a general: a little too thin, a pair of gold-rimmed glasses eternally perched on the tip of his nose, a penchant for sleeveless cardigans. Over time, Annibale had formed the idea that the reason he'd joined the army was that it allowed him to reenact his true passion: playing with toy soldiers.

In the big house in via Caffaro (to be honest, it was his mother's), the largest room was called 'the diorama room'. The general had recreated some of the biggest war scenes from history with wood and papier-mâché: Cannae, Pavia, Lepanto, Austerlitz, Gettysburg, Stalingrad, D-Day. The two brothers were admitted to that giant wonderland and allowed to play, touch, move, make-believe, but never to change the course of history. When they'd finish playing, everything had to go back as it was; no changes were allowed on the field. History was not a game.

One day, just as Marshal Soult's corps were surprising the Austro-Russian army on the Platzen at the climax of the battle of Austerlitz, Annibale had asked his father, 'Why isn't there a Waterloo diorama?'

Kids know how to be mean, but the general had simply smiled. He'd appreciated the question.

'Because Austerlitz is the triumph of human genius and strategy, while Waterloo was decided by external factors. Starting with the weather. There was no trace of intelligence or cleverness, only good and bad luck.' Annibale had never bothered to find out whether that was the truth, or simply his father's opinion.

The brother he'd pretended not to love for years in order to protect himself was sitting at a table in the middle of the restaurant. Each time they met up, Annibale felt naked before the pretence. He pretended, to himself most of all, not to love the kid who was almost a son to him. That's how he'd treated him after their mother's death.

The place was humming and the music blaring, but all the better. Young men and women, students waiting for their trains with bags and rucksacks, laughter and hugging, hearts made lighter by the Christmas holidays about to begin. No one paid attention to him. Verde was right, Annibale thought: the country was changing, and now, Canessa could walk through a crowd of young people who only a few years ago would have been screaming insults at him or retreating from him as if he were contagious. He could walk in without being noticed, just another guy.

Napoleone Canessa's eyes shone with a sad light. He was sitting with his knees together, a worn leather bag between his feet. Annibale sat down without a hello, thinking that his brother would be a lousy terrorist: he'd placed himself in the most exposed spot in the entire self-service area, wearing the guilty look he'd had since he was a boy, even when he was totally innocent. Napoleone's melancholy had forced Annibale to defend him constantly from the bullying of the older kids from the Cinque Terre, where they spent their summers with an aunt, always on the lookout for foreigners to pick on.

'I've got some papers here for you to sign.'

No greetings, no small talk. Annibale opened his bag and pulled out a pile of documents held together by an elastic band.

'I'm sorry I missed the funeral. I asked for time off but they said no.'

'I know. It was probably better that way.'

Napoleone looked at him but without surprise. 'You hate me that much.'

It wasn't a question.

'I don't hate you, Napoleone, quite the opposite: I can't bring myself to hate you. I don't know where we went wrong, what the breaking point was. Maybe I've always been too demanding. But we've drifted apart and I'm probably the one who's suffered most.'

'How would you know? Jesus, even now you're being patronising.'

'I said "probably". But if you'd come to the funeral, I would probably have hugged you, defended you once more, and rekindled

72

a relationship that's only ever brought me pain. That's what it is – pain – and I can't stand it. Napoleone, I see everything you do as a form of rebellion, and I don't get it. It makes no sense. It just feels like you're punishing me and Dad. Maybe not. You're actually probably very consistent in your beliefs. But I want to stop chasing after you, rescuing you, protecting you. From today onwards, to each his own.'

He removed the band from the papers. 'Dad removed you from the will entirely, leaving you only the legal minimum, but I convinced him to change it because even though I know you wouldn't have argued, I want you to have half. I'm keeping some furniture, a few old colonial trinkets, the books and dioramas, but I have buyers for everything else. It'll be a decent sum. It'll allow you to get a house and live comfortably. If you know how to invest, you won't even have to work. Just sign where I've marked.'

'I don't want the money.'

'But you'll take it, all of it. It's not dirty money, it used to be Mum's and now it's yours. Don't be an idiot, and don't do as I would in this sort of situation. You might have a family someday, maybe kids, and the money will be useful.'

'You're still scripting my life, Annibale.'

The waiter walked over with the coffee they'd ordered. The lieutenant colonel took his black, swallowing it down in one gulp and smiling to himself as he watched his brother add three spoons of sugar. *Undrinkable*, he thought.

'If that were the case, then this is the last scene I'd write. But I know you better than you think. You've always been *against* everything, but once I'm out that door, you'll be relieved to see life from another perspective. You'll start building something, and you're someone who can do that successfully. This is the irony that links us: I'm the antisocial one, despite my uniform. I bet you'll be married with kids way before me.'

Napoleone started signing. Annibale handed him the documents one by one, slowly. At the end of the pile, he gave his brother the ones to keep.

'Good. That's it.'

But he couldn't bring himself to stand up. Something was bothering him.

'There's something else, isn't there? I know you just as well.'

'You're right. Yeah. Before I go, I want you to tell me about your arrest.'

'I was acquitted, you know. "Sorry, our mistake, case closed, forget about all this." Nothing to add, really.'

Annibale Canessa waved away the objection.

'I'm interested in your version.'

'Why?'

'Personal reasons. I've never believed in coincidences. I don't know how much coincidence there was between your arrest and Petri's capture.'

'Annibale, you'll never stop believing the world revolves around you, will you? But like I said, there's nothing to add. I've never been a terrorist or a sympathiser. Sure, like others, I praised the armed struggle, went to meetings where there might have been some fugitive passing through. But that's it.'

'So what happened that day?'

'I was visiting a friend who was leaving for Greece, and he decided to go and say goodbye to his old comrades in Modena at a social centre in an occupied villa with a nice garden. I tagged along for the party. Eating, drinking, singing, making out. Joints. Lots of joints actually. Other than that, a very bourgeois thing.

There were around forty of us. Suddenly, the police special unit was there, black suits, balaclavas, assault rifles, the lot. They shoved us against a wall and searched the house, claiming that it was a hideout for a new terrorist cell. We laughed, but a gun and some old leaflets turned up in the search.'

'They could've been there for some time.'

'True, but my friends said no, they'd been planted, and maybe by the police themselves. It wouldn't have been the first time.' He grinned at his brother, but the Carabiniere didn't bite.

'There were forty of you, so why did they hold only you and five others?'

'We were the only ones on record as "autonomous". The others were students, younger than us and there for fun. I got three months in jail. Then one day they call me to tell me there's no evidence against me, the gun can't be traced to any shooting, the leaflets were like, really old – we couldn't've made them. "Nothing more emerged after a thorough investigation. You're free and clear, but you'd better toe the line." End of story.'

Annibale Canessa slid his documents back into his bag and stood up. He put his coat and beret back on, and looked at his brother. 'One last question: who was the magistrate in charge of the inquiry? You must've met them.'

'Someone from Milan, the one who sent the police, apparently following an anonymous lead from a supergrass. His name's Salemme, Giannino Salemme.'

'Never heard of him.'

Annibale Canessa headed to the door of the restaurant without looking back. It was the last time he saw his brother alive.

*

Rome was beautiful as always, but around Christmas it had something extra, something magical. Annibale Canessa drove his Porsche towards the small hotel in via Sistina where he'd been a regular for several years now whenever he wasn't in the barracks or some safe house. He handed the keys to the valet and locked himself in his room, exhausted from the trip. He showered, put on his civilian clothes and headed to a restaurant behind Piazza di Spagna, walking down the famous stairs. Compared to the snow and fog in the north, the weather was lovely. Cold, but clear. The streets and squares sparkled with festive lights. It felt like forever since anyone had celebrated a proper Christmas.

This year he'd leave his thoughts behind and not think about the future. Finally. But there was something to sort out.

On 23 December 1984, at 10.30 a.m., Annibale Canessa was sitting outside the office of the commander general of the Carabinieri. His uniform, dry cleaned at the hotel, was impeccable. To his breast he'd pinned all of his ribbons, his carefully polished medals and the arms of the paratrooper branch of the Carabinieri.

'Sir, the general will see you now,' the secretary said.

Lieutenant Colonel Canessa stepped into the office, clicked his heels and saluted the flag before bringing his right hand to his forehead and saluting the generals waiting for him. Verde sat in one of the armchairs in front of the commander's desk.

'At ease, Colonel Canessa. Please sit down.'

Annibale didn't move, though he relaxed his posture. He held his beret tight under his left arm, and pulled out a piece of paper with his right hand. The officers stared at him, bemused.

Verde broke the silence and tension that had fallen over the meeting. 'I was just discussing your future assignments with the general, Canessa. Maybe it's too soon to talk about Sicily. With your résumé and experience, you could be an excellent ambassador for us. You might work abroad in a consulate, with your fame and pedigree. I'm told you speak many languages, is that right?'

Canessa brushed past without looking at him and set the folded paper on the desk, addressing the commander general.

'Sir, this is my official request for final discharge. I would like to thank you, General Verde and the force for everything you've given me. As of today, I am a civilian.'

'Are you joking?'

The commander general was shocked, and he didn't like the feeling.

'Not at all, sir.'

Verde interjected, switching to the informal, fatherly tone he'd often used with Canessa, especially in delicate situations like this.

'Annibale, don't be rash. Your brother's situation has blown over. You can't still be angry about the Petri situation…'

'No sir, I'm not angry about the Petri case. You helped me to understand something. I've been thinking about what you said for the past five months: "There's life out there"—' he pointed to the trees along the Tevere '—and I think it's time I looked into it.'

'Annibale, what the fuck…' Verde was furious, but the commander general waved his outburst aside.

'If this is your decision, we will not force you to reconsider. I hope you don't come to regret it. You were born to be a Carabiniere.'

Annibale smiled. The commander general was good at his job. He'd always admired him.

'Thank you, sir. You may be right, but I won't go back on my decision. There are too many people in this country who regret their life choices.'

He clicked his heels with deliberation, saluted the other two officers, the flag, and left the room.

The moment he was outside, he undid his tie, unbuttoned his uniform and pulled out a plane ticket. Addressing the secretary's curious look, he said: 'For now, it's the Maldives.'

2

The Third Millennium

I

THE LOBBY boasted a couple of worn wooden benches, full of splinters, and a plastic ash tray half melted by countless cigarette butts. Visitors to the morgue obviously kept smoking despite the ban, but could anyone honestly deny the comfort of nicotine to the people in that sad place? Whichever way you looked at it, ending up here was a tragedy: you either came in for work, or your 'work' was a loved one.

Admittedly, the décor was utterly depressing. On one of the flaking walls was a poster decrying the dangers of drug use. *A bit ironic*, thought the police officer standing guard at the door of the morgue: entry was forbidden to the unauthorised. *It's taking the piss*, he thought, *posting something like that here. Most of the bodies coming through over the past thirty years were those of junkies who'd OD'd or were otherwise drug-related. Maybe less true now.* But the poster was undoubtedly from the 1970s–80s.

He was about to share this with the woman, but then considered the young girl beside her and the sorrow that united them. Still, that didn't stop him from taking in the light wool dress which buttoned in front and fell to her ankles. A blue cardigan was draped over her shoulders. He couldn't help detecting her curvy shape through the sombre outfit.

I mean, nothing wrong with that kind of attention in a place like this, is there? He tried to justify his thoughts. *Faced with death, we should all be clinging to life. I'm hardly a monster!* Fortunately, he set those thoughts aside in his effort to be kind. 'Miss, would you like something to drink? There's a vending machine in the other room.'

Before she could reply, the door banged open and a tall man with short grey hair and a searing gaze charged into the room as if someone had shoved him. He had on a very dated jacket which seemed excessive for a warm afternoon in late April. Under it, however, he was wearing a blue polo shirt and a pair of canvas trousers.

'Where are the victims from the Centrale station shooting?' he asked with unquestionable authority.

The police officer pointed to the door behind him.

The man pushed through and walked into the morgue, taking a long corridor that turned onto a shorter one. Two beds stood against the wall, and the bloodstained sheets revealed the presence of the victims.

A volley of laughter came from one of the rooms ahead. The man poked his head round and found three assistants playing cards.

'How could you abandon those poor souls? Move them into the autopsy room. Immediately.'

The assistants stood up quietly and followed orders, wheeling the beds into another room along the first corridor before walking away. One whispered something to the others, another

80

tried hiding a snort, but the man's look silenced any further comments.

Alone at last, he lifted one sheet first, then the next. A spasm of pain ripped through his chest as he looked at those massacred bodies, opening up a sudden, destabilising abyss in his life. It was a revelation.

2

'What are you doing here? Who are you?'

Two men had come through the door. The speaker was in his thirties, wore a leather jacket and clearly hadn't shaved that day.

'Who let you in? Can I see some ID?'

The other, despite being better dressed in jacket and tie, must've been the subordinate. An old cop trick: the scruffy one is the boss, dressed down so he can discuss things more easily and unseat people's defences by pretending to be their equal. He looks more like you, more approachable than his associate – but of course that's not the case.

The man wearing the dated jacket saw through them. He let the sheet fall back onto the body, and talking as if to himself, pointed his left index finger to the wall, almost as if at some other dimension beyond it. 'They shot Petri first. That much is clear: he was the target. The spray went from right to left and it didn't hit his right arm, whereas the other guy is almost shredded. He was trying to save Petri, move him aside, to no avail. AK-47, one of the recent mods – I'd need to see the bullets. Explosive, probably, given the damage. Undoubtedly used a silencer. I doubt you found any shells. They had a bag around the ejector.'

The police officers were dumbfounded, their mouths gaping. The one in the jacket was the first to collect himself.

'Who the fuck are you?'

'Knowledge, history... They're power, my friends,' a voice behind them proclaimed. The speaker was a stocky man, completely bald, with a belly so taut, it threatened to rip open his nice white shirt – clearly tailored and expensive, with the initials *SC* embroidered on it. He dabbed at his shiny head with a linen hanky and, falling into a chair by the wall, remembered enough of his manners to speak.

'Colonel Canessa, my sincerest condolences. I'm sorry to see you again in such sad circumstances.'

Annibale smiled, nodding in return.

'Thank you. You haven't changed, Calandra. You must be commissioner, if not chief magistrate by now.'

'The latter, Colonel, the latter. For what it's worth. But I still act like the good old days, and you'll remember I'm the type who prefers something of a free rein. In all things...' He left the sentence hanging.

The officers listened in on the conversation, not knowing whether to interrupt or not, and increasingly curious. Calandra went on to explain in a didactic tone.

'Colonel Canessa – or do you go by something else, now you're retired? Maybe a fancy inspector? – is the brother of one of the victims. Does his name mean anything to you? No? Your loss.'

He gestured vaguely.

'The wife of one of the victims is out there,' said the well-dressed one.

Annibale felt a pang of sorrow. Dull, but painful all the same.

'The woman and girl are related to Napoleone Canessa?'

'Wife and daughter,' replied the rough-looking one.

'I don't think they should be let in right now. This is my brother, if you need to identify the body.'

'Okay,' the police officer replied.

Canessa and Calandra left the room. Annibale leaned against the wall for support.

'You got here fast.'

'You too, Calandra. One of your planes?'

'Touché. Though my channels are fresher, Colonel.'

'You sure about that?'

Chief Magistrate Sergio Calandra was a member of the Secret Service. He always had been. The two met in the late 1970s and it had taken Annibale some time to consider him an ally, especially after the via Gaeta affair. During the Years of Lead, even the institutions played dirty and, more often than not, fought with each other for a variety of reasons, sometimes even plotting against the State they'd sworn to protect. But he'd always liked Calandra. He was fun, a Sicilian with a love of life. In his heyday, he'd had a wife he called The Widow, as they spent only a couple of days a year together, and a string of more or less regular mistresses he fooled around with in hotels and fancy restaurants. He had even more casual lovers, all of them very young. He liked good food and nice clothes, and what he had on now was clearly a suit from Piombo, though a size up wouldn't have been a bad idea. Annibale had always suspected that Calandra used service slush funds to pay for his vices. 'Well no, it's not ethical, but better used on this stuff than doing something awful or covering it up,' he'd justified it to Repetto when the latter once expressed his concerns.

'I still have some good friends here and there, Calandra. And news travels fast these days. Napoleone and I hadn't seen each

other for some time. We weren't close.' He paused. 'But his fate...
this got to me.'

Annibale tried to speak about his brother with some detach-
ment, as if that bloodied body in front of him hadn't stirred a
bundle of feelings.

'Him and Petri together,' said Calandra. 'That's quite the
coincidence.'

'Yes, you're right. I can't figure out what might have brought
them together. Maybe they ran into each other somewhere ages
ago. But now...' he shook his head. 'Are we sure this isn't pure
coincidence? My brother may simply have been in the wrong
place at the wrong time.'

'I don't believe that. And neither do you.'

Annibale smiled and offered his hand to the chief magistrate.
'Will you be around?'

'I'll be looking into it,' Calandra replied, non-committal. 'After
recent events, you understand, even the least indication that an
armed group might be forming needs to be thoroughly investigated.
We might cross paths again. Soon.'

'Yes, of course. I'm glad to see you're keeping well. I should
probably go speak to my sister-in-law.'

'Likewise, Colonel, despite the circumstances.'

As Canessa walked away, one of the police officers joined
Calandra, who was taking a half Toscano from a small leather
cigar holder.

'Pardon my question sir, but who is that?'

'Someone playing dumb. It's not working on me,' Calandra
replied. And he lit up his cigar right under the NO SMOKING sign.

3

Annibale Canessa took a deep breath before pushing against the doors and stepping into the small, filthy waiting room.

The girl was huddled up against her mother, looking for protection. She couldn't have been more than ten or twelve, and she was holding a book. She really was his brother's daughter: looking at her he could see a striking resemblance to his own mother, her grandmother. It sent shivers down his spine.

'Excuse me, madam, could I speak to you outside please? Your daughter, too.' He spoke coldly, stepping into the police role, because he had no desire to discuss the matter there, to deal with his sister-in-law and niece in front of the uniformed officer.

The woman stood up, took her daughter's hand and followed Annibale down a series of labyrinthine corridors and stairs. When they got to a long, dark and foul-smelling passageway underground, Napoleone's widow moved the girl behind her as if to protect her, and stopped walking.

'Where are we going?'

'I apologise for the route, but I'm taking you to an exit in the building next door to avoid the press.'

She nodded, but took her daughter's hand again. They kept walking until they emerged into the courtyard of the neighbouring wing. Annibale led them to a small park where there was a swing and a slide, even a drinking fountain. The adults sat down on a bench under a chestnut tree, and let the girl head for the swings.

The man inhaled the fresh, clean air and thought about this trip to Milan, his first in almost thirty years. A high-ranking officer, once part of his team and now part of the Canessa network, had told him what had happened. He'd called just after 9 a.m., and

Canessa had got a lift to Rapallo on the skiff, then picked up his Porsche for the drive. It was now 2 p.m., and the weather had worsened, threatening rain.

'She's a beautiful child.'

The woman studied him carefully.

'Child? She's almost twelve. You don't look like the police, though you behave like one, almost as if—'

'—I used to be one? I was a Carabiniere actually, but a long time ago. Maybe it's true what they say: born a cop, die a cop. I'm not sure how to tell you this' – his tone was suddenly more intimate – 'but I'm Annibale, Napoleone's brother. I'm sorry we had to meet this way.'

The woman ran a hand through her long, dark, shiny hair. Rather than seeming angry or surprised, she almost seemed to have expected the revelation.

'He told me about you, though not much. He wondered if you'd ever see each other.' Her eyes welled up.

The girl called her from the slide, waving. 'Mummy! Look at me, like when I was little!' Her mother waved back, forcing a smile.

'We went our own ways a lifetime ago. It was a form of self-defence for both of us.'

She sniffed and nodded, talking to him as if they were discussing an everyday matter, as if the situation weren't steeped in death and tragedy. 'Yes, I knew, but maybe it was also a form of cowardice, don't you think? Refusing to address the cause of your disagreement, the suffering that smothered the love. Because I'm ready to bet on that for Napoleone.'

At least my brother was lucky, thought Annibale. *He had a life, a family, and lived with a woman who understood him, made him feel good, got him to stand on his own two feet.* As he put these thoughts together,

86

he ran through his own life experience: fragmentary, a series of occasional relationships, alienated from himself as much as from others. Now it was his turn to give in to emotion, to the weirdness of that meeting, the uncertainty into which they'd both stumbled, which bound them and would continue to do so even if they went their separate ways.

'What's your name?'

'Sara, and that's Giovanna.'

Their mother's name.

'She looks like her grandmother.'

'I know: we have photos at home.'

She suddenly burst into tears and Annibale found it came naturally to him to hug her.

Giovanna ran over to her mother. 'Mummy! Why are you crying?'

They spent a few minutes with their arms around each other, before Annibale realised they weren't alone.

4

Carla Trovati was watching the scene from a distance out of respect for what was clearly a delicate moment. She'd been wise to look there, on the corner between two apartment blocks. Her journalism teacher had pointed it out to her.

'Very few people know about that passageway,' he told her. 'It's the best way of getting out of the Institute of Forensic Medicine without using the main doors. It's usually taken by VIPs' families to avoid journalists. I'm telling you because you deserve to know about it, but keep it on the down low.'

Surreptitiously, she'd stepped away from the huddle of colleagues – print, web and TV – pretending to head into a café for an espresso. Instead, she'd snuck round the corner and taken the small alleyway. And what a scoop. She'd recognised Annibale Canessa immediately. He'd changed very little from the photos she'd handled while preparing her thesis on terrorism and the media.

'And the others must be wife and child of the second victim, the one whose identity they've kept back. Why is he talking to them like they're family?'

Even before any formal announcements, it would be an excellent piece. She needed it – she'd been in a rut for a while now. And it was the best way to get past her feelings from the previous night.

She'd been there since 9.30 a.m., first on the scene. When she answered the call and heard Giulio Strozzi's voice, she'd been tempted to slam the phone down, but he'd predicted her reaction and opened with 'It's about work'. The managing editor had been in the office since 7 a.m., when she'd kicked him out of her place. 'There's been a shooting near the station. Two dead. Ready for it? One of them is Pino Petri. No ID on the other. See? Always a silver lining,' he'd added smoothly. 'I thought you'd be up and showered, and you're the one who can get there the quickest. A good thing for you, but also for the paper.'

So there she was, a detached observer, waiting for the hug to end so she could move closer and grab a comment from that family she couldn't fully place.

Annibale saw her from the corner of his eye. Cute. Actually, a lot more than that. She was wearing low-rise jeans and a white t-shirt under her suede jacket. He didn't have a good eye for this sort of thing, but he was sure they were all high-end brands despite their low-key appearance. She was pretending to have stepped out of the medical building for a phone call, but she'd been spying on them for a while now. A journalist for sure.

He released his sister-in-law from the hug.

'Sara, listen to me. What did the officers tell you?'

'They said the magistrates want to ask me a few questions and that they'd pick me up from the morgue.'

'Why was Napoleone in Milan?'

'He got a call last night, over dinner. He was on the phone for a few minutes. When he hung up, he seemed weird, as if he'd been talking to a ghost. He told me an old friend needed him and he was going to come up to Milan to help him out. He slept really badly and spoke your name a couple times in his sleep.' She dried her eyes with a tissue. 'That's it. That's all I know.'

'Okay, thanks. You should go back in now – the police are no doubt looking for you. Look, don't lose your patience, though the police and magistrates will seem cold and distant, and pretty unpleasant. If they still play it as we used to, they'll start out treating you like criminals. It's not out of meanness. Not always. They just think it's the best way to get you to tell them all the details. Stay strong and tell them the truth, nothing but the truth.' A flash of gratitude came over Sara's face. 'But maybe don't mention his mentioning my name in his sleep, okay?' She nodded. 'Good. See that woman? She's probably a journalist. I'll handle her, you head back.'

He squeezed her shoulder and handed her a card. 'These are my contact details. Phone as soon as the questioning is over. Though I'm worried they might call me in too. Do you need anything?'

'Only the truth.'

'You'll get it.'

They stood up and Sara, holding back all of her other questions, took Giovanna's hand and headed for the door they'd just come out of.

Carla saw Annibale Canessa coming towards her. His wasn't a face you'd forget easily: it looked sculpted by a neoclassical master, with an expression of placid strength. But she didn't let it get to her. She wasn't like that.

'Hello. I'm Carla Trovati from the—'

'What happened to that poor guy you outed?'

Carla wavered. Partly because like all her colleagues, she suffered from a feeling of invisibility, and finding someone who'd actually read your work was exciting. The question, however, also implied a fierce disdain for her job. She caught herself in a moment of weakness and tried to make up for it. Direct stare, direct tone. 'He's great, actually, living a better life than before. He's free. So, what are you doing here? Who's the woman with the child, Colonel? If that is still your title…'

Annibale managed a wry smile. The girl had guts.

'Listen, here's the deal: I spill some beans and in exchange you take a walk around the block, leave those two alone, and don't reveal the existence of this passageway to anyone else.'

'Deal. So, my first question…'

'No, no questions,' he interrupted. 'I'll only tell you what I can. Pino Petri was killed while he was with another man. That man was my brother, Napoleone. Last night Petri contacted him and asked him to meet him in Milan. He didn't tell his wife the reason they were meeting, nor do I know if he knew it himself. They were shot with AK-47s. I hadn't seen my brother in over twenty years and I don't know if he had any enemies. When you write this down, remember: Napoleone may have served three months under suspicion of terrorism, but he was released when they couldn't find any evidence against him. Acquitted. There was no crime.' He spoke clearly. 'He was clean. Don't use the word "terrorist" when you speak of him, or anything like it. He wasn't one then, and he isn't one now. Like many at the time, he inhabited a grey area to the left of the Italian Communist Party, that much is true. But he never went against the law.'

Carla was frantically writing everything down in her notepad. 'Anything else?'

'Nothing yet. However, in exchange for your discretion and honesty, I promise you first-hand information from here on out. Leave me your number.'

Carla pulled a business card out of her bag. Annibale pocketed it, then offered her a handshake.

'So, we have a deal?'

'We do. Can I have your number too?'

He smiled.

'Maybe later, when we become friends.'

Carla nodded. 'Thank you. And I'm sorry for your loss.' She watched him go back into the building, and then made a swift exit from the courtyard. She pulled out her phone to update Strozzi, unaware of the man on a scooter. He was pretending to look through the flowerstand. But he was actually eyeing the entrance to the Institute of Forensic Medicine.

5

Nando Panattoni dropped Rocco off at the Rogoredo train station, fifteen minutes before the high-speed train that would take him back to Naples. No plane, no security checks, no name or ID. Tickets paid for in cash, every time.

Rocco had changed his clothes and looked almost like everyone else now. *Don't judge a book by its cover*, Nando thought, watching – and worrying about – his accomplice. Barely out of the car, Rocco was already glued to a red-haired woman in tight leather trousers, his eyes boring into her behind. *Please don't do anything stupid.*

Nando abandoned and set fire to the car in the Idroscalo area, which was populated by sex workers and cross-dressers, and then fetched the clapped-out scooter he'd hidden there the night before. He rode back to the city, stopping in a café in via Negroli not just for the amazing custard pastries and Illy coffee, but also because it was one of the very few that still had a payphone.

He dialled an ex-directory number in the Corso Magenta area.

'Everything go well? Any problems?' asked the voice on the other end.

'It all went fine.'

'Good. Now focus on monitoring police headquarters, the morgue, courts. Your target's the brother. I want to know what he does, who he talks to, every little detail. Briefing is at 6 p.m. Don't call unless it's an emergency.'

His stakeout at the Institute of Forensic Medicine had been worth it. Annibale Canessa was here. He wouldn't lose sight of him.

He called his partner to let him know where to find Canessa.

Judge Astroni's knock at the door of the prosecutor's office was more like a caress. Without waiting for a reply, he barged into his mentor's room.

Antonio Savelli was sitting behind his desk reading through documents. He was a tall man, shockingly thin, a bit like Kojak and famous for his moral integrity. In the troubled years of the corruption inquiries, he'd often spent his nights on a makeshift cot which was now gathering dust in a storage room on the third floor. Savelli had never had any help. He was an inscrutable man who'd got where he was by keeping his distance from all political parties. In Rome they'd say: 'When he goes on the attack, he pulls no punches.' And so it was: the man who'd got him his position had received several notifications of impending investigation followed by arrest warrants. He regretted having voted for Savelli's nomination.

Unlike many of his colleagues, Savelli spoke very little, but his rare interviews regularly shook the foundations of power, both political and financial. He'd inherited a villa from his maternal grandfather, along with a sailing boat on Lake Maggiore. He'd settle into the cockpit any time he could and chase the wind alone, followed by a cautious police escort.

He thought of himself as a fair man without weaknesses. He had one, though: his assistant, Federico Astroni, now sitting in one of the leather armchairs in front of his cherrywood desk. Savelli had taken that desk with him everywhere he went, from the outer suburbs all the way to where he was now. Some people keep family photos, some their qualifications, still others, paperweights: Savelli kept his desk. And it would soon follow him upstairs and into the large office of the solicitor general.

'Such a shame,' Astroni said, feigning a lack of interest.

Savelli knew his protegé well. He was there to give his opinion on the Petri-Canessa case, not for small talk. So Savelli cut to the chase.

'I was just thinking: the case falls to Guidoni, but we're talking about a famous former terrorist and we need someone with more experience alongside him. I had Lorenzo in mind since he's led three Petri-related cases already.'

'True, but I'd suggest someone who wasn't directly involved and has no preconceived notions. Someone less biased by past experience. Someone who can go down other paths, not just the obvious terrorist one. Maybe the reasons for the double murder are different, more…' He searched for the right word, 'recent.'

Savelli looked at his protégé. As usual, his reasoning was sound, but removing someone from the investigation when they were already familiar with it was an odd move. It went against his pursuit of what's right, especially given that left to himself Guidoni was already a loose cannon. He was presumptuous and inexperienced, had powerful backers and could count on their helping him through seemingly insurmountable obstacles. The judge wasn't aware of any ties between Guidoni and Astroni, so it struck him as peculiar that Astroni was considering keeping him on board. What his right-hand man said next, however, clarified things.

'We could assign Marta Bossini to him as support and incentive. She's already dealt with terrorism cases.'

It all made sense now. Despite the demanding trial that awaited him, Astroni also wanted control over this important and delicate case. As always, he'd mapped out every detail. Guidoni had little experience, but with a Rottweiler at his side who'd lead the chase and be guided as necessary by Astroni's counsel… As Federico's current lover, Marta Bossini was perfect, loyal in every respect.

Well played, Federico. You want the Petri case; it's yours. Savelli smiled at Astroni, who was still feigning ignorance, as if the final say didn't really matter to him.

'It seems like a good solution. Do you want to tell him?'

6

Annibale sat beside Giovanna in the small office next to the one belonging to the magistrate following the case. He was planning his immediate future, and not really paying attention to his niece. The niece he'd only just discovered he had.

Eventually she complained, 'You're not listening to me!' in a tone so adult it made him jump.

He gave her a weak smile, feeling out of his depth in the role of babysitter yet knowing full well that his relationship with her wouldn't be ending any time soon. Nor would it get easier after their time together in that depressing place, its files packed with stories that saddened him to his core.

Despite having served his country for a long time, he still got sharp, stabbing pains in his stomach when he looked at that dark, grey building jutting out of Milan's city centre. It was almost an allergic reaction. At first he thought it was just an isolated case, but he'd noticed the same symptoms in Turin, Genoa, Rome, and realised it was something else. Inside those buildings, the law (and he was intimately acquainted with its injustice) had revealed time's real trick: everyone may be equal before the law (though that wasn't true), but time is an inescapable sentence for everyone; it doesn't play favourites. Time got lost; a second, a minute, an hour – it didn't have the same meaning in there that it did outside. Time was lost for ever. Not only did it move more slowly, it actually took you to a different dimension. Point in case: how long had they been there? He had no idea. *And if it happens to me as a former Carabiniere, what about others?* So he'd avoided courts of law whenever he could, opting to meet magistrates and judges in barracks or literally anywhere else.

'Of course I'm listening,' he replied to Giovanna.

'Are you my uncle?'

'I am.'

'So why didn't you get me a Christmas present? My friend, her uncle got her tickets for the Laura Pausini concert.'

The kid's reasoning rattled him, but he played along. 'Because I'm a new uncle, so I start doing uncle things now. I'm going to get you a pen and a piece of paper. Here. Will you draw me something?'

Giovanna took his offerings with a condescending look, letting him know that they were for babies. But she accepted her task.

'Okay. I'll draw Mummy.'

Annibale smiled at her. He cast his thoughts back to when he was sitting in the back seat of a police car with her and his sister-in-law (it was still very strange to think of them like that), and he'd realised they were being followed. The driver and his colleague hadn't noticed. When he'd been on the front line, it was precisely that attitude, that kind of distraction that had most infuriated him. 'Each attack is preceded by a string of daily tailings and stakeouts – and not one of you bastards has noticed,' he'd scolded his team at the time. Of course, it had been difficult even for him, but his senses had come out of hibernation fairly rapidly, engaging the cycle of attention-prevention-defence-attack.

Their followers were good, but they'd made a space-time mistake. There were a couple of them, one on a scooter and the other in a nondescript car. They delayed at a critical moment – what Canessa had always termed 'the changing-of-the-guard': the scooter had fallen behind in traffic, so the car had to stay behind them a little longer instead of turning down a side street. It blew their cover.

So they weren't police or the press. They were something to do with whoever had killed his brother and Petri. Maybe… but why would they be coming after him now? Was he a threat to them? If so, something deeply troubling was afoot. Petri knew things that could harm powerful individuals, not just terror-related tales. Were the Secret Service behind it? He didn't think so. Calandra wouldn't have shown his hand this soon. It was something else. But what?

Sara came back from the office next door, interrupting his thoughts. She looked almost relieved.

He stood to greet her. 'How did it go?'

'It went well. They were kind and understanding, nothing like you described. They said I can go home, and they'll let me know when they'll release Napoleone for the funeral.'

She covered her tears with a sneeze.

A brigadier appeared at the door. 'Madam, whenever you're ready.'

'They're giving me a lift to the station. There's a train in half an hour.' She looked to him for reassurance.

'Go, look after your daughter. I'll sort things out here, the funeral too,' he replied. Sara hugged him and took Giovanna's hand. Giovanna turned to him and handed him the paper. 'It's for you.' And she left with her mother.

Alone, Annibale looked at the drawing. There was a slide with a boy on it, and a man and a woman under it. A family on a happy day. Really well done.

'Mister Canessa, please.'

The clerk formally invited him to step into the office of Deputy Prosecutor Fabio Guidoni. Annibale folded the drawing with care and slid it into his jacket pocket.

Carla was tapping excitedly on the keyboard in the cupboard of an office they'd carved out for her when she was hired. It was her personal oasis: clippings were sorted into files stacked with precision, and each article backed up on the PC's personal folder, easily accessible. There were no signs of her personal life. No photos, no posters, no trinkets – all things that profoundly irritated her.

The article was flowing smoothly, easily, filled with facts and images. Carla was feeling great, the previous night with Giulio Strozzi already a faded memory. It only reappeared now at longer intervals, but it still brought some lingering nausea with it. It felt like leaning over the abyss, teetering on the edge and feeling the draw and pull of the fall, if only for a second. Then the feeling would leave, she'd take a deep breath and collect herself again.

Across from her, Salvo Caprile was typing up a profile of Colonel Canessa, which would be printed alongside the scoop she got from the former Carabiniere behind the morgue.

'Shit, Carla, this guy was a cross between Rambo and the Terminator,' her colleague exclaimed, highlighting a clipping from the archives.

Carla smiled. She really rated the small Sicilian guy who'd joined them a year ago as a sub and had immediately been offered a full contract. He was quick and flexible, even if not the greatest writer. Strozzi called him a 'mouse', but it wasn't a put-down: whenever they needed to locate a story, a resource, a paper trail from the past, Caprile was like a mouse with cheese.

'The via Gaeta story is incredible. I was two years old. I never knew all the details.'

'I was three. My mum told me years later that when my dad got home from work that day he said: "Someone finally got him."'

'Shit, that's cool. Can I put it in?'

'Don't fuck around, Caprile.'

'Shame.'

Carla stared at him with a mixture of tenderness and pity before her gaze moved to the Monica Bellucci poster behind him.

She returned to her typing, but the screen showed a new email notification. She opened it. 'Well done, an excellent piece.'

Giulio Strozzi was live-editing her article, reading it while she was writing it. Technology: a double-edged sword, both extremely useful and incredibly invasive.

Maybe her boss was just trying to cover up his guilt, but even without his flattery she knew she was doing a great job. Her colleagues had discovered the identity of the other victim with Pino Petri, and that the former Colonel Canessa was in Milan and about to be heard by the prosecutors as an informed witness. But she was the only one who'd talked to him, so her article would lead the front page. It had been Strozzi's idea, and the chief agreed.

The memory of her night with the managing editor returned to dampen her mood.

8

Annibale Canessa was surprised – and not pleasantly – by the diplomas festooning the wall behind Deputy Judge Guidoni. He already had a strong dislike of people who paraded their accomplishments, but this one really pushed the meaning of 'accomplishment': they weren't just work-related – law degree, Master's from an American college – he'd even included a bungee-jumping certificate from New Zealand and third prize in a Hawai'i triathlon.

He had to admit that Guidoni was well-built, with the body of a weight-lifter. There was nothing about him of the stereotypical magistrate. *Not that it makes a difference*, Annibale muttered to himself, a firm believer in the book and cover adage for any role, *but this wall display of testosterone isn't promising.* He spotted a revolver stuffed into the man's belt, and the picture was complete. *Jesus! He thinks he's a sheriff.*

The woman next to him was something entirely different. Her gaze was piercing, and though her face wasn't what you'd call pretty, there was something seductive about it, like Medusa's head. She was squeezed into a beige trouser suit that hugged her body. Repetto would charmingly have called her a prick tease. The term made him smirk.

'What's so funny?' Guidoni asked him. He couldn't have been that dumb, then.

'Actually, I've been trying all morning to think of something,' he shot back.

Guidoni nodded. The woman watched him carefully.

'*Mister* Canessa,' the words underlined his point that, in here, previous rank no longer mattered, 'may I offer first of all my sincere condolences for your brother's death. That said, I'd like to take a statement.'

'I'm all yours.'

Annibale had decided to play the part of the retired Carabiniere who'd never forgotten the force's motto: *Usi a obbedir tacendo*, to follow orders in silence.

'How long had it been since you'd seen your brother?'

'Twenty-five years, give or take.'

The prosecutors looked at each other in confusion. The woman spoke next. 'Not even a phone call, a card?'

'Nothing. The last time I saw him was on the 22nd of December 1984, for less than an hour, in the self-service restaurant in the train station in Modena. And then today, as a corpse.' He spoke like a police report. The colleagues in front of him knew he was telling the truth: Canessa realised they'd have checked his calls, emails, confirmed his movements.

'Your brother's wife confirms your story. Yet I must admit, I'm surprised. It's not that I don't believe you, of course. But your hatred for each other must have been fairly strong to keep you apart like that.'

'I wouldn't call it hatred. More resentment of each other's life choices. From my point of view, his behaviour towards our parents played its part too. Ever since we were kids.'

Canessa wasn't entirely happy about divulging that painful domestic reality to the prosecutors, but he needed to concede some truth in order to get them to believe the lie: that he was indeed sad and dejected.

'What about Petri?'

'The last time I saw him? Same year, in July. I arrested him in Spain, brought him back to Italy, and never saw him again except on the news. He eventually disappeared from there too.'

'Did you know he was on parole and close to release?'

'I hadn't thought about him for a long time. And I haven't really followed the news for the past couple of years.'

'You're in the hospitality and food service business now,' Guidoni said, looking at a document. Probably a police report.

'Yes, I'm helping my aunt.'

'But you're also a member of the Genoa bar association.' The woman was also holding a folder, a blue one, and pretending to look through it.

'Yes, after leaving the force I went to university and graduated in philosophy and law.'

'Two degrees? Good god.'

The macho prosecutor seemed impressed.

'So, coming back to us, can you imagine why Petri might have met with your brother?'

'No. Do you have any ideas?'

'We're pursuing various lines of inquiry. But that meeting between two former terrorists is definitely unusual.'

Annibale was irritated by the woman's provocation but he swallowed, not taking the bait. Instead he stated, slowly and clearly, 'However distant we were, I must point out that my brother, in all honesty, was never a terrorist.'

'He spent a five-month sentence on suspicion of belonging to the armed wing of the party,' she reminded him.

'Three. It was three months. They did arrest him, but he was let go for lack of evidence, and when we last saw each other he told me he'd received a written apology. As far as I know, he was clean.'

'We're at an impasse then, my lawyer friend – if I can call you that,' Guidoni smiled, with no trace of malice. 'Is there anything you can do to help us?'

'If I could, I honestly would, but I've been out of the game for a quarter of a century and have no more contacts. I'm in a different industry. I'm sorry.'

'No hunches, theories?'

'All I can tell from my own experience is that Petri was the target. My brother must've been collateral damage.'

It was true, but sitting in that room even he didn't fully believe it.

'Are you sure?'

'Of course not, but Petri was a former terrorist on parole, a lifer with multiple sentences. My brother was a librarian from Reggio Emilia with a wife and daughter and a false arrest behind him. If you're looking for a motive, then Petri's your man.'

'My dear sir,' Guidoni couldn't resist the lure of titles, even if he meant it cuttingly. 'You simply can't imagine how many families turn out to be viper's nests. Maybe your brother had a secret life. Even at the time, his arrest surprised you, right?' Presumptuous, insinuating, Guidoni thought he'd just scored a point against Canessa, whose very silence urged him to continue. 'Did your brother use drugs?'

'Not that I'm aware, but again, I hadn't heard from him in quite some time.'

'You know, it wouldn't be the first time a former terrorist moved up the social ladder by dealing heroin, cocaine – or something else.'

Annibale held hard to his self-control to stop himself giving a piece of his mind to this arrogant bastard who was already advancing some inane theory without a scrap of evidence. He kept quiet, grinding his heels into the floor.

His sermon over, Guidoni offered, 'I hope you don't mind, and I told your sister-in-law the same, but we won't be eliminating any possible lead.'

It sounded like a threat rather than consideration. The prosecutor looked at his colleague for backup. She was still standing, pretending to be busy with something else.

'I think that for now we can dismiss Mr Canessa.'

103

She resurfaced from her thoughts, as if only half-involved with proceedings. 'Yes, sure. Just one question, please. You got to Milan pretty quickly. Who told you?'

'I still have friends on the force. They heard my brother was involved and called me out of respect.'

'I suppose you won't be telling us who told you.'

'You suppose correctly. They have nothing to do with this and I'd rather not drag them into it.'

The woman replied with a cutting glare and turned to the clerk, saying: 'For the record: *Mister Canessa refuses to collaborate.*'

'Very well, you can go,' Guidoni cut the tension, 'for now. Of course, we'll have to talk to you again, once we uncover more evidence. You're not planning on leaving the country, are you?'

Canessa looked at them both and then stood up, asking flatly, 'Where would I go?'

Back in the corridor, Annibale took a deep breath and made for the exit. The afternoon had almost yielded to evening, and the courts were quiet. It was a Saturday, too.

No one offered to walk him out, nor did he ask for help. Though he'd been away for a lifetime, he recognised the old routes, the labyrinthine staircases and corridors of that large building dedicated to the pursuit of the law. He went to the public phone in the lobby and dialled a number he'd learned by heart a long time ago. The clear voice of a young woman replied, and was immediately disappointed. She was clearly expecting someone else, maybe her partner.

'Hello, this is Max. Is your dad home?'

'Hold on, please.'

She put the receiver down carelessly while Annibale considered what right he had to involve his friend, dragging him into a game that was showing every sign of turning dangerous.

'Max! It's been a while, how are you?' No sign of any kind of emotion in his voice.

'Not too bad, thank you, except for some sudden business – I imagine you've heard?'

'I did, of course. I was truly saddened and surprised.'

'Do you have the time to talk about it?' Annibale held his breath.

'Of course! When?'

'I'm in town only briefly, but I have time. Do you remember our old café? That should work for both of us, right?'

'That'll do. I'll see you there in an hour, just need to sort a few things out.'

'See you later, then.'

Annibale looked around. Darkness was creeping into the building. It was time for him to leave, but he still hadn't solved the matter of the people on his tail. He didn't want to face them in the open. He needed to disappear, without letting his guardian angels know that they'd been spotted.

What I need is a stroke of luck.

Just then, he heard the sound of footsteps behind him. Lorenzo Giannini made his appearance from a side corridor, along with three agents acting as a security detail. He was one of the few magistrates with whom Canessa had always had a good rapport during the war on terrorism. Younger by a couple years, he was a large man now sporting a white beard. He'd always lifted Canessa's spirits, one of the few in that place who could. Canessa bumped into him, pretending not to see him and hoping that the giant in jeans and flannel shirt would do so instead.

'Annibale!' Giannini thundered, his baritone voice carrying a decidedly Tuscan accent.

'Lorenzo! Of all people…'

They hugged under the confused gaze of the security escort. The magistrate suddenly fell serious. 'I heard about Petri and your brother. That was bad news. I'm so sorry for your loss.'

'Thanks. I've just been questioned by the prosecutors in charge of the case.'

The magistrate snorted. 'Guidoni and Bossini, an odd pairing.' He added nothing else, already regretting saying that much.

'There used to be a time when a case like this would be yours. Petri especially, you've dealt with him several times…'

'True, but things are done differently around here now.'

He clammed up, aligning himself with his peers; respectful of rules, just as Canessa remembered him.

'What are you up to now?' the magistrate asked.

'I was just looking for the exit. My memory of this place is a little foggy,' he lied. 'I'm getting old.'

'You on foot? I'll give you a lift! Where are you headed?'

'Towards Corso Sempione, but you can leave me anywhere near there.'

Giannini placed a large hand on his shoulder and started walking towards the underground car park. 'Come on, no problem. Also, and I don't want to appear insensitive by changing the subject, but do you really have a restaurant these days?'

The magistrate had always loved fine food. His barbecues, with meat ordered personally from Val di Chiana, were legendary.

Panattoni saw one of the magistrates' cars pull out of the car park, preceded by the security, but he didn't bother to look at its passengers. A couple of hours later, when Guidoni and Bossini also left the building, he realised he'd been played. Shocked, he wondered if the target had noticed them, but soon dismissed the thought: that would be a disaster. He called his associate on the other side of the building and dismissed him. Then, using the burner phone, he dialled the number he'd called once already, expecting a violent reaction from the other end.

'We lost him,' he opened, with as much apology in his tone as he could muster.

9

Annibale made himself comfortable at one of the tables in the café run by Sardinians, halfway down the large avenue. Customers came and went, often forced to stand at the bar for their order, and glaring at him for hogging a whole table. He was too busy envying a couple enjoying their plate of spaghetti with sea urchins.

He'd been there for the past fifteen minutes, ever since Giannini had dropped him off on the corner of via Procaccini. The fine Saturday had drawn almost half of the city's population outside; the air was crisp, skies were clear. It was the ideal weather to head out, stretch your legs, laugh, forget. Ideal weather to blend in, and not be noticed.

Annibale kept a watchful eye over his surroundings, all senses on the alert. Which was how he noticed a familiar presence before it stepped into his field of vision.

Ivan Repetto recognised his old comrade-in-arms from a distance. He smiled, noticing that he'd chosen a spot with several exit points. Canessa hadn't forgotten the teachings, the rules, the commandments regarding survival in a world that wanted people in uniform dead and buried. He was alert, but only those who knew of his obsessions, like Repetto himself, would notice. Anyone else would simply see a man waiting for someone, maybe a partner, to join him on that mild spring evening.

A light breeze rustled the leaves on the street. Repetto made himself known from a distance, waved, and came to sit opposite his old friend. They shook hands. He hadn't changed since the last time they'd seen each other over ten years earlier.

After they left the force at the end of 1984, almost at the same time (Verde had called it the 'Laurel & Hardy Farewell'), they'd continued to meet up for a couple of years. Or rather, Repetto had forced Canessa, every now and then, to come to his wife's family's summer house in Inverigo. He remembered him as a restless man, lost without his uniform, full of doubt, a mature university student without any real direction. Someone with no financial problems but equally no idea how to spend his time or money. The visits had dwindled until they were phone calls at holidays, then cards in the post. The last one was from 1999. Then... nothing. Now here he was, with the same grey hair he'd had the past twenty years and a web of lines around his eyes. But those eyes hadn't lost any of their sharpness.

Max was his nickname, like Vittorio De Sica's character in the old film Annibale had forced him to watch over and over again during long stays in the barracks, country hotels or safe houses, every time it aired on TV. It was the name of a young soldier who dreamed of fighting with style, an officer and a gentleman, with both military and life skills.

Annibale ordered some beers and a plate of spaghetti 'like the one that young couple are eating'. The pair turned around and chuckled, and he saw the woman give him a look that reminded him of his younger days. Now, however, he had other fish to fry.

Repetto didn't offer his condolences. He didn't believe in platitudes. There was no need for that sort of thing between them.

'This whole shooting thing is complicated. I have a feeling about it. It was ruthless, planned. A professional job.'

He gave Repetto a short summary. Beers and spaghetti arrived in the meantime, and Repetto declined to partake of the pasta.

'Someone was waiting for them, and they knew that Petri had called my brother. They were worried he'd say something, which is why they took them out. They were watching them. This isn't a small matter.'

'Petri never talked, never became a supergrass, never disavowed his actions. He didn't even claim to be a diehard or a political prisoner. He's always been quiet. A wall. What could he possibly have to say now? All his exploits have already been traced and recorded.'

Annibale set down his fork. 'Yes, Ivan, that's our first question. And the answer? We have no idea. Second question: we have no idea *who* he would say it to. My brother? It makes no sense. He was a librarian in Reggio Emilia…'

Repetto took a sip of his cold beer. 'Maybe he needed something… or someone, a middleman.'

'I thought of that too. He wanted to talk to me, but couldn't track me down. I'm not in the phone directory, and it's not easy to find me. But he knew my brother lived in Reggio Emilia, because they were arrested on the same day; it was all over the news. He wouldn't have forgotten that detail. Maybe he thought we were still in touch and sought him out to ask him to meet with me.'

'Why not phone?'

'No, never on the phone. Maybe he wanted to be sure I'd be willing to listen, gauge the interest. Maybe. Another detail we'll never know. We do know this though: anyone who kills so brutally has some horrendous thing to hide from their past – and something big to defend here, now: money, power, reputation.'

'Again: Petri was arrested in the 80s. Why not take him out then, if he knew all this? From your speculation, these are people with resources and means.'

'Maybe they didn't know back then. Maybe they thought he didn't know and they've now realised that actually, he did.'

'Maybe Petri was blackmailing them,' Repetto suggested, 'or he gave them the impression that he wanted revenge and they pre-empted him. Possibly?'

'That would be a stretch, and it still wouldn't cover everything.'

'What else, do you think?'

Annibale didn't reply, lost in his own thoughts. The air was full of voices and laughter.

'Young people are much better looking these days, don't you think? Your kids must be grown up by now. Do your daughters go out at night?'

'Of course! My eldest has already made me a grandfather, and the youngest – she's the one who answered the phone – is nearly twenty and almost never in the house any more.'

Annibale smiled. 'If I had a daughter, I'd be worried sick every time she left the house.'

Repetto shook his head. 'You torture yourself if you get wound up in that thought. Sure, I worry a little when they're away, but they have to live their own lives.'

They fell silent for a while, and finished their dinner with a coffee. Repetto waited for his friend to break the silence.

'Those two prosecutors, Ivan… you should've seen them. What a pair: a dickhead who thinks he's Big Jim and a woman you'd have called a prick tease.'

'Names?'

'Guidoni and Bossini.'

'She's quite famous. Haven't you ever heard of her? She's been following a lot of corruption cases, part of Astroni's pool.'

'I don't know anything about her, but Mr Muscle seems unfit for this inquiry. And she's clearly trying to control him, manipulate him, get him where she wants him. She seems to have been put there specifically to influence the investigation, but I can't figure out why.'

'A cover-up?' Repetto was shocked.

'I don't know, but something rings hollow. Something's off key, murky, something's not being said. To top it off, Calandra's involved.'

'The Secret Service? I mean, yeah, with a former terrorist gunned down…'

Annibale paid the bill and they headed for the city centre, while the couple who'd been waiting for their table silently thanked them.

The time came for Repetto to pose the question that had been looming over them since the start of their reunion. 'Why did you call me, Annibale?'

Annibale stopped walking, and placed a hand on his friend's shoulder. 'I need help. I'll be looking into this case, but I don't want to drag you into it more than I have to. I was followed today, all the way to the courts. This is dangerous. There's more than one person behind it, and they have resources. I want you to stay out of it, but I'm hoping you'll help me from the back benches, with the logistics.'

Repetto raised a hand. 'I won't shy away from this.'

'Look, I can't have you on the front line again. I need you in the background,' Canessa replied.

'I'll come along with you, like old times, but don't forget you're no longer in uniform. What authority do you have to look into the matter?'

'None, but that won't stop me. The story here is muddled, all out of order. I want to focus on the details and set them straight in my own way, if necessary. I got the feeling in the prosecutor's office that they're not going to see it through. I'll need to do it. You stay in the background. Just find me what I need.'

'We used to have the means, an infrastructure, loyal people,' Repetto objected, but Annibale's wry grimace stopped him.

'We can set things up again. We have a number of favours to call in. Start with Rossi – it's time to collect.'

They'd reached the Arco della Pace. The square was all lit up, and the trees on the opposite side cast their shadows over the cobblestones. Young people were hanging out on the stone benches and outside the bars.

'They have guns,' Repetto sighed.

'So do I.' Canessa grinned.

He's still the same, thought Repetto.

10

Cosima, Maggese's widow, had spent all afternoon watching people coming and going on her quiet suburban street. She'd also attended the funeral, in order to pay her respects to the kind man who'd helped her with her shopping. But she hadn't come forward, and instead stood in the shade of the wall tombs – there was her husband's, bless his soul. Now night was falling, and everything was settled again, calm and quiet.

Peering from behind the curtain, she could see the swing where she'd spotted her neighbour exactly one week ago, absorbed in his thoughts. It was another Saturday. Not as nice as the one of the tragedy, but warmer.

Cosima wasn't all that fond of children, but she was impressed by the composure of the 'little orphan' (she'd automatically decided that's what she was). In the middle all those people, she'd been able to maintain a touching gravity. And it suddenly hit Cosima that there were now *two* widows in the houses opposite one other on her road in the suburbs of Reggio Emilia.

She cast one last glance across the road and saw a man walking around the swing. It must've been the brother. But unlike poor Napoleone, who never looked towards her window, it seemed like this one could read minds like they do in films, because his eyes shot up to meet hers. Mrs Maggese nearly screamed. She let go of the curtain and went back to the news report on the preliminary hearings involving the head of the opposition. 'The last big corruption trial,' the journalist called it. Judge Federico Astroni was explaining why the politician (what a shame, she really liked him) deserved his sentence. *What a handsome man*, she thought.

There was very little news from upstairs. The last of Giovanna's friends had left a while ago and apart from a short break for supper, she'd kept to her room, quietly reading.

'She mumbles to herself, making up stories. Napoleone and I were worried when we found out, but then we realised that this fantasy world of hers wasn't closing her off; it was actually opening her up,' Sara told Annibale. They were sitting in the vast kitchen, in what now seemed to her an unbearably empty space. She'd wanted it that way originally because it reminded her of her family's farm in Bassa.

Canessa was washing up after the meal he'd made for his sister-in-law and niece: spaghetti with clams and salted cod. Zia Mariarosa had brought the ingredients directly from Camogli. She'd come over the previous morning with the rest of the family, thinking, as Annibale had, that the funeral would be a small, close-friends-only affair. Instead, there had been at least five hundred people, and as he set the last plate on the rack, Annibale had another wave of regret at having shut down all communication with Napoleone. For his stubbornness in denying all possibility of a reunion, and his cowardice. But there was something else troubling him, too. He'd been surprised by how few nosy strangers there'd been at the funeral. Surprised and even a little envious.

Napoleone had lived a full life. He hadn't run away, he'd built something – and in so doing, he'd *left* something. Annibale had known he would. He'd said so the last time they'd seen each other: that of the pair of them, Napoleone would be the one to start a family.

From a practical point of view, the worst thing about the funeral was that he hadn't been entirely sure about who was a friend and who was there out of nosiness. He'd tried to get a look at each face, but he'd only recognised the police officers. A pair of them had had recording equipment. He wished he'd had the authority to ask for copies of the tapes so he could go through them and identify anyone, a face, an expression that might help him move forward in his pursuit of the truth.

He joined Sara on the couch. She'd kicked off her shoes and was leaning head in hand on the armrest, with her legs stretched out next to her, still draped in the elegant black trousers she'd worn at the service. She flashed him a tired smile.

'Are you staying over tonight?'

'I should go. I need to pick up some stuff at home and head back to Milan.'

She seemed surprised. 'Milan? Why? For the investigation?'

'For *my* investigation.' He ran his hand along bookshelves almost groaning under the weight of the books they held. All used, all read. 'Did Napoleone like his job?'

'He did. He found peace and answers in the library. He lived for us – and his books. He even had one in his pocket when he was shot.' Her eyes welled up. 'Annibale, what are you going to do? One of the few times Napoleone told me about you, he said you were like a Panzer tank. His word. You lose control, run over everyone and everything. Wouldn't it be easier to leave it all to the people in charge of the investigation? When we met in Milan, I wanted the truth from you. Now that Napoleone's buried, I feel like I'm ready to put it aside if it means they'll leave me alone.'

He turned a tough look on her. 'The truth will bring you peace. I abandoned my brother once before, unwilling to confront our shared history. I owe it to him, and also to myself. Listen to me, Sara. I'm up against some dangerous people and the only thing that holds me back is the thought of you and Giovanna somehow getting dragged into this. They may not think you know something, but they could hurt you to get to me. I don't know who "they" are exactly, but I know they're ruthless.'

Sara shifted her feet back to the floor and looked straight at him.

'Are we in danger?'

'I don't know, but please be careful. Keep an eye out. If you spot a face a little too often in different places, make a note of it. Check the house to see if anyone has been in here while you were out.' He pulled a piece of paper out his shirt pocket and handed it to her. 'Here are two phone numbers. You should memorise them if you can. One's a friend of mine: ask for Max, and he'll put you in touch with me. The other belongs to Flavio Cordano, a lawyer in Genoa, another friend, and very good at his job. If any legal issues come up, any at all, call him. He knows what's going on.'

Sara took the paper and stared at it for five minutes, committing the numbers to memory.

'I really need to leave now.'

'Don't you want to say goodbye to Giovanna?'

They went upstairs together. Giovanna had fallen asleep in her pyjamas on top of the bed.

'She's sensible, your niece,' Sara said, tucking her in. 'You should try to be the same.'

With a mixture of fear and excitement, Annibale realised that he had a family now.

11

Piercarlo Rossi stepped out of the building in via Borgospesso, taking in air cooled by the recent rain. The bad weather had returned in early May, but he'd already switched over to his summer wardrobe and had no intention of pulling out the winter one. He headed towards the city centre, planning on breakfast in via Broletto, even though it was noon already. He knew a café where the waitress had eye-popping cleavage and tattoos that pointed to all the right bits of her body. He'd been trying to chat her up for some time. *Not long now*, he told himself, *then I'll take her to Santa and Bob's your uncle!*

At that very moment, his past collided with his present.

'Hello Vampa, you seem to be doing well.' The voice was only a few steps behind him, but actually came from years ago.

Rossi froze in the middle of the pavement, uncertain whether to turn around or not. There were only two people in the world who'd call him that. Marshal Repetto had given him the nickname because of his lush, arched eyebrows, and the mane of hair surrounding his shiny dome. Like a Transylvanian vampire.

He was the sole heir of an extremely wealthy family of silk workers from Como. Orphaned at an early age, he'd grown up with his grandfather, who told him on his deathbed: 'Even if you try really hard, and I know you will, you'll never be poor.' He'd managed to do some serious damage to the family wealth in the late 70s, but he'd only got it down by about a third. He then fell in love with a girl from Dario Filippi's circle, the terrorist group known in Milan as the 'weekday bandits'. They'd made history for the cowardly murder of a journalist and for never spending more than a couple of months in prison, thanks to the new collaboration law – they all ratted each other out.

He'd put a lot of effort into getting into their circles: he knew nothing about politics, the imperialist State, multinationals, that bullshit. He did care about women, and that brunette had a backside that truly moved him. He'd almost managed to bankrupt himself for the one woman he'd ever really felt attached to. Served him right.

His contribution to the revolution, however, had been negligible. They'd kept him in the dark for most of the action: at most, he'd been a 'postman', delivering memos. Obviously they never divulged their plans – and he didn't want to know – but when they'd killed Giuseppe Ardito, the journalist, he'd been shocked to the core. It was too late though. Canessa had arrested him along with the rest of the group in a single operation at break-neck speed all over the city – his trademark approach. Annibale didn't trust anyone apart from his own team, and when he made multiple arrests, it wasn't a coordinated raid: he ran like the devil and caught everyone himself.

At that moment, stock still on a pavement in central Milan, the passers-by brushing past him as they went about their daily business, Rossi thought back to his night in the barracks in via Lamarmora, first in solitary, then in the interrogation room. After a short wait, he'd been hauled in to face Canessa and Repetto, one tall and chiselled, the other stocky, but both tough as nails.

'What are you smiling about, you piece of shit? Wipe that grin off your mug or I'll do it for you,' Repetto hissed, his face almost touching Rossi's.

'You don't look like a terrorist, you look like a pillock,' Major Canessa said, scanning some documents. 'You don't look like an intellectual. What were you doing with those arseholes?'

He'd told them the truth for an hour.

When he was finished, Canessa turned off the recorder, removed the tape, and handed it to Repetto.

'I hope you got to fuck her!'

Rossi held up his thumb and index finger. 'I was this close, but that's when they started shooting.'

With a smirk, Canessa stood up, grabbed the papers and shredded them.

'Piercarlo Rossi, your sins are forgiven. You're lucky: I'm like God these days, I can do anything. Go in peace. You were never here. You never existed. But if I catch you being a pillock again, even just driving through a red light, you'll pay for every last thing.'

Rossi had practically kissed the Carabiniere's hands.

'Can I really go?'

'Yes. Piss off, we never met. And remember: I don't do this for nothing. You owe me big time.'

Rossi turned round at the door. 'You won't regret this. Good luck, and if you ever need anything, look me out. Honestly: you want something, I'll do it. House in the countryside, a holiday, a loan.'

'Get out, pillock, before I change my mind.'

Here they were, now, in the third millennium.

Behind Rossi, Repetto was smiling. He'd noticed the trimmed eyebrows, the shaved head. 'Looks like "Vampa" is outdated. We'll have to come up with something else. You busy? I'm here to remind you of an old promise you made.'

Panattoni was sitting in his flat-cum-office in via Bergamo. It was in a 1960s building and boasted all the kooky features of that architectural period. In his loft on the top floor, a spiral staircase wound up from a large open-plan room to a terrace with a stunning view over the city. At that particular moment, however, the PI wasn't interested in urban landscapes.

He was waiting for new orders from his retainers. He'd been to a funeral in Reggio Emilia, where he'd blended in with the crowd, careful not to be caught on police camera, then returned to Milan. 'All clear,' he'd reported. The brother wasn't in a hurry and he was still in the dark, that much was clear. But according to Nando's retainers, Canessa would soon be coming to Milan to start his own investigation. They were sure of it.

'You're in charge of finding out when he arrives. Which is why we need to keep tabs on the people he may contact.'

They gave him a list. The first name on it was Ivan Repetto, a former marshal.

He liked afternoon sex; it reminded him of his youth. Back then, the right time to meet girls was the afternoon, not the evening. During Milan's wintry, grey hours, it really excited him to lie in bed knowing that everything was still going on outside while he was naked inside with the latest young thing who'd fallen for him, and whom he wouldn't see again. He felt like he was floating.

He had the exact same feeling that rainy afternoon as he lay under the sheets watching Marta get dressed. They were in what used to be his parents' room and was now his. Well, it was their furniture, but the actual house was different. The large walnut bed, for example, was from the Thirties, a piece of Fascist Modernism. An architect he knew had told him how much it was worth – definitely more than all those fussy nineteenth-century reproduction pieces that adorned the bedrooms of Milan's wealthy.

Marta Bossini was sitting in front of the mirror that used to be his mother's. He loved her back, and he loved taking her from behind so he could caress her spine.

She'd slipped her skirt back on, but she was still topless. Feeling his gaze on her, she turned around and gave him a faint smile. No, definitely not love, but maybe devotion.

Astroni threw out a question with studied casualness. 'So, how's the Petri-Canessa case going?'

It was the first time he'd mentioned it. He'd held back for a while, playing down his apprehension and curiosity, but he couldn't keep quiet any longer.

Marta reached behind her to hook her black bra.

'It's tricky. We don't have any leads yet, but it was obviously a professional job. So far, though, we can't figure out the motive. We're digging through their pasts to see if there's any crossover, any point of contact. It's time-consuming.'

Astroni sighed and sat up in bed.

'I get it. But if it were down to me, I wouldn't rule out recent elements. All three main characters in this triangle had new lives. And I don't like having Canessa's brother, the former Carabiniere, in the background.'

Marta weighed up his words, filed them away mentally and nodded.

'I didn't like him at all during the interview. He was kind of numb and lost, but his eyes kept flashing with what I'd call rage…'

'You're right. Rage,' he interrupted, 'is a form of renewable energy. Don't underestimate it. Just like the need to be in the centre, to play a starring role.' Almost to himself, he added, 'I wonder where his pride has got him this time. Maybe he's crossed his own line.'

Marta slipped her arms into her jacket and moved closer to Federico for a quick kiss.

'How and why would he have crossed it? To get close to the man he arrested?'

Astroni spread his arms. 'Oh, I don't know. But I do know he's dangerous, and he might intervene, might even tamper with evidence, for good or ill. Trust me: he'll get in your way, so watch out.'

Marta pulled on her raincoat and stopped at the door. 'Did you know him well? In his prime, I mean?'

Her lover flashed her an evil grin. 'Fortunately not. We judges were cannon fodder back then. They were police, prosecutors and judges all rolled in one. Only obedient little judges worked with the likes of Annibale Canessa.'

'And you weren't one of them. But those days are over now, right?'

Federico stepped out of bed, naked and defiant.

'You bet they are.'

12

A long line of cars hovered over the sun-baked countryside, headed for Milan. But they were speeding along in the opposite direction, aided by a fog-free morning.

Annibale was studying the documents Cordano had given him. He was the defence lawyer for the prisoner and Annibale had contacted him to get an interview in the Opera Prison.

Rossi was driving, playing his part. He and Annibale had met five days earlier at the Marchesi Patisserie, while Repetto kept watch. With no time for nostalgia, Canessa had explained what he needed. 'Somewhere remote, but not completely isolated, with space for a car, more than one exit. Not in the centre, but not too far out in the suburbs either. It absolutely cannot be traceable back to you. Two clean phones, a satellite with a foreign SIM, a fast car for me – not flashy – and another car that you'll be driving when I don't want to. In case someone comes looking for us, we need to have time to disappear. Oh, and when you find the house, do a supply run. Non-perishables.'

Rossi, somewhere between amusement and irritation in his new role of prop finder, set down his cappuccino. 'Anything else? Women? Weapons?'

Annibale granted him a tired smile. 'I'll arrange the women,' he joked. 'Can you also get hold of some machine pistols and some automatics? Clean, good quality stuff.' Thinking back on the conversation now, he grazed the stock of his trusty Beretta at his waist, felt his revolver strapped to his right ankle. He was sure that even if they had to open fire, he wouldn't need to use his old friend. Then again, you never knew.

Rossi had been swift and thorough, just as expected. He'd suggested a renovated warehouse made into a luxury loft in the 1980s. It was near the canal, just down from the Canottieri Milano sports club but on the other side, and surrounded by a high wall. Accessed via a small door on the Alzaia, it had a gate onto the alleyway for vehicles. There was an even smaller door, well hidden, that opened onto a vacant field. 'It used to belong to an idiot who lost it on crack. He gave it to me to repay a debt, and it's still in his name, registered in the Virgin Islands. Even if they're good, they'll still only find the company. They'll have to work much harder to figure out which partner it actually belongs to.' He handed over the keys to an Alfa 156, almost new, waiting for them in the yard.

'Colonel, this one's yours. I found a slightly older BMW for myself, so we can be a little more chic. Rented under a false name from a Swiss society I've got shares in. Company card. They'll have to travel all over the world to actually catch me.'

Annibale put a hand on his shoulder. 'Great. You're hired. Pick me up tomorrow morning at 7.30. We have things to do.'

He'd spent the night in the loft, in a large bed on the mezzanine. He immediately clocked the skylight, which offered a fourth emergency exit: over the roof, and a quick leap into the neighbouring allotment. Someone was clearly taking care of that, so he'd need to note down who it was and what their routines were. He then hid his weapons in a cupboard: a couple of Sig Sauer P226s and the two MP5SD3 Heckler & Kochs that Rossi had procured for him.

He made himself a plate of pasta with *bottarga* he'd brought from Liguria. He decorated sliced Sardinian tomatoes with anchovies, and paired it all with a Pigato Rossi had put in the fridge.

He was alone again, but it wasn't the loneliness of the past twenty-five years. He liked this new feeling. It was his choice: the inevitable suffering before a battle, when you won't back down.

All night he was tense and alert, just like when he was a soldier preparing for action. He was ready. Half-asleep, he tightened his grip on the Beretta he'd placed under his pillow. Old habits are hard to break.

He was now in the car with Rossi, and they had nearly arrived at the Opera Prison.

'Who am I?' he asked abruptly.

'Anni— *Max*.' Rossi caught himself immediately, but not soon enough to escape a slap from Annibale.

'Me – Max, you – Vampa, Repetto – Angelo. Remember: no names or surnames.'

They reached the prison gates. Annibale pulled out both guns and slid them under the seat.

Rossi couldn't take his eyes off them.

'Are you going to leave them there?'

'I can't take them into the prison, can I? Look, don't worry. Just don't stay out here. Go into town, grab a coffee and keep an eye on the car. And remember—'

'—to note down everything that seems out of place, anyone looking at me too closely, same car driving past more than once. I got it.'

'Good man,' said Canessa. He got out of the BMW and approached the prison gates.

13

Pasquale Cammello had consented to speak to him.

He was a *camorrista*, a criminal working with the Camorra in Naples, and he had two life sentences and one pending re-evaluation. More importantly, he'd been Pino Petri's cellmate. Annibale hadn't been confident he'd agree to talk, but he'd tried to fix it up all the same. Surprisingly, Cordano, the lawyer for the case who'd acted as middleman, had given the green light for the interview and now Cammello was waiting in a room whose walls looked filthy but actually weren't: the colour was naturally ugly. Annibale sat wondering how they'd got that colour when the iron doors opened, and Cammello stepped in.

The guard uncuffed his large wrists and pushed him into a chair on the other side of the table. No one suggested a handshake.

Cammello spoke first. He was tall, thin and balding, and he looked more like a school teacher than a criminal.

'I know why you're here, Cop: you want information on Pino,' he began fairly aggressively. 'In any other situation, I'd never sit here and talk to you. But I liked Petri. He was a good lad. He had balls, he was honest. He thought the same of you.'

Annibale couldn't mask his surprise. A mistake, but he didn't catch himself in time.

'So he talked about me?'

The *camorrista*'s disdainful stare made him realise this wasn't a conversation; it was a favour he was granting to the former Carabiniere. No questions allowed. Cammello would talk, Canessa would listen.

'Couple of months ago, I spotted an envelope with your name on it among his things. I said: "I know that name!" He stuffed the envelope under a book and looked at me in a way that terrified even the likes of me, the rare times he'd give me that look. "He used to be a Carabiniere," he admitted. "What, you're writing to cops now?" But he didn't say a thing, and I learned that when he went quiet, that was the end of the conversation. Fuck all left to say. But he did respect me some, and he told me how out of all the cops he'd met, you were the only one who impressed him. He told me about that woman you left out of things in Spain. He goes, "He tracked me down for three years, finally found me. I never hated him. I would've liked to know him better, but it wasn't possible at the time. Maybe now..." That's it. He never talked about you or your brother after that. Then he got shot down.'

He mentioned it as if that were a natural consequence, as if he and Petri were bound to go that way: taken out in the middle of a road. He stood up and called the guard.

Canessa tried his luck. 'Had he changed at all recently? Anything strike you as different about him?'

Cammello froze. Without turning around, he said, 'For the last eight, nine months he was always lost in thought. He read a lot, but lately he was focused on one book, wrapped in newspaper. Everything else was the same: always alone, barely trusting anyone, no condescension. I liked the guy.' He stepped forward before turning round at the door. 'Oh, there was one more thing. I heard him muttering to himself once about some judge or other.'

Canessa felt an electric jolt. 'A judge?'

Cammello shrugged. 'Yeah. And some other word, but I couldn't hear.' He put his hand on the door. 'You know what? This might be the first time I'm rooting for a cop. Petri was a man of honour. I wouldn't mind you skinning those fuckers who killed him like a dog.' He disappeared behind the door, and the locks were bolted into place.

Canessa thought about people like Cammello and the 'dogs' they'd killed, dishonourably. But he'd stopped trying to understand the criminal code – who was honourable, who wasn't. As Canessa saw it, their world was devoid of honour. It had nothing.

The *camorrista*'s words confirmed what Annibale already knew: that the Canessa to whom Petri had meant to reveal his secrets was Annibale. Napoleone was just the middleman.

He backtracked mentally. Eight or nine months earlier, Petri changes his tune, something happens in his life. He keeps a book wrapped in newspaper, maybe a notebook. Something on his mind. What is it, and what's in the book?

The former terrorist had a sister somewhere. She would receive his personal effects. He had to get in touch with her: that story about a judge needed confirming now, even if he only turned out to be the one overseeing his parole. He felt renewed hope. He was on the right track.

It all crumbled, however, as he was leaving the prison. He spotted Rossi standing by the BMW on the other side of the main gate talking to a bald, elegantly dressed man with a bulging belly and recognised Chief Magistrate Calandra in his grey woollen two-piece suit and regimental Marinella cravat.

He should have expected it. He steadied himself and crossed the paved area separating him from the Secret Service agent. As he did so, he scanned for any other presence in the area, but came up with only the one car and its driver, clearly Calandra's security guard.

'Colonel, I was just talking to your *driver*,' the word was loaded with sarcasm, 'and I mean I was doing the talking because he's got your style: very tight-lipped. Nice day for an outing, isn't it?' His arm swept across the landscape, stopping at the prison. 'But that's a stinking eyesore, any way you look at it.'

Annibale played along, looking up into the clear sky. 'Good spring so far, yes.'

'A bit buttoned-up yourself, aren't you! Almost summer, my friend, almost summer.'

Annibale smiled. 'Fair enough. Are you on a day out as well, or are you visiting?'

'I came to see you. I knew you'd be here – don't ask me how.' He grinned. 'Not only is my hearing excellent, but if I were you – if you don't mind my comparison – I would have started here too. Except Pasquale Cammello wouldn't have given me a minute of his time.' His jovial expression faded, and he became serious. 'Can I steal a few minutes of yours?'

'Are you hoping to ask what Cammello told me?' Annibale kept to the same light tone, trying not to come across as defensive.

'Oh, if you want to keep me updated, I won't say no: I'm certainly curious. But no, what I want to talk about is more complicated. How about you let your "driver" join mine, and I'll drive for us, so we can talk?'

'Sure.'

Canessa asked Rossi for the keys to the BMW. Rossi, a little perplexed, handed them over reluctantly before heading over to the Croma. Through its tinted windows he caught a glimpse of Calandra's driver and felt even less reassured. Calandra took the keys like a child with a new toy, grunting excitedly as he settled into the car seat. 'It may not be the latest model, but this car's a joy,' he said as he got a purr out of the engine.

Calandra enjoyed the drive. Canessa had always admired, if not outright envied, the Secret Service officer's ability to navigate life by latching onto its more appealing aspects: a signature tie, a nice car, a good restaurant. He took it in with gusto, and a look that embraced all the positives. Never left anything out.

He kept quiet for a while, his eyes on the wheel. As the traffic increased closer to the city, he said nonchalantly, 'You're set on carrying along this road.' It was a statement, not a question. He shifted gears and stopped at a red light. 'You know, Colonel, I think this is quite a significant matter, something you can't see through on your own.'

Annibale automatically brought his hand to his belt, but realised his gun was still under the seat. 'Are you offering to help?' he asked, unable to hide his sarcasm.

'For what it's worth, yes. Or at least some impartiality.'

The answer caught Annibale off guard. He was tired of this foreplay.

'Do you know something I don't?'

Calandra took one hand from the wheel and held it up as a gesture of peace. 'No, not all. But I am, you might say, an outsider. Whereas you're right in the thick of it. So you may need to focus on the whole, and you might be fast – I know you're good – but I have the advantage. I've followed this country's history for several years, up close, and in all its dark corners. You've stayed on the sidelines, Colonel.' He fell quiet, as if expecting an invitation to continue.

Annibale was a good listener, and he was definitely interested. 'Go on.'

'You seem intent on not letting go, and so you'll keep going. That might involve my superiors, especially its consequences. Which is why I wanted to speak with you: to invite you to continue.'

Annibale was surprised, almost shocked. He'd thought Calandra wanted to tell him off, warn him, even threaten him. He was expecting anything but a green light, an invitation to plough right ahead.

The Secret Service man chuckled. 'Please don't look so surprised. I do admit that I'd be worried if you got hurt. But we don't want you to stop.'

'I honestly don't understand what use I can be to the government,' Annibale said.

Calandra cut in front of the number 24 tram, setting off a concert of blaring car horns. 'I'll be honest with you. You've met the prosecutors in charge of the case. A couple of unsettling characters, if you catch my drift. Guidoni's mediocre, Bossini is ruthless – motivated by some resentment I can't place. A Jacobin of the worst kind. Black and white, the exact opposite of how I see life. There aren't any shades of grey as far as that woman is concerned.' He paused. 'My dear Colonel, we're only at the opening skirmishes, but you'll soon be clashing with them. And not only them. Look: the prosecutor's office has become extremely powerful over the past few years, especially in Milan. It does what it wants, and it often goes against politicians publicly. They don't accept interference from Parliament, and I doubt they will from a former police chief – no offence. Canessa the Tank on a collision course with the magistrature: I'd like to see that!'

It was all starting to sink in. 'You think we'll have a run-in on account of my investigation and my personality, and you want something out of it. You're hoping I'll do something to hurt or weaken them. But what if I don't? What if I make an agreement with them? Have you considered that?' He paused. 'What I don't understand is this: doesn't this government support the magistrature's actions, both out of principle and as a political strategy? They've dealt some serious blows to their opponents. Aren't they currently trying the leader of the opposition?'

Calandra took the outer ring road, heading towards Ravizza Park. He brought the BMW to a halt under an oak tree and the second car stopped behind them. The chief magistrate opened the car door. The air was cool, despite the exhaust from the cars on the street next to them. They got out and headed into the park itself. Calandra took a deep breath.

'Times change, my dear Colonel. One can't deny the usefulness of the magistrature for the current government, of course. Initially, actually, it was almost a political task. It swept away the old powers favouring those currently governing the country, though I don't think that was actually the goal of the majority of magistrates. But we can't always delegate to judges the duties that belong to others. Power holds on to power. Do you understand what I'm saying? You can't hide behind judges as a long-term strategy. Plus, people are afraid of uniforms, an invasive State. First you get the applause, and then they're bored and become unsettled. Legacy of the Bourbons, the Austro-Hungarians, the Vatican. And the war is over.'

'I swear I've heard this already, many years ago…'

'Indeed, it's just like when we finally finished with terrorism. We got tired of indignation, too. People change; it's life. Revolution is followed by a period of calm, the people want to have fun again, they want peace. And the government doesn't want the judicial system breathing down their necks. If they continue to grill the leader of the opposition, they'll turn him into a martyr.'

'And you're hoping that this case will unravel in their hands, maybe with a nudge from me.'

Calandra stopped walking and pulled out half a Toscano from his cigar holder. He offered one to Canessa. 'I didn't know you smoked cigars,' Calandra commented, surprised.

'I used to every now and then, with my friend Repetto. When you retire, things you never thought possible start happening. You'll see.'

Calandra laughed, then went serious. 'Yes, that's what we hope, Colonel: that you'll do what you were famous for thirty years ago: some dirty work. Drag this prosecutor's office into a war it might lose, or that'll at least weaken it. Make it look bad, get it to make mistakes. What I think is more likely is that it will be the first to find out the truth.'

The Secret Service man let out a cloud of smoke and sighed. Annibale Canessa didn't like being used, nor did he care to wage a war against the prosecutors. All he knew was that he would stick to his path, single-handedly (or nearly), against everything and everyone. If Calandra could help, all the better.

'I'll do what I have to, Calandra. My war may cross over with yours, maybe not. But your help could be useful to me, and this is where we circle back to my first question. Do you know something I don't?'

Calandra raised his hands. 'Trust me, I would tell you if I did. All I know is something you've also figured out. These are muddy waters, and the magistrature are more involved than it seems. Putting Guidoni and Bossini in charge is the sign. Something's rotten in the state of Denmark. Be careful.'

'Who's that?'

Rossi and Canessa were stopped at a welcoming *osteria* in viale Montenero for a bite to eat. It was noisy, packed and steamy. Maybe it was the *pasta e fagioli*, but Annibale suddenly felt snowed under by responsibility. He often felt the weight of the world on his shoulders. For now, he focused on his duty to the man in front of him, happily devouring a *burrata* cheese from Andria.

'He's from the Secret Service. Maybe I shouldn't have brought you into this. Things may definitely go the wrong way. There are more people involved, and they're more dangerous than I had imagined.'

Rossi's fork stopped between his plate and his mouth, a string of white cheese swaying from it.

'You're getting rid of me?'

'I'll keep using your skills and resources, but I don't want you on the front line. I can't have you as a chauffeur unless it's unavoidable.'

Rossi knew the decision was final. *Damn*, he thought, *just when I was getting used to it.*

14

Panattoni was desperate. For the past few days he and his partner had been staking out the company run by the former Marshal Repetto. They were in an industrial area filled with warehouses, outlets, supermarkets, appliance stores. Not a cheery place, but not as filthy or terrifying as some of the locations he'd been sent to on the edge of Milan.

Panattoni was from Tor Bella Monaca originally, but had got used to the city centre and its amenities, its comforts. He hadn't been back home in years, and every time he ended up somewhere that reminded him of it, he felt blue. His nostalgia, however, would always be reserved for the balcony in via Bergamo.

It wasn't the stakeout that made him restless, but the phone call he had to make to his employers every evening at 6 p.m. They got angrier every day.

They wanted him to bug Repetto's office, and it had been extremely difficult to explain that bugging a company that produced, installed and maintained security systems would be a suicide mission.

In his rear-view mirror he spotted a Punto coming up behind him. His partner. Finally he could get out of there. If only he didn't have to make that damn phone call.

'He spoke to Cammello, the son of a bitch.'

Marta Bossini slammed her new handbag down on Guidoni's table.

'Which one's the son of a bitch, Canessa or Cammello?' Her colleague clocked the expensive accessory and attempted to lighten the mood. 'Did you go for some retail therapy?'

Bossini sat down and glared at him, but got the opposite of what she wanted. Guidoni chuckled.

'It's not against the law. He asked to talk to him and he was granted access. We can't force that "nice" *camorrista* to talk to us. And he can't have talked that much anyway. He doesn't know anything.'

Marta was unable to keep her surprise from erasing her frown. 'Are you hiding something from me?'

Guidoni was enjoying upsetting her. 'What do you know, for once the useless Guidoni has an ace up his sleeve, but all in good time. Now we need to shake up our Rambo here, remind him of his place. And the first thing we need to do is call the place where Petri worked and let them know they're about to receive a visit, and to let us know when it happens.'

Marta was surprised. The gym rat with few friends in the judicial branch was revealing himself to be up to the task. Almost on *her* level. He needed to be reminded of his place.

She crossed her legs, letting her skirt ride up to the dark line on her tights and drawing a poorly concealed glance from Guidoni.

'Couldn't have said it better myself. Go ahead and make that call.'

15

'A good start, but we're going in circles now.'

The comment – actually a criticism, as only Strozzi could deal them out – was bouncing around Carla Trovati's brain. She'd been at her desk for the past two hours nursing her irritation at this way of pointing out a mistake or something missing. All journalists who made it up the ladder had to put up with its banality. The ridiculously asinine plural. *We're* going, *we're* doing… Who's this *we*?

Carla had believed, for a while, that it was all teamwork, shared responsibility, and they all won or lost together. Then she'd realised it was a deceitful, gloating, fucker of a system, designed to make you feel even more of a loser, a traitor to the cause.

'We all lose, because of you.'

Carla hated that plural. And when they asked, 'Why didn't we have this?' with feigned kindness, instead of slagging you off, what could you say? 'Your honour, I didn't have it because I'm an idiot? Please just tell me off.' Too easy, huh?

She was mulling this over one morning in the office. As the first to arrive, she'd walked across the empty room that was local news and sat down at her cupboard desk to wait for an idea. It was almost noon and even in her small room she could feel the damp, heavy air that threatened the arrival of summer heat. Caprile wasn't there, the whole office was practically deserted: journalists on the trail of stories, press conferences, pacing up and down the courts of law. Maybe she should go too. But Carla had been tasked, from day one, to follow Annibale Canessa's every move, and she'd gone a whole week without losing track of him. She'd been to his brother's funeral, but she hadn't been able to get close again since the morgue. Canessa had stopped replying to her, started avoiding her. He avoided everyone else too, if that was any consolation.

Out of the entire team working on the Canessa-Petri story, she was the only one to have got any actual news out of it. But Strozzi had warned her: if she didn't come up with anything else, it'd be fair game and she'd be back to her previous tasks. Thank you! Next…

After their night together, their relationship had entered a sort of limbo. Formalities, small talk, no hint of anything more, a smile, a joke. Strozzi was smart. Maybe he'd got what he was after, another notch, or maybe he was waiting for the right moment for another fuck. He wouldn't show any signs of weakness until then. *I'm a nice guy, we slept together, but nothing changes between us. I'm the boss, you're the employee.*

In any case, she still couldn't track down Canessa. No idea where he was, no idea about anything. He'd disappeared, though she knew he was out there, and almost definitely in Milan pursuing his own investigation.

She looked up and noticed that something was different on the wall in front of her desk: Caprile had swapped the calendar photo of Monica Bellucci's butt, October 2019, for the generous bosom of a small blonde from some TV show. *Even Caprile moves on, updates things.*

She was the only one hanging on.

16

Claudio Salemme knocked gently at the heavy office door before turning the handle. He hesitated to widen the crack he was looking through while he waited for an invitation. His father, Giannino, finally waved him in as he finished off his phone conversation, accompanying his goodbyes with annoyed gestures.

The large desk was tidy. There was no computer, because Giannino Salemme hated all 'modern contraptions', as he called them: emails, mobile phones, the internet. 'The only net I want to know about is the one I use to catch sea bass,' was one of his regular technophobic comments. 'Nothing can replace a working human brain.'

A series of shelves ran along his office walls, all in dark cherry wood, with sliding glass panes protecting volume upon volume of antique books, some extremely rare.

There were no pictures apart from a single family photo showing his wife (*with her sickly face, poor Mum*, thought Claudio), and even that was relegated to the one spare nook in that extravagant display of bibliophily. These weren't just legal texts – the collection boasted art catalogues, essay collections, novels and poetry. And Giannino Salemme had read almost all of them, unlike many who surrounded themselves with books as if they lived in an abbey, and yet never pulled out a single tome, not even to use as a paperweight.

His son Claudio, on the other hand, considered himself a practical man. He wasn't prone to flights of fancy, and he'd never in his life touched a book that wasn't a university textbook – and that only after turning a corner following his rebellious youth. He'd ruined eyes on them, and burned them all after graduation in a sort of personal catharsis. It was his belief that literature, the arts, familiarity with stories, history and feelings made people too sensitive and therefore too easily controlled. He was convinced, without a shred of proof, that only the uncultured could have the cold blood, the ruthlessness and determination to order the most extreme acts, to make the harshest decisions. His certainty, however, cracked a little whenever he entered this dark temple to knowledge. Maybe Giannino Salemme was the exception to the rule…

Lost in this reflection, he heard only the end of what his father was telling him.

'—worried.'

'I'm sorry, I didn't catch that.'

'I was saying that I see you looking worried. When you knock on my door it's usually because you've done something stupid or because something is bothering you.'

Claudio was always annoyed when his father saw through him. He could never get used to this power dynamic, despite being smart enough to understand that his moment had yet to come, and that his boss was someone else.

'I don't think Panattoni is up to the task with Canessa. Maybe we need to do something more drastic. Maybe we should call back his Neapolitan colleague.'

Giannino Salemme shook his head.

'No. Panattoni has done an excellent job thus far. Let him work. He'll find Canessa again soon, you'll see. We can't fall back on extreme measures unless there's a real, tangible threat. We have to be cautious.'

'Canessa has been to prison to talk to Pasquale Cammello – isn't that a threat?'

'No, the meeting didn't go anywhere. Cammello can't have told him anything.'

'You know him that well?'

'I know, or rather knew Petri that well, yes.' Giannino Salemme broke into one of his predatory grins. 'He wasn't one to talk much. Not with his comrades, not with anyone watching his back. He was a loner, suspicious, prickly.' He leant his heavy arms on the desk and smiled. 'Things are fine as they are. Let the whole thing blow over, and keep an eye on the field from a distance. We have good radar and good allies. They won't surprise us.' He picked up the phone. Claudio knew their time was up but he still had something to say.

'I get that he's an old friend of yours, but I've never liked him. I don't trust him. He'd kill his own mother to get what he wants.'

Giannino Salemme put the phone down. The gap between his lips formed a grin that was truly disturbing.

'We would do the same, my son. But that is precisely why we are in no danger. We're in this hand in glove. To get what he wants and keep what he has, he'll have to defend us and we'll have to defend him.'

17

The building was like any other around Centrale. *Not far from where they massacred my brother and Petri*, Annibale thought as he looked at the ghostly monolith of the station. He ran through the brass plaques that named law firms, medical practices, insurers, even a comics publisher that populated the building. None of these buildings served as a private home. They emptied out no later than 8 p.m. and stayed that way over the weekend, holidays and summer.

A light rain was falling again, and the traffic was hosting another concert of car horns. It was a Thursday evening in mid May.

Annibale had asked Rossi to leave him out there a couple of hours earlier and had let Rossi go.

Recent events – the meeting with the prosecutors, his conversation with Cammello, the unexpected chat with Calandra – had left him feeling powerless.

He'd thought it would be easy to get back into the fray, straightforward like it used to be, when he had the strength of the State behind him and his moral strength within, or at least what he considered to be some kind of consistent morality. All of that had combined to create a bulwark against the troubling scenarios he'd had to face while on duty. He'd thought that by jumping back in the game, he could identify his target, go after it and get to it, steamrolling every obstacle. Just like all those years ago. But circumstances had changed.

Back then, there was a war on, with all the corner-cutting allowed in a state of emergency. He'd been a uniformed soldier and somehow, at the same time, a free agent despite procedures and hierarchy, willing to turn a blind eye. There were regular compromises, the path was sometimes unclear, and the differences between the State and its enemies blurred. This was a new season, and though it seemed the war was over, the road was still full of pitfalls and traps, even more than actual enemies. He was more of a detective inspector than a colonel these days. Yet no matter how many people still called him that, the army and the force were no longer behind him. His father, the general, historian and military strategist, would have drawn a parallel between World War I and II: on one side, the trenches, the advancing enemy, and no option for failure; on the other, a shifting battlefield, threats from all sides, ambush and retaliation.

With these thoughts swirling in his head, Annibale stood waiting to get into the third-floor office in the sad, grey building Petri had walked into every morning at 8.30 a.m. and walked out of at 5.30 p.m. The plaque read ACCOUNTANCY, ADMIN AND WEB SUPPORT. From what Repetto had told him, it was a modern accountancy business using practical financial software for supermarkets, small businesses and private companies with varied investments and interests. Petri had studied IT in prison and this was one of the places that employed people on parole. The director's name was Flavio Spano.

Annibale was hoping the office would clear out a bit, and he waited for some of the employees to leave. He kept an eye on the second-floor offices, to escape notice as he entered. He needed news on Petri that he couldn't get through official means, a fact that frustrated him. He was a nobody, these days, even as he played detective.

The bravado he had felt at the start had abandoned him. But he would press on, as he always did. He checked his watch and stepped into the building.

Spano left the fish tank he'd fashioned for himself at one end of the open plan area crammed with a dozen desks.

The space wasn't enormous, but it was cleverly designed. A long corridor stretched all the way to the wall where there was an office on each side with glass partitions, just like you see in American films. One was dark now, and the other belonged to the owner, something Annibale had worked out when he asked to speak to him and the receptionist dialled him. The man in the first fish tank had lifted the receiver and looked up. The reflection on the glass had prevented him from seeing the reaction to the woman's message. Was it resignation or cooperation?

He walked across the work space, followed by the only other person still there on that rainy evening: a pale young man with greasy blond hair and a face pitted with acne. Spano, on the other hand, looked like a fifty-year-old who meant business: sure of himself, his thick moustache balancing out his receding hairline. He had the look of a holdover from '68 who'd abandoned his hopes of changing the world, and become jaded as a result. That first impression would turn out to be not far from the truth.

Spano offered his hand with detached courtesy. A regular grip. The I-know-who-you-are-and-I-have-my-eye-on-you type, Repetto would've said.

'What can I do for you?'

Spano knew who he was, Canessa realised immediately, just as he realised he wasn't going to breach that wall. He tried anyway. 'My name is Annibale Canessa. I'm the brother of the man who was killed with Pino Petri. I'm looking into the reasons behind this whole mess, and I wondered if you—'

Spano raised a hand to interrupt, as if that information was of no importance. Behind him, meanwhile, the young man with acne had stood up and was gathering his things into a bag. 'I'm sorry, but there is nothing I know that can be of any use to you,' he said, dry but polite. 'And even if I did, I wouldn't tell you. I've already spoken to the prosecutors in charge of the case and I believe there are correct procedures to follow. I'm sorry about your brother, but I don't think there's space for personal investigations. There's the magistrature, there's the prosecutor's office, and in my opinion the people working there are good. This country needs to trust its legal system.'

It was hopeless. Canessa realised he was up against someone who'd exchanged revolutionary purity for judicial rectitude and ruthless moralism. There was no wiggle room, no nuance, no points of contact. The boy behind the inflexible Spano, however, was looking at him with interest as he slipped on his raincoat. Annibale smiled weakly, bit his tongue, and tried hard not to slip out of his humble and submissive amateur-detective persona.

'You're right, of course. I'm no bounty killer, and I don't mean to stand in the way of the law. We're on the same side. I've had some experience and I put myself at their disposal. Sometimes it can help to have another set of eyes, a different perspective on the same information.'

'Maybe I wasn't clear.' The man's tone turned sharp and threatening, as if he were still the old activist despite his corduroys, cashmere vest and tie. 'I know who you are and who you were, the methods you used back then. They warned me you might be paying me a visit. You didn't follow the rules thirty years ago and you're not going to follow them now. Now please leave, or I will call the prosecutors – actually, I'm calling them right now.'

He pivoted and headed towards his office. Annibale clenched his fists and dug his heels into the carpet to stop himself from following as he would have done in the past. He was tempted, but he realised that no good would come of the temptation, only trouble.

He saw the secretary squirm, felt her terrified gaze on his whitening knuckles. Her horsey face looked apprehensive. Canessa took a deep breath, relaxed and walked back towards the glass doors.

The last thing he saw was Spano on the phone before he turned around and headed for the landing. Only when he could no longer be seen did he run down the stairs to the exit, looking for somewhere to catch his breath and release his anger.

18

He didn't immediately realise he was being followed, and when he did he was furious. He stepped out of the front door and blended into the crowd, worried that he might suddenly see a policeman or, worse, Carabinieri car patrol. They would undoubtedly invent some excuse to stop him – obstruction, tampering with evidence, anything would do – and he'd never be rid of them. After his questioning, he'd promised never to have anything to do with those two: they'd pursue their investigation, he'd stick to his.

He was already on via Vitruvio when he noticed someone following him. He avoided turning round so as not to scare them away. He was determined to turn the tables this time, to be the hunter instead of the hunted. He kept walking along the pavement, away from the station. He crossed at the traffic lights, looking for the perfect window to reveal his shadow. Oddly, the guy was disappointingly unconcerned about being spotted. Clearly not a pro.

Pausing in front of a shop with bathroom mirrors on display, he recognised him. It was the pasty-looking guy from Spano's office and he seemed nervous, huddled in his raincoat and holding on to his tote bag.

Canessa realised that he wanted to talk, but something was holding him back. Maybe they were still too close to his workplace, or maybe he was looking for somewhere more private. So he led his shadow down a twisting path of streets, cars, people on their way home, and rumbling trams to a quiet mooring. A clean café with a large woman who had a twinkle in her eye behind the bar. He stopped at the door, as if in invitation, then stepped onto the neutral ground and sat down at one of the three tables, all empty.

'Good evening.'

The woman's cheeks lit up with a cheery smile. 'Good evening! Horrible weather, eh? I'm closing in a few minutes. Do you want a coffee?'

Canessa looked towards the entrance.

'I'm waiting for someone. We'll order together.'

The boy hesitated at the door, as if trying to gather his courage and his strength to take the final step. The café owner came to his rescue. 'Please, come in, come in, don't just stand there in this weather! Your friend's waiting for you!' And so the boy, smoothing down his greasy hair, walked into the café and hurried over to Canessa's table.

'Hot chocolate?' Canessa asked.

The young man shook his head, and spoke to the owner. 'A Martini please, no ice.'

Weird, Canessa thought. 'The same for me, please.' He'd imagined him a health-nut, a vegan, the enemy of all vice. He was proved wrong again as his interlocutor fished a pack of unfiltered Gauloises out of his bag and placed it on the table.

'It's a shame you can't smoke in public any more. At least I can still put them in front of me and savour the moment I'll light up, as soon as I'm out of here. Do you smoke?'

'Not really, no. If I'm with friends, I might partake of half a Toscano.'

'Good for you.' He paused. 'I'm Davide Alfridi.' He offered a sweaty hand, a weak but sincere handshake. 'I'm sorry about the way Spano treated you.' He spoke quickly, downing his drink and ordering another from the owner, who was keeping an eye on them, worried she might be dealing with a couple of drunks. 'He's obsessed with justice, rules. Ironic, since he went around smashing things to pieces thirty years ago.'

'Have you worked with him for long?'

'Eleven years, since the beginning. We were partners, equals back then.' He lifted his glass to toast the old company. 'Then I realised I wasn't cut out for the fish tank, for giving orders and dealing with other people – especially being ruthless with them, the ones who don't pay or try to defraud you. Spano still has some of his old… intimidatory ways. So I handed over my shares and stayed on as an employee. It's a little embarrassing for him, but he can't be without me. The software, our programs, they're my design.' His smile wasn't triumphant. 'It's just… Spano, he was in some gang or other back then, played security during demos, one of those guys with a crowbar who now hang off every word from the prosecutors they used to call slaves of the system. He told me as much; he finds it funny, almost. Well, he took a strange turn, but he's not alone. He's not a bad man though. He helps so many people.'

A sudden, almost imperceptible note in his voice gave Canessa a clue to Alfridi's sexual orientation. He didn't think he'd betrayed any change of expression, but Alfridi read his thoughts and his face lit up. He smiled, dropping all his shyness. 'We were lovers, yes. Many years ago…'

The young man – whom Canessa now realised was in his mid-thirties – downed another Martini and looked at him. 'Petri talked to me about you. He admired you, even if he had no idea where you'd gone. I'd like to help…' His voice dropped to a whisper, as if something were weighing on his heart.

Annibale took the lifeline that had been thrown to him from that uncertain ship. 'Had you noticed any changes in him recently?'

'Maybe seven or eight months ago. He was quieter, more distracted. He carried this book with him – it could have been a notepad, one of those larger ones, covered in newspaper.'

The same thing Cammello had said.

Canessa insisted. 'What was it? Did he tell you?'

'No, he was very protective of it, and he was very clear about his personal boundaries.' He smiled. 'I was curious, of course, but I never pressed. He had a personal attachment to that book.'

'Do you think someone less respectful of boundaries might have taken a look?'

'I don't think so. Petri's past scared a lot of people, but also his present.'

The noise of the evening traffic wafted towards them. Alfridi added quietly, 'Just like you. Spano is right about that. You can be scary even when you're trying to be kind.'

Annibale didn't reply. He didn't show it, but made a note to revisit his own behaviour going forwards.

Alfridi continued. 'If he didn't tell me, I can't imagine he would have told anyone else. I was the only one he spoke to in the office. He was good, fast, did everything we asked him. But other than Spano, who's given so many ex-cons and paroles a job, or me, Petri had no connections to speak of. Partially due to his colleagues, mind you, but also his own aloofness. In any case, as I was saying, he seemed different, but I wouldn't be able to tell you what was pressing on his mind.'

'What did he tell you about me?'

'He asked me if, after all these years, you would agree to meet him. I told him yes, that he should look you up, try finding you. That's all.'

'Did he ever mention a judge or a magistrate?'

'A judge? No. What would he say about that?'

'I don't know.'

'I'm sorry.' Alfridi picked up his bag and stood to go.

'Wait, one more question: did you ever talk about anything besides work? Anything that might be useful.'

The young man checked his surroundings – it was only the two of them and the owner, who was now busy cleaning the coffee maker – and sat down again. His hair fell back into his face, covering one eye.

'Actually, yes, though I don't know how useful it might be.

Right after he changed, seven months ago, he asked me how to access the *Corriere della Sera* archives from his computer.' He almost whistled. 'It's not that hard.'

Annibale was all ears. 'What was he after?'

'He didn't tell me, and I didn't ask.' He cleared his throat. 'I just taught him how to get around the system and into the archives. That's it.'

For Annibale, the cogs started whirring, processing the new data. 'Maybe we can access that information in his computer memory?'

'We could have, but the police took it away. Do you have access to them?'

'Unfortunately not.'

Annibale could feel his frustration mixing with the impatience coming from behind the bar. The owner was huffing and sending them clear signals: she was closing, they needed to leave. Alfridi insisted on paying for both of them.

They stepped out onto the wet pavement. At least it had stopped raining. Alfridi hesitated again before lighting a cigarette. 'Actually, there is another way. His search might have left traces in the target system. But we'd need a device directly connected to the archives, one of the *Corriere*'s computers.'

'Would you be able to find something out if you had one?'

Alfridi smiled, gratified. This was his field of expertise.

'It would be easy, but we'd need to know someone from the paper, to let us use one of their computers.' He sighed, as if to indicate the impossibility of the task. 'I wouldn't know where to start.'

'I do.' Annibale patted his coat for his wallet, and asked Alfridi for his contact details.

19

'I don't like it.'

They were sitting in the car, in piazza Piola. It was dark, and it was raining again. Repetto wasn't sure he'd lost whoever was following him, but Annibale told him not to worry: they were here to follow *him* and he would get rid of them later if he had to.

'You can't trust that journalist. How do you know she won't publish it as a story? Or worse, she might go tell them.'

'I have no other choice, and she seemed ambitious and open to compromise. She'll help me in exchange for an exclusive.'

Repetto shook his head and looked out, wiping the window with his sleeve to see if he recognised any of the cars parked around them.

'The fog is lifting. Petri went the *Hansel & Gretel* route, and left me a trail to follow to find the truth. He knew they'd try to stop him from meeting with me, and he knew he was in danger, so he left a trail of crumbs.'

'I'm not getting the metaphor.'

'What he wanted was to meet me: he wanted to tell me about a secret he was holding on to, something from when I was hunting him down as a terrorist. But he was wary. He knew that the people with things to hide would play dirty, so he protected himself. He left behind a skeleton key, and a string of signs to decode. He was sharp: he didn't leave them any old where, only in places where I would find them. As insurance.'

'You seem very sure about this, but I still don't understand.'

'Bear with me. He talked about me with the only two people he trusted: a *camorrista* and a colleague; a criminal who wouldn't speak to anyone but who thought of him as a man of honour, and an invisible man nobody notices. Opposites in many ways, but similar in their aloofness, for entirely different reasons. He didn't do it randomly: he didn't speak to anyone else. He knew I would start there. I'm a man of the law like they are. But he also knew that these people – who esteemed him as a criminal and possibly felt some affection for him, who knows? – would speak to me and me alone. Why? Because he'd let them both know that I was the only one *he* could trust. He also knew they wouldn't say anything to the people investigating, and he was right: Cammello and the young man only told me about the book, about Petri's change of demeanour, his request to access the *Corriere* archives and this mysterious judge. Which reminds me: look into the people who follow his case, starting from the parole judge. That's our next target.'

Repetto lowered his head. 'I wouldn't be so sure he did all of this intentionally.'

'I'm telling you he did. This is a scavenger hunt, and the prize at the end is the truth. We'll get there.'

Annibale opened the car door.

'And who are these fuckers following us?' Repetto asked.

'I don't know, but it must be someone who'd be destroyed by this secret. They're keeping an eye on us for now, but they can't find out if we're getting anywhere…'

'Couldn't we just turn the tables? See where they lead us?'

'Later. We're in no rush. We can catch them whenever. What matters with this whole thing is the why, not the who. Once we get to the treasure, we'll figure what to do with them too.'

Before Repetto could open his mouth, Canessa had disappeared into the rare spring rain falling over the city.

*

Panattoni watched Canessa run quickly down the steps of the underground station. For a moment, he considered following him, then changed his mind. He was resigned to the fact that Canessa was allowing them to follow him, and could easily get rid of them whenever he wanted. Figuring out what he was up to wouldn't be easy. But he didn't want to mention it to his employers.

He was also restless. He was thinking about the tanned beauty waiting for him in his via Bergamo loft and how much he enjoyed her company, not to mention her long legs. More with every day, in fact. *Maybe it's old age creeping up on me.* Every time he thought about seeing her again he felt a mixture of desire and tenderness. He'd probably never find anyone else like her, willing to be with him for nothing. But the pleasant feeling was marred by the fear of having to tell his employers that Annibale Canessa was not amenable to surveillance. He wasn't going to be a pawn like those he'd taken care of in the past. He wasn't like anyone else, in fact. He was the one keeping *them* under surveillance: letting them get close – and then losing them when he got tired.

He had to tell them. If he didn't, sooner or later they'd find out themselves. That's what scared him. He thought he'd wound things up with the killing at the station, but he was right back at the beginning. And with all those cops around, nothing good could come of it.

Nando Panattoni, locked in his car in piazza Piola, watched the rain cascading down his windscreen.

I was probably better off when I got paid in steaks.

20

Carla Trovati was watching the idiot waffling on the phone. She'd been sure she'd be alone tonight since it had been an extremely slow day for news. A night shift with no one to bother her.

But Saverio Martelli, one of the middle managers, had stopped for his monthly plug for the dog magazine he worked with. Caprile always snorted, 'By dogs, for dogs', and Carla's opinion was that they were the only people who'd let him write something. She couldn't keep her eyes off the clock behind the man. It had been years since he'd written something, if he ever had, for the *Corriere*. He was basically employed as a caterer.

Twenty past midnight. Ten more minutes and Canessa would be here. But if Martelli hadn't left by then, she would have to intercept Canessa and postpone the meeting.

When he'd called her a few days earlier she'd nearly fainted. The former Carabiniere's offer had excited her more than a date or a hookup. He was running a parallel investigation and offering to share it with her. She'd be allowed to follow him every step of the way, as long as she didn't write anything about it until it was over.

Carla was nervous. That was *the* story, the one that would turn her career around. The councillor's outing was nothing in comparison. If only Martelli would finish his dog piece...

With that, Martelli switched off his computer, stood up and grabbed his coat. 'Carla, I'm done here – you okay closing up?'

Always the same question, always the same answer. 'Of course! You go home. I'm good, thanks.'

She watched him walk the length of the corridor, and when she saw him disappear into the lobby, she called the doorman.

'I'm expecting two people. When they show up, please let them through.'

She caught Canessa eyeing up her legs. She hadn't put any thought into her outfit that morning, but clearly something was working for her: black tights ringed with horizontal stripes, black miniskirt and a white shirt.

Gentle, distracted, barely there… Carla felt his look all the same. *Maybe what they say about him is true after all – he's a heartbreaker, with a taste for women…* She smiled as she led her two guests into the office.

Canessa's friend hadn't even looked at her; he'd barely said hello. He was a little unnerving. Initially she had him down as younger, but now that she was closer, she saw that his baggy clothes, the tote bag, the post-grunge look topped off with greasy hair – had deceived her, and he was actually older than she was. What was a man like that doing with Canessa, with his chiselled looks?

'The *Corriere* headquarters… I've always wanted to see them!' Alfridi was looking around in awe, overexcited, like a clueless tourist. Carla changed her mind pretty quickly about that.

He sat down at one of the desks and before she could tell him that it belonged to Ferraroni, the journalist covering local politics (now there was an annoying bore), the not-so-young man had already turned on the computer, bypassed Ferraroni's password and hacked into his personal account with a laugh.

'Impressive porn collection,' he commented, opening one of the folders, 'but no kids or weird stuff. He's just a perv.'

'Please don't leave a trace,' Carla reminded him, worried that Ferraroni might notice something. Though she did appreciate the irony, as he rode a moral high horse around the office.

'Sorry, the habits of a hacker are hard to lose. But don't worry, he won't notice a thing. I'll get to what we're here for.' His fingers started flying over the keyboard. 'Just give me a couple of minutes.'

Carla took some time to study Canessa, who was leaning against one of the other desks, checking the open area around them. He was wearing a casual outfit, but underneath the light jacket she could make out a well-built body. She was sure he carried a gun, but she couldn't figure out where. Being so close to him and not being able to ask any questions, not even why they were there, was extremely frustrating. She didn't protest, though: they'd made a deal and she would stick to her side of it. It would be the making of her career, after all. She just needed to be patient.

'Has it always been like this in here?' Canessa seemed genuinely interested, not just making polite conversation.

'No, it used to be smaller before our section expanded quite a bit.'

He walked over to another desk and picked up a newspaper, pretending to look through it as he scouted out the corridor and various access points. *What a freak*, Carla thought. Just when she was about to ask him something, Alfridi called her over.

'There's a problem here.'

Canessa quickly joined them. 'What do you mean?'

'Well, I'm working from a *Corriere* terminal, yes, but I might as well be working from mine. I can access the system but I'm not *inside* the system I asked for, the archive. I'd have to use the archive computers to find any trace of Petri.'

Canessa turned to Carla. 'Where is it?'

'Downstairs, but we can't get in there now. It closes at midnight.'

'Good. Fewer archivists around while we work.'

Carla felt a wave of elation mixed with fear. On one hand, she was drawn in by all of this, while on the other, she knew it could be dangerous – for her in particular. She knew what Canessa was saying, but at the cost of coming across as naive, she asked, 'How do we get in without keys?'

'That's the least of our worries.'

Canessa patted Alfridi on the shoulder and gestured to him, then turned back to Carla. 'Come, show me the way.'

'We're taking a quick tour of the *Corriere*.'

Carla felt the need to tell the doorman where they were going, but she knew she wasn't all that convincing given the time of day. Alfridi's smile was rewarded with a grunt. Canessa sidled across the lobby, as he had done on his arrival, to avoid giving the security cameras full view of his face.

They walked out into the courtyard and Carla turned right, heading for a small door between some large recycling bins filled with newspapers. She stopped. 'First closed door,' she announced, but before she could finish her sentence, Canessa had pulled out a set of keys. He tried one of them in the lock, then heard a *clack*. 'First open door,' he replied with a grin.

They felt their way down a corridor, since Canessa suggested it would be better not to turn on lights that could seen from outside. They turned on the overstairs light. Two flights later, they were standing in front of a large, sturdy wooden door, double-locked.

'The archives.'

Carla was extremely worried. If someone found them here, she would lose her job, or at least any chance of a career. But she couldn't stop herself. The excitement of what she might discover was winning out over her worries. Adrenaline had started to course through her. It took Canessa a little longer, but he managed to open this second door too.

They were in.

2 1

Calandra answered his phone, clearly annoyed. He was lying on a king-sized bed in the penthouse suite of a nice hotel on the Lungarno, in Florence, and he was sharing it with a woman young enough to be his daughter, even his granddaughter. Entirely naked except for a red thong, she was stretching languidly in front of the window, in the light of the moon, and boy was he enjoying the show. Calandra preferred it when she danced, admittedly, but this was her choice today. He was considering whistling an appropriate tune for the scene, something like *Firenze sogna*, when the phone call snapped him out of his bliss.

It was one of his most trusted men, someone who didn't officially exist – on the books or anywhere else – and wasn't employed by the State, though it was the State that paid his egregious monthly salary. No one had ever seen him outside the place he was calling from. Not even Calandra. For years, he'd lived in a basement in Rome, a sort of techno bunker that allowed him to listen in on other people's lives. Maybe he didn't even have a home; maybe he lived there.

'What?'

'Two pieces of news, neither good.'

Calandra sighed. 'Tell me.'

'The prosecutors are getting antsy, especially the guy. He's been to the Opera prison several times.'

'Cammello?'

'Nah, Cammello's tough. Another one, the cellmate, used to be with Petri too, when he was alive. RIP.'

'Amen. Interesting, keep an eye on the situation. Do we know anything else about him?'

'A smalltime dealer, a nobody. But if the guy's pressing him, it means there's something of interest, something that might help him out, right?'

'True,' Calandra agreed. He was starting to feel prickly, nervous. They were moving ahead, out of the picture, and it was troubling him. 'I don't believe in coincidences. Can we intercept them?'

'It's difficult, you know, with prosecutors. There are protection levels and special checks, but I'm moving in that direction. Mr Muscle isn't as dumb as we thought. He might actually pose a challenge to our star inspector.'

'An unpleasant surprise, I agree. He's cooking something up and it can't be good. I should warn Canessa. We can't afford to lose him. Do you know where he is?'

'Ouch. That's the second piece of bad news. For all I can see, it's as foggy as January, and he's as slippery as an eel. Not even a ping on our radar.'

'Let's wait. Focus on the prosecutors. Warn me if they have any strokes of genius. Are we clear?'

'Crystal.' The man-who-didn't-exist hung up.

The young woman had finished her session and was looking at Calandra with eyes as murky as the river three floors below.

'Come here, babe. Life is full of bad people, and I want to feel good.' He gestured for her to move closer. He knew she wouldn't be able to soothe his mind, though. He couldn't stop thinking about Canessa.

Where was their detective, damn it?

Annibale was fascinated by Alfridi's work. He looked like a pianist, as light on the keyboard as if he were playing a sonata. Carla was keeping watch. She was tense, but Canessa had been through similar situations and wasn't worried. He didn't want to get her into trouble, but it was a risk he had to take. He couldn't stop now.

'Here, I've found something.'

Alfridi wiped the sweat off his brow, then dried his hand on his trousers. Carla was disgusted; she didn't like the guy. Canessa, on the other hand, seemed to enjoy his presence, or was at least amused by him.

'What is it?' he asked his personal tech wizard.

'He looked into some old stuff, pre-1984.'

'That stuff isn't in the archive. We've only got the headlines – the actual articles are on microfilm,' Carla said, checking her watch. It was 2.30 a.m.

'So?' Canessa asked.

'So I need to get the references and find the right reels.' Alfridi gestured to the size of the archive. 'It's going to take some time.'

At that moment, from somewhere in the building they heard a voice shouting, 'Trovati?!'

'Oh my God, it's the doorman. He's looking for me. I'll go and buy us some more time.'

Canessa listened as her heels clicked into the darkness.

Alfridi kept working on the keyboard. 'Switch that printer on for me, the green button,' he directed Canessa. Above them, the sound of footsteps on the stairs. Alfridi had stopped typing and was holding his finger down on the Enter key. 'Come on baby, wake up.'

Canessa wasn't sure who or what he was talking to, but before he could ask, the printer hummed and spat out a piece of paper. Alfridi was lightning fast: two taps and the computer was off. He put the printer back to sleep as he leapt to his feet, grabbed the paper and shoved it into his pocket. 'Okay, we can go,' he said triumphantly. Canessa closed the archive door behind them.

Footsteps were moving down the staircase, putting him on alert.

'This way.'

It was Carla. 'I told the doorman that you're waiting for me on via San Marco. Quickly! We need to leave before he gets back to his post and checks the cameras.' She led them down a series of corridors towards the underground car park. They met a couple of locked doors, but Canessa didn't disappoint: he opened those too. They resurfaced behind the secondary exit, panting. They caught their breath and left while the other doorman was looking the other way.

A giant moon seemed to be shining a spotlight directly over them. Carla felt like she was being watched by a thousand hidden eyes.

'It's really quite big,' Canessa commented, taking in the *Corriere* building. 'It was different when I used to work around here.'

For a second, Carla thought she was dealing with an idiot. *With everything we've just been through, he's playing the tourist now?* she thought, and then she noticed the doorman behind him. Canessa was playing a part for her.

'Oh, you're still here? Miss, I was worried you weren't coming back, and I saw your stuff still in the office.'

'I'm sorry, we lost track of time. We're heading off now.'

'Your guests left their IDs at my post. I brought them back for you.'

Carla and Canessa thanked him. Once they were alone, Carla turned to her companions in that strange adventure. 'Can you wait here for me? I'll go and get my things.'

As soon as she was gone, Alfridi pulled out the paper he'd printed and handed it to Canessa, who appreciated the IT expert's discretion. He'd hidden it from the woman. *Good idea, best not to risk it yet*, Canessa thought. He gave Alfridi a friendly punch on the shoulder and looked at the results.

11 November 1977

7 February 1978

10 September 1978

9 January 1979

18 June 1979

13 December 1979

21 April 1980

Canessa looked at Alfridi. The dates meant nothing to him.

'Those are the editions of the *Corriere* that Petri looked up. He was searching for something published on those dates.'

'But we don't know what?'

'No, there wasn't enough time. But I didn't want to leave empty-handed. At least next time we won't be driving in the dark.' Alfridi smiled.

Canessa stood looking at the piece of paper. 'You're right, this is already something.' He pocketed it just before Carla reappeared, breathless, but happy to have survived a close shave.

'Sorry, I had to chat to the doorman for a bit, to make everything seem normal. We don't usually get visitors around the building this late. What's on that paper?'

'The key to access the system,' Alfridi lied, proving himself an excellent ally. 'I'm good with computers, not at remembering things. At least we'll be speedier next time.'

Carla hazarded a smile.

'I hope there is a next time. If someone realises what we just did, there'll be questions.'

They left the vehicle entrance area and walked into the clear, cool, rain-washed Milan night. The air was crisp, and summer was on its way. A couple of cars ran up via San Marco. They heard cries and laughter.

Alfridi shook Carla's hand. 'Maybe with the key and some extra info, you could try yourself, during the day,' he told her, warming up and losing his formality.

'Maybe, yeah.'

Then he turned to Canessa. 'You have my number if you need anything else.'

'Do you need a lift?'

Alfridi was already on his way, heading towards largo Treves. He didn't turn around. 'I like the walk; it's good for me.'

Annibale and Carla turned to look at each other.

'Do you need a lift?'

'I'm not that far from here,' she answered, a little embarrassed. 'I can walk too…'

That man was a living piece of Italian history. She'd only

seen him in books and newspapers, and he was barely a couple of years younger than her dad. She wanted to talk to him, to ask him about the past and the present. And yet she stood there, her wish hanging in the air because of the unusual reticence she felt just then.

Canessa smiled, as if understanding her thoughts.

'It's late, but if you want to, we can go and grab a bite to eat, maybe some early breakfast.'

Carla laughed.

'Actually, I do know this place that shifts seamlessly from caipirinhas to cappuccinos.'

22

Gerardo Vicini watched them on the screen of the security camera for the entrance on via San Marco. He was one of the last on the night shift, and one of the last from the old guard, hired when the *Corriere* was still a family business. Everything was changing now, and the owners were outsourcing security to a different firm, a *service*, damn it. Vicini had come in when '*la Signorina*', as everyone called the original owner, was still in charge. He'd felt personally recruited, a part of the company – despite continuing to vote for the Italian Communist Party – at least as long as she'd stayed on.

He chewed on some liquorice, uncertain what to do, his right hand hovering over the phone. Maybe what was going on in his mind was just silly; after all, it was almost 3 a.m. It could wait until morning. On the other hand, Christmas might still be some time away, but if he turned out to be right, his end-of-year bonus would be definitely heftier if he showed himself as zealous, diligent, and vigilant. *Sod it*, he told himself. He grabbed the receiver and dialled a number he had scribbled down on a scrap of paper.

'Sir, I apologise for the time, but you told me to call you no matter the hour...'

They took her car. Carla drove him to one of those trendy pseudo-pubs in the Navigli area that are actually timeless and classic. It stayed open all night, especially when the days started getting warmer. She'd been here with Giulio Strozzi and a few other colleagues on one of those neutral evenings, until everyone else had drifted away. Now she was sure that that had been her boss's plan all along, and she wondered if any of the others had helped him. Coming back here was a form of healing, a detox.

Wooden tables, the atmosphere of an old *train*, a popular 1950s eatery. One day, Carla would write a book on Milanese trends, forgotten fads, the ones that persisted, clubs and places that were swallowed by nothingness and those that never went. This particular one was buzzing, even at this hour.

Carla spotted an empty table and led Canessa through the crowd. Annibale couldn't help looking at Carla's backside, and he wasn't the only one. A man suddenly jolted up from his chair, hoping to chat her up, and as his chair shifted, he hit the colonel in the left side. Carla noticed his pained grimace, which seemed out of all proportion to the impact.

'I'm sorry, did I hurt you?'

Canessa waved him away – he was fine – before sitting down at the table with his back to the wall. Carla studied him again. He looked at least fifteen years younger than he was, and his deep green eyes drew her attention. He might seem like a puppy at times, but she knew that behind an expression that would've charmed many a woman, whether sincere or affected (she felt a little something herself, she had to admit), a dangerous man lay in wait.

She noticed Canessa massaging his side. 'Did he hit you hard?'

'It's an old wound. Every now and then I forget it's there, but whenever I get closer to kissing it goodbye, it gets jealous.'

She ordered a Greek salad and he asked for spaghetti *cacio e pepe* ('with a caipirinha, before the cappuccino'). While they waited for their dinner-breakfast, they killed time with some rather leaden small talk. Carla, though, was dying to probe, and she couldn't resist as soon as she finished her salad.

'From via Gaeta? The wound, I mean.'

'You've done your homework, I see, despite your age.'

The man was somehow both attractive and unsettling. Carla waited in pained silence for a bit before continuing.

'I was still a child at the time, but I read a lot. About the raid, the man behind it, and what came after that. For all intents and purposes, you brought down terrorism in Italy.'

'Terrorism ended with the supergrasses and the 1980s, when supporters became entrepreneurs and armed groups became rock bands. Would you like to know the full story of via Gaeta, from a witness's perspective?' he teased.

'You weren't just a witness. But yes, I won't pretend I'm not interested. Off the record, as it were, of course.'

'Of course.'

She had the feeling Canessa was mocking her, especially when he suddenly said, 'Stand up.'

She stared at him in surprise. 'Why?'

'Please stand up. I'll show you.'

She did so. Someone in the place turned round to look at her. Annibale continued, 'Turn around, full circle. Okay, you can sit down again.'

Carla offered him a sly grin. 'You didn't get a good look earlier?'

He didn't react. 'I did, but apart from never missing an opportunity, I also wanted to make sure you weren't wearing a microphone.'

'You're pretty paranoid, huh?'

'And I'm still alive. Give me your phone.' She pulled it out of her bag and handed it over. 'Okay, now put your arms on the table, palms down.'

Completely enthralled by now, Carla followed his commands.

He took out the BlackBerry, checked something, then placed it between them.

She waited. 'So?'

'What I'm going to tell you – though not here – is the shocking truth. You can't repeat it to anyone, not until this whole thing is over, and definitely not until I tell you so. Do you understand?'

Carla, quivering in anticipation, raised a hand from the table. 'I swear.'

'Ah! Don't move your hands, or the deal's off.'

'Okay, okay, but can I at least get a preview?'

He gestured to the waiter to bring the bill over.

'Yes, you're allowed to check out the merchandise.'

He leaned towards her and whispered, all in one breath, 'The people who shot me in via Gaeta weren't the terrorists – they were mostly dead – but someone from the Secret Service. I was shot in the back, and not in the stomach, as was reported. I'm not a hero, I'm a fool. Or, as you say in Milan, a *pirla*.'

1980

'I DON'T LIKE IT, not one bit.'

Amelia Ferri couldn't look away from the window. She'd been fiddling with the curtain, shifting it as little as possible to look down on the narrow street filled with people. She didn't want to be seen – accidentally or otherwise – by anyone.

She'd been chanting that mantra for several days now, and her three flatmates had started mocking her. 'I don't like this, I don't like that,' Gennaro Esposito echoed to the tune of *Funiculì funiculà* and from the sofa, where he was indulging in his favourite pastime: a toothpick pedicure.

The scene was disgusting enough to begin with, but Esposito had somehow managed to make it worse: at the end of each session, he'd take the toothpick, wipe it off on his trousers, and put it back in his mouth, where it stayed until the next pedicure.

He obviously did it on purpose to tease her. The first time he'd done so, Amelia had rushed to the bathroom, gagging. When she realised that Esposito did it just to goad her, she'd mustered all the willpower and self-control that had made her – second daughter of the wealthy, famous cardiologist to Turin's car-owning 'royal family' – one of the most ruthless and wanted terrorists in the whole country.

At the sound of Esposito's Neapolitan melody, she dropped the curtain and went over to the sofa, where her partner waved at her with the same hand holding the toothpick.

Amelia stared at him with clear and obvious disgust. Esposito was her complete opposite. They would never have met had it not been for the war they were fighting on the same side. His parents were 'nobodies' (according to Corrado Perfetti, another member of the hit squad, former literature student from Florence and underground cabaret performer), his only residence was a cellar in one of the most derelict neighbourhoods of the Spanish Quarter, 'even rats won't go there'. Brown-noser (the only accusation he'd plead innocent to), thief, robber, killer, and terrorist.

Whenever Amelia thought of herself with Esposito, she couldn't help but remember *The Persuaders!*, a series she'd watched when she was younger, mostly because she liked Tony Curtis. The opening credits always showed the parallel lives of the main characters, who were as different from each other as possible. Just like her and Esposito.

Amelia had had everything: money, private-school education, British tutors, nice clothes, skiing trips, coral beaches, jewellery, a white Spider for her twenty-first birthday. Gennaro was poor and desperate. His sister had died of cholera one summer and the streets had been his only form of schooling. She was beautiful and tall, her swan's neck brushed by long hair (short now out of necessity); he was short, dark and dirty, even limped a little. But he was incredibly loyal to the cause, and no longer cared about money. He was fierce and obedient. He'd got involved in armed direct action during a prison stay from which he'd made a bloody escape, and had embraced the Idea without hesitation and without flaunting any intellectualism, unlike others. He was a cold-blooded killer.

Amelia thought about the glory of the revolution that had brought them together: only their desire to bring down the imperialist state, only loyalty to their principles could have induced them to live under the same roof, her and that street rat. To Amelia, that's what he remained. She still dressed with sombre elegance, which was why they called her 'the Czarina'. She loved all the things she'd been given, and didn't want to let them go – *One day I'll be taking them all back, with interest* – but she always added that everyone would benefit from them because of what they were doing. The meaner comments were about her joining the cause so she could continue to dress well. Elegance was often useful for duping the dumb slaves of power, the police and the Carabinieri. 'If you'd stopped at the autonomous stage,' Perfetti would prod, 'you'd've had to dress like the *komrades*. Ripped jeans, shapeless jumpers, parkas.' The Czarina agreed: she wouldn't have been able to.

Gennaro had stopped looking at her mockingly. His eyes now spoke of something else entirely: pure lust.

Amelia smiled. She would exact her revenge for his mockery and teasing that evening when she did it with Adelmo Federzoni, a former Latin and Greek professor from Modena and the leader of their group. She'd enjoy it, too – Federzoni was a good-looking man and a decent lover – but she would make sure to add some extra noise to torture Gennaro who, Perfetti had told her, always put his ear to the wall to listen to her moans. The four of them had split the two bedrooms in the flat, with Federzoni suggesting that the men take one room so she could have her own space, but the Czarina had refused, both on ideological grounds and those of her own pleasure.

The night she'd gagged over Gennaro's pedicure, she'd been teasing him by telling him about how much she loved sex, how many people she'd slept with, and what her favourite positions were, until Federzoni took her aside.

'Amelia, enough. Gennaro is crass and gross, but he's not that smart. He doesn't know you're playing with him, and it could harm the balance in the group. He plays a crucial role in what we need to do. Leave him alone.'

Amelia went back to the window. 'I don't like it, not one bit,' she started saying again, tugging at the curtain. The street below was swarming with people wearing the AMGA uniform, the Genoa gas and water company, police and Carabinieri. All those cops were making her nervous. Via Gaeta was too narrow a street, running along the hill above Genoa's Piazza Principe train station. To be fair, all the roads were narrow there. She was used to Turin's large boulevards and she felt so clumsy in the car that she often refused outright to drive, letting the others do it for her.

'I mean, this is just bad luck,' she said, still looking out of the window. A shiver ran down her spine. Despite the heating inside and her heavy jumper, Amelia was feeling all of the effects of the season, which was turning out to be particularly harsh. Especially that early February: the city was in the grip of an icy wind blowing in from the forts to the north.

'Amelia,' Federzoni coaxed, 'you need to learn to look at a situation from a different perspective.'

'And what would a different perspective be in this situation? You don't think it's unlucky for two gas pipes to have blown up so close to us? And that they're worried about more of them bursting, so AMGA's people will be roaming around, and come to check up here too? And why are the police involved?'

Federzoni made everyone some coffee. He was tall and greying, and he didn't look like a man who was active on the front line. But the planning division still thought of him as their best field commander: a cunning strategist, smart, even cruel at times, despite his professorial demeanour and affability.

He grazed her shoulder, sending another shiver down her spine. He always had that effect on her. 'Put it this way: the pipes could've burst right beneath us, and they would've come in the middle of the night, like they did with our neighbours. How would we carry all that stuff in our pyjamas?' He pointed to the chest with the secret compartment that held their arsenal.

Perfetti poured himself a coffee, and flung a snide comment her way. 'Especially you, in that little thing you wear – if you even do.'

Esposito laughed, and even Federzoni smirked. Good old-fashioned sexism, just as in any military enclosure.

Amelia didn't bat an eyelash. 'So why the police?'

'They need to check that there aren't any other leaks in the area – it's routine. And it can be problematic if they have to evacuate a building in a hurry. Not everyone's happy to leave. Would you be?' he asked Gennaro.

'Fuck no.'

'See? It's okay, don't worry. They're scheduled to come in tomorrow, expecting three students. I won't be here, you'll be studying for your exams; they'll check the kitchen and boiler and then they'll leave.' He picked up a biscuit and chucked it over at Gennaro, who caught it, whooped like a monkey and settled back onto the couch.

Amelia tugged at the curtain again. 'If you say so...' She focused on one of the gas company vans parked just beneath them. 'What if it's a trap? They come in with the excuse of a gas leak check and they round us up without firing a single bullet.'

This time, Federzoni burst out laughing, and the others joined in.

'Am I that amusing?' The Czarina felt insulted.

'Amelia, Amelia, there's no cop smart enough to plan something that complex, with all these actors and in this setting, without someone noticing that something was off. Not in Italy. Come on, have some coffee.'

'I don't like it, anyway. I don't like it at all.' Amelia looked out of the window one more time before she sat down again.

Ivan Repetto saw the curtain move, and wondered which of the four terrorists was becoming curious, or worse, suspicious. He was sitting inside the AMGA van that wasn't an AMGA van. It was a Carabinieri surveillance van, equipped with all the recent tech: listening devices, cameras, videocameras. Repetto zoomed in with the Canon he was using, waited for the sliver of face to appear again, and took the shot. The woman.

'I think they're becoming suspicious. They've noticed something's off.'

Canessa smiled at Repetto's worrying. 'They're just concerned about the whole mess. It's to be expected. They're not fans of complication, but they haven't figured it out. They'd have moved if that were the case.'

Annibale was sitting at the back, reading some papers and chewing on a Toscano. It wasn't lit, but the entire van stank with it all the same. None of the three Carabinieri in working overalls dared protest. They were surprised he wasn't smoking already, and they knew that if they irritated him, he'd definitely light his cigar.

It was one of the first supergrasses, the first fruit of the new law the general had pushed for, who'd revealed the existence and location of the safe house. After a couple of stakeouts, led personally by Canessa – he didn't want someone else to ruin it by getting caught or leaking info – he'd found out it was currently occupied and who was inside: a hit squad composed of some of the most wanted and most dangerous terrorists around. He'd recognised two of them almost immediately: Adelmo Federzoni and Amelia Ferri.

Annibale had been opposed to a direct attack, the usual raid. 'If we go in all guns blazing, besides risking our own people, we might kill them. We – or I – need them alive for the most part, and I know we can make it. Imagine the consequences: a couple of them might talk, and then the whole edifice would crumble. We'd have the whole organisation in our hands.' With the general's approval, he'd got the green light for his plan from the relevant ministries. And so, despite Repetto's universal pessimism, every-thing would go according to Canessa's design.

Annibale was confident. He knew it would work. He'd laid out every detail. A small team of eight trained and trusted men. They would go round knocking on neighbouring doors, getting people out quickly, then head to the terrorists' flat. Repetto and himself first, the others on the stairs, ready to intervene. Canessa was sure that these members of the Red Brigades would not be armed. In their position he wouldn't be either. They'd be calm, relaxed, prepared for something, sure, but without guns. It would just be a safety evacuation, wouldn't take longer than a couple of hours, best course of action would be to cooperate. Everything would be over faster. Once the four were out on the landing, the team would spring into action. They'd bring them in as they were, no guns fired, no one wounded, no violence. Nothing more than a well-aimed kick, maybe a punch.

Canessa had planned every detail. He'd wanted everyone to wear work shoes and gloves, to remove all watches and any sign of a life different from the one they were currently playing. They were gas workers. After they'd rehearsed, he'd personally checked every single agent. He'd even got them to perform some manual labour in the days leading up to the raid, to roughen their hands. If the terrorists were as good as he thought, they'd be cautious, and they'd notice every detail.

'Everything will be fine.' He smiled at Repetto, but the marshal's hunch persisted.

He wasn't asleep. He was dozing, half-alert, in a state of vigilance that allowed his mind to wander a little. Annibale Canessa was always somehow in control, even if his mind was drifting else-where – like now, when his random thoughts started materialis-ing around the form of a young blonde, the daughter of a stern colonel from the Guardia di Finanza. When he'd met her at an army officers' dinner in Turin, she'd struck him as demure, but she'd soon shown herself to be surprisingly feral. Annibale wasn't a regular at those sorts of military social events, but he did use them to scope out women, as Repetto put it. Where else could he do it? After the general, he was top of the terrorists' list, so he couldn't just wander around, hang out in public, looking for company and conversation. What other people his age did naturally was out of bounds to him. And so, every now and then, he'd respond to an official invitation to an event with colleagues in the armed forces, maybe some politician or representative of the Church. Women seemed to be attracted to him not only because of his looks, but because of the smell of danger emanating from him, the scent of steel and blood that followed him. These occasions furnished all of Annibale's relationships, which were usually very short-lived since he lived on a knife-edge. Anything more complicated or requiring more effort than a fling would tip him over. It was impossible for him to have a true connection; he couldn't give out his phone number, book a restaurant, take a walk on the beach, go to the cinema. He wasn't like anyone else. He was someone who had to whisper, 'I'll call you' at the end of his flings – usually in a hotel room with two Carabinieri guarding the door. And then he couldn't.

Maybe it would be different with the blonde, he thought, and he really wanted to believe it. He and Repetto were assigned to the general for some delicate operations. The second day, his mentor had called him and insisted he go to the party.

When Canessa replied with his usual 'Thank you, I'll consider it', the general had looked at him with ill-concealed frustration.

'Please go to this one, Canessa. Get your mind off things. That's an order.'

He was taken by her, literally. He'd worn his uniform, something he rarely did, a fact that both angered his colleagues and aroused their jealousy. As he wandered around a room full of ladies and officers who'd put too much effort into their outfits, he'd spotted the young woman and was struck by her appearance: she looked like a student in her knee-length tartan skirt and a blue cardigan over a white shirt with an embroidered collar. *A convent girl?* he wondered. She looked to be about seventeen (instead of

175

twenty-one, as he found out later), so he decided to engage her in conversation and nothing else, to distract himself from a tedious evening of married women fawning over him. He was done with them, he'd told Repetto (who did not believe him, of course). He headed over to her.

Canessa came up behind her as she was getting herself a drink from the buffet. Her name was Giuseppina, and she turned out to be a bit special, placing him immediately and catching him off guard. Without turning round, she said, 'You're better looking than they say. Are you also better at fucking?'

Twenty minutes later they were in the storage room between the wine bottles, crates of food and waiters coming and going. They'd moved, or rather, she'd dragged him behind the crates and fallen to her knees in front of him.

'I wanted to taste you. I like you, but now that I know what you taste like, I expect more from you,' she whispered when she got back to her feet. He just stood there, trousers round his ankles.

They started seeing each other, their sessions increasingly passionate. Canessa was intoxicated by her alchemy of innocence and perversion, and he borrowed a friend's flat for a while. One night he took her dancing at the Murazzi, overturning the established order of his existence. It was packed with people, some of whom would have taken him down had they realised who he was, but Annibale was disguised in a studded leather jacket, jeans, and fake reading glasses. In her tight leather trousers and black shirt (no bra underneath), Giuseppina ground against him to the rhythm of the pulsing strobes. Annibale floated off into a world far removed from his own, happy, guard down. Mostly.

She gave him a sly smile and slipped her hand into his trousers, holding his penis; her other hand found the Beretta 925B, still an unofficial release, stuck into his belt. Slowly she removed both hands and whispered, 'You're harder than your gun.'

Five minutes later they were in the toilets, he was taking her from behind and she was growling like an animal.

Annibale was positive he'd planned every last detail of the raid, and he closed his eyes, letting his mind flip through the images of the last night he'd spent with her. They'd started out along the Po, and moved on to a flat next to the Grande Madre...

The sound of the door slamming open dragged him out of his filthy dreams. He grabbed a gun from the table in front of him and aimed it at whoever had just walked in.

A colonel.

His first thought, to be honest, was that it might be Giuseppina's father, coming to settle the score with the man who had taken his daughter (and how!). But he wasn't a Carabiniere. He belonged to the Guardia di Finanza.

'Who the fuck are you, you idiot? Why the fuck are you in uniform? If they see you, this all goes tits up!'

Repetto had actually fallen asleep next to Canessa, and now he was trying to figure what was going on in front of him. Was Canessa shouting and pointing a gun at a superior officer?

Without losing his calm, the newcomer shut the van door behind him, removed his hat and sat down on one of the benches. He was tall and almost entirely bald except for a ring of hair crowning his shiny skull.

'Put your weapon down, Captain. I'll pretend I didn't hear what you just said. I understand the delicacy of this situation.'

Canessa lowered his gun but didn't retract his attitude. 'Politeness doesn't alter the facts: you have no authorisation to be here, this operation has been planned for months, and you risk blowing our cover with that uniform of yours.'

The colonel attempted a smile. 'You're not the only one who knows how to follow procedure, you know. I made sure no one saw me come in here. Calm down.'

'Fantastic. That means you can leave the same way you came.'

Canessa stood up. The other man did the same, much more slowly, and still smirking. They faced off. Canessa clenched his right fist.

'What? You're going to punch a superior officer? Don't be stupid.'

Annibale realised that this man wasn't one of those ambitious careerists who knew nothing about the trenches, the sweat and fear of the battlefield. He was rumbled. He also had eyes in the back of his head: he saw things it seemed he hadn't noticed.

'So what?' he asked, changing his angle. 'Are you here to supervise? Right. Make yourself comfortable. It'll all be over in a couple of hours.'

'I'm sure it will, but not in the way you think.'

'And why's that?'

'We're moving in now.'

At that, Repetto also stood up and moved threateningly towards the colonel. 'Excuse my wading in, but it's only a couple more hours. What's the rush?'

Canessa added, 'Not to mention that a sudden raid will put the lives of my men at risk.'

'Your men will run no such risk,' the officer calmly objected as he slid an envelope bearing the stamp of the Minister for the Interior out of his jacket pocket. He handed it to Canessa, who held it out so that he and Repetto could both read it. The minister and the commander general had signed written orders stating that Operation Arpione was now under the command of Colonel Marco Baccini and his team.

'*Your* team?' Canessa hissed.

Baccini was amused by his anger.

'You're not the only Carabiniere in Italy, and you're not the only one capable of running this sort of operation. I'm sure you're aware of the GIS.'

'The Special Intervention Group. But it's not been activated y—'

'That is where you're wrong, Captain,' Baccini cut him off, clearly enjoying himself, 'because in a van parked just out of sight are nine of its best assets. As I said, you're not the only one in the country tracking down terrorists.' The officer looked at his watch and did up his coat. 'Well, this conversation has lasted long enough. You're out of this, Captain. Don't do anything rash. Think of your career.'

Annibale stood rooted to the spot, orders still in hand. Furious but powerless. As the colonel opened the van door, he blocked him.

'Why?'

The officer flashed him a smile. 'Because the State needs a win, and it needs it now.'

They watched him disappear into the night.

Repetto had to struggle to keep Canessa from chasing Colonel Baccini. The captain was furious, and Repetto knew him well: in that state, he might well do something incredibly stupid. He lunged for the sat phone and tried to get in touch with the general: no luck. Canessa just kept staring outside at a street made even darker by the absence of the moon and the intentional dimming of the lights. It had all been meticulously planned, and for what? He was frustrated. He didn't understand and he wanted to leave – to see who made up this special team, to find out if they were prepared. But his sense of duty held him back. He might blow their cover if he suddenly ran outside, no matter who they were. It had already been incredible risky for the colonel to show himself.

Several minutes had gone by, however, and nothing had moved. No light in the terrorists' flat. From up there, the men sliding along the walls towards the door of the building were practically invisible. Baccini was almost certainly leading them, though they were all wearing black trousers, turtlenecks and bulletproof vests. Every man had an automatic in his holster and a short assault rifle in hand.

Canessa squinted. 'Those are Uzi.' Repetto nodded.

'The latest model, too. Is that the one assigned in the GIS?'

It was strange. Even Repetto was confused. The whole situation was starting to look skewed. Confirmation arrived in the shape of Baccini's gun, revealed by a cone of light.

'Annibale, that's a—'

'—Makarov PB 6P9, with silencer, eight rounds. Definitely not standard issue,' Canessa confirmed.

'You use the Walther, though.'

'Yes, but never in official operations. It's just backup. No, there's something wrong here. Those aren't Carabinieri.'

'Who are they, then?'

'I don't know. All I know is that this reeks of a conspiracy. This "colonel" has shafted us.' And before Repetto could stop him, he'd grabbed the Beretta and launched himself out of the van, running towards the door that had just swallowed the men in black.

*

Gennaro Esposito got up every night at least twice to take a piss. Three, if you counted the times the Czarina's moans woke him up. He'd started worrying. Not about the bitch, but his own bladder.

It can't be my prostate. I'm too young for that. He'd even seen a doctor from the Workers' Aid. 'Definitely not your prostate,' he'd confirmed with a smile, making Gennaro's day. 'But there's too much salt in your diet, and that's not good. You should eat less in the evenings.' Gennaro, however, never got enough food during the day. The evenings were his big moment. There was never time for lunch. Everyone was always rushing around at lunch, especially up there, in the north. Everyone always bustled around in the north: if you took more than a minute at the bar to enjoy your espresso – which you couldn't, because they were bad at making them – there was always someone behind you, huffing, and you had to down it and let them through. *What's the rush?*

He flushed the toilet. On his way back to the room he shared with Perfetti... was something moving on the landing?... nothing more than a slither, a brush against the door. If Gennaro had reached the age of thirty-five, first as a *camorrista* and then with the armed struggle, it was only because he didn't believe in coincidence, and he didn't trust anyone.

He tiptoed across the living room and stopped. Should he go and get the P38 from under his pillow – Federzoni allowed him to keep it nearby in case of emergency – or shout to wake up the others?

Those seconds of hesitation killed him.

The door exploded in a shower of broken wood. One of the shards, about thirty centimetres long, pierced his eye socket and drove itself through his head. He died instantly, but one of the

181

men in black now swarming through the flat still sprayed his chest with gunfire as he passed by, just to make sure.

Corrado Perfetti was shot down coming out of the bedroom. He'd tried to grab his comrade's P38, but the gun had slipped between the bed and the wall. He'd walked out, but he hadn't stood a chance. The gunmen were already moving towards the room occupied by Federzoni and the Czarina, though Colonel Baccini's team didn't know their names, or their plans. Their only order was to kill.

They must've blown up the locks. Scaling the stairs two at a time, Annibale saw some of the other doors cracked open, faces peering out. 'Lock yourselves in!' he shouted.

He reached the third floor to find the door shattered; Gennaro Esposito's corpse lay on the floor, blood pouring from his chest and a splinter in his eye. He heard a muffled volley of shots and spotted the men in black looking down at Perfetti's body. A few metres away there were more of them, ready to burst into the other room, from which they all heard gunshots. One of Baccini's men lay in front of the door convulsing, his hands over his left eye.

The men closest to Annibale spotted him and raised their Uzis.

Annibale held up his badge and shouted, 'Carabinieri! Put your guns down!' Gun low, badge high, he inched towards them.

'Carabinieri,' he said again.

The men seemed confused. They lowered their machine guns. The gunfire from Amelia's room gave way to a moment of complete silence. A heartbeat – then the shooting erupted once more with increased ferocity as the remaining men rushed into the bedroom. The room was large enough for a bed, a sofa, several chairs and a wardrobe. The sofa, capsized to form a makeshift barricade, was now gutted by the machine-gun fire. Federzoni's body lay on the side of the bed facing the balcony. There was a hole on his forehead. On the other side, the men were watching the Czarina bleed from a wound in her side. She looked bad, but she was still alive. One of them raised his Uzi to her head.

Annibale aimed his own Beretta at the man: 'Down, or I'll shoot!' His yell was cut off, however, with a sudden sharp pain, a blaze of heat to his left side. Instinctively he brought his hand to the source of the heat, and pulled it back covered in something wet. Blood? He collapsed to the ground while the man with the gun finished off the Czarina.

In his last moments of consciousness, Annibale saw someone standing over him with a gun to his temple. He closed his eyes. As he fainted, he thought he heard hurried footsteps... voices... then Repetto nearby.

'What are you doing!? Have you lost your minds?!'

The first thing he noticed was the light flooding into the room. The blinds were practically shut, but somehow the sun had found its way in, scorching everything in its path. He'd fallen asleep. How could he? This never happened to him. It was the morning of the raid, he had to get ready, check that the men were ready. He tried to get up from the bed but fought against a leaden tiredness and what felt like ropes, or ties.

I'm tied to the bed!

He checked, and found that he actually had tubes and IVs attached to various parts of his body. Captain Canessa was still very drugged up.

A voice yelled, 'He's awake!'

But he'd gone back to sleep once more. When he woke up later, the sun was back again. They'd opened the blinds, and he could feel a sunbeam piercing his left eye. Then his right. Those were some strange sunbeams.

'Major, can you hear me?'

'I'm a captain,' he slurred.

Muffled laughter.

'Okay. Can you see me?'

Annibale squinted, and as the haze lifted, a smiling, bearded face materialised in his field of vision.

'Where am I? Who are you?'

'You're in the intensive care unit at Galliera Hospital, in Genoa, and I'm Professor Guidi, the surgeon looking after you. The bullet didn't damage any vital organs but you lost a lot of blood and you were this close to dying. Good thing you're made of sterner stuff, Major. There are no complications, so we should be able to let you go in a week. You'll have to go through some rehab, of course.'

Annibale suddenly remembered.

'I need to speak to Marshal Repetto,' he said.

'Yes, there are many people who want to speak with you, too, but you need to rest first, Major.'

'I'm not a major. Why do you keep calling me that?'

'I'm sure your colleagues will explain.'

'There's nothing we can do, Annibale.'

Whenever Annibale was called by his first name, he knew the conversation was over. There was no chance of appeal without eroding the general's patience entirely.

The general had refused to sit. He was standing by the window, looking out on a dark winter morning in Genoa. The blinds were open, but the sun – had it been there, or had he imagined it? – had disappeared. Canessa wanted to tell him to move away from the window: he was too exposed. But thinking about it, the Red Brigade never used snipers; it wasn't their m.o. Repetto, on the other hand, was sitting down. When the general had refused, he too had remained standing, but his superior officer, annoyed, had pulled rank. 'Glue your arse to that chair.'

Two weeks had passed since the massacre in via Gaeta. Only the three of them, and a few of the general's close assistants, called it what it was. As far as the rest of Italy was concerned, it was a success story, the first tangible result in the war on terrorism. Four members of the Red Brigade dead, a dangerous group shot down when they refused to surrender. The papers were scattered over Canessa's bed and he leafed through them, baffled. His photo was splashed across all the front pages, and he was dubbed a 'hero'. He'd come back to his senses quite quickly and was ready to jump back into action, though not against the terror cells. Or rather, not against the ones threatening the State, but the ones who had lied to him, working from within. Including the one who'd shot him from behind, almost killing him. The 'colonel'.

'I bet he wasn't even a colonel.'

The general shook his head.

'Who was he, then? His men were strange too. It was almost as if they didn't understand when I spoke Italian.'

'Good old Canessa instinct, huh? You're clearly feeling better.' The general offered Repetto a smile. 'Mercenaries, probably, former special forces on a new payroll. The "colonel" and a couple of others were Secret Service. The others were contract. Who knows where they came from, or where they've gone.'

'Why?'

'Why the massacre? Because the State needed *this*.' He pointed to the newspapers. 'It needed to show its teeth, prove it could turn things around. The State is slow to wake up, it's an unwieldy beast, but once it picks up speed, it tramples everything.'

'You and me included.'

'You and me included, if not for the marshal.'

Canessa was still confused. He'd always thought of himself as an intelligent man, hard to surprise. He thought he was living behind a shield, one that protected him not so much from bullets – the one with his name on it was still out there, he knew that much – but from ambushes, betrayals, double-crossing, traps. And yet, here he was, knee-deep in one. They'd tricked him.

'Why?'

The general finally dragged the second chair towards him and sat down on the right side of the bed.

'Because last week there were six attacks and five dead in six days. Because we've been held hostage by the Red Brigade for the past four years and someone, up there, needed to show the people, voting people, that the State is present and it knows how to mete out punishment.'

'We could've taken them alive. We would've got so much more out of this.'

Annibale was stubborn, and the general knew it.

'Major, the idea that any of them would've talked is entirely your imagination. I was prepared to support you, and I did, but there were others who didn't believe in you. The faction that wanted a show of force from the State eventually won.'

'Who's that? The commander general?'

'He swears he never signed that order, the one you and Repetto mentioned. Where is it anyway? It could easily have been a minister, even the prime minister, if not the entire chamber or a parliamentary coalition, or something else entirely. It doesn't matter.'

'I'm not a hero. I don't want this promotion. I didn't do anything – on the contrary, I failed. *Carte blanche* is what you told us.'

'Enough!' The general never raised his voice, but everyone knew when he'd lost patience, when a conversation was over and there was no more room for negotiation. 'I've had enough of these complaints. They're pointless, and they get us nowhere. Plus, they remind me of the fact that I've also been played like a fool, and I don't have "special powers" as I was led to believe, which is infuriating. *Carte blanche*? You need a pen to write on blank paper, and someone else is holding it.'

The general was a pragmatic man. He didn't like to linger over victories, losses and defeats, even less the debriefs that accompanied them. He expected you to skip to the next square, the next step. There was no 'back to square one' in his game.

He leaned against the mattress and stared at Annibale. 'We need to embrace the positives in this story, even though it stinks. First of all, strategically speaking, it's been a critical result. However it went down, one of the most dangerous Red Brigade hit squads has been neutralised, and among them were some of Judge Lazzarini's killers. Additionally, you get all the credit, you were promoted – the youngest major in the history of the force. You'll be famous, you'll have prestige, references, and power, and all that will end up being useful when you need it. You'll get a medal. Repetto too, of course.' He waved towards the marshal, who performed a mock-bow.

'I don't want the promotion,' Annibale insisted, looking at the badges lying on the small table beside the tissues and a bottle of water.

'You'll wear them, you'll smile about them, and you'll ignore everything else about this whole thing. End of story.' The general stood up, grabbed his loden and headed towards the door. He opened it, and then turned back. He was an intimidating man, with a square jaw and a pair of dark, burning eyes behind heavy glasses.

'Annibale, don't do anything stupid. We have a job to finish.' With that he left.

Repetto looked at the door and back at Annibale with concern. He knew that the newly promoted major wouldn't give up that easily. There were interesting times ahead.

'So what do we do now, Major?' he asked, light-heartedly. But he knew his direct superior officer well.

Annibale went back to looking at the seagulls looping around the sky.

'You heard the general. We have a job to finish.'

An uncomfortably hot July evening. A Volvo estate surreptitiously slipped away from Rome's traffic and into a knot of empty tree-lined streets in the Prati neighbourhood. Rome was emptying out, and the heat was driving everyone towards the coast or the countryside, cooler areas. But the family of the man currently at the wheel would get to their villa in Ansedonia a few days later. His eldest daughter had her high-school exam the following Monday, so they'd all decided to wait for her, including her sixteen-year-old bookworm brother. *What a bore! This year is dragging on and on*, he thought as he pressed the button on the remote for the wooden door. Inside were a few parking spaces reserved for special tenants. *Like me.*

Colonel Baccini, who also went by several other names, felt his life was good, if not fabulous. A smart, elegant wife who was also good in bed. Two polite teenage kids who did well in school and were good-looking like their mother. A satisfying fake job as an insurer (amazingly, it actually paid), and another – he couldn't talk about it but it definitely brought him more money – as a Secret Service agent. Together, they ensured him his own personal *dolce vita*. Alongside the 250-square-metre property in Prati, he also had a loft in Parioli, unbeknownst to his family. He'd set it up for his lover, a twenty-two-year-old Greek woman of statuesque beauty. While studying abroad at university, Aria had ended up in an unfortunate group of right-wing extremists, and when Baccini's team had notified the police of their existence, he'd kept her out of it. He'd had his sights on her, but was surprised when she was the one to approach him: she realised that someone had helped her out. She was smart. She'd posted a note on the university board: 'Looking for the person who saved me. Aria.' The board was under surveillance, to weed out the 'grey areas' where supporters of the terrorist cells might be communicating. And so he'd contacted her, excited about not having to coordinate their meeting.

That's how their relationship had started. Baccini had put her up in the Parioli loft. She studied at the university, even brought friends home, and he'd come up with a cover story for her: she was the daughter of a wealthy arms dealer in Greece which explained her clothes, the house, the sports car, the trips. When she and Baccini fucked, he made her call him Onassis.

He was heading home after seeing her that Friday night. They hadn't had much time because his family was waiting for him in Prati for dinner at 8 p.m. sharp, the time when the perfect family man usually came home from his insurance job. The real one. He actually met clients every now and then to discuss policies. A hobby. But it was his other job, especially during these troubled times, that made him feel like a god, with the power of life or death over mortals at the throw of the dice. That job completed him. The money, the power. Everything else followed from it, including the women. Because along with the Greek woman, part of the 'available' faction, there were also the 'difficult' ones, as he called them: all the women who were unhappy to be with him initially, and who needed some convincing: he might reveal some little secret about them or their loved ones…

His Greek goddess, on the other hand, was always there, grateful for his help and all the wealth, and he never had to press with her. He even thought he saw her looking at him with adoration from time to time. *Maybe she loves me a little. Maybe.* In any case, he hadn't been able to stay long that evening. Short but sweet, and it still made him smile.

'I only dropped in to say hi, babe,' he said.

'Let's be quick then,' she replied. She let her silk nightie fall to her feet, leaving her entirely naked, and she dropped to her knees, on the spot, with the door still open… Before he could protest about that dangerous and embarrassing situation, she'd sucked him off so well and so quickly that for the first time in his life he'd yelled as he came. He looked around, worried someone might have noticed. The top floor of the building seemed empty.

She always surprised him.

Maybe I love her a little. Maybe.

Monday, Monday, Monday. His family would leave and he'd have fifteen days with her before joining them on holiday. He'd redirect all calls to his phone, too, just to be sure.

There were two lifts in his building. The one he took led directly to his flat. As the doors opened, a strange silence enveloped him.

'Darlings, I'm home,' he called. No answer. When he reached the enormous living room, he shuddered. His wife and children were sitting on one of the twin sofas, custom made for him by one of the best artisan firms in Brianza (whose owner had one too many skeletons in his past). They were perfectly still, hands in their laps, terror in their eyes. On the sofa opposite them was a man dressed entirely in black: trousers, long-sleeved polo, shoes, socks, even the balaclava that covered his face. He was stroking the Smith & Wesson calibre .22 in his lap. *A professional. A revolver means no shells left behind.*

The man who currently wasn't Colonel Baccini was worried.

He tried to keep calm, trusting in his experience, though he'd never been in this type of situation. He liked easy wins, being ahead of the game.

'Manuela, are you okay?'

His wife nodded, first checking with the masked man, who gestured for her to reply.

'We're fine. They've treated us well. They haven't touched us and they haven't taken anything. They said they won't harm us as long as we don't try anything.'

'Good. It's a bit warm,' said the man on the sofa, 'and we didn't want to turn up the air-conditioning, as Eva' – he pointed to the eldest – 'has a bit of a sore throat.'

The man talked with no real inflection, as if he were a family friend over for a visit. Hearing his daughter's name, Colonel Baccini felt a prick of anger. He was considering the best option for neutralising the intruder (though he wasn't a man of action) when he felt a gun silencer pressed against the back of his head. Another man materialised beside him, dressed identically to the one on the sofa, but short and stocky.

'Take a seat,' the sofa man said, as his cohort pushed Baccini onto a chair and cuffed his hands behind his back.

'Apologies, but we don't trust you. You might do something brash and someone innocent could end up getting hurt. Your family has been extremely helpful so far. We just want to talk. We talk, we leave. No one gets hurt.'

'I don't know who you are, but you don't know who I am either,' he protested.

'Oh, but we do know. And now it's time for them to know too.'

The fake colonel's eyes widened in terror as the sofa man pulled a hefty file out of a briefcase.

'You know this man as Carlo Rosconi, and that is his real name, yes. But that's not his only name.' He dropped several pieces of ID onto the glass coffee table: passports from different countries, national IDs, driving licences, credit cards.

'Please, help yourselves, but don't get too excited and make sure you take a good look.'

The woman and the two teenagers started cautiously, moving more quickly through each new document. They'd pick one up, study it, pass it on, looking first at each other, then at Rosconi.

'They're setting me up! Those are fake, Manuela. Please don't believe what this bastard is saying.'

'Fake? I doubt it, in your line of work. Madam, isn't your cousin in the Guardia di Finanza? Customs, if I'm not wrong, so he's used to these documents. Take them to him for confirmation. I appreciate that you might not believe me, but he can confirm that what you're holding is an authentic Greek passport, and so are all the others.'

The woman seemed confused. Rosconi realised that she was starting to doubt him and soon, so would their children.

'What do you want? Money, jewellery? I have a safe.'

'Excellent, let's talk about the safe…'

He extracted more documents from an envelope.

'These were in your fake insurance office. They show what you look like when you go by "Marco Baccini".' He handed the family a set of photos of a man dressed in a Carabinieri colonel's uniform. 'You own a loft in Parioli. Please, take a look. These are photos of him leaving the garage in a Mercedes Pagoda, a nice collector's item. Antique.'

The photos were clear, and showed a young, dark-haired woman with some impressive cleavage sitting next to Rosconi-Baccini, and wearing a black evening dress. She couldn't have been much older than his daughter, and was holding on to Baccini's arm with joyful abandon. The masked man with the revolver had omitted to mention her, and he got the reaction he wanted.

Rosconi's wife and daughter stared at the photos, in shock.

'Dad, who is that? And who are you?' Eva asked, her voice cracking. The man in black had known that the betrayal would hurt her the most.

'He's lying to you. Don't fall for it! They're clearly faked!'

The man in black chucked another envelope on the table. 'These are the films. We don't care about them. We're not here to blackmail anyone.' He looked at Manuela, pulling out another file of photos.

'The boy's a minor, so you might not want him to see these. He can go to the other room with my partner.'

The boy didn't move, and stared straight at him. It was clear he wouldn't be leaving. A minor, not a child.

The man then handed over the explicit photos of Baccini and his Greek lover in bed. Uncensored. The daughter gagged and someone handed her a bucket.

'Bastard! I'll kill you!'

'Shut up!' his wife cried. 'I don't know who these people are or why they're doing this, but this is something *you* caused, something *you* did. To *us*.' She threw the photos in his face.

'Manuela…' He was grasping at straws now.

'Who the fuck are you?!' his daughter screamed in his face. The bucket was now full and reeking.

'Go and take care of that,' the man on the sofa ordered his partner. 'I got this.' His partner took the bucket and left the living room. The man on the sofa turned to the girl.

'I'm sorry. We've been the bearers of unpleasant news, and I'll be the first to admit my shame. But this man, who started out as a police inspector, is a traitor: of the State he swore to defend, of the people he swore to protect and of his family. Your husband, your father is a Secret Service agent of the worst kind, a sellout and a coward. He's used State money to live the high life, and not just that. He's bribed and killed.' He handed Manuela the last of the envelopes, the bulkiest. 'In there are more photos, encrypted bank accounts and access details, keys and addresses of the Parioli place and others outside of Rome, photos with other women. The flat in Parioli is the main one; there are too many others to keep track of. Plus newspaper articles on massacres and tragic events he's dirtied his hands with in recent years. He's always served the slimiest, most rotten side of the country. Of course, it's my word against his. But I was telling the truth about everything else, so you'll believe me on this. I'm sorry about the pain I'm causing. I wouldn't have come here had you not been an intelligent, honest person. You had to know.'

The man in black stood up. His job was done. Although it

hadn't cost him much effort to move, he still flinched with the pain from his left side.

Powerless and fuming with rage, Rosconi-Baccini found an opening. 'You fucker, I know who you are! You'll pay for this! I'm not going to ruin your life – I'll take it!'

Annibale, unfazed, slowly aimed his gun at the man's leg and shot him in the calf. All they heard was a *plop* and Rosconi collapsed to the ground. Someone yelled, and Manuela and the children jumped to their feet.

'Silence, please. Sit down.' Canessa moved closer to Rosconi-Baccini, who was writhing in pain on the floor, and removed his handcuffs. He stuck his face an inch away from the other's and hissed: 'I never want to hear anything else from you, Rosconi, Baccini, whoever you are. If I do, I'll send all of this material, photos, accounts to your colleagues and to the prosecutor's office. I believe the Secret Service are the ones who'll be angriest with you since you opened a hole in their net. When you've finished dealing with your family, you'll retire. Are we clear?'

'You said no one would get hurt!' Rosconi's wife was less upset about the harming of her husband than she was about their broken promise. The man had, after all, destroyed their family.

They would be quite comfortable, Canessa was sure, even without the flat and the swish life they led there.

'It's true, I did lie – to you, not him. I hurt you, and for that I'm truly sorry.' He turned to Rosconi. 'Quit whining. It's nothing that disinfectant and some gauze won't fix. The bullet came out clean. Speaking of.' He used a pocket knife to dig into the hardwood floor and extract the bullet. 'I also apologise for this damage.' Once again to her husband: 'You won't even need the hospital. I didn't shoot to kill, and I looked you in the eye when I did it. Unlike you.'

Repetto only spoke once they'd left the ring road behind them and were driving on the Aurelia. They were chasing the blue and orange light of the sunset, with little traffic to hold them up. Major Canessa was driving calmly, half a Toscano between his lips, seemingly free of worries. Repetto, on the other hand, was full of them. He had to spit them out.

He put as many as he could into a single question. 'Annibale, do you think we did the right thing?'

The major inhaled a mouthful of smoke and blew it into the night air, already swelling with the scent of the nearby sea. He face remained immobile.

'Right has nothing to do with it. It was something we had to do, and we did it. And now, as the general said, we can finish our job.'

Repetto settled into his seat and shut his eyes. He starting silently humming a song by Roberto Vecchioni, one of his favourite musicians.

> *Oh Velasquez, if only I hadn't followed you,*
> *With you there's no turning back.*

3

The Third Millennium

I

C AN I, in all honesty, call myself a slut?

Carla Trovati asked herself this question as she woke naked in her own bed with a man by her side. At the sound of his light breathing, she'd rested her head on his chest, and was now gently caressing the bullet wound from the shooting in via Gaeta. The entry point was on his back. A coward's shot.

With Strozzi, she hadn't really wanted it. She'd been naive and he'd duped her – she wouldn't have been so yielding, so inept even if he'd drugged her first. But she'd wanted Canessa from the moment she'd met him. A strong attraction that she hadn't even admitted to herself. Strozzi was predictable, really, while Canessa was the opposite: filled with secrets to uncover, distances to bridge, voids to fill. Strozzi hadn't looked at her with a raging fire inside. He was insincere. Canessa had undressed her with his eyes from the first moment. Maybe not the very first one – at the morgue – but when they'd met again later. When he'd come along with that strange hacker, his gaze was like an x-ray.

She absolved herself, eventually. *Okay, I know I've got looks. But I've never used them as a weapon. I'm not a slut. I slipped, once, and allowed myself to have a petty, clever man. What happened last night was natural, organic, something we both wanted. Sure, the colonel has his own way with words, and he told me the story I wanted to hear, but god, what a difference. Strozzi was all fluff. Canessa's stories are the stuff of real life, and an incredible one at that.*

And so she made peace with her own heart.

They'd stayed in the club for half an hour, just enough time for the *cacio e pepe* that Canessa ruled 'edible', based on his experience as a restaurant owner. Right after the guy bumped into him and they'd sat down, the whole via Gaeta story had unravelled. Annibale had looked at her, his eyes once more boring right through her armour.

The nightowls on that first summer's night were chattering, drinking, laughing. Everyone was young, good-looking and carefree. Canessa, despite his age, had never had so much fun or lived so fully, and he felt strange acting like a thirty-year-old given that he was almost twice that. When he'd been Carla's age, he hadn't had the time or the chance – he saw himself with Giuseppina, in those fleeting, worried moments – but he was never that age at the time, and he never had been since then. Sometimes he thought he'd lived through a different Italy to everyone else. Or rather, he was the one preventing his reality – the one filled with terrorists, criminals, a corrupt Secret Service, all ranks of scum and villains, a reality where cruelty happened every day – from spilling into the other. In his parallel dimension, everyone was at risk – even those who didn't know, didn't care, couldn't imagine… who read the news and thought it would never happen here, or to them.

That was why – because not everyone knew, not even that beautiful woman who hadn't even been born in the 1970s – he'd smiled at Carla's professional curiosity, and asked her to 'stand up'.

2

'We can talk while I take you home,' Carla suggested as they left the club. The night smelled good. Summer was on its way.

Canessa looked at her and slowly shook his head. 'Better to talk indoors; it's safer. I'd take you to my place, but it's better for both of us if you don't know where I live. I'd suggest your place, if that's okay with you.'

'But how will you get home?'

'I'll call the driver, or I'll walk. I like walking.'

She'd tried to figure out whether he was messing with her ('the driver'?), but Annibale was unreadable.

Once in the house, he didn't make a beeline for the couch, like Strozzi, but sat down in a chair. Carla tried very hard not to look like an innocent child when he undid his ankle holster and removed the revolver.

'Sorry,' he said, 'it was starting to rub. Are you okay?'

Carla couldn't know that it was a Ruger LCR .22, but she did know that this thing belonged to real life. She was shocked, but she wasn't afraid or disturbed by it. They'd come to her place for a reason.

She sat down on the couch, crossing her legs and hoping to catch Canessa taking a peek but he didn't, absorbed as he was in his own thoughts.

'You have a nice place here. Do you live alone?'

'If I had a partner, I wouldn't be here with you now, would I?'

'I was thinking a friend, a colleague.'

'No, it's mine.'

'It must have been quite the expense – just like those shoes you're wearing. Sergio Rossi, right?'

This time Carla couldn't help showing her surprise. This guy was incredible.

'You know your shoes too?'

'Not really, but my aunt reads a couple of magazines and she leaves them around the place, so I pick them up every now and then. They're fun.'

'I wouldn't have thought top inspectors went in for that kind of reading.'

Canessa smiled wryly. 'When you miss out on your youth by fighting a war, and spend most of your adult life in self-imposed exile, you end up wanting to have fun. You start looking at red carpet photos with all the latest celebrities. I don't even know who they are, but it's harmless trivia, keeps me busy. I know something will happen, eventually, like it did back then.'

'Which was…?' Carla had lost herself in the sound of his voice.

He stood up, and walked over to the drinks cabinet. 'Is that Laphroaig? It was all the rage back then. I always had a bottle in the car and wherever I was staying. Do you mind if I…?'

'Please, help yourself. A friend gave it to me for my thirtieth and I've barely drunk any of it.'

Canessa found himself a glass and poured some whisky. He took off his jacket and sat down again, closing his eyes with his first sip and letting his head drop back.

Oh God, he's going to fall asleep. Carla began to panic, but then he asked, 'So, you want to know about via Gaeta? Stand up again.' They went through the same show from the restaurant.

'Do you need to pat me down?' she teased.

'No, I can tell if someone is wearing a hidden microphone.'

He gave her a swift and straightforward summary of the massacre on via Gaeta. His account contained nothing of the boring, bureaucratic report. He did go into the details, but he never got bogged down in them. His emotion came across, captivating her completely, as if his story were a fully immersive virtual reality game.

With a bourgeois belief in the State handed down to her by her father, Carla was nonplussed. The story was shocking enough before the punishing strike against the fake Colonel Baccini. She couldn't help asking, 'Do you think you did the right thing?'

'My marshal asked me that, and I'll give you the same answer: I don't know, but it doesn't matter. Sometimes the question isn't whether something's right, but whether it needs to be done. That did. I have no regrets.' Without another word, he stood up, picked up the ankle holster and his jacket. 'It's late… actually, it's early. You probably need to head to the paper, and I also have things to do.'

Carla stood up then. She didn't know what to say to keep him there, so she blurted out the first thing that came to mind, a journalist's question: 'What do you think about all this happening now? Do you have any thoughts on the big picture, any ideas?'

'It won't end well, and lots of people will get hurt. Thank you for the evening, your company, and the whisky.' He made for the door, before suddenly turning back and flashing her another wry smile. 'I don't want you to be one of those who gets hurt. Please be careful.'

'I think I would've preferred it if you'd said, "You won't be one of them, since I'll be there to watch over you." Much more knight in shining armour.'

Canessa stepped closer, and her spine tingled.

'It would've been more romantic, but untrue. I've only made one promise in all my life, and it was a mistake.'

'Because you broke it.'

He objected. 'No, I kept it, I really did. But these situations don't allow for promises.' He paused. 'I can't protect you, not in the way I'd like to. But you're right, I should've said something else.'

'What?' Carla was a blade of grass, swept away by her feelings.

Canessa let the gun and his jacket fall to the ground and put a hand on her side, pulling her towards him. She melted into him.

'I wish I'd met a woman like you in another life, a life I've never had but one I would've liked to live, if I had known you. It sounds complicated, but...'

Carla kissed him, interrupting a train of thought that made no sense but which she understood perfectly.

Flinging their clothes aside, they found themselves on the bed in a flurry of hands and lips, and she was only sorry that Strozzi had got there before Annibale.

He was as she'd expected him to be: strong and tender, even when he turned her over and took her from behind, slowly at first, then harder, faster. He refused to remove her stockings, enjoyed caressing them, rubbing his fingertips against them before moving up her back and, finally, holding her breasts. She could feel his tummy pounding against her bum, his fingers on her nipples. She'd never had sex like this before, and when she came, she wanted it to last forever.

3

She fell asleep, her head on his chest, and when she woke up, Annibale was gone, though his scent lingered. Even on the note she found in the kitchen, next to the espresso pot he'd set up for himself and washed before leaving.

You're something else, and I really want to see you again soon. But please, be careful. A phone number, which she realised was Swiss. *For emergencies only.*

What about for urges? she smiled to herself, and headed for the shower.

It was late. She threw on a pair of jeans, a light blue shirt, tossed a jumper over her shoulders and ran to the *Corriere*. She was feeling good, contented. She stepped into the office, her eyes still hidden by her Ray-Bans, tired but happy.

Giulio Strozzi's voice called out to her from the fish tank and she stumbled, as Canessa would've said, into another life.

'Carla, can you come in here a second?'

She walked in with her head held high, convinced that the discomfort of their meetings was finally behind her. Not even his inscrutable face could dampen her mood.

'I wanted to touch base with you on the uh, Canessa *affair*, and talk to you about something else that's come up, if you have a moment.'

'Of course.' She took a seat.

Federico Astroni was glaring at the two phones sitting on the leather desk pad he'd taken with him to every new office. One was his BlackBerry, the other an old calls-only model. He'd lined them up perfectly next to each other in a touch of OCD that he found calming. He'd been putting off a task that was now unavoidable.

The thought of having to use the one to the left, the 'ancient' phone, exasperated him; worse, it consumed him. He'd come into his office at 7.30 a.m. as always, walking the few metres that separated the Taveggia café from the courts. The season was changing, the heat was on its way, and Astroni was already thinking of his sailboat, a passion he'd picked up from the chief judge. The *Falco* was waiting for him, docked in the Rapallo marina, with its two masts, clean lines, and prow he now imagined sprayed with surf.

This year, after July and the first hearing in the trial of the last politician to hold out on him, he'd take a long holiday like he hadn't done in years, nothing short of forty days. To those who complained about excessive holiday allowance for magistrates, he always replied that a job like his was twice the burden of anyone else's. His forty days were effectively a regular person's three-month break.

Six weeks across the Mediterranean. Just him and a companion to be confirmed. It wouldn't be an easy choice: there were many suitors for the position of cabin hand, cook, sailor, dishwasher, escort, sex partner, but – alas – no one could cover all those roles. He expected a complete woman, ready to trade her mani/pedi for calluses on her hands and feet, and to accompany him on the adventure he'd been dreaming of for so long. He wouldn't put up with an escort, and he'd already let everyone know, raising quite the hubbub in the ministry, law enforcement, and the courts. He wouldn't back down. Everything was down in black and white, the only security compromises he would accept: 1. they could install GPS, radio or whatever damn tech they needed to track his location, 2. he would contact them once a day to confirm he was alive. The end. No escort, unless they had a submarine, a quiet, unobtrusive submarine. Did they? No. *So leave me the fuck alone.*

He pored over the route he'd mapped, ran through an imaginary casting for his fellow adventurer, with his usual Americano and toast. During the big corruption inquiries, one of the TV stations owned by people who disliked the judge's office had aired some clips of him eating toast. Someone had mocked him. *Breakfast of champions of justice.* Big whoop.

He was thinking about that episode from his past, but right now, in the present, those two phones sat there waiting for him.

That story.

That cursed story was following him, as insidious as an obscene mantra, as unexpected as winter in May. The story had resurfaced like an iceberg just when it finally seemed to have been left in the past. What had he done to deserve this? Nothing, or very little, maybe a conversation, a couple of careless words. The worst part of it all was that phone call. The contact who needed contacting, the voice he had to hear again.

Federico Astroni stared at the two phones a little longer and then yielded. He grabbed the one on the left with his left hand. The devil's hand for the devil's work.

4

Annibale Canessa stepped off the 94 bus in front of the Sormani Library and realised as if seeing it for the first time how close it was to the courts of law. He'd never been inside, always brushed past it. He hoped he wouldn't bump into anyone he knew – a prosecutor, a police officer or worse, someone who knew him, a reporter or blogger, one of those new journalists who hadn't existed in his day.

An old criminal contact from the 1970s had explained how using buses and trams was the best way to escape being noticed or followed. Despite what you learned in films and on TV, there never actually was anyone ready and waiting to recognise you and call the cops: everyone minds their own business, and if you accidentally lock eyes with someone, they turn away; if someone is following you, they'll lose you in the crowd.

Canessa had memorised the dates of the papers Pino Petri had looked up. It had been risky but necessary to visit the *Corriere* last night, and he called Alfridi to thank him profusely.

'Don't worry about it! If only we could drop in again, we might even be able to find out what Petri was actually looking for,' the IT technician replied, keeping his voice low so Spano wouldn't overhear the conversation.

'No, seriously, you've risked too much already. I just have one thing to ask: keep an eye out, and if you notice anything strange, call me.'

'Wow, a spy story! I like it,' Alfridi chirped.

'I'm serious: there's nothing good about any of this. Please, Davide, be careful.'

Here we go. He stepped into the library, where several piles of paper awaited him. He wasn't even sure what he was looking for.

5

Giannino Salemme sat caressing the leather chair, lost in thought while he waited for his son, who was taking his time. Again.

Over the last thirty years, Salemme had always blocked the cops, especially that one, but this time he'd had to go even further. This time the situation was serious, maybe the worst it ever had been. In the past, Canessa hadn't known who he was up against, and he probably still didn't, but something was up: he had an idea, a lead. His *Corriere della Sera* visit had confirmed it. So what would he do next?

When his son finally stepped into the room without knocking, as per usual, Giannino sighed.

Claudio had on a very fine blue suit. At least he'd learned something from his father. He learned some style, given up on the tackiness of his youth. Of course, if his mother had still been around... He looked at the photo on his desk. Maria had passed away when their son was only three years old. He'd never been faithful, but he had respected her in his own way. For him, respect meant keeping the family safe, expanding it with her: they would have had more children, and he would never have left her. Maybe Claudio, with both a mother and some siblings, wouldn't have followed his father's path, or ended up even more ruthless than he was. Maybe he would really have paid attention to his studies, and now he'd be somewhere in the States, with an American family, and Dad would be invited over for stuffed turkey every Thanksgiving. Hopefully his children would take after their mother, and be honest, clean. Maybe all the dirty work would have fallen on Giannino's shoulders...

But instead, his only son was the spitting image of his father, only more impulsive. Giannino hadn't been able to keep him out of the business or this endless saga.

'Canessa is a threat,' he said once his son had taken a seat.

Claudio looked at him, surprised. 'But he knows nothing,' he objected, 'and anyone who knew anything is dead. You said so yourself a couple of days ago.'

'Before he died, Petri hacked into the *Corriere* archives, looking for something. Canessa went to the archives himself with that journalist, Carla Trovati, and an actual hacker who used to work with Petri. He's found something.'

Claudio smiled. 'Well done, Dad. You're still the best. How do you know all this?'

Salemme senior took out a Toscano, special President's reserve, and lit up.

'We have a mole. We have to use our advantage.'

'So what do we do?'

'According to the mole, Canessa still knows nothing. But I don't trust anyone: he could've withheld information from those close to him. We need to find out more.'

'Do we need to "ask" someone?' Claudio's smile was like a knife. 'The journal—'

'The journalist will not be touched.'

'The computer guy, then.'

'Yes. He's gay. Call Panattoni.'

'What should I tell him?'

Salemme senior opened his arms, affecting resignation. 'To do whatever he needs to do with the queer, as long as he finds out what Canessa knows.'

I know fuck all. I could really do with a team and resources right about now, Annibale thought, stretching his legs under the table. Yet another microfilm was running before his eyes, and the piece of paper with Alfridi's *Corriere* results lay on the table beside him:

11 November 1977

7 February 1978

10 September 1978

9 January 1979

18 June 1979

13 December 1979

21 April 1980

He'd already run through each of those editions, twice, top to bottom, but nothing had jumped out at him – no clues, hints or ideas. None of the articles or names were ringing any bells. Two thoughts were torturing him: one, that he was missing something, and he didn't like that; and the other, that this was no way to work, without digital archives and no cross-references. This wasn't a job for one person. He considered sending the information along to the prosecutors following the case. He wasn't pursuing a personal vendetta, after all, and he didn't care that much about justice, either. What he needed to do this time was find an answer. Annibale wanted to *know*. Not for his own sake, but for his brother's, and his family's: they deserved to know why he'd been killed. All he had to do was walk the few steps over to the courts of law, and hand over the list. But something in his gut, his instinct, wouldn't let him. Even the wound on his side, that mark of betrayal on his flesh, kept warning him against it.

So he handed all the material back to the librarians and left the building. He'd lost track of time in there, shut up with the smell of old wood and paper. The sunset was already washing the city in crimson waves. Uncertain what to do next, he headed towards piazza San Babila, walking along via Durini, and did what he always did in situations like this: used a public phone to call Repetto. He needed his advice, his perspective. The marshal picked up after two rings.

'Is everything okay?'

Repetto sounded worried.

Canessa reassured him. 'I need to talk things through with you.'

'Same place?'

'No, the bowls club.'

The bowls club was an old bar in Greco where they used to hang out during their life on the front line. It got crowded in the evenings, because the restaurant was good value and the bowls lanes were covered and lit up. It was easy to blend in. You just needed the right clothes – and to avoid showing your inner cop.

6

'How do you feel about mazurkas, Colonel?'

Ivan might have been stocky, but he showed off his agility with a graceful twirl. The club was definitely still there, and it was thriving, only it wasn't actually a bowls club any more. The first long evenings had brought dozens of people out under the arbour for dinner and the new dance floor that had replaced the bowls lanes. There were several couples over fifty, as well as young people, even teenagers, men leading wives and partners and also their own children, showing them how to dance.

'What is this, a revival? Did I miss something?'

'Annibale, you miss out on a lot of things – remember, ballroom dancing never goes out of fashion.'

Repetto had on a light linen jacket and flared trousers – very 1970s, as if he'd somehow expected the situation. Canessa didn't dare ask if he'd worn them specially for the occasion or if they were relics from his own cupboard...

They found a table. The *osteria*'s prices had stayed more or less the same, though the quality of the food had dropped a bit. The rice was overcooked, the wine barely passable. Canessa's palate had developed since he'd started running the restaurant with his aunt, and his taste buds were now more critical. His standards had been so much lower back then, when he'd survive on stale sandwiches for weeks.

The air was warm, and the breeze carried voices, colours, music. He was always fascinated watching people having fun, and he relished a feeling of the absence of threat, something that seemed to belong only to others, not people like him.

'So?' Repetto asked.

Canessa had already told him about the *Corriere* visit, but he had to admit that after his initial enthusiasm, he'd run out of ideas. 'I don't know where else to look. Maybe there's nothing left.'

'If Petri was looking for something, it must be there. You – we – have to keep looking.'

A reality check. Just what he needed.

'What if we followed the people following you?' Repetto added, lighting himself a cigarette.

'You're obsessed. It's too complicated now. I'd have to make a point of going somewhere they know and letting them spot me. I don't think we should, yet.' Canessa waved the smoke away from his face along with the idea. 'I told you, they're just pawns.

But you're right, the key to this whole story lies in those papers. If Petri was killed now, after so many years, it's because he was hiding something and, for some reason, the people behind that secret suddenly felt threatened. I knew something like this would happen. Remember the day they took him away from us in Milan? If only I'd got him to talk… There was already something rotten about the whole thing.'

'This is the Canessa I know and love,' Repetto commented, sarcastically. 'Paranoid, just like in the good old days.'

Canessa smiled. 'My being paranoid has lengthened both our lives considerably. But back to Petri. This is what I think.' He leaned forward to whisper. 'All I need is one clue from those papers that links up to him. One detail, a tiny hook. I don't need it to show up in all of them. Just one, and then I'll have the key to the rest.'

Repetto found himself looking into the spirited eyes he'd seen in his colleague for so many years, before they suddenly disappeared. Canessa was about to lower his head and charge.

'Colonel, look,' he pre-empted him. 'Put your research on pause for a day, sleep on it. They're not going to burn down the library, right? Take a break, trust me. Go to the cinema, relax.' He picked up a crumpled copy of the *Giorno* and started leafing through it. 'I'll find you a good film. Remember? We used to do this. You'd hunker down in a cinema in the dark. I'd sit a few rows behind you, watching your back. Sure, the films weren't always great, and you did doze off several times… Where on earth is the local news section?'

Canessa suddenly jumped to his feet, tipping a chair over and almost trampling a waitress. She glared at him, certain he was drunk.

'*Shit!*' he exclaimed. 'Local news! That's what I was missing, that's what I skipped. Repetto, you are a gift from Heaven! I have to go.'

'You realise the library's closed now, right? They're not going to open it for you personally.'

Deep down, Canessa knew Repetto was right. Times were not as interesting now that he was a free agent, a self-styled detective inspector. So he looked at Repetto with resignation.

'You're right. I'll head in tomorrow. Thanks, Ivan. But I still need to go. I'll be in touch soon.'

Repetto was curious about the sudden rush.

'How's it going with the journalist?'

'You should never kiss and tell, but I will say that she's something special.'

Repetto hoped she was the right one. He saw a new Canessa: he was glowing. If they hadn't been embroiled in this blast from the past, he would have been happy for his friend.

'Okay, you head off. I'll stay a little longer and enjoy my evening. But be careful, and call me as soon as you find anything.'

7

Every time he headed to the station or the airport to pick up Rocco, Panattoni ended up sweating buckets, no matter if it was actually hot, as it was that Friday. His ability to put up with the younger Neapolitan killer just got worse with time, not better. He never got used to him.

The truth was that this was no longer the life for him. Sure, he was still a retired fascist enforcer, former Lazio hooligan, someone who'd never done anything legal in his life, never had an honest job, never kept his hands clean. But there was one crucial difference between Rocco and him: Rocco was a killer and criminal to the bone. It wasn't a job to him – *he had fun with it.* Panattoni saw himself as a victim of circumstance and necessity. Rocco would never change his ways. Crime was all he knew. He was an animal. Panattoni believed himself made of different stuff, and he longed to get out of all this. He truly felt it was possible to leave all of this filth behind him. There was nothing in it, except for the money, and everything was fake. He wanted to change before he died. Even that fucking Petri had changed, hadn't he? He'd tried to, anyway, until Rocco killed him like a dog. *With my help.*

I never technically killed anyone, he insisted, absolving himself, as if smashing bones, driving cars, gathering intel, and setting up ambushes didn't put him on the same level as the ones pulling the trigger or plunging the knife.

His mood was made even worse by the fact that he'd have to put Rocco up somewhere for the evening, and *somewhere* meant at his place. Hotel was out of the question. Before leaving in the morning, he'd told *his girlfriend* – he loved being able to call her that – to spend the night with her mother (best option) or with one of her friends (second choice, but he wasn't too keen on it due to jealousy). He had to put someone up for work, he'd told her. And it was the truth. He'd even admitted, 'This guy is a maniac, a madman, and I don't want you under the same roof.'

She'd kissed him, slipped on her tight jeans, and packed her stuff into a nice Louis Vuitton bag (he'd bought her an original, worth over a thousand euros). She kissed him again, offering him a glimpse of her loose breasts under a white shirt, and left the house.

Panattoni pulled up next to the Garibaldi station entrance and prayed for Rocco to be quick.

He'd asked the Salemmes if it was truly necessary to bring in the 'boy' – that's what *they* called him – for a job like this. He was enough, surely? He just had to put on a balaclava, pick up Alfridi, and make him talk. He even had a couple of syringes filled with hallucinogenics, a modern variant of the hyocine the Nazis had used.

'Rocco can take things too far, you know.'

Claudio Salemme had stopped him. 'Nando, Nando, you're getting soft. How else should things go? If we don't push "too far"—' he'd raised his voice to an irritating falsetto, '—the guy will just call the police or Canessa as soon as he wakes up. Even if he doesn't see anyone's face, it'll still tip him off. Can we run that risk? No. So call Rocco.'

The car door burst open and he nearly banged his head, bringing him rudely back to the present. Rocco chucked his bag in the back and settled into the passenger seat. He reeked of sweat, even more than usual due to the heat, the train journey, and the early wake-up call that had stopped him from taking a shower (if he ever did).

'Let's get moving, mate. I need to down a couple of cold Cokes. I'm dying of thirst.'

Panattoni sighed. The clock on the dashboard said 10.20 a.m. It was going to be a long day.

Chief Magistrate Calandra adored his new summer Prince of Wales blazer, custom made for him by a tailor he knew in Naples, right behind piazza dei Martiri. He adored the tailor, he adored the square, and one of his favourite cafés was there too, La Caffettiera. 'These are the things that make life worth living,' he'd say.

It was a cool wool in all senses of the term. Rome was starting to get unbearable, except in the evenings when the wind – from the north or who knew where, he'd never figured it out – snuck into every nook. In there, two floors below a government building – formally assigned to another office with another purview entirely – the man who didn't exist was waiting for him in the lobby of the control centre, where the temperature was perfect. Whenever he went down there, and it wasn't very often, Calandra would take a box of *gianduiotti* to his valuable collaborator, who loved those chocolates. He got them sent to him from an old Turin chocolatier, custom-made, of course. One of his first teachers had told him: 'Remember, if you want to tame a human being, a gift always works better than violence or seduction.'

The invisible man, in his always out-of-season clothing – today it was a full winter three-piece suit, complete with heavy vest – unwrapped one and popped it into his mouth, savouring it and giving Calandra a grateful, devoted look. He handed over a file stamped with the information services seal: a bright sun casting light over the city walls, on a black background with the Latin motto *Scientia Rerum Rei Publicae Salus*. Knowledge of issues is the salvation of the Republic. Sure, the Republic, but mostly the people to whom Calandra dedicated his work ethic.

While Calandra looked through the file, the invisible man explained. 'We found Canessa in the Sormani Library in Milan, but with a six-hour delay due to a technical issue. Not that much, but just enough to lose him again.'

Calandra came across a page with seven dates.

'What's this?'

'The *Corriere* publication dates he's researching.'

'Excellent.' Satisfied, Calandra handed back the file.

The man stared at him in surprise.

'But we still don't know what he's looking for, or where he is now.'

Calandra patted him on the shoulder.

'You've done an excellent job. Don't worry. Keep up this surveillance. What he's looking for doesn't matter. Leave him to his research and make sure no one disturbs him. It means he's still pursuing his private investigation. Canessa the Tank is on the move, and that's all we need to know. The rest will follow.'

He did up his blazer – he was starting to feel cold, and didn't like being underground for too long – and headed for the lift, anticipating daylight and lunch at the Hassler's Imago. Good food, and Rome at his feet. No better feeling.

8

Panattoni gave the steering wheel of the Fiat Doblò he'd stolen from the long-stay car park at Malpensa airport a little squeeze. The chances of its owner noticing its absence that day were almost nil. Once his job was over, the car would end up in a ditch, cleaned up and torched, just to make sure. All he had to do was watch it around the security cameras in the car park; everything else was child's play. It wasn't the first time he'd stolen a car, after all.

A damp, sticky heat had descended upon the city, earlier than forecast. Panattoni had never fully got used to Milan's climate, with its erratic seasons. And since he didn't believe in climate change, all the fault lay with that fucking city. Rome, for example, was something else entirely.

Speaking of oddities, Panattoni was starting to realise that he'd never really got the hang of so much of the action, behaviour, and situations he'd lived through after... how many years in Milan? Almost ten now. Was his a crisis of conscience? Hardly! Too late though... *Maybe more of a mid-life crisis*, he told himself, adding *Fuck that*. Whatever it was, he wanted to quit. Had to.

That whole thing was proof of that. Experience was telling him something was off: all the other dirty jobs he'd done on the Salemme payroll had been quick, even the ones that had ended in violence and bloodshed. Surgical, not a trace. This one was different: it was dragging on. And they weren't confronting just any old person, a witness to silence, a lawyer to bribe, a business competitor to warn, not even a low-list criminal with a loose tongue that needed cutting. Those were all easy to deal with. Too easy.

Panattoni wasn't a rookie. He knew about Annibale Canessa, knew his story, and he'd found out even more about him in the past couple of days. Canessa might have been out of the game for the past twenty years or so, but he was a tough nut, a former high-ranking Carabinieri officer, trained and trigger-happy. To judge by his movements, he was also still in shape. After all, you don't forget some things, and it takes little to get back into your old habits.

Rocco opened the car door, making him jump. Again.

'Panattò, what's up, why you so jumpy?'

'I don't like any of this.'

'Eh, you'll get over it,' Rocco teased, cracking open yet another can of Coke.

They'd spent the past two hours in the Bonola shopping centre car park. Never together for more than a couple of minutes, that was the rule. Now that Rocco was back, it was his turn to stretch his legs, get a coffee, or buy some lingerie – he'd spotted a get-up that would look mouthwatering on his girlfriend, and wouldn't last long on her. It was a good distraction from his job, which was to grab the queer, chuck him into the van, drive to some out-of-the-way location, and make him sing.

This time, he hadn't brought a gun.

'We should be clean, just in case we get stopped.' He started mumbling a good-luck chant. 'We won't need more than this baby for the sucker.' He pulled a leather-grip Laguiole knife from his jacket pocket and waved it around with his usual soulless grin.

Panattoni shuddered. He hoped the fruitcake would show up soon. Sitting there next to Rocco was making his stomach churn.

Davide Alfridi walked up the steps of the Bonola underground station at 8.15 p.m., at least two hours later than expected, and started walking briskly along via Cechov. There'd been an issue with a tractor company's online banking, and he'd had to work overtime. He was worried for his 'doggy', as he called his new Jack Russell. He'd only had him a couple of weeks, and was still trying to find him a suitable name. He'd noticed that the pup suffered from separation anxiety, and that was enough to convince him that dogs were better than people. He needed to find himself a boyfriend, someone he'd love and trust enough to ask him to stay at home and take care of the furry new arrival.

The sun was setting, but it was still pretty hot, and Alfridi tried to stay under the trees and their shade. He'd never been so excited: the *Corriere* mission, working with that super inspector – he was definitely not what the online articles said – and Canessa's warning to watch out. He looked around, just in case. No one. Maybe he should have asked the Carabiniere what to look out for.

'Excuse me!'

A van pulled over on his left side and a man waved at him. They were going in the opposite direction, and it wasn't easy for the driver to lean out across the seats to talk to him. Alfridi thought it might be a courier, someone with a delivery. There was some space between two parked cars, so he stepped off the pavement to hear him, leaning towards the car door.

'Hey, sorry,' said the person behind the wheel, a large man in a mover's uniform, 'but do you know how to get to via Ojetti from here?'

'Of course!' Alfridi gave him directions.

'Thanks a lot.'

Alfridi turned to step back onto the pavement – *at least there are some people around with good manners* – when he heard the van's side door slide open.

Two hands grabbed him and he found himself handled like a parcel – though they might have taken more care with a parcel – and slammed against the side of the van.

Everything went dark as he lost consciousness.

9

The number 94, again, the Sormani Library, again. Annibale Canessa was troubled. He kept checking around, his eyes scanning for any possible threat. He was doubly troubled, and that just wouldn't do. He'd adopted one golden rule all his life: limit the time you spend being worried, and if you're troubled, limit your reasons to one.

The first reason was tactical. Coming back to a place where he'd consulted material using his real name and real ID wasn't a wise move. But thinking about it, only Chief Magistrate Calandra had any way of knowing what he was up to, and he wasn't dangerous at this stage. The prosecutors? According to the news, they had no interest in keeping tabs him. Not yet, anyway. Some of the journalists closer to the courts had written that there was some illegal dealing going on (weapons? drugs?), but almost as if they didn't believe their own words, or had been forced to write them. Canessa knew they wouldn't write something like that without the explicit consent of the relevant prosecutor.

Despite his concern, he calmed down somewhat when he spotted Repetto among the crowd of people waiting for the number 12 across the road. He was disguised as a lawyer; he'd even brought a small briefcase. He'd promised to watch Canessa's back like the good old days, and he was sticking to his word.

The second reason wasn't tactical, and that made it even more dangerous. Carla Trovati. They'd just spent their second night together, and he'd ended up sleeping by her side, unable to let go of her and her soft breathing, her beautiful, naked body. He still wanted her, all of her: he wanted her company, her words, her lips, her scent. They'd made love as soon as they woke up, with passion and tenderness. She really got to him. He was trying to hold back, but most of his thoughts were currently – and dangerously – focused on her.

'One thing at a time. Right now, it's a second round with the papers.'

Scanning his environment one last time, Annibale walked up the steps.

Carla sat at the table in her t-shirt and underwear, her *New York Times* mug empty before her. God, that man also made the best coffee she'd ever had.

She was troubled. She'd bumped into him waiting for her outside her building, and as he headed into the bathroom for a shower ('Do you mind? Sorry, it's been a really long day'), she'd tried surprising him with a minimalist (that is, practically invisible) matching silk lingerie set. Annibale, with hands that were clearly capable of anything, ran a finger along her panties' waistband, arousing her like never before.

As he'd moved lower, to her buttocks, he murmured, 'It's very easy on the eye, even easier to take off, but I much prefer what's underneath, not just here.' His fingers brushed lightly against the black silk triangle, causing her to shudder. 'But also here.' He'd kissed her forehead, then her lips.

Carla wasn't one for morning sex, never had been. *Once you're up, you get going* was her rule. She'd told Annibale too, but he'd pulled her on top of him. She'd straddled him, and when he slid inside her, biting her nipple, he smiled. 'Surely it's better to come than go?'

They chatted through breakfast together, and she'd been struck by their shared gestures, their easy domesticity. Then he'd told her about his fruitless research, revealing Alfridi's findings in the *Corriere* archives and the dates of the editions Petri had looked up.

She froze. 'You didn't tell me you'd found something in Petri's access trail.'

Canessa stood up, leaned over to kiss her, and moved towards the door.

'I didn't know if I could trust you yet.'

Carla gave him a faint smile.

'Well, I didn't make it that tough.'

Rocco lit himself an unfiltered Camel, leaned against the Doblò and nodded. The sun was already high and they needed to get going, but the Neapolitan killer was in the mood for smoking and chatting.

'He's the first queer I've met who's got balls as well as arse.'

His maniacal laugher swept across the empty countryside, with its scattered empty farmhouses and ruined warehouses, and only birdsong and the buzzing of bugs in reply. The clear sky was enough confirmation of being outside of Milan's greater metropolitan area.

They'd been there all night, beating up Alfridi. At first, he was so scared he'd pissed himself.

'Fuck, that's disgusting!' Panattoni had yelled, holding Alfridi's thigh down. They'd used the Rocco method. 'You work them with no real reason, and they cry *Why?* and you say nothing. After a while they lose their minds. Some of them even think they deserve it.' Two hours later, however, when they'd told him why he was there, when they'd asked him what Canessa was looking for at the *Corriere*, and, most importantly, if he'd found it, the young man's gaze – emerging from two heavily bruised eyes – had hardened. It suddenly became clear – to Nando at least – that they wouldn't be getting any more information out of him.

They moved on to more brutal techniques, with no response. At dawn, when Alfridi had lost all resemblance to a human being, Panattoni had left, resigned. On his way he'd kicked the man's bag, spilling its contents. Out rolled a pack of biscuits, which he'd ignored earlier. Looking at it now, however, he had an idea. Sure, they were only biscuits, but not just any kind: they were dog biscuits.

All he had to do was walk back in and say, 'I wonder who these are for? Is there maybe someone waiting at home, feeling all alone? Let's go pick him up, bring him over here, and have some fun together...'

223

Alfridi had tried widening his eyes in fear, but the movement was rendered impossible by the bruising. After a final, half-hearted refusal, he'd spoken. About Canessa, the newspaper, the dates. And his torturers knew he was telling the truth.

Rocco complimented Nando – 'Well done, nice idea!' – unaware that Nando had only tried giving Alfridi a way out, a means to end his suffering. He'd been genuinely impressed. However, he was also currently in the grass, wiping clean the knife he'd used to slit the man's throat.

'Glad you appreciated it,' he'd replied non-committally. By this time, Panattoni was completely fed up with himself and his monster of a partner.

'What do we do with the body?'

It was halfway through the morning, and getting hot. They needed to hightail it out of there.

'Leave him. We're going.'

'But they'll find him and Canessa will know we're after him.'

Panattoni spread his arms and shrugged.

'Rocco, he's gonna figure it out anyway when he looks for Alfridi and can't find him. He'll know what happened.'

'Maybe he'll think he's on holiday, or he went to see his mum, or...'

Panattoni wasn't listening. He was ready to leave and he headed for the Dobló. But he stopped in his tracks after a few metres. In front of him stretched a tract of uncultivated land, fading into tall grass and lines of poplars.

'Canessa is going to fuck us over, I can feel it. We're going to pay for everything, even our *antecedents*,' he muttered. 'Good word, that one, who knows where I read it.'

'The fuck you saying?' yelled Rocco.

But Panattoni was already in the van.

10

Canessa froze.

On his third run through Milan's local news on 21 April 1980, something caught his attention. A name. He thought he recognised it, but he didn't stop in time and it disappeared again in the sea of lines. Admittedly, there were several names he'd recognised since he started looking through the newspapers: politicians, actors, singers, sports personalities and criminals. The right name, however, had eluded him like a balloon floating away from a child.

He focused. It had to be someone with ties to Petri. But how, since Petri was one of the most dangerous terrorists around back then? He was a ruthless killer. Could the name he was looking for belong to another terrorist? He rejected that theory: Petri knew everything about his former comrades, and he wouldn't have been ambushed by one of them. So if not an accomplice, what about a victim? Who had he killed in that time period? In March 1980, Petri and Antonio Malerba had killed a doctor from the San Carlo hospital, a left-leaning man famous for his progressive ideas but critical of the Red Brigade and the armed struggle in general. Just the sort of target the terrorists preferred. Canessa and his team had arrested Malerba soon afterwards, though not before spraying a volley of bullets at his legs. He'd survived, but he was pretty roughed up.

Tommasi. Was that his name? Canessa wasn't sure. After another fruitless run through the microfilm, he decided to break for lunch.

It was way past time, but his stomach had started complaining. He would talk to an 'expert' while he ate, he told himself. He left his post as it stood, with the microfilm still in the reader, told the librarian and headed outside.

Corso di Porta Vittoria was surprisingly quiet, with very few pedestrians and only a couple of cars. He checked the clock on the corner: 3 p.m. He looked for Repetto – who had obviously changed his location and disguise – and spotted him without jacket or tie sipping a coffee in a café near the courts. His leather briefcase had been replaced by a small rucksack at his feet. Canessa walked in and leaned against the bar. They both looked around. Canessa ordered two of the fresher looking sandwiches and a beer, and they sat down at one of the tables furthest from the entrance.

'Do you remember the doctor Petri killed in 1980? It was the first attack after via Gaeta. I was still in hospital.'

Repetto smiled. 'Of course. Moscati. The San Carlo one.'

'That's the one!' Canessa exclaimed. 'I could only think of Tommasi. Thanks.' He wolfed down his food and made for the exit.

'Are you going to be in there for long?' Repetto asked. 'I do have a family, you know…'

Canessa turned around. 'You're right, Ivan. Head home. I still have quite a bit to do, but I don't think I'm in danger. Not at this stage.'

Repetto didn't budge.

'I'll wait. I don't think it'll take you too long.'

He was right. Canessa found the name, and with it a lead.

Now that he knew what he was looking for, he started scanning the newspapers, sure that the name would show up in a title or subtitle. And there it was. A small piece, bottom right of the page, almost drowned out in all the other slugs. That particular piece of journalism jargon still amused him; after all, the news was also about slugs, though a different type entirely: 'Moscati back in Novara. To be buried tomorrow in family plot.' The article spoke briefly about Francesco Moscati's coffin which, for those who hadn't been able to attend the funeral service, would stop in the Famedio in Milan's Cimitero Monumentale, before continuing to Novara to be interred in the family tomb. The Moscati were a well-known dynasty of doctors.

Canessa was sure that Petri had stopped at that point. There was nothing else in the paper that could be of the least interest to him. But why had he been looking for that article? Why, after thirty-five years, did he care where one of his victims was buried?

Canessa whirred the film back, one, two, eight days. There was the news of the killing, right on the front page:

THE RED BRIGADE STRIKE AGAIN.
DOCTOR MOSCATI KILLED.

'Shit!' he exclaimed. One of the librarians glared and silenced him with a finger to her lips.

He still needed to find a link between the dates Alfridi had provided. He picked one at random: 18th June 1979. He flicked back, scanning only the first pages. Ten days earlier, a giant headline:

NO END TO TERRORIST MASSACRE.
TWO POLICEMEN KILLED IN TURIN.

Of course. Tartaglia and Collini. The former a Neapolitan brigadier, the latter an officer from the Brescia area, a young man described by all as a great guy, passionate and full of life. They'd been killed like dogs, lured by a phone call into an ambush in Turin's Vallette neighbourhood, an area of council estates and industrial warehouses not far from the prison.

Annibale quickly flicked back to the 18 June edition and checked for both names. He eventually found one in the regional news, a small piece at the bottom of the page:

COLLINI, PRIVATE FUNERAL
IN GARGNANO CEMETERY

Collini's family had refused a State service and his sister had been very critical of the institutions, blaming them for not keeping their citizens safe.

Petri was searching for his victims' burial spots. Was that the link? What did it mean? It made no sense.

Canessa stretched his legs under the table and laced his fingers behind his head. It was getting late.

As he pulled out his phone to text Repetto, he heard one of the librarians behind him.

'I'm sorry sir, you can't come in. We're closing in twenty minutes.'

Repetto turned on the charm. 'I'm not looking to come in, love, I'm trying to get my friend over there to come outside.' She eyed him suspiciously but let him in all the same.

Ivan, you old dog, Canessa thought. In a flash, Repetto stood at his side.

'So?'

Canessa spoke quietly. 'He was looking for the cemeteries. I'm not sure why.'

'The cemeteries?'

228

'Yes, the burial places of the people he'd killed. I found two almost identical articles in the list of dates. I was about to check a third.'

Flicking through the editions prior to 10 September 1978 brought a result. Another of Pino's murders, in Genoa: Marchetti, the judge. Canessa lingered over the photo, feeling emotional. Marchetti, gentle and quiet, had been a friend of his father's; they'd known each other their entire life and he'd been nearing retirement. Of course it was his duty, but Marchetti's death was another reason Canessa had chased Petri so doggedly.

He flicked quickly to 10 September. It took him a little longer this time, but eventually he found Marchetti again, this time in an obituary, which reported that the body was resting in Staglieno.

Annibale leaned back in the chair. 'This is a lead, an actual lead,' he told Repetto.

'But why did he care about where they were buried?'

Canessa rewound the microfilm and replaced it in its box. He paused. The sun slanted further through the window.

'I have an idea, but I need to confirm it. Call Rossi. I'm going to need him to drive tomorrow.'

I I

'Panattoni is strange.'

Claudio Salemme offered his father a flute of champagne. He prided himself on his expertise, having taken a wine-tasting course. Unlike all his other misguided hobbies, he'd actually seen this one through. His interest in wine seemed to stem from an actual passion, and it was confirmed by the care he took to nurture it, just like a vine.

They were in the kitchen of their enormous house, which occupied the entire top floor of a building in via Caradossi. Along with the champagne, they were also enjoying their view of Santa Maria delle Grazie, its Bramantesque dome ablaze in the summer sunset.

'This is very good,' Giannino Salemme commented, downing the entire glass. The kitchen was gigantic, and the Salemmes enjoyed spending time there in the evenings before going out to pursue their actual passions: young women, picked up in trendy new clubs, chi-chi restaurants, discos and exclusive bars.

They each had independent access to the kitchen, which served as a barrier of sorts. They had silently agreed to live under the same roof, as long as neither invaded the other's space. This was their neutral zone, and their evening drinks at the American-style bar were a good way to recap the day, talk about work and sound out ideas.

The champagne was chilled and accompanied by a selection of olives from Calabria, slices of ham and walnut bread.

'It's a cuvée special, 1999. Classy stuff, produced in a small *maison*, six hectares of modern, biodynamic techniques,' Claudio explained, glad the wine had hit the mark.

'What were you were saying about Panattoni?' Salemme senior interrupted him. He didn't really care about the wine's story. He just wanted to drink it.

'He's paranoid, talking too much. I don't think he's going with the flow.'

Giannino Salemme swallowed an olive and spat the pit into the sink. The cleaner would deal with it in the morning.

'I can understand why. We've never asked him to push this hard.'

'There was no other way.'

'I'm not denying that. I'm just thinking that we've done plenty of nasty things without regrets, but they all ended quickly. Wham, bam. This one is dragging on and on.'

'Why not get rid of Canessa then?'

'You young people! Always rushing. No. There'll be no more deaths, at least for as long as we can keep on top of the situation, stay one step ahead of him.'

'Do you trust your sources?' Claudio watched his father crack an ugly smile and raise his glass for more champagne. He poured out some more, adding, 'Clearly you do, since you're keeping them all to yourself.'

A little irritation there. Giannino Salemme patted Claudio's shoulder. 'Son, it's better if you don't know everything. We need to compartmentalise. I'll tell you when you need to know. Don't worry. Now my apologies,' he hopped off the stool, 'but I need to freshen up. I've got a lady waiting for me.'

I2

'Slow down!'

Rossi was so startled he nearly swerved. God! Canessa still scared him, even after all this time. It seemed like he was asleep, and maybe he actually was – but with one eye open, like in films and novels. Or both eyes closed, mind churning.

Admittedly, Canessa was trying to get some rest, making the most of travelling as he'd always done. That was why he had someone else drive him whenever he could. He stored up sleep like an animal stores up food before hibernating. A reserve for all the times when he might not be able to sleep for a while. He was doing so now, despite having slept for ten hours straight.

He hadn't spent last night with Carla, unlike the two before that. But they'd chatted on the phone when he left the Sormani Library and Repetto had gone home.

'How are you? Any news?' Carla asked immediately.

'You know what? I miss you,' Annibale replied.

Carla's stomach somersaulted. *Good lord, am I really in this deep already?* 'I miss you too,' she said.

They lingered in silence for a moment, and then they both started talking at the same time, 'I wanted to tell you that—'

They laughed.

'You first,' she invited.

'Listen, tomorrow morning I need to head outside Milan, and I'm leaving early. I don't think I can see you this evening – I mean, if you want to see me, that is.'

I really do, she said to herself. 'Look, you beat me to it. I can't either. I have a night shift, and I'm off to the courts in the morning. The case prosecutors have called a press conference.'

Canessa took a sharp breath. 'Have they found anything, do you think?'

'I don't think so, but they have to have something to show for themselves – people are already complaining. It's like: "Courts Silent on Shooting in Milan". Where are you going?'

'Unlike them, I have an idea but I need to check it out. If you invite me over for dinner tomorrow…' He left the sentence dangling, 'I'll tell you what I found.'

Carla smiled, sorry that he wasn't able to drop by right then.

*

232

That morning, Rossi had picked him up at 6.30 in another BMW, a newer model with a Swiss numberplate. The air was crisp, the morning sky clear. Canessa had directed him towards the southern entrance to the Don Lorenzo Milani overpass, as a meeting point for pick-ups.

'In case someone's following you, so they won't know where I'm based.' Canessa walked there, going through a private residential garden by picking the lock on the gate. Rossi might have understood all those precautions in the 1970s, but now it felt more like paranoia than secrecy. Sure, they'd killed his brother, but this whole civil war game seemed out of place, dated. *We're in the third millennium, for Christ's sake.* But he'd never contradict Annibale, not even under torture.

When he opened the car door, Canessa saw immediately that Rossi was agitated. 'Bad night?' he asked, buckling up. He pulled the SIG from under his jacket and slid it into the pocket in front of him.

Rossi sighed. 'Where to?' he asked, fingers poised over the satnav screen.

'Gargnano, Brescia, the western branch of Lake Garda. But before we leave the city, let's stop somewhere good and grab some breakfast.'

'Not a fan of the service area caffs?'

'Not a fan of their cameras. Unless I have access to them.'

Despite being Italian, Rossi drove like any Swiss driver in Italy: 200 kilometres per hour. And just like the Swiss, he believed that speed cameras were ornamental: even if they did work, the fine would never reach him.

We're all the same, aren't we, Canessa thought as he dozed. *The only difference between innocence and guilt is whether the speed camera is working.*

*

They reached their destination in under an hour. Rossi parked the car behind a bend in the road so it wouldn't be visible from the entrance, and they made their way into the Cimitero Monumentale in Gargnano. It was a beautiful site, spread over the side of the mountain and dominated by a chapel that seemed in danger of being impaled by the rocky peak above it. To Canessa it resembled a theatre, with the dead on separate stages, so they all had a good view of the lake.

Despite the early hour, they spotted a man limping between the gravestones, broom in hand. He must have been the custodian, or one of the cleaners.

'Follow my lead, and don't talk even if he speaks to you directly,' Canessa ordered.

The caretaker's eyes followed them as they walked up the steps. When they got to the top row, just beneath the chapel, they started walking down again, peering at the terraced rows.

Right on cue, the caretaker called out, 'Good morning! Can I help you? Are you looking for someone?'

His voice was as strong as his body was weak: his right leg caused him obvious discomfort. He couldn't have been more than forty, but he looked much older. It wasn't his body so much as his face, which was lined and disappointed, as if he'd suffered some sort of deprivation. His clothes, however, retained some dignity: beige trousers, a light blue shirt, a blue vest, all clean and ironed.

'Good morning! I'm Major Zanella, Carabinieri,' Canessa replied, waving his old badge as deftly as a street magician.

That was all the man needed. He stood to attention and

would undoubtedly have clicked his heels together had he been wearing shoes instead of sandals. Chest out, chin high, perfect posture.

'Brigadier Camastri Davide, retired, at your service, sir.'

'At ease, Brigadier.' Canessa looked at his leg once more. 'Injured on duty?'

The man smiled bitterly. 'You could say so. We were chasing a car here on the lake, near Riva. A group of robbers after a hit. The driver was fresh out of the academy. He'd just started his shift and I was giving him some driving lessons when we got a call about a robbery. A moment later their car cut in front of us. There was no time to change seats, I just told him to floor it. He seemed to be doing well but then he must have got nervous. He lost control and we crashed into a tree – the only one for two kilometres around. Couldn't have aimed better if he'd done it on purpose. Good thing it was there too, or we'd have ended up in the lake. I ended up like this; not a scratch on him. He left the force a couple of months later.'

'I'm sorry,' Canessa said. He pulled out Petri's photo. 'Do you recognise this man?'

'Isn't that the terrorist, the one they shot down?'

'That's the one. Giuseppe Petri.'

'The photo makes him look younger. He looked older when he came here.'

Canessa didn't visibly react. 'When was that?'

He thought about it for a minute. 'It was still cold. Maybe end of February. I didn't know who he was then, of course. Or rather, I knew the name like everyone else, but not what he looked like... You know, I still have some of my old cop skills,' he chuckled. 'I studied him for a bit – there aren't many new faces dropping in here. He started looking around, just like you. But before I could ask, he'd found the tomb.'

'Can you show us?'

The custodian turned around. 'It's right over here,' and he set off along the row, broom in tow. He stopped shortly after, pointing with his arm. The tombstone bore only a name and dates:

BRUNO COLLINI

22 FEBRUARY 1955 – 2 JUNE 1979

'It's strange, you know. When I heard the news on TV, I was almost sad, despite his history. I was happy to see him here.'

'Why's that?'

'Because everyone else has forgotten about this kid. He was all right, kind and positive. He had a lovely girlfriend. They were going to be married at the end of summer. She still got married a year later to a rich boy from Toscolano. Likes his Ferraris. And I can't shake off the idea that there was something going on already. In any case, she's never been here since I've been on shift, and I haven't heard anything different from the others. Collini's parents both died in the early '80s. His sister kicked up such a fuss when it happened, but she maybe comes only twice a year. I'm the one who changes his flowers – I use the ones thrown out by all those self-righteous sorts who come once or twice a week to refresh their relatives' graves. Some have too much, others have nothing. Poor kid.' He paused for a while, genuinely moved. 'So when that guy came with a big bunch of irises and some candles, well, I was pleased. Then I found out he was a terrorist, and he'd killed a bunch of people. Does that make any sense to you, Major?'

'It does. Thank you, Brigadier. You've been extremely useful.'

The man didn't respond, though he must have been curious. A cop to the bone, even while holding a broom. Back in the day, someone like him would have ended up on Canessa's team, despite his limp. Loyal, reserved, alert: he'd have done his job well, limp and all.

13

All he needed now was the final confirmation. On the way back to Milan, he made a phone call to Marchetti's widow. Petri had killed Marchetti in Genoa, 1978, in front of the Svizzera patisserie in via Albaro. Canessa had stayed in touch with his wife, a spritely eighty-year-old woman who lived in Portofino from March to October, in the house she'd inherited from her second husband. She'd got married again about ten years after the murder, and twelve years after that she'd been widowed again. At that point, she'd decided to live in Genoa only four months a year, in winter, when Portofino was too sad. As soon as spring was on its way, she'd move back to the Riviera. She'd refused a slew of offers to buy the house, including the ridiculous ones, as she called them. She was too fond of opening her blinds onto the Piazzetta and watching the celebrities and the wannabes parading just below. Despite multiple attempts from children and grandchildren, the house was firmly in her hands, and she had a tight grip.

'They'll be able to enjoy it or sell it on later.' She'd wink at Annibale whenever he dropped in on his skiff from San Fruttuoso. The trip was one of his rituals: he'd bring her a fish on the hook, and she'd offer to cook it. Theirs was a special relationship, the only one he'd ever nurtured with the family of a terrorist victim, and that was because the Marchettis had been friends of his father. Annibale had known them forever.

When he'd arrested Petri in 1984, she'd called him to say, 'Thank you, Annibale.'

She picked up almost immediately, as if she'd been waiting by the phone.

'Oh, my dear, I wanted to call when I heard about your brother. I'm so sorry, though I know you were…' she searched for the right word, 'distant. How are you doing? Are you coming to see me?'

'Thank you, Madame,' he always called her that, 'but I'm not in Liguria. Can I ask you something? I hope it doesn't bring up bad memories.'

'Annibale, what's going on? Talk to me. You're worrying me.'

'This conversation needs to be confidential. I'm sorry to even mention that.'

'Of course, silly.'

'The question may seem strange, but have you noticed anything different about your husband's tomb in the past few months?'

Marchetti's widow was quick to respond. 'Annibale, Annibale. I don't know how, but you already know my answer. One morning, towards the end of winter, I found a bunch of irises and two candles. Someone had visited his grave, but no one knows who it was. You know though, don't you?'

'I do.'

'And you're not going to tell me.'

'No, not yet.'

'Look after yourself, Annibale.'

'You too, Madame.'

Carla Trovati almost crashed into Caprile as he ran out of the entrance on via Solferino. She lost her balance dodging him, and she would have ended up on the floor if he hadn't grabbed her arm.

'Salvo, what's up?' she asked, gathering herself.

'Sorry, Carla, I'm in a rush. Strozzi has finally given me something interesting since you were at the courts for the press conference. Any news?'

She shrugged. 'Nothing really. They're following a couple of leads, but they're denying any links to terrorism, despite Petri. I think they're hiding something. They're not willing to talk. It feels like someone higher-up forced them to hold the conference.'

Caprile was listening distractedly, looking around, as if waiting for someone.

'What's up with you? Did you hear what I said?' Carla snapped.

'Yeah, no, sorry… I'm waiting for the news car. I need to get there fast.'

A blue sedan turned onto via Solferino from largo Treves.

'What's the story?'

'A big-time murder, up in the west. Serious stuff, looks like someone was settling a score. Might be linked to male prostitution – or worse.' Caprile lowered his voice conspiratorially. 'A serial killer, or a hate crime. They killed a gay guy, and it looks like he was tortured.'

The car stopped in front of them. Salvo opened the door and got in.

On a hunch, Carla asked, 'Do you know the victim's name?'

'Davide Alfridi. See ya.' The car pulled away.

Canessa received the call on the Swiss sat phone as they were nearing Milan, and he was about to remind Rossi to slow down yet again.

'Are you sure? Are you okay? Look: not on the phone. I'll call you later and we'll arrange something. Let me know if you have any more details.'

'Something wrong?' Rossi asked as they passed the San Raffaele, on the eastern ring road.

Canessa answered him with a question. 'Am I right in thinking that you have somewhere in your portfolio: shares, and therefore influence in a huge pharmaceutical company?'

Rossi was surprised, though by this point he was getting used to Canessa's knowing every detail of his life (and maybe even death, but he'd never ask about that).

'I do.'

'Good.'

Canessa started jotting something down on his notepad. He tore off the sheet of paper and handed it to Rossi. 'Can you get hold of these things? Just buy whatever your company doesn't supply, but not all at once, and not around here.'

Rossi glanced at the list. He couldn't help his reaction. 'You could set up a field hospital with this stuff. Are you expecting a war to break out?'

Canessa stared ahead blankly. Then, as if speaking from somewhere else entirely, 'It already has.'

14

On the plasma screen in his private office, Judge Federico Astroni watched in horror as the body was wheeled from the abandoned farmhouse to the coroner's van. This mess wouldn't rebound on him. He had nothing to do with it, apart from making the call with the phone supplied to him. He'd been absolving himself for decades, with the rhetorical skill that distinguished him not only in Milan, but in courts all over Italy. If he could convince everyone else, surely he could convince himself as well. Every time the situation resurfaced, he told himself he was blameless: he'd been dragged into it by someone else, some despicable person who'd got to him the one time he was down. He'd seen him a number of times since then – after all, they both belonged to the elite of Milan's judiciary system – but he never thought their paths would cross again. He needed to get out of all this, but his only option was going part of the way with that man.

Brief phone contact was tolerable, but he had no intention of meeting up with him. 'We need to talk, in person,' he'd barked last time they spoke. Astroni had given him a resounding 'No'. He still didn't know the details of Alfridi's terrible fate.

Astroni stood up and walked over to the sofa. He tried to slow his breathing, but he was too nervous.

Chief Magistrate Calandra stroked the naked back of the brunette on his right. The cool evening breeze caressed her skin, and she shivered excitedly. Another perk of a Mercedes convertible.

His regular lover, she was in her forties but looked younger. Not a striking beauty, but a brilliant and exciting one. The man from the Secret Service relied on having someone he could actually have a conversation with, covering a variety of topics with insight and intelligence. She filled the role perfectly.

They were currently on their way to his house in the Maremma area for a long-awaited weekend getaway. She was married with two kids, and it wasn't easy for her to find the spare time. Otherwise it was a win-win situation: no money was involved. They simply shared the pleasure of each other's company and the sort of gifts lovers exchange.

He was about to turn off his phone and disappear for two days when he saw a call from the 'overseer'. He plugged in his head set. His lover realised she was being excluded, but she didn't object.

'Yes?'

'They killed someone.'

'And?'

'He worked at the same place as Petri.'

'Ah…'

'They're currently treating it as male prostitution.'

'A front. They'll find out eventually, just as you did. Did you check the victim's phone?'

'There were three calls from an encrypted Swiss number.'

'That's our Horseman of the Apocalypse.'

'That's what I thought. What do we do now?'

'Nothing. He can look after himself, and we keep watch. Keep me updated, especially if you think there are actual, direct threats.'

He hung up a moment before turning onto the tree-lined drive that led to his corner of paradise. The sunset was lighting up the surrounding hills and the villa, with its crown of olive trees and vineyards.

'How beautiful!'

'I'm glad you're here with me.' Calandra took her left hand and kissed it.

'Will you be able to leave your work at home?'

He smiled at her as he parked the car under the arbour. 'No one's invited, my dear, except you and me.'

He switched off his phone.

15

Canessa was planning to meet Carla in piazza Napoli. From there, they would go to a restaurant in Gaggiano famous for its rotisserie chicken. Something to share.

He called Repetto before leaving the loft. His friend had heard about Alfridi on the news.

'How did they get to him?' Straight to the point, as always.

'I don't know. They may have followed us without our noticing.'

'I doubt that.'

'So do I. They tortured him to get him to talk.'

'Are we ruling out a random killing?' Repetto asked, sarcastically. 'If they were following us, they would have gone after the journalist,' he never used her name, 'to deflect suspicion. Killing two people from the same workplace doesn't look like a coincidence. The case is even more confusing now. Why didn't they go after her? No one besides us would've made the connection, not this quickly.'

Repetto was right. Annibale tried to mask his worry with silence. His friend had struck a nerve once more. He'd always been good at spotting Canessa's weak points, and they were often linked to women – like his relationship with Giuseppina, his lover in Turin right before he was shot. Annibale had always thought it might become something serious and, when Repetto had voiced doubts about her actual commitment, Canessa had brushed them off, annoyed, and sulked for a week. Later, in the hospital, his first thoughts were about her, and he'd asked Repetto if she'd come to visit, or maybe called. But she'd disappeared. His friend hadn't stooped to petty comments like *I told you so*. Once Annibale had felt better, he'd tried calling her more than once, but the reply was always the same: *She's not home*. Eventually, Repetto had discovered that she'd left to complete her studies in the United States.

This time, Repetto sensed danger for Carla.

Canessa didn't doubt for a second that Alfridi had been killed because of his ties with Petri. But also with him. What Repetto said was dramatically clear, and provable. But he tried to get around it with a logical explanation.

'If it hadn't been for the jogger, who knows when we'd have found Alfridi's body. No one would have noticed he'd gone missing. But the disappearance and murder of a journalist on the *Corriere della Sera* would be big news. Whoever they are, they don't want that.' His reasoning made some sort of sense, but Canessa knew perfectly well that it was also an attempt to silence any suggestion of a threat to Carla.

Repetto kept quiet. From where he was calling they could hear one of the grandchildren whining for his grandpa.

'Look, Ivan…'

'Don't even try it,' Repetto cut him off. 'I'm not backing down. Keep Rossi out of it. Let's avoid collateral damage. I'm moving in tomorrow, and we'll be a team, 24/7.'

Carla was there on the dot.

He'd waited for her in front of the Ducale cinema, constantly alert. He was still on the lookout, his eyes moving rapidly from one mirror to the other. For the first time since they'd started seeing each other, Canessa had brought along his SIG as well as the ankle Ruger. She couldn't keep her hands off him when he got in the car, but he moved her away from the holster.

'Should I be scared?' she teased, trying to lighten the mood.

The humidity from the canal rolled in through the open car windows. Canessa revelled in the temporary respite. Such moments were a way to escape reality, the string of deaths. He'd already felt something like this before, but here was something new, a joy he'd rarely known before. Reality wasn't slipping away. On the contrary: reality was this woman almost half his age.

Carla had on a grey tube dress, elegant and unpretentious. *Some famous designer*, he thought. She looked amazing. He stroked her thigh, meeting her smooth, firm flesh. No tights.

'No, not scared, but if anyone approaches you in a van or a large car asking for information, stay at least two metres away from it. Lock your doors; don't use the underground; walk in crowds and try not to park too far from home or in dark places. No underground car parks. Better to risk a fine if you don't have a choice.'

Canessa realised he'd slipped into his cop voice. She laughed in response.

'Wow, *okay*! Remind later so I can write it all down.'

After dinner, they parked beside the canal. There was no time for notes in between kissing and fondling. He felt like a teenager, and she was more convinced than ever that she was falling for this man floating in a sea of secrets.

Later, as he lay in her bed, far removed from his worries, Carla asked how the investigation was going.

'Petri was apologising for the lives he'd taken. In his own way, he was making amends.' He told her about the irises and candles, the trips to the cemeteries.

Ever the journalist, she asked, 'If he was on parole, how did he get so far out of the city?'

'He risked it. He probably had someone covering for him. If you ask me, it was his boss. He might have forfeited all his privileges, but he was always a determined man – it's what made him one of the most dangerous killers in Italian history.'

'Okay, but why the rush, why now?' She hopped out of bed and pulled on his shirt. Something fell out of his pocket. She bent over again to pick it up, offering Annibale a view of her perfect behind.

'That's a good question. I have no idea. But I do know that it's the clue to his murder.'

Canessa got up and started to dress. He needed to leave, and he had to find some way of telling her that he'd be disappearing until the entire matter had been wrapped up. It was too dangerous for her. He already had one death on his conscience.

He was searching for the right words as he walked across the other room in the flat. Carla was on her way back to him, holding the object that had fallen out of his shirt.

A piece of paper.

'Sorry, but there's a mistake on this list. I know I shouldn't have, but I took a look.'

16

Behind the kitchen bar, Carla was busy with the kettle, which had begun to whistle.

'Would you like a lemon balm and tarragon tea?'

Canessa took a look at the paper. It was the list of *Corriere* editions Petri had collected in his search for his victims' resting places. He stared at it.

11 November 1977

7 February 1978

10 September 1978

9 January 1979

18 June 1979

13 December 1979

21 April 1980

He didn't even remember putting the list in his pocket. Once he'd figured out the pattern and tested his theory, he'd forgotten all about it. He was angry with himself: scant attention to detail, lacking in rigour. He didn't like it. He'd thrown himself into the investigation with his usual zeal, but without the careful attention that went with his uniform. Canessa the Tank wouldn't have made that sort of error.

'What's the mistake?'

He spoke with noticeable irritation, though he obviously wasn't angry at her, and Carla preferred to overlook it.

'How many people did Petri kill?' She answered with a question of her own.

'Eight.'

'In what groupings?'

'It sounds like you already know the answer.' Canessa was trying to keep his cool, but he was about to lose it.

Carla turned to face him. 'I do, but I also wanted to show you my reasoning, so you could reach the same conclusion.'

'Fine.' Canessa thought for a second. 'Four single murders, two double. Six attacks in total.'

'On there,' Carla pointed to the piece of paper Canessa was still holding, 'you have seven dates.'

'Shit.' The former Carabiniere quickly checked. 'I'm such an idiot, I hadn't noticed!'

'Maybe it's a technical error…' Carla sat down and handed him his mug of tea. 'Careful, it's hot. Do you remember his murders, or should we look them up?'

Canessa searched his memory. 'I remember who he killed, but I'm having difficulty connecting names and dates. Let's see…' He handed her the list. 'You check them off, okay? His first victim was the prison guard in Vallette… Rossetti, Paride Rossetti, in 1977.' He paused. 'Process of elimination. Marchetti was at the end of the summer of 1978. The two police officers, one buried in Gargnano, were June 1979. The last one was the doctor, Moscati, in 1980. What's left?'

'February 1978, or maybe late January, if the dates are all from after the murders. Then January 1979 or late December 1978, and December or late November 1979.'

Canessa sipped his tea. His face lit up. 'End of January 1978, Professor Saldutti, vice-president of the High Council of the Judiciary, and his driver-bodyguard, Ferroni. Early 1979, security guard Presatti, in Modena, during a robbery to fund their operations.'

'Saldutti was buried in Rome, in Verano. Do you think he travelled that far?' Carla pointed out a detail from her own research on Petri.

Canessa smiled. 'Well remembered. You're good at this. He may have sent flowers to the more distant ones, or asked someone to take them over, or maybe he went in person, but it's irrelevant. We know that even if he didn't go, and I believe he did, he definitely wanted to. So, what's left?'

Carla stared at the paper. '13 December 1979 is the edition, but we already have eight murders.'

The noise of Milan's nightlife filtered in through one of Carla's open windows. Canessa seemed to be listening to it, as if seeking inspiration.

Suddenly he stood.

Carla also got to her feet. 'What's up?' she asked, worried.

He took her hand in reply and gently pulled her towards him, unbuttoning her shirt. Sliding his hands under the fabric and across her shoulders, he let it drop to the floor.

Completely naked, she looked at him with a twinkle in her eye. 'What are you thinking?'

Annibale traced her nipple with his finger, making her shiver.

'Thanks to you, we may have found an even stronger lead, and I wanted to thank you appropriately…'

17

Annibale Canessa was religious. Maybe not observant, but definitely a believer. His morning ritual involved diving into the sea and swimming out as far as the statue of Christ of the Abyss, resting at the bottom of the San Fruttuoso bay. He'd dive down to the base of the statue and pray, for the living and the departed.

As he stood in front of the building on the corner between via Caravaggio, via California and piazza Bazzi, he realised that he missed that swim. He should take a break and head back there with Carla. They would eat pasta with pesto and white bass roasted with tomatoes and Ligurian olives. They'd sit on the terrace of his aunt's restaurant, and in the evening, when the tourists went home, they'd go for a swim. Instead of that view of urban Milan, he flashed on Carla in a bikini, with a backdrop of San Fruttuoso bay at sunset. A black bikini. The image he liked best, though, was of her diving into the water wearing nothing at all.

Annibale knew very well that he wouldn't be taking any breaks, not now. He was simply putting off the inevitable with those fantasies. Carla's research had led them nowhere. There was nothing in the online phone registries. There were no articles or news about the family. All the material was old. Over time, people's memories coalesced around a killer rather than his victims, unless the latter also became famous somehow.

There was no proof that anyone from the family still lived on the fourth floor of this corner building. But there was no proof to the contrary either. The internet really wasn't the oracle it was supposed to be.

They had to move, look, knock on doors. *Pull a finger out*, as Repetto would say. And Canessa agreed: that was the best way of finding the truth.

It had been exciting to discover the anomaly. The date was no longer a mistake. Instead, that extra line from the past was the key to understanding the killings in the present. But after his initial enthusiasm, Canessa had ended up here, and the details of the story had overwhelmed him, drowning his enthusiasm.

He could see it all over again. He had been there only once before that humid afternoon, fast becoming a muggy evening. It had been a dark, cold, filthy morning. A leaden, grey day, as only Milan's winter can offer. *Even if it had been as nice as today*, Canessa thought, *no one would have noticed*. It had only been his oversight, his laziness that had prevented him from seeing that extra date, the anomaly.

The building's main door opened onto via California, but the windows of the flat looked onto the piazza and the street behind it. Looking at them now, he remembered being here in early December 1979. He remembered everything. Over the years, he'd glazed over the memory of what had happened in order to protect it. A cover that would help him keep the pain at bay. When he was on the front line, he'd always maintained some form of emotional distance from the dead in the street – whether they lay under a sheet or on full display – and from their grieving families. He'd always told his subordinates to treat the families as they would the killers. They often omitted, concealed or forgot details that could be crucial to an investigation. 'No emotion, no kindness. Cold determination.' That was his motto.

But on that cold morning in 1979, something had breached his defence. The family, the man lying on the ground with only one white sock on, his shoe a few metres away... yes, they'd got to him. And he'd repressed it, but it didn't take much for Canessa to access those violent emotions all over again.

A woman walked out the door. Smiling, he held it open, and let her out first. The caretaker had already closed up. He'd chosen his time, between 7 and 8 p.m., since it would be easier to find someone at home. But he had no luck finding the surname on the doorbell.

The lift was one of the old models with a seat. He resisted trying it out, though he'd always liked the style. He opened the double doors first, then the metal cage, and stepped onto the landing. He remembered the door, though it also lacked a name plate.

He didn't know who he might find there, if anyone.

But he was here now.

He rang the doorbell.

For a few minutes that seemed to last forever, he heard nothing. Then, his senses – now back to full power – noticed something, or someone, rustling across the floor on the other side, and the door opened.

Canessa found himself facing a young woman, or so he thought. She couldn't have been more than thirty, with blonde hair falling over her shoulders. She was wearing a baggy blue silk shirt. A short denim skirt revealed her long, tanned legs.

Canessa looked her over. She was clearly used to such attention, and she seemed not to notice or mind. But Canessa wasn't there for her looks. He wanted to know if his hunch was correct.

As if in confirmation, the young woman's face lit up with a smile. 'It's you!'

He returned her smile, and it took him back to that day. To a different life, and to the pain that had never truly left him.

'Yes, it's me. Hello, Caterina.'

DECEMBER 1979

'CATERINA!'

Investigating judge Rodolfo Lazzarini checked his watch first, then his reflection in the mirror. He smiled. He was sporting his trademark crumpled look, his white shirt coming out of his trousers and ready to fall to his ankles any second. He tucked it back in. He needed to get another hole punched in his belt: it was new, but he always forgot how skinny he was and his trousers inevitably ended up sliding down. If only that were the extent of his problems.

Some men boast a certain innate elegance. Lazzarini thought of his friend and colleague Federico Astroni, who was always impeccable. He'd be more at home in London's Old Bailey than the old courts of Milan. Lazzarini, on the other hand, was a small man who dressed badly and looked worse. He was aware of it, but it didn't faze him. Even if he'd been George IV with his own Lord Brummell on hand for advice, he knew he wouldn't look any better.

He looked at his watch again and raised his voice. 'Caterina!'

It was late, but his five-year-old daughter was still in her room. When she'd checked that same hallway mirror and noticed an imperfection in her hair, unlike her father, she'd headed back to her room to sort it out.

Seven-year-old Piero was fidgeting by his side. 'Daddy, we're going to be late!' Even at that age, he was already serious and precise like Rodolfo. His paternal grandmother called him *a little gentleman*. She was so proud of this grandson. And Piero was beautiful, like Mama and Caterina.

Teresa Aliprandi, now Lazzarini, was tall and blonde, with mesmerising green eyes. Her only flaw was her name. At least, that's what students and colleagues thought when they met and fell in love with her. She'd always been the main topic of conversations, first in the Law faculty at university, then at work. Teresa wasn't really a fashionable name, and it definitely didn't suit that goddess. Her beauty was legendary. Everyone asked the same question when they met her for the first time, and the answer was always the same: she would never be a model. Rumour had it that her parents rejected the scouts from fashion firms who wanted her to model for them. The truth was, all she cared about was her studies and becoming a lawyer.

When she crossed via Festa del Perdono, she looked like 'the only force capable of stopping the revolution', a leader of the student movement used to say. In common with all the other men she met, he had only three things on his mind, and not necessarily in this order: 1) catch her attention, 2) start a conversation with her and 3) get her into bed.

Teresa had a few close friends, but she was kind to everyone and even if she was aware of her looks, she never showed it, a fact that only enhanced her reputation.

Rodolfo Lazzarini knew her, but he wasn't interested in her. He was methodical, a planner, and during his first years of university his plan was to change his looks for the better. He didn't care that much, but he figured it was something he could do. The point was, there were other priorities and his primary focus was his studies. He didn't worry too much, as he'd had his fair share of adventures since school. He'd always been an exceptional student, never swotty or snobby. He was kind and selfless, reserved yet charming. With his intelligence, his sense of humour and a self-deprecating streak, he was a magnet for girls rejecting film stars in favour of intellectuals. In his parka and carrying a Marxist philosophy book, Lazzarini offered an entirely unique experience.

So when he quite literally crashed into Teresa Aliprandi, it was love at first sight. Not for him, however. She was running out of a classroom and she tripped over him as he was walking down the corridor, lost in his own thoughts. The man of her dreams suddenly emerged from a flurry of papers and books. He didn't have the slightest inkling that the person in front of him would eventually be his life's companion.

Their first kiss took place in a dark cinema showing a film neither of them would remember. It was that kiss, more than her beauty or intelligence, that snapped Lazzarini out of his obsessional focus on his studies. A new, unknown world was opening up to the future judge, an unexplored universe: that of physical pleasure born of love and desire.

Later in life, he got laughs from friends and light slaps from his wife when he admitted that he'd entered their relationship in the spirit of a researcher taking on a new subject.

Against all predictions, their union was cemented with the birth of Piero, and shortly after that, of Caterina. Though both had law degrees, they'd taken different paths. Rodolfo won the competitive magistrate exam, and after two years in Apulia, they moved back to Milan. Teresa was employed in the legal department of a multinational pharmaceutical company, where she earned twice as much as Rodolfo. The Italian offices were based in Lainate, so Teresa was always the first to leave the house. That morning, she'd left even earlier to catch a plane to Zurich for an important meeting in the company's central offices.

Whenever Rodolfo talked about his wife's job, everyone – *everyone* – looked at him as if he were a madman. He understood why. They all thought that a woman that gorgeous could easily have found some 'distraction' in her position. 'A woman like that…' a lawyer once said to him, 'I'd lock her up at home.' Lazzarini just shook his head. No one really understood what united them, from ideas to values, from educating their children to sex, which everyone else obviously saw as disappointing for her. All unfounded, ridiculous rumours that Rodolfo and Teresa Lazzarini dismissed, strong in the knowledge of what held them together.

With Teresa leaving so early, he was the one to get the children ready, give them their breakfast and take them to school. They were always pressed for time, chiefly because of Caterina's dawdling, and that particular December morning he was sure to be even later, despite both schools being practically downstairs.

The little girl finally emerged from her room. Lazzarini tried to detect what had induced her to go back and change her hair at the last minute. She had on a black, knee-length skirt with dark tights, gym shoes, and a polo neck jumper. There it was: the woolly hat! The previous one had had a pompom. Her blonde hair, just like her mother's, poked out from beneath it.

Lazzarini couldn't help himself. 'Caterina, did you change your hat?'

She stared at him with her piercing green eyes, almost pitying him. 'Daddy, it didn't go with the jacket,' she replied, as if it were the most obvious thing in the world.

Rodolfo avoided looking at himself to see just how little of his get-up went together. He gently nudged his children onto the landing and called the lift.

Rodolfo's penultimate thought came to him in the form of an adjective. *Opaque.*

'This city is opaque.'

He was formulating the sentence as he opened the door to his building and found himself assaulted by the grey smog that blanketed Milan in winter. He was used to it, having been born in Barona, but Milan was the one, unspoken dissatisfaction of his life – even before his two years in Apulia, and the discovery of entirely new flavours and smells, before he developed his penchant for windy, briny days with a view of the sea. He didn't have a single drop of southern blood, and yet he felt like a southerner, and would proudly become one if he could. On mornings like this, he imagined what it would be like to walk his children to school in an explosion of colour, even in winter. Apulia. If he hadn't been married to Teresa, he'd probably have stayed down there.

Lazzarini walked to the left and emerged in piazza Bazzi, just opposite the school on the other side of the road.

'Lazzarini!'

Rodolfo's final thought was *I hope they can aim*. He'd turned round to see who was calling, only to find two guns pointed at him. Piero was holding tight to his right hand, while Caterina was walking on his left.

Lazzarini was afraid for them, not for himself. More than anything, he was surprised. There had always been a trail of blood across the judiciary sector, and though he'd considered that he might be a victim, he reasoned that moving into financial crimes would remove him from the list of targets. Clearly not.

He was shot eight times in total. The first bullet caught his arm, but the second had already fatally hit his lung. He shoved his children aside, silently apologising to them. Caterina ended up on the pavement a few metres away from him while Piero held even tighter to his father's hand. When Rodolfo fell, Piero went down with him. He saw one of the two killers come closer for a final shot to the man's head – but the shot never came. The killer turned and walked away.

Piero Lazzarini uttered a howl of despair. As one of the witnesses reported: 'I've never heard anything that sounded less like a human.'

'Are you animals? Cover that body immediately!'

Captain Annibale Canessa's yelling washed over the Carabinieri standing next to the corpse of Judge Lazzarini, along with some high-ranking officers of the special branch of the police.

Canessa and Repetto had been in Milan following up a tip about a Red Brigades hideout when they'd heard about the ambush. Canessa was baffled by the name 'Lazzarini': he had no idea who the man was.

'Who is this poor guy?' he'd shouted to the team, as they organised themselves in the via Moscova barracks.

Silence. The only thing moving in that filthy, unused room was the dust. Everyone knew the real reason behind the captain's fury. A few months earlier he'd compiled a list of potential terrorist targets, and Lazzarini did not feature on it. He couldn't have, not even with the best will in the world. They couldn't protect *all* of

Italy's judges and magistrates. The 'Canessa list' contained only the names of those who might be active targets. It started with people on the front line against terrorism, be it red or black, and included any who might somehow represent the State. Lazzarini belonged to neither category.

'He dealt with financial cases, tax evasion, insider trading, laundering, that kind of thing. He was good, best in his field. Everyone had great expectations for him.'

'Who said that?' the captain asked, clearly impressed.

A young brigadier, a recent addition to the team.

Canessa didn't wait for an answer. He'd already moved on.

And now Investigating Judge Rodolfo Lazzarini lay on the ground, his head and chest in the grass and his legs on the pavement. His great expectations had been drowned in a pool of blood, and he had fallen victim to a group of ruthless fanatics, certain they could change the world by killing and maiming in order to draw it in their own image.

Canessa would never get used to it, to human stupidity. Those bastards would go nowhere. He'd catch them all himself if he had to.

Lazzarini had fallen with his right leg at an unnatural angle, a shoe flung from his body and only one white sock still on.

A police officer finally arrived with a white sheet, bought in a nearby shop. None of the magistrates, officers, or agents present at the scene had reacted at all. Not even the major, in theory Canessa's superior.

In theory, but not in practice.

Everyone knew Canessa's reputation, his ties to the general, his incredible success, the shooting in Rome when he'd saved Verde, the freedom he enjoyed. But as one chief constable put it: 'Sure, he has help, he has friends in high places, he has freedoms we can't dream of. But even without all that, it's how he looks at you: as if he could blow your brains out on the spot. The man is terrifying.'

One of the police officers explained, 'There were two of them waiting for him. They called out his name. Usual m.o. But they've never killed anyone with children nearby. The bastards!'

He raised his voice on the final word. But Canessa didn't even notice. 'Children? *Where are they?*'

Canessa left Repetto downstairs to deal with the scene.

'Make sure they're doing things properly. Given that for once we got here pretty much as it happened, we can't overlook anything. I doubt there'll be much, but if there are any interesting clues, we need them bagged and tagged.'

He sent a young brigadier to a toy shop he'd spotted in via Foppa on the way over. He called the lift and headed to the fourth floor.

A uniformed police officer stood at the door. Fortunately he recognised Canessa immediately, since Canessa was famous for demolishing cops who wasted his time by not keeping up to speed. Inside the flat were the usual crowd of people who turn up after a tragedy, all playing their part. Family, friends, police, colleagues. Canessa knew how grief worked. He observed from afar, but without playing a part.

The flat was large, with four bedrooms and a vast living room, all of them opening onto a long corridor that led to the front door.

Captain Canessa removed his coat and hat and hung them up with all the others. A commissioner he'd met before came up to him. One of the few he liked, because he didn't get bogged down in preambles.

He cut right to the chase. 'The wife just landed in Zurich. They sent someone from the consulate. Efficient for once. They're bringing her back to Milan.'

'The kids?' Canessa asked.

The police commissioner shook his head.

'The eldest was still holding on to his father's hand. They had to pry him away. He's got a small wound to his arm. Nothing serious, but he was covered in blood and in shock. The doctors wanted to take him to the hospital, but his grandmother—' he pointed to a woman in her sixties, her eyes puffy from crying '—didn't want him to go. He's in his bedroom with a paediatrician, Lazzarini's cousin. He's not ill, but he won't speak.'

'And the girl?'

'She cried. Then she said that her dad is dead because some bad men shot him and she wants someone to do the same to them. After that she too went quiet. *I'm waiting for Mummy*, she said. She's in her room with her preschool teacher. The school's just across the road and the teacher came over to help almost immediately.'

The commissioner paused, looking around to make sure no one was listening. 'You want to know what I think? She isn't even five, and she's tougher than some people I know. She might be able to help with a police sketch.'

'Hm,' was Canessa's reply. The young brigadier came back at that moment, holding a bag. Canessa looked inside, then squeezed it. 'Good, nice and soft.'

'It was quite pricey, sir,' the young brigadier offered him the sales tag.

Canessa looked at the receipt and nodded. 'Let's hope they'll cover the cost for us!' He turned back to the commissioner. 'Which one's the girl's room?'

The police officer pointed it out. 'Do you have something in mind?'

'Actually, I do. I want to try something.' Annibale pulled the stuffed lion out of the bag, looked at it, put it back and walked to the girl's bedroom.

The hardest part, Canessa thought when he left the Lazzarini home, had been removing the teacher from the room without kicking her out, insulting her or having her cuffed as an obstacle to an ongoing investigation. That was his usual method for dealing with rioters, people who crossed him or wasted his time. The teacher wasn't more than twenty-two or so, and not a fan of the cops or law enforcement. Like most of her peers, she obviously belonged to the far left, and way farther than the limit marked out by the Italian Communist Party.

'I'm not leaving,' she'd said, smoothing her velvet skirt and pressing her Camperos boots together. 'I'm not leaving her alone.'

I'm not leaving the girl alone with a fascist pig like you, her defiant look said. But Canessa hadn't fallen for it. He wasn't there for a pointless fight. It was nothing personal, all part of the job.

He had to convince her to leave, and he didn't have much time to do so: he wanted to talk, however briefly, to the girl, who was leaning against her pillow looking bored.

'Listen: you know her. I don't. But it didn't take me long to figure out that she's tough. She saw her father die, and she has the strength to help us figure out who did it. You might not believe me, but I'm actually great with kids and' – he smiled – 'with teachers. If I'm not seducing them, I'm arresting them. You'll be out of here in a few minutes either way, but one method will be

262

more problematic for her. We don't have much time, so please…
I'd rather you left by choice.'

The young woman looked at him with a mixture of hatred and curiosity. She left the door ajar and stood outside.

The girl seemed interested in Canessa's uniform. She kept quiet a little longer and then said, 'My daddy is dead.'

Canessa nodded. 'I'm sorry, Caterina.'

Her face lit up. 'You know my name?'

'Not only your name. I also know you like stuffed animals. So I brought you this one. His name is Leo.' He handed her the toy.

Caterina grabbed the lion. She hugged it, bringing it to her face.

Canessa knew he only had one chance, and time was running out. As soon as her mother got back, she'd take the child away and her memories would fade, if not vanish entirely. This was the time to find out what she knew.

'Caterina, I know this isn't easy…'

'Are you going to get the bad men?' she interrupted.

'I'll try, yes.'

'Promise.'

'I promise,' he said, regretting it immediately.

She hugged the lion again, brushed some hair out of her eyes, and looked at him. 'You have a bad face too. I think you'll get them.'

'But I'm with the good guys,' Canessa protested, feeling ridiculous.

She made a strange face. 'It's a compliment! To get bad guys you need a good bad guy.'

Canessa couldn't hold back a smile. The child was incredible.

'But I need your help to catch the bad guys. Do you remember anything about the people who fired the shots?'

He worried that he might be stirring up some appalling memories, but if that was the case, she didn't show it.

'I didn't see one of them very well. He had a beard, but not as long as Merlin's. I saw the other one: he was short and had a cut from here to here.' She touched under her right ear.

'A scar,' Canessa suggested.

'Yes, a scar.'

The captain stood up. 'Thank you Caterina. You've been very helpful. You're a very special kid.'

'Will you get them?' she asked again.

Canessa turned back to see her staring at him with her green eyes. He shoved his hands into his pockets, then did something he had never done. It went against the Canessa Commandments. It was something a police officer should never do with anyone, least of all the family of a victim.

He made a promise.

'I'll get them.'

4

The Third Millennium

I

ANNIBALE CANESSA still remembered Teresa, Lazzarini's widow. She was hard to forget, not only because of her looks, but also because of the circumstances in which they'd met. Eight months after her husband's death, they'd had a coffee at Milan's Cova café in via Montenapoleone. He'd just got back into service after recovering from the via Gaeta massacre, and had been in town for a meeting with a judge.

Teresa had visited him in Genoa, while he was still in intensive care after the shooting. She'd come specially from Milan, bringing a pack of *gianduiotti* with her. Had Annibale been conscious, the Carabinieri watching over him would have let her through – no one could say no to her. But he wasn't, so she left her gift with a note asking him to call her as soon as he was back on his feet. She wanted to meet him.

And so, the night before his return to Milan, Annibale called and they'd arranged to meet in the historic Cova café in the city centre. It had been warm, and ignoring protocol, Canessa showed up in jeans and a t-shirt.

'You look like a teenager,' Repetto said.

'I am one.'

'You wish! You're older than I am!'

It was a month since what Repetto had dubbed 'the trip to Rome'. Milan was half empty, and would soon be entirely so.

Canessa wanted to walk from the courts to the meeting. Repetto had tried to talk him out of it ('Let's take the car, it's got air-conditioning'), but nothing doing. After his near-death experience, he wanted to get back to his simple routines, such as a walk in the city centre.

They'd formed a strange convoy: Canessa on one side of the street, Repetto on the other for a wider visual, two Carabinieri in a patrol car behind them (one holding a PM12 machine gun, finger at the ready).

Given the time and day, Cova was almost empty. Teresa had chosen a table in the corner. Her blonde hair was hidden under a foulard tied under her chin, and she was wearing sunglasses indoors. She had on blue silk trousers and a baggy green shirt, with a light cashmere cardigan over her shoulders to shield her from the air conditioning. She'd stood up and shaken his hand in one fluid motion.

'I ordered a cappuccino. Can I get you anything…' She paused, thought about his rank, and finished, 'Major?'

Canessa glanced at his watch. 5.35 p.m. 'A gin and tonic,' he told the waiter.

She removed her glasses and looked at him, smiling with the incredible green eyes she'd passed on to her daughter.

'I thought you couldn't drink on shift?'

'I do whatever I want on shift.' Canessa smiled provocatively, and immediately regretted doing so.

Lazzarini's widow held back a laugh. 'Yes, they told me what you were like.'

'And…?'

'A Carabiniere to the bone, as far as commitment goes, but as for the rest…' She paused. 'Well, a little idiosyncratic.'

Canessa was still recovering and he tired easily, but Teresa's extraordinary beauty was arousing some vital, physical instinct. He kept his mind on the thought of her as a widow and the mother of Caterina, his formidable little ally and witness. His gaze, however, revealed an undeniable attraction to her.

Teresa smiled again – a symphony in itself – clearly not insulted by any of the thoughts Canessa's eyes betrayed.

'You're an unusual man, Major. However, I am here to thank you personally for having kept your promise to my daughter. You got my poor Rodolfo's killers.'

The man with the scar had been Gennaro Esposito. Tough little Caterina had recognised him in a photo. The taller, bearded one had been Adelmo Federzoni. Several supergrasses had confirmed that the men had been in Milan at the time, and that they usually worked as a pair.

'If we're talking the letter of the law, I suppose I did get them. But I'd rather have taken them alive.'

Teresa remained silent for a moment. 'I understand. Still, at least Caterina is sleeping again now. You know, as soon as I got home, she told me about you and showed me the lion. She was practically quivering with a mixture of sadness and excitement. She was thinking of her father and the horror she'd witnessed, but also about being part of the investigation. Before the via Gaeta operation, she'd stay up all night. She didn't have nightmares like Piero. She said she had to be ready, in case they came back.

She kept a piece of paper on her bedside table with the phone number you gave her.'

'That child is incredibly strong,' Canessa commented. 'How is Piero?'

Teresa leaned against the soft chair and closed her eyes. 'He's still terrified. He stopped wetting his bed, but he's started again. He'll only go to school if we walk the other way round. We can't go through piazza Bazzi any more. He's been assigned a psychologist. Let's hope it works.'

'I'm sorry.' Canessa didn't know what else to say.

Teresa removed her foulard, and her blonde hair fell over her shoulders and into her eyes. Canessa did his best not to react, despite realising that even a simple gesture from such a woman was enough to stir him up.

'Life goes on. And knowing that my husband's killers are no longer around is an even better reason not to look back. I didn't want them dead, but this way we'll skip the whole ordeal of a trial. And considering my children, that may be best. In any case, the fact that you spent a whole month in hospital must mean there were no alternatives.'

Canessa simply nodded. He was about to stand up and bring the meeting to a close when she blurted out, 'I really miss my husband. My life feels so empty since he left us. I know how men look at me. I know what I could have with someone else' – she looked at him – 'and every now and then I do meet someone who makes me feel something. But I'm afraid of getting back to my life. There was an alchemy with him that I doubt I'll find with anyone else. Are you married? Sorry, silly question. How could you be, with your life? I don't know, maybe I'll re-marry, maybe not. Rodolfo always told me that only fools say "never".'

Annibale nodded.

'But the feelings I experienced in the ten years with my husband… I'll never have those again. I may find someone to share a bed with, but that's all. I don't think I can stay alone for too long. I need warmth, like I need food, drink…'

For years, Canessa wondered if that had been an invitation. Maybe, if he'd said the right thing, he would now be in a room at the Grand Hotel et de Milan with that goddess in his arms, and Repetto holding a gun outside the door.

Invitation or not, Canessa had stood up and kissed her hand, an officer and a gentleman. His action wasn't motivated by a sense of morality, his position or the uniform he usually wore. Not even respect for a widow in her moment of grief, but respect for himself.

After via Gaeta, he'd decided to change his ways. He'd had it with superficial flings. No more one-night stands, no more chancing it with his colleagues' wives or girlfriends. He would wait for someone who truly excited the whole of him, and not just his desire.

'Madam, it has been a pleasure to meet you. And thank you for the *gianduiotti*. I'm a big fan.' He walked out swiftly, forcing Repetto to leave half of his fourth soda.

2

Annibale couldn't look at Caterina, sitting on the other side of the sofa, her arms wrapped around her long legs, without seeing her mother in her. They were identical, and he was overcome with the memory of their first meeting: the woman, Cova, the walk, her invitation…

There was a similar awkwardness with her daughter, now. They sat in silence, exhibiting a shyness that was out of character for both of them.

The layout of the flat had changed completely. The entrance and long corridor had merged into one large living area. The furniture was modern, mostly IKEA. The paintings, rugs, books and objects scattered around the house spoke of refined taste. Rather than a family home, it looked like a single person's spacious refuge. A professional drawing table in a sunny corner revealed Caterina's passion for her work.

'You're just the way I remember you.' She was first to break the silence, brushing a strand of hair from her face.

Canessa smiled. 'Thank you. You've obviously changed, but I still recognise the strong young girl I met all those years ago.'

Caterina didn't blush or react to his words. She seemed lost in thought. She got up from the sofa and walked into another room. She came back with the stuffed lion, and placed it on the sofa beside Canessa.

'I've always had him with me. One time when I was about twelve, I went on a school trip to London and I left him somewhere. I had to move heaven and earth to get him back.'

'Where are your mother and brother?' he asked.

Caterina blew her hair out of her face. 'Mum got married again, seven years after Dad's death. She had two more kids. Her husband is a good man, and he was amazing with us. But he's from Florence. Do you know what Florentines call their city?'

'The Capital.' Canessa laughed, remembering a Tuscan corporal who'd always said, 'I'm on leave, going back to the Capital.'

'Exactly!' Caterina giggled. 'While we were both young, Mum forced him to live up here, but when we were older, *whoosh!* moving out. Piero and I stayed here. Mum's down there with my stepsiblings, and she seems pretty happy.'

'How is Piero?'

Caterina hugged her knees tighter, her knuckles whitening. Her voice stayed calm, but there was something wobbly behind it.

'He never really came to terms with it. His life was shattered that day. He went through alcohol, drugs, rehab, therapists. He's not even forty and he looks sixty. But recently he does seem to have found some peace. He's on a Taizé Community farm in Provence.' She noticed Canessa's expression, and pre-empted him. 'No, we haven't seen him. That's how he wanted it. I last heard from him two years ago, and he said he was doing well, that he'd finally discovered the best therapy for him. He had to leave here, so he'd never see any place or person who'd remind him of the past. A clean slate and a new language too. We haven't been in touch since, and he hasn't called, though we do check in with one of the community leaders. Apparently he's doing really well, seems a lot lighter.'

Caterina fell silent for a few minutes, as if the brief recollection of her brother's situation had cost her something. She shifted, letting her eyes wander along with her mind, and then looked back at Canessa. Curious, examining him as she had been ever since he'd walked in. She had questions, no doubt, but was waiting for him to ask his first.

'What about you?'

'Nothing, no aftermath for me. What did you call me? Super tough. I wanted to be a Carabiniere until my last year of school, but then I signed up for architecture. I graduated, I travelled to Germany, South Africa, Australia. When Piero tried committing suicide again, I came back here to live with him. Our grandparents on Mum's side left us quite a sum. Whatever Piero got, he split and gave half to the Taizé Community, half to me. I am,' she smiled, 'what you might call a good catch. I work as a freelance interior designer. Do you want to know if I'm single?' She looked at him with her mother's eyes.

For a second, Canessa considered letting her go on, entranced by her life story and the strangeness of talking to someone he'd met when she was only five years old. But then the real reason for his being there took over.

'Listen, Caterina, I'm about to ask you some questions that may seem very strange. Is your father still buried in the Famedio, at the Monumentale? You said your mother and brother aren't in Milan, but do you ever go to your father's grave?'

'You know, I'd thought of various reasons for why you might be here. But not that. This is a surprise.' Caterina seemed sincere. 'This is about your brother and Petri's murder, isn't it? Are you back in action?'

He couldn't lie, not to her.

'It is, and I am.'

'I go to see Dad maybe once a month. Mum comes along sometimes too. She comes up to Milan just for that. Yes, it's the Famedio.'

Canessa nodded. 'The third question may seem even stranger, but have you noticed anything out of the ordinary on the tomb? Flowers, candles, something else you couldn't explain?'

Caterina couldn't hold back her surprise. 'You know, for several months after his death, people brought all sorts of things to Dad's tombstone. They were all so shocked by how brutal, how ruthless it had been, with the two of us kids there... And also because Dad wasn't an obvious target like all the more prominent judges.

It really was one of the most cruel attacks during the Years of Lead. But then it all just faded, as these things do. So Mum and I were both surprised when we found a bunch of irises and two white candles. One was still burning. How did you know? What's this about?'

Canessa leaned over and gave her arm a paternal squeeze. Then he stood up.

'You'd be a good Carabiniere. You've got what it takes.'

Caterina remained on the sofa. 'But won't you tell me what the flowers were for?'

'Not yet. I'm sorry.'

'Don't you trust me?' Carla's sarcasm didn't bode well.

He usually didn't mind that side of her. He'd noticed it the first time they'd had sex, and he'd said, 'Like there's no tomorrow.' She'd laughed, and mimicked him. 'That's a quote from one of the 007 films with Pierce Brosnan. He says it to Halle Berry.'

'I missed that one,' Canessa replied, kissing her. But she pulled away, teasing him some more.

They'd made plans to meet at Porta Genova after his visit to Caterina Lazzarini, and then they'd gone to eat seafood in a pricey restaurant. Canessa wondered if the other customers actually appreciated the excellent dishes, or if they merely went there because it was famous. Its most annoying feature was that it was impossible to have a conversation there, since it was unbearably noisy. Carla's mood had soured because she was expecting updates from Annibale and she'd been under pressure for a couple of days now, with Strozzi breathing down her neck. She'd have to turn in something soon or lose the piece to a vulture.

'I do trust you, but for your own safety, I'd rather you didn't know where I live,' Canessa replied.

Carla, however, was nervous. She didn't want to hear his reasons. 'You're just being paranoid. I don't think you trust me enough, or you think I might let something slip. I thought you'd be different…'

She turned her back to him and disappeared into the night.

Shortly after, Repetto appeared at Annibale's side. Despite the trench coat hiding his MP5, he wasn't suffering from the heat.

'Trouble in paradise?'

'Our first fight.'

'You want to run after her?'

'I do, but it wouldn't help.'

So now you understand women? Well, you really have grown!'

Canessa allowed himself to smile.

'Come on, let's go. We need to make some discoveries if we can.'

3

Repetto had made himself a plate of spaghetti with garlic, pepper and olive oil.

When Canessa caught a whiff of the garlic frying in the pan, he realised he was still hungry. 'Add some for me too, will you?'

They ended up eating outside the loft, protected by tall walls and an arbour. 'This is a nice place,' Repetto said. 'A bit out of the way, but nice.'

There were two sleeping areas in the loft, essentially screened-off corners of the large living area. Sharing the space proved no issue; it was as if the past thirty years hadn't happened. How many times had they eaten pasta together in the evenings?

Repetto had shown up at the door with two large boxes of groceries. He'd put them in the large fridge, which was empty apart from five or six bottles of good wine, a couple of champagne, and a half-eaten can of tuna.

'Canessa and tuna: an old pairing makes a comeback. The bottles aren't your doing though, are they?'

'A house-warming gift from Rossi. He has a secret cellar downstairs.'

Repetto had always been a drinker, but only the good stuff. 'See? It was a good idea for me to come here!'

Annibale was still upset by his fight with Carla. But after he'd polished off half a pack of spaghetti and a bottle of Alsatian Gewürztraminer he was feeling much better, at least physically.

'I still think this is at least a couple of hundred retail,' Repetto said, draining his glass. He cleared the table and came back with two shots of grappa and two cigars.

'To old times,' Canessa said.

His friend raised his glass. 'To brainstorming, or should that be fried brains?' They were recapping the investigation.

Canessa began. 'He went to visit Lazzarini's tomb, too.'

'But why?' Repetto was surprised. 'Was he making amends for other people's murders too?'

Canessa drew on his cigar. He wasn't really a smoker, but enjoying a cigar with an old friend was a good way of clearing his mind.

'Or maybe he was behind Lazzarini's murder too, and we got everything wrong.'

A long silence followed.

Repetto suddenly slammed his hand on the table. 'No!' he said, 'We weren't wrong. The one with the scar was Esposito…'

Canessa interrupted. 'There's no doubt about him. Caterina recognised him too. But remember, we never really got confirmation about the other one.'

'The supergrass…' Repetto's voice rose.

'Supergrasses are criminals who snitch. The absolute worst. We've all used them – in droves – but I've never fully trusted them. Especially if there's no tangible, external proof. And in this case, there isn't. They said the other man was Federzoni. Do we believe them? Okay, let's. Maybe they didn't intentionally lie, but they knew nothing, and proceeded by deduction. Federzoni was protecting Esposito because he saw him as a promising asset. They were always together, in life as in death.' His thoughts went back to via Gaeta and his mood turned dark.

Repetto poured out another shot of grappa. 'So what if Petri was there with Esposito that day? What does that change? Did we cause everything that's happened in the past two weeks by pinning a judge's murder on the wrong guy?'

Canessa offered him a wry smile. 'Yes.'

'If that's the case, it means that all these murders – Petri's, your brother's, Alfridi's – have happened to hide the fact that Petri was involved in the attack on Lazzarini. But why?'

Canessa stood up, strangely calm. 'I don't know, but what I do know is that it's not about one killer instead of another. Clearly all this revolves around Lazzarini. Nothing else comes into it. Petri was part of the hit squad, Petri pulled the trigger. Then the murder was pinned on Federzoni and Esposito, and I shot them in via Gaeta…' He went on, sarcastically. 'Petri never said a thing. He never collaborated, never disavowed his actions, never claimed them, never said a word. He kept quiet from the moment we got him. Then, a few months ago, something happens, and he's handing out flowers and candles, as if begging forgiveness. That change of heart isn't relevant right now, but it might be later. All that matters now is that he was trying to tell me something, and it must have had to do with that murder. He was looking for my brother because he needed to get to me, and he didn't trust anyone else. And it can only be about Lazzarini, the only anomaly.'

'You have no proof though.'

'Not yet. It'll come.'

'When?'

'When they try to get rid of me. Because whoever they are, they don't want the truth to emerge. They've made that clear over and over. And to make sure the past stays buried, they'll have to kill me.'

Repetto pulled the MP5 from under the table.

'They'll have to kill me too.'

4

At any other moment in time, even just a couple of days earlier, the view of prosecutor Marta Bossini's back would've excited him. Right now, though, Astroni was too troubled by other problems. The last text he'd received had pushed him right over the edge.

He'd hoped that Marta and the gym rat they'd assigned her would find something – anything – but no, their investigation had hit a dead end and he had no other choice but to yield to that phone, to the call that brought him so much pain.

Marta also seemed distracted, even annoyed. They'd had sex without any real passion, and she'd faked her orgasm. Noticeably. The whole thing had been pathetic.

'What's up?' he asked before she could explore his feelings.

Marta turned to face him. 'We're stuck. There are no leads. I was really happy to be working on this case – something special – but now...'

'What about the murder of the gay guy? That can't be a coincidence.'

'True, but we don't have anything on that either, other than the fact that he worked in the same office as Petri. They maybe had three conversations out of office hours in five months. They weren't close. That's it.'

Astroni reflected. 'Maybe it's just that he knew something about Petri, and whoever killed Petri wanted to silence him too.'

Marta agreed. 'That's the most probable scenario. But what did he know?'

Astroni was quiet for a second. 'What about Canessa, our former Rambo? From what you told me, he visited Petri's office as well. Maybe he met Alfridi. Maybe he questioned him.'

Still naked, Marta stood up and went over to open a window. She'd hoped someone might see her, but all the windows on the opposite building were shut. Damn Saturday!

She sat on the windowsill. 'He's still around, running his own investigation, but he'll come across us eventually, and we'll have to deal with him then.'

Unless, Astroni thought, *someone else deals with him first.*

*

'Lazzarini, Lazzarini…'

Calandra was fidgeting with the light blue folder his man had handed him. He spoke the name a third time. 'Lazzarini. It does ring a bell.'

Even if it hadn't, Canessa had definitely got to the crux of the matter. If he'd stopped on that particular square, it had to be the right one. That Carabiniere was a real force of nature. He was born with it, and exile – no matter how long – would never take it out of him. He just needed to loosen up.

He'd done well to bet on him. Canessa would end up being the winning horse.

Calandra opened up the file and quickly read through a couple of pages. He looked quizzically at his collaborator. 'I don't see anything out of the ordinary here.'

'Because there isn't,' he confirmed. 'Murder solved, killers buried. Literally. The end.'

'No, it can't be. If Canessa is looking into it, it means something's up. Maybe the truth was buried with the killers, so you need to focus on the Lazzarini murder. You need to rummage through everything, and pull out any story on this Lazzarini guy that doesn't appear in official records: gossip, a cutting that ended up in the wrong file, any relevant notes. If Canessa is betting on him, we need to stack up our poker chips too.'

'Place your bets,' said the man. He left.

Calandra noticed that he'd changed to his summer outfit. He also realised that if he'd asked anyone else to look into a thirty-year-old case, they would have objected. Youths and their impatience. And yet his mouse hadn't squeaked once.

Invaluable. Calandra lit up a Montecristo. Fuck the bans.

5

Nando Panattoni had decided that if he survived (and he was seriously doubting that right now), he would leave Milan, Italy, maybe even Europe the very same day. Whenever he emerged from the situation. The money in his Zurich account (under the name of a ga-ga Swiss eighty-year-old) wasn't exactly the amount he'd hoped to retire on. The Salemmes never paid until the job was done, and after this one, he was out. Job done or not, what mattered was getting out alive. Those two were worse than a mafia clan. He wondered how Rocco would take it if they offered him a contract to kill him, Nando, after all this time.

On the other hand, the money he'd made after twenty years of dirty tricks would be more than enough to disappear to Santo Domingo with his girlfriend, leaving no trace and living pretty comfortably for the rest of his life. Her family over there would protect them. Put an end to all this shit.

If he made it out alive. Because those two sons of bitches had just told him he was about to take on the hardest job in his life. And to prove just how much of a suicide mission it was, they'd even arranged to meet him in person, at a famous restaurant in the San Siro area. A personal farewell.

Of course, it wasn't an invitation to lunch. They'd be eating: he was supposed to come in, make himself known, go to the bathroom and they'd meet him there in their own sweet time. Then he'd disappear.

'Nando, Nando, you seem tense! Is your stomach cramped? You got your period?!'

Mr Big – Nando's name for Salemme senior, though only with Rocco – was still trying to squeeze himself into suits that were definitely too small, no matter how cool they might have been. Did he really think he scored women with his looks? At his age, power and money were the only pull.

Standing in the small bathroom with the Salemmes, the warm air ramping up the stench of piss, Panattoni felt his anxiety spiking through the roof. Father and son were dissecting him visually and reading his fears, as if they knew about his plan to flee: car to Zurich, withdraw money, train to Munich, plane to Miami, three or four days in the Keys getting used to time zone and climate, boat to Santo Domingo. Four vehicles, three passports. All ready.

Claudio's eyes were full of contempt. The young bastard was just like all rich, spoiled brats. But his father… he looked like he could actually read Nando's mind. He was truly dangerous.

Nando Panattoni was waiting.

'So, Nando, you've always been a good worker.'

'Yes, really good,' Claudio chimed in.

'So what we're asking of you now is the final test.'

'A love token.'

Mr Big laughed. 'Good one! *A love token*. I like it.'

Nando decided to play along. He laughed too, but his laughter soon turned to whimpering when he heard what that love token entailed.

'You need to kill Canessa and that pesky marshal of his.'

Panattoni had been expecting something more like Petri, or Alfridi, a job with some chance of success.

'Canessa…' he sputtered, the sweat spreading under his arms.

Mr Big slapped him on the shoulder.

'Come on, don't tell me you're scared?'

'I'd be a fool not to be!'

Salemme senior laughed again. 'Good point, good point. You're a wise man, and that's a good start.'

'Canessa is who he is, and you have two targets,' Salemme junior cut in. 'So you'll receive double the usual fee, and we're allowing you to bring in reinforcements. What about that associate of yours?'

'Carletti? He isn't up to this. He's only good at snitching,' Nando whispered.

Giannino Salemme spread his arms, and gestured to his son for him to open the door.

'C'mon, it's getting too hot in here. If Carletti can't do it, ask Rocco to bring someone. He's bound to know one of those guys in Gomorrah who walk around in their pants with AK-47s. Make sure they wear trousers though.' The Salemmes burst out laughing.

Panattoni interrupted them. 'What do you think's the best way of catching him?'

Claudio stopped laughing. 'Good question. We could say that's your fucking job, but what about this: on his way to or from his girl, the journalist. That's when he'll let his guard down.'

'And his pants,' his father put in. They laughed again.

'As for the girl,' Salemme senior turned deadly serious. 'I don't want you touching a hair on her head. Is that clear?' He pinched Nando's cheek. 'Good lad. Do the best you can. Get backup. Money's no problem. But,' he stopped at the door and patted his cheek, 'you need to get Canessa on the first try. He's like Tex Willer. You know Tex?'

Panattoni shook his head.

A sigh. 'Do you read anything other than porn? Comic-book hero Tex, with his sidekick Kit Carson, never gives you a second chance.

And neither do we. Panattoni, from what Rocco tells us, you've been doing a lot of the driving and very little dirty work recently. Take a weapon. You're going to do the shooting this time. Now get out of here. I've ordered a Florentine steak and I need time to enjoy it.'

6

Every now and then, Annibale heard from Sara and Giovanna. Life in Reggio Emilia had gone back to normal. But his sister-in-law would tell him (and sometimes Giovanna, too, when she took the phone) that things were different from the way they used to be: there was an empty space. Canessa was always surprised and moved by the strength of the bond between husband and wife. It was something he'd never experienced.

Now and again, whenever the conversation touched on Napoleone's memory, there was a crack in Sara's voice, and she held back tears. Because she was strong, she managed. She would soon turn back to the conversation at hand, telling Annibale about what a help Giovanna was and how mature she had turned out to be despite her twelve years. Canessa liked talking to Sara.

Their conversations were moments of respite from the worries of his investigation. He wasn't worried for himself, but for the people around him. He couldn't stop thinking like a soldier, something he hadn't expected to be again. Yet here he was. His suspicion that his calls might be bugged grew stronger every day. He knew there weren't any bugs in Carla's flat – he'd swept the place while she was asleep.

Still, he made a point of not saying anything over the phone to Sara or Carla. But it upset him to think that someone might be sharing their intimacy, recording it, transcribing it for someone else to read and file away somewhere. He thought of giving Sara a burner phone, but he didn't want to worry her.

Annibale decided to pay Carla a visit. He and Repetto had spent the past two days on the internet looking into Lazzarini, but the little there was they knew already. They'd moved on to the files on the murder but didn't turn anything up.

Would Carla see something they didn't? After all, they had got this far thanks to her. A different pair of eyes might help. He smiled, knowing that this was an excuse. He wanted to talk to her, to make up after their fight.

Dog-tired, Repetto had collapsed and was snoring from behind the screen. Canessa knew what a telling off he'd get when he returned – but with any luck he'd be back before his friend realised he was gone.

Friday evening in late May, and Corso Garibaldi was still busy thanks to the unseasonably warm weather. Carla always walked the corso to and from the *Corriere*. New places and businesses were cropping up all the time. She read some of their names and wondered how long they'd been there.

She was wearing a pair of skinny jeans (maybe too skinny, given the looks she was getting) and a light blue blouse. One of her favourites. She was a bit down about Annibale's disappearance. Okay, she was the one who'd stormed off in the middle of the road, but he'd really narked her with all his paranoid safety precautions. And then, he'd taken her *fuck you* literally when she drove off. Jesus, he really was a Carabiniere. So where had he got to?

There he was. Right in front of her.

Leaning against the door next to hers.

She felt like she was in a romcom. She walked past him and did a double-take, unable to believe her eyes. She walked back, and Canessa was still there, smiling at her.

Kissing him furiously seemed like the most natural thing in the world.

'So, what was the "little girl" like?'

A cool breeze lifted the curtains and got into bed with them. Annibale was admiring Carla's perky, youthful breasts and shaved muff. The first time they'd had sex, he'd been a little surprised by it; he'd suddenly felt old. Was that the norm now? A fad, or her personal style?

He smiled at the thought, and Carla pounced.

'So, my questions amuse you?'

She plunged a sharp finger into his side.

'I was thinking of something else. Sorry. Caterina? She's four, five years older than you.'

'You're squirming, Colonel. What is she *like*? Blonde, brunette, short, tall, a dog, pretty?'

Canessa placed his hands behind his head and closed his eyes.

'Tall, blonde, sparkling green eyes, gorgeous.'

Carla looked at him. He looked for a smidgen of jealousy in her eyes, but there was almost nothing. Almost…

'Really? And she still has the stuffed animal you got her? So sweet.'

So sarcastic.

'It's true, she was a kid, but she was strong. She was five when she watched her father die, and she described his killer perfectly. Gennaro Esposito.'

'And now you think the other man was Petri.'

'I don't think so, I know it.'

Carla got up and slipped on a t-shirt that barely covered her bum. She went to the kitchen and came back with two mugs of herbal tea (Canessa was a convert).

'So?'

'So, nothing. If I'm right, there's something else behind the murder of Lazzarini.'

'All because of a case of mistaken identity concerning the hit squad? How is it relevant?'

'It's not just that. If Petri was the second killer, then that would be the only murder that has never been credited to him. There's never been any doubt about the identity of the killers in all the others. Even before the supergrass spilled. There have been confirmations, debates, witness reports, even confessions. The only oddity about Petri's atonement is his visit to Lazzarini's tomb.'

Canessa got up and started getting dressed.

Carla said nothing. She'd realised he wouldn't be staying the night.

He was the first to speak. 'I need you.'

'What do you mean?'

He leaned in and kissed her.

'In every way. Can you get into your archives? During the day, this time. See if you can find anything odd about Lazzarini's murder. Maybe some gossip in an old cutting, a photo that catches your eye. Follow your instincts.'

Carla jumped to her feet and pretended to click her heels.

'At your service!'

7

Rocco and his associate arrived on separate trains at different times, one at Centrale, the other at Rogoredo. To avoid risk – if a hotel was unthinkable for Rocco himself, there was no question of booking in two of the same species – Panattoni had set them up in a small flat in via Teodosio, a former janitor's quarters converted into a two-room flat and rented out to business people needing somewhere to fuck their new lovers, or visiting managers who hated living in hotels (there were more of the former than the latter).

He'd rented it out for a week. Hopefully that would be enough. Cash payment, no documents required. He'd stocked the fridge – sandwiches, ready-made pizzas, Coca-Cola and other soft drinks, couple of light beers but no other alcohol – and had left a stack of porn films on top of the DVD player. He'd also installed a small camera connected to his smartphone, to keep an eye on the killers. He was particularly keen to know whether they'd disobey orders and head outside to cause havoc.

He picked them up in a single trip, stopping at Rogoredo first, then Centrale. He'd drop Rocco's associate at the flat on the way. He didn't show up in his underwear, as Salemme had joked, but it was clearly visible under his rapper-style jeans. He was even wearing a snap-back cap and a couple of heavy gold chains around his neck.

'Jesus, what a chav!' Panattoni muttered to himself when he spotted him coming out of the station. No one else seemed to notice him.

They hadn't agreed on a signal to recognise each other – a newspaper, a flower, a certain colour – but it wasn't necessary. The guy headed straight for Panattoni and slapped a hand on the car.

'Hey mate, you Nando?' he asked in a loud voice.

'I am, but why not raise your voice a little? That way everyone can hear you and remember we were here.'

The guy flashed him a terrifying smile, just like one of Rocco's.

'Let's hope not, huh, or we gotta kill them all!'

At least this one has a sense of humour. Panattoni sighed.

Rocco dropped the fake Louis Vuitton luggage in a corner. He grunted at his associate, gave him a high-five and then sniffed out the place. Literally.

'Panattoni, this place smells of whores but I see no whores, what? Can you sort that out?'

Panattoni collapsed into an armchair. He'd briefly considered moving in here himself to keep an eye on them. He didn't trust them.

But no, fuck them. Fuck the Salemmes. He wasn't going to play babysitter to these psychopaths.

'With this sort of contract, you have to look sharp. The rule is: look, don't touch. And don't be seen. It's a delicate situation and you need to make an effort. Do you understand who we're dealing with?'

'Oof, how hard can it be! We got the brother, we'll get him.'

Panattoni ran his hands through his hair. They didn't get it.

He stood up.

'Okay, well. The fridge is stocked, there's porn over there, rest up, and get ready. We could be moving as soon as tomorrow evening.'

Fabio Guidoni sauntered into Marta Bossini's office wearing his regular jeans with a preposterous cream-coloured jacket and a black tie sporting green giraffes. Marta, in her designer suit, stared him up and down. He looked like he'd just been to London to learn how to 'be eccentric'. He hadn't brought it off.

Guidoni seemed oblivious – or maybe he didn't care.

'I've got fantastic news!' he announced. 'Interesting developments on the Petri case!'

Marta was all ears. 'I'm listening.'

'Nope, not here. For this sort of fireworks, we need a drink. No security. I'll take care of us.' He opened his preposterous jacket, revealing a gun in its holster.

8

A couple of hours later, 'fireworks' lit up the night sky on Milan's west side, though Guidoni and Bossini couldn't have predicted it. Explosions, not unlike those on the closing night of traditional festivities, were heard from a couple of kilometres away. A famous TV channel called it one of the most violent shootings in Milan's criminal history, a 'bloody settling of scores'. No one actually knew if organised crime was behind it, but reporters started citing Chicago in the '30s, Palermo in the '80s, even Beirut. Eventually, when the investigations were complete and the results made public, the conclusion was this: there might have been more victims in other cases, but never had there been so much shooting.

Forensics had recovered from the scene a hundred and twenty-six 7.6x39 calibre shells spat out from two AK-47s (the only weapons left behind), a hundred and four 9x19 calibre parabellum, presumably from one or more MP5s and several other guns: a SIG P226, a Beretta 92. According to experts, not all the bullets were recovered, but the ones from the bodies of the two men on the ground and those from the blazing car and nearby scooter were easily recovered by the white suits. Several had fallen into the canal. Five were found embedded in the façade of the Canottieri Olona sports club on the other side of the canal. Witness reports and fingertip searches confirmed that at least four men had been involved. Two had died on the spot and two were wounded, one severely. None had ended up in hospital. According to forensics, there was blood from four different sources. A probable fifth suspect had not been injured; there was none of his blood. There was insufficient information to determine the direction that the fifth person and the two wounded had taken after the shooting. Two cars had been involved, but only one was left in via Lodovico il Moro. Investigating officers agreed between themselves – though certainly not in public – that there was little hope of finding it after all that time, and certainly not in a state that would permit a full investigation. It had probably ended up in a lake or reservoir outside Milan, or locked in an old building on the outskirts, undoubtedly torched.

No one would have imagined, however, that the car missing from the site of the shooting (colour: grey; make: Alfa Romeo; model: unknown) was currently parked behind the high walls surrounding a former printer's-turned-high-end loft. No one would have imagined, or believed, that the car had moved only a couple of hundred metres. So no one looked for it close by.

A few hours earlier, Canessa had been making his way home from Carla's place. She'd come to terms with their routine and no longer complained about his secrecy about where he lived.

'For now,' he insisted, 'it's better if you don't come to my place. It's still too dangerous. Later, after I've figured things out.'

'Maybe I won't care "later",' she teased.

Annibale would leave just before dawn, and he'd done so this time too. Repetto had been waiting a few parking spots away from Carla's front door, and he was now driving with one arm draped out of the window. The MP5 lay between the two seats, hidden under a cloth.

The former Carabinieri sat in silence, wrapped in the sounds of a city neither slumbering nor awake.

Repetto was on edge. He'd had yet another fight with his wife, who was understandably upset about the amount of time he was spending away from home. Barbara Repetto knew her husband well, and she'd realised that this wasn't technically to do with work, whatever he might have told her. When she got out of him that his former boss was also involved, she'd blown up. 'That man's middle name is Danger!' she yelled. Repetto had tried to reassure her that times had changed and she had nothing to worry about, but even if it had been true, she wouldn't have believed him. The phone call had ended badly.

Annibale, for his part, was thinking about Carla. By now, it was clear that there was more between them than physical attraction, and even that was a long way from 'fucking'. He knew he felt something more for Carla, but he was torn. What sort of a future could he have with a woman half his age? He'd seen relationships like that, of course, long-lasting ones where the age gap didn't matter. But they each had their own situations, their own outlooks. Carla was a young journalist on the rise, he a former Carabiniere living in a small town in Liguria, a place far removed from the world and accessible only by boat or on foot. He worked in a restaurant – or not at all, while her job took her all over. She wasn't confined to one place, and definitely not to his place, as beautiful as it might be. So what future was there for them? Where could they put down roots? It was hard for him to even think about the word 'love'. He'd always been afraid of it.

So the two former colleagues had found themselves stewing in their own juices on a night that would prove to be pivotal. Maybe nothing would change, however, since this time, Panattoni (on a scooter) and Rocco and his associate (in an Astra stolen from Linate airport) had perfected their tailing. Their timing was spot-on, and Canessa only noticed when the scooter overtook them and lost control, skidding a few metres ahead of their car as they sped down via Lodovico il Moro near the Canottieri Olona sports club.

Panattoni didn't know what direction Canessa would take as he left Carla's place. So he'd placed the two Neapolitans in largo La Foppa, even though he was sure Canessa had parked on the opposite side, near Foro Bonaparte. When he saw the damn Carabiniere walk down the corso and turn onto via Tivoli, he knew his hunch had been right. Canessa got into a car with its engine on. Nando called Rocco and told him to meet him immediately on Cadorna: he was sure they'd pass that way.

'When the time is right, I'll overtake them and pretend to fall off the scooter. They'll focus on me and you'll get them from behind, got it? Don't mess up. They're not new to this.' Panattoni hoped that Rocco's man was at least good at killing people. He wanted it to be over quickly.

Then all this shit would be in the past, and he'd disappear without a trace.

*

The shooting didn't last long, maybe three minutes.

When Repetto saw the man overtaking them and losing control, he instinctively slammed on the brakes. Canessa, shaken out of his thoughts by the car jerking to a halt, turned around while his partner checked in front of them – old habits were hard to lose. That was how he spotted the two men with AK-47s getting out of the car stopped behind them.

'Look out!' he shouted to Repetto.

The shooting started a fraction of a second before Canessa could grab his friend and drag him down to the space between the seats and the dashboard. The splashes of blood told him that Repetto had been hit. He couldn't waste time. He had to get out of there immediately.

What the attackers didn't know was that Canessa never lost his cool under fire. He was trained to think and act with lightning speed. A general once said: *He is the only person I know who sees things from above.*

He leapt into action, Canessa style: no hesitation, no guesswork.

He grabbed the MP5 and threw himself out of the car on his side, while the Alfa was being riddled by bullets. Lying down, he had a good view of the feet of one of the shooters behind the cover of their car, and he opened fire in that direction.

The killer swore and fell to the ground, nursing his foot. Canessa gained a small advantage, since the man from the scooter – he still had his eye on him – was a poor shot: he emptied an entire Beretta in front of the Alfa, into the Naviglio canal and beyond. Too high, too low. Canessa ranked him as the least dangerous of all three. He'd take care of him later.

Meanwhile, the third killer, angered by the shot at his associate, had let loose with his rage, destroying what was left of the car boot and windows with his volley. Canessa decided to bring the whole thing to an end, as half the world would be there soon and he had no intention of explaining things to anyone. Especially not where his weapons came from.

He stood up from behind the right side of the car, and with his back to the Naviglio, he riddled the killers with bullets, the SIG in his right hand and the MP5 in his left. He heard a moan and watched as the driver of the scooter clasped his side.

Panattoni had fired a few shots when he felt a sharp pain in his side. Running his hand down to check, he found his shirt drenched in blood.

His blood.

This was the first time he'd been shot. He was shocked. He pulled the trigger two more times without aiming, then shoved the gun in his jacket and started running down a side alley that came off the main road. He could hear the bullets flying behind him, and Rocco shrieking insults: 'Panattoni, you mother-fucker!'

He didn't stop. He was just being practical. They'd failed, but he could still save himself.

Rocco, killer for hire, working for the Camorra and whoever else could afford him, fired one more round before reaching the end of his deplorable existence. It was aimed not at the man he'd been contracted to kill, but at Panattoni, the coward who'd run away and left him.

Canessa cursed himself for having been surprised by amateurs. People who only felt good when they snuck up from behind.

When he saw one of the killers turn his back to aim at the one on the scooter (definitely the worst of the pack), he reloaded the MP5 and left cover, opening fire on the pair of killers with both the SIG and the machine gun. The one he'd already hit had got up again, and was now using the car door as a shield. Pointlessly, since Canessa unloaded the entire MP5 on him, hitting him eight times, twice in the head. His rapper cap fell to the ground as he slid against the Astra.

Rocco – yelling and swearing – was now firing at random. Canessa trained his remaining bullets on him, hitting him three times in the head, and four in the chest. He died on the spot.

Silence fell over the road, but sirens could be heard moving closer. Canessa tossed his two guns on the front seat of the Alfa before moving Repetto onto the back seat, as gently as possible. In the rear-view mirror he watched as the other car burst into flames.

With a sudden screech of tyres, he sped down a side alley.

9

The first to be alerted was Chief Magistrate Calandra. The man from the Secret Service had a home in Testaccio, a nice flat he'd shared with his wife for twenty-seven years until she passed away. Despite the regular affairs with beautiful young things while she was still alive, Calandra had always been in love with her, a contradiction he could deal with only through self-justification and indulgence. Since his wife had passed away, he'd rarely slept in the place. The house was a sort of mausoleum he returned to whenever his daughter came back to visit from the States.

That night, Calandra was sleeping perfectly well, his memories for company, and no dreams. When his man called him, he realised it must be something big.

'What's up?'

'Shooting in Milan, extremely violent, shower of bullets, two dead.'

'Who?'

'Not our hero, don't worry. Two young killers. But he's involved. I checked the tapes on several cameras, and his car turned onto via—' a brief pause as he found the note '—Lodovico il Moro, a few minutes earlier. The car that was tailing him was the one from the shooting.'

'Has anyone asked for the tapes yet?'

'Not yet, but they will soon.'

'Soon, maybe, but they'll be too late. Wipe everything. System failure, hydrogen bomb, plague. Whatever the fuck you have to do, but I want no trace of Canessa in this. In fact, where is he?'

'Disappeared.'

'Good. Keep me posted. Constantly.'

Giannino Salemme indulged in the company of young women he preferred not to call 'escorts'. As with his American 'girlfriend', he liked to think they'd chosen him for his miraculous powers of seduction. Of course, there were gifts – jewellery, gadgets, trips, money and in particular, his contacts, possible favours – but nothing was ever agreed in advance. Salemme senior was strict about two things: those were gifts, and he would not meet them in his home.

It had been his lucky night. The brunette he'd snagged at the bar in via Savona came from a good family and had agreed to take him home with her and do it on Mummy and Daddy's bed. The foreplay had lasted a lifetime and had got Giannino Salemme particularly aroused. But right when the pill he'd popped to keep him going had started to take effect, his phone buzzed. He glanced at the screen: Claudio.

Begrudgingly he told the girl he had to take it. She shook her behind in front of him to show him what he was missing out on, and headed to the bathroom.

'This better be important.' Salemme senior made no effort to hold back his frustration.

'It is. A shooting in via Lodovico il Moro, along the Naviglio. Like a scene from a film. Two dead.'

'Well, that's good, isn't it?'

'We don't have IDs yet.'

Salemme senior huffed, 'Son, I appreciate this caution of yours, but please don't give in to paranoia.'

Claudio didn't flinch. 'Panattoni has disappeared without a trace. He always calls me after a job. But not this time. I'm going after him.'

The girl reappeared at the door. She paused, gave him a naughty look and started teasing her nipples. Salemme senior swallowed hard.

'Look, Claudio, be careful okay? I need to go now.'

He hung up.

Federico Astroni didn't want company. The law student who'd come over to talk about her thesis – yet another on the Kickback Affair – would have been an easy catch – her adoring eyes told him as much – but the judge needed to sleep. To rest. He'd only got snatches of rest ever since this thing had started.

There wouldn't be any comfort tonight. He'd been looking out on his beloved square and counting cobblestones instead of sheep, but sleep hadn't come. A stroke of luck, in hindsight, since the phone – his own, not the other one – rang. It was his mentor, Judge Antonio Savelli.

'Federico, forgive me calling at this hour, but there's been a terrible shooting in the Navigli area. Two dead, and we don't know how many others were involved. The anti-mafia agents are already on site, but I want you to coordinate the investigation. I know you're busy, but…'

'Antonio, please, it's my duty.'

'Thank you, Federico. I'll see you in the morning.' Savelli corrected himself. 'It's already morning, I suppose.'

'I'll see you later, Antonio.'

Astroni's reaction was in line with Giannino Salemme's. Two dead: it added up. He immediately dismissed the thought.

He had nothing to do with this.

Carla wasn't asleep yet. Canessa had left an hour ago, but she lay there staring at the ceiling, wondering what to do. Her lover was basically her father's age.

But the point wasn't that Canessa was too old, actually. She imagined introducing him to her parents in their sanctuary on corso Magenta. Her mother would polish the good cutlery and china like a madwoman. The two men would study one another, each counting the hairs on the other's head (Canessa would win), especially the grey ones (a draw?). Just imagining it made her feel extremely uncomfortable.

She sensed they were headed for the inevitable showdown, a scene that would sort out feelings and emotions, and it scared her. One of her friends at university, someone who fell in love at least twice a year (or so she claimed), had explained her theory. 'When people start a relationship, they're not thinking about making it permanent. You meet a guy, he's good-looking, you start hanging out. You just have fun together. You don't think about getting engaged, moving in together, weddings: you're just two people. You don't talk about love, even if the word is hovering in the background. But then there's this random moment when you suddenly ask yourselves: so now what? do we say that word, and all the ones that follow?'

For Carla, everything was very real, especially that June night.

Suddenly the darkness lit up.

Is this a sign? she wondered.

Actually, it was a picture of Caprile illuminating her phone. What was he doing calling at this hour?

'Carla, hi, sorry,' – she heard wind in the background – 'I'm on my scooter. Listen, forensics have just been called out for an emergency: sounds like a big mess, a shooting. I'm headed there, but you're on my way so I can pick you up if you want? Five minutes?'

Carla jumped out of bed. 'Three!'

'Carla, you're a maniac. On my way.'

I O

Repetto needed surgery. Canessa had cleaned his wounds immediately and given him a massive blood transfusion with medical packs procured by Rossi, but it wasn't enough. The bullet to his side had gone through, but the one to his left shoulder was still in there.

Annibale had good first-aid experience, but Repetto needed medical help. The wounds didn't look bad, but there was a risk of infection. He needed a specialist, a surgeon, but no hospitals. It was time to resort to the Canessa network. He dialled a number on his Swiss phone.

It rang three times before someone on the other side emerged from sleep.

'Professor De Micheli, it's Annibale Canessa, do you remember me?'

There was a pause. Then a voice, remarkably alert given the hour. 'I thought you'd never call.'

During the Years of Lead and the dark period of kidnappings, Auro De Micheli was a skilled young surgeon, not yet rich and famous. When his first born, only six years old, was kidnapped, De Micheli didn't have any money. His wife, however, was heiress to a vast property empire, so they had been able to pay the ransom.

The boy had not been returned. The following day, a young Carabinieri lieutenant had shown up at their door, barked orders – including some to his superiors – and sent everyone home.

'Let's start over.'

Within thirty-six hours, he'd flushed out the kidnappers. He'd started with the notion that there had to be a mole for a job like this, someone deep inside. De Micheli's wife's family didn't have a factory or any sort of public image, only an office that dealt with their business. Though their wealth was considerable, it was invisible: so someone must have tipped off the kidnappers. Someone who knew exactly how much they were worth. Canessa had interrogated all the insiders, fingered the right one (an accountant with an expensive lifestyle and a brother with addiction problems). Two days after the ransom had been paid, they conducted a dawn raid of the boy's location. He never told the family about the small hole prepared for the child's corpse, had it come to that.

As he was leaving the surgeon's house that afternoon, Canessa felt a tug on his jacket. It was the doctor, his scruffy face still marked by tension and fear.

'I know you won't accept a reward or payment, but if you ever need anything in the future, I'll do anything I can.'

Canessa looked straight at him, his gaze penetrating.

'I'm going to say to you what I say to everyone who offers me help.'

'Of course.'

'Words have weight. I'm going to hold you to it.'

'You were expecting this.'

It wasn't a question. The doctor tossed his blood-stained gloves in the bin. He'd lost his hair but not what lay beneath, nor the legendary hands that had earned him the nickname of 'the Michelangelo of the scalpel'. The only difference between him and the genius of the Sistine Chapel was that De Micheli expressed his creativity by saving lives.

He'd found a full surgical set-up in the loft, improvised behind a screen but stocked with all the necessary. He'd brought his own tools, carried in an IKEA bag as requested, and come over on a scooter.

'He's good. Strong fibre,' De Micheli said, dropping onto the sofa. The day was filtering in through the large skylights. 'He'll be able on his feet in a week.'

Annibale, who'd been the perfect nurse, offered him a coffee.

'Do you have any whisky?'

Canessa opened a cabinet. 'Peated, eighteen years.'

'Perfect. Make it a double, thanks.'

Annibale poured a glass, and sat next to him.

De Micheli took a large swig. 'You know, I was waiting for you to call me one day. I really wanted to repay you, even though you've left the force. To be honest, I'd almost lost hope. But I certainly wasn't expecting something like this.'

He threw back the last of his drink and stood up.

'I was never here, right?'

I I

Via Lodovico il Moro remained closed for several hours. The last of the forensics team left at around sunset, and only then was the road reopened to the public.

At roughly the same time, Panattoni left his safe house, a two-room flat in Quarto Oggiaro officially registered to his girlfriend's brother. He'd effectively brought her entire family into a web of various fronts. If Marita ever left him, he'd be ruined. But Marita was his girl, his young, beautiful girlfriend. He was going to build an entire new life with her, away from all that scum.

His wound was little more than a scratch, and the sawbones he'd called in had cleaned it up, put a couple of stitches in and handed him a bottle of antibiotics and some painkillers.

The place was minimally furnished with a bed, a table, one or two chairs, a TV and a small kitchenette. Panattoni kept some cash there. He also had a gun hidden away and a stock of non-perishable food.

Once the doctor had left, it was late afternoon. He was a good person overall, small coke habit aside – he'd been struck off and survived by taking jobs like this. The doctor had watched over him for a few hours while he slept. Maybe he shouldn't have slept so much, but he'd been tired and unable to think straight.

When he woke up, he realised it was late, and he turned on the TV to listen to the news reports. The two Neapolitans had been dubbed Camorra killers. They had nothing on Rocco – he'd always avoided jail.

His worries and adrenaline kicked in. He called Marita one more time. No reply. He decided to try her brother.

'She *no está aquí*. She go to your place.'

'What do you mean, my place?'

He heard a muttered 'arsehole' from the other side.

'Your place, your place. Where are you? You no estaying with her?'

All at once Panattoni twigged. She'd gone to via Bergamo, his official home. He swore loudly and hung up on his future brother-in-law. He paced the flat. He'd told her to never go back there: it wasn't safe. But she hadn't listened. He'd have to go back too, since all his belongings were still there.

Fuck.

'Ah, here's good old Panattoni.'

He should've expected the little shithead to be involved. Panattoni had come in, Beretta in hand, but he hadn't been ready for the scene before him. He vomited onto the glass table by the sofa.

Marita, his girlfriend, was lying on the table, half undressed, with bruises and cuts all over. She'd clearly been tortured: he saw cigarette burns and a bullet hole in her forehead.

Nando stood there for three interminable minutes, catatonic. His future, the world he'd built for himself – his escape, the pizzeria on a Caribbean beach, love, sex, children – all erased in a second. He was gutted, useless. He didn't notice the gun at his head.

Claudio Salemme's voice droned on.

Despite the scene before him, all he could think of was Santo Domingo, a bungalow on the beach, Marita walking out of the water, an orange bikini on her tanned skin… His very own Bond girl.

None of that would happen now. Die another day? The film was fucking *wrong*.

The voice spoke again, as if from a great distance.

'Nando, Nando! You know, I actually wasn't expecting you here. I was surprised to find her, too. Your girl was tough, she didn't rat on you. If you hadn't come in just now, we would've missed each other. I was about to leave just when you opened the door.'

Still in a stupor, Nando turned his head to the right. Only then did he feel the cold metal of Salemme's gun at his temple.

For a second, he considered his options. He even put his hand back to grab his Beretta, momentarily proud. But Salemme took it off him easily. What did it matter anyway? What was the point of reacting?

'Were you going somewhere, Nando? You wanted to drop it all and leave?'

Panattoni wished he could explain. Not to save himself, but to let Claudio know how little he cared about them and their business. He'd never betray them, never say a word. He just wanted to leave and start a new life. A life away from the shitshow they ran, with their nice homes, their designer clothes, cars, money. Vermin, that's what they were. Vermin. Worse than him.

'Scumbags!' he spat out.

The bullet bored through the void that was Panattoni's life without Marita, shattering the upper half of his skull.

Claudio Salemme, wearing a plastic raincoat, pollution mask, latex gloves and polyethylene shoe covers, placed the gun in Panattoni's hand, making sure to press his fingers on the stock and trigger. He took the man's Beretta for himself. Murder-suicide, another case of gender-based violence. The police wouldn't probe too deep, not with everything else going on.

He opened the door of the flat and looked around. No one. He took the stairs, pausing between the second and third floors to remove the protective gear. He stuffed everything into a paper bag from a high-street shop. Night had fallen by the time he stepped outside again. He strolled towards viale Lazio, where he'd left his bike. Bikes have no number plates.

He was proud of himself. He hadn't thought killing would be so easy. His first time had been excellent; he'd behaved like a professional. Maybe he should have been the one to deal with Canessa instead of the three stooges they'd hired. He'd mention it to his father, though he knew that was a dead end.

In any case, the old man would have to give him this much: you can't argue with conventional wisdom. If you want something done right, do it yourself.

12

Canessa had two phone calls to make. He opted for the most difficult one first.

He called Barbara Repetto from her husband's phone.

'Ivan, I'm worried about you! Where are you?'

'Barbara, it's Annibale, not Ivan.'

He heard a noise on the other end of the line, as if Barbara had just grabbed hold of something to steady herself. She gasped. So he hurried his explanation.

'Listen, Ivan has been injured but he's fine. He's not in danger, and I'm sorry that—'

'Bastard.'

She delivered the insult calmly, without raising her voice.

Canessa waited for her to continue, to let it out, but Barbara said nothing else. So he spoke again. Without offering excuses or explanations, only logistics and instructions.

'We're not in the hospital. Ivan is resting. I'm sorry, but you can't come to us. He'll be able to call you tomorrow, and I'll bring him home in a couple of days. I'll never seek him out again after this, I promise.'

He used the Swiss phone to call Carla, withholding the number. She answered on the third tone.

'It's me.'

'Where are you?'

'I'll explain later. How are you?'

'All good, but I'm drowning in work. Things are manic here. Did you hear about that organised crime shooting? Salvo and I were the first on site.'

Canessa bit his tongue to stop himself telling her the truth.

'I heard. Crazy, huh? So maybe we shouldn't see each other yet?'

'Why not come over around 2 a.m.? The night is still young!' Her tone was full of energy, and he loved what it stood for: her passion for her job, her love of life, no game-playing.

'You're probably tired. Listen, I need to head to Liguria to sort a few things out. I'll call you again tomorrow, okay?'

'I'll be here! Love you.'

Carla hung up quickly, as if the words coming out of her mouth had surprised her more than him.

She was wrong. On the other end of the line, Canessa stood as still as a statue.

13

The head of the rapid response team was watching the two prosecutors and trying his best to appear merely confused by their behaviour rather than outraged as he actually was. Flying in the face of all evidence, Marta Bossini and Fabio Guidoni were following their own path. But he had no intention of challenging them. They'd be the ones carrying the can.

Silvestrin had just brought some sensational news to their attention, plus a few smaller, but still interesting pieces. First of all, the second killer, whose prints weren't in the national database, had finally been identified, thanks to their colleagues in Naples. His name was Ciro D'Alletto, aka 'Rocco'. Unlike his associate, who was linked to a clan in the Vesuvius area and had a criminal past, Rocco worked for the best offer, whether Camorra business or not. A rare case of a freelancer in Naples. No boss wanted him around for long. He was a ticking bomb, only good as a killer, and dangerous in the long run. According to Silvestrin, he'd been the one with the contract in Milan; the other had been brought in as backup.

'Because the job was bigger this time. Good precaution, but clearly not enough.'

'Why "this time"?' Bossini interrupted. She hadn't sat down like her colleague, and instead she was leaning against the window looking into the office courtyard.

'Because one of the two AK-47s—' Silvestrin went for the suspenseful tone of a noir film, complete with dramatic pause '—is the one that was used to kill Pino Petri and Napoleone Canessa.'

'Well, damn,' Guidoni said, unable to contain his surprise. Bossini, on the other hand, maintained her icy calm. She moved away from the window and joined her colleague behind the desk.

'Are you certain?'

'Complete match: weapon, shells, bullets.'

Guidoni slapped the desk, practically shouting, 'Bingo! That proves my theory. It's nothing to do with terrorism. It's a turf war between gangs, for control over drug-dealing. Like so many former terrorists, Petri turned to other criminal activities.'

The head of rapid response took a deep breath. 'I'm sorry, your honour, but drugs up here are usually linked to the 'Ndrangheta or foreign interference. The Camorra has nothing to do with it.'

'They're trying to expand, my friend, and went against the current dealers.'

'I'm sorry, I have to insist: it's just not plausible. The Camorra attacking the 'Ndrangheta in Milan? Not possible. That's not how organised crime moves. There's no precedent. They agree on territories and treat it like a business.'

Marta Bossini cut in, her tone glacial. 'You let us decide what is and isn't plausible, Silvestrin. The two killers may very well have been employed by the 'Ndrangheta. We'll see, but at this stage it's not relevant. What we're interested in right now is how it ties in with the Petri case. Before the shooting, we received crucial information about the drug trafficker behind it all. Now we have confirmation that it's not Petri's past that's connected with it; it's his present. Thank you, Silvestrin. You may go.'

The head of the rapid response team nodded and left the room. He found his right-hand man just outside.

'So? How did it go?'

'To hell with all of them!' he blurted.

As soon as the police officer had left the room, Marta called the judge, as Astroni had instructed. 'From now on, you need to make two phone calls every time. Savelli first, then me. Be efficient and loyal. Ask him for help and suggestions. Your career will greatly benefit. Then call me immediately. Don't wait any longer than it takes you to dial my number.'

She told Guidoni what Savelli had just said on the phone. 'The two cases are connected, so we'll work alongside the anti-mafia agency, but we'll be in charge.'

Her colleague was excited. He couldn't wait to show the ace up his sleeve.

'Excellent. And the other thing?'

'We'll play that card as soon as we have more on our final player, our dear Canessa.'

Astroni was waiting for her call.

14

'I'm the one who killed them.'

Carla pulled away from a long kiss, and looked at him in shock. She was even more shocked than when he'd told her the

309

true story of via Gaeta. It wasn't about the deaths, but the danger he'd been in.

Canessa had cheered up. Yet although she'd repeatedly shown him her affection (and maybe something more), his life on the edge might become an obstacle. Weren't there enough of those already?

He'd suggested they spend the night in a hotel, 'to celebrate our reunion after all this time apart. We'll pretend we're on holiday somewhere nice. Dinner on the balcony, breakfast in bed, and in between…' They'd booked into a junior suite on the top floor of Hotel Gallia, she in her name, while he'd used a real ID card with a fake identity.

The temperature inside was perfect. Annibale had an urge to open the window, to let the night air come in. He settled instead for the excellent view of the gorgeous square beneath them, the sky turning electric blue behind it.

Canessa had spent days in the loft, never leaving Repetto's side. Luckily, Repetto's wounds healed quickly.

'We're even,' Repetto said when he came to. 'It was my turn to be the fool who got shot!'

'Well, I was there too, so technically it's two-one for me,' Canessa teased.

Repetto wasn't having it.

'It was my job to be alert. You were recovering from passionate sex and weren't in the right state of mind…' His laugh turned into a grimace: the wound was still fresh.

After the call to Barbara, and in spite of Repetto's complaints and stubbornness, he'd taken him home to Monza.

'Very nice,' Repetto commented as he lowered himself cautiously into the passenger seat of the BMW Series 1. He'd tried convincing Canessa one more time. 'I need to watch your back.'

'It didn't help much last time.'

Repetto hadn't taken it as well as he usually did. His pride hurt more than the wound.

'I was an idiot,' he kept saying.

'We both were,' Canessa reminded him. 'We were distracted. That's why we need a breather. We can't let anxiety take over. You head home, I'll go to Liguria for a couple of days. I've been away too long. It's high season and I need to help my aunt.'

He hadn't told Repetto – he wouldn't have been able to drop him off – that that very afternoon he'd seen a photo of the third killer on TV. Fernando Panattoni. According to the news, he'd been found dead in a flat in via Bergamo along with his foreign girlfriend, legally resident in the country. Everything pointed towards a misogynistic murder-suicide, and the politicians and psychologists started having a field day.

But it was a cover-up and he knew it: his handlers had tied up a loose thread. Panattoni had been nothing but a pawn. Plus, the news cited a revolver as the murder weapon, but Canessa knew that Panattoni had shot him with a Beretta. Sure, he might have changed weapons later, but it seemed unlikely. Someone who's just taken part in a shooting in which he was wounded doesn't go home, change weapons, then top himself and his girlfriend.

He'd been killed.

Barbara Repetto emerged from the family villa, set within a magnificent garden, to help her husband get out of the car. Canessa spotted Repetto's grandchildren looking at them through the windows. A small girl with red hair pulled a face at him. Was she angry at him, like her grandmother? Barbara hadn't even greeted him, but Repetto firmly reminded her: 'Manners. Please say hello to my friend.'

Barbara held his gaze, but Repetto was as stubborn as a mule.

'Hello, Annibale. Thank you for bringing Ivan home.'

Husband and wife walked down the cobbled drive lined by the flowerbeds that were Barbara's pride and joy. They were almost at the door of the villa, where the grandchildren had gathered, when Ivan turned round and signed for Annibale to phone him.

Canessa smiled. *He just won't quit.*

She let her dress slide to the floor, and stood wearing only her panties.

'Fuck me,' she whispered. She kept her panties on as he entered her, over and over again, from every possible angle.

Eventually, when they woke up towards dawn, she asked him to tell her everything about the shooting. He told her about Panattoni's death too, and the connection he'd made between the two.

'Now what?' she asked.

'Now we need to find the connecting thread in all this. I'll head to Liguria, for real this time, and try to piece it together as I deal with *trenette al pesto* and seafood fry-ups.'

Carla sat on the bed. 'Two Camorra killers and a private investigator with PTSD who kills himself or is killed along with his girlfriend. It doesn't make sense.'

'It does. Petri and Judge Lazzarini are the keys. I'm sure of it.'

'It seems pretty clear that you're on the right track if they tried to kill you. But these people clearly have money and contacts. You can't just look up people like Rocco and his accomplice.'

Canessa agreed. 'It's true, they're powerful. But more than the who and the how, I want to know why. I'm old school that way: motive is the most important thing.'

Carla stood up and opened the window, breathing in the fresh air. She took off her panties and stepped onto the balcony, completely naked. She leaned against the railing, slowly, offering him a view of her behind. Then she turned to face him, opening up her legs.

'Come here and fuck me like there's no tomorrow.'

15

Five hundred people were invited to the wedding of Renata – daughter of Nicola Frugoni, private healthcare king in Lombardy and one of the wealthiest men in the country – and Anton Giulio Castravano, son of the chancellor of Bocconi University, law and business economy graduate and one the leading experts in Italian civil code and family business inheritance.

Both parties were hoping that the guests wouldn't turn up en masse for the religious ceremony in the small hill church above Bellagio – it held no more than fifty – and would only show up for the reception on the terrace of a glorious villa on the lake. It was quite the event. As it happened, word got around, and they had their wish. Everything went according to plan and the illustrious guests, dressed to the nines, threw themselves at the dancing and the buffet provided by a three-star chef.

It was sunset. The villa's garden hosted three gazebos, each far enough from the other to offer some privacy, and close enough to the water that you could hear it lapping against the shore. It was refreshing, in all aspects.

Astroni sat, alone, under one of the gazebos. The other two were packed with inebriated guests, laughing and talking raucously.

'Don't you think buffets are a great invention? You grab, you eat, you grab again, you eat more. You leave plates and glasses around. You do the rounds. You take your own time and when you've had enough, it's an Irish goodbye!'

Giannino Salemme, squeezed into a white suit that really needed to be let out (alternatively, he could have lost some weight), grabbed the chair next to Federico Astroni, who was picking at a plate of pasta tubes with tomato and parmesan, one of the chef's signature dishes.

'That one's taken,' Astroni said, clearly annoyed.

Salemme pretended not to hear, and settled in next to Astroni.

'Have you lost your mind?' he almost jumped to his feet, then thought better of it. 'Everyone can see us!'

Salemme spread his arms. 'Federico, relax! We're some of the top guests at a boring wedding. We're chatting, we've known each other for forty years, who do you think will care? Give me a break, please.'

Astroni glanced around, but everyone was still eating and drinking. No one was paying them any attention. He still couldn't relax, however: his mind was spinning with problems, and the presence of this uncomfortable person made it worse.

Salemme moved his chair closer. Astroni tried to appear as normal as possible.

'We need to talk.'

'About what?'

Salemme lowered his head.

'Federico, Federico… still the same I see. Always waiting for someone else to fix your problems.'

'What do you mean?'

'Why do you think you're famous? Was it an act of courage? The brave prosecutor up against the powerful? Come on. You started locking people up when the system was in crisis, and the *people*,' Salemme spat out the word while gesturing at the guests around them, 'started standing under your window to praise you. You've wallowed in the muck for years, doing nothing, never making a clean sweep of it, cursing in private while publicly praising the politicians you sentenced to the scaffold when the opportunity arose. You only made your move, you and your accomplices, when you knew you had your backs covered. Not a moment sooner. And now, you're doing the same.'

'I don't have to take this from you. I'm leaving.' Astroni made to stand up, but a hand pushed him back down onto his chair.

Claudio Salemme flashed him one of his reptilian smiles. 'Listen to my father, you tosser,' he hissed.

Astroni was furious. 'Get your hands off me!' He turned to Salemme senior. 'I want nothing to do with this arsehole.' He knew all about young Claudio's résumé, though not his recent exploits, or he actually would have fled the scene in horror.

Giannino was more accommodating. 'I'm sorry, Federico, we got off on the wrong foot here. Let's keep it civil and quiet. Listen. Whether you like it or not, we're linked, and it's a heavy chain. One of us falls, the other is dragged down with him.'

'What do you want?' Astroni felt the first drops of sweat rolling down his forehead, despite the cool breeze.

'We've tried containing the problem…'

'I saw that…'

'Shut your mouth!' the man behind him threatened, inching closer.

315

Salemme senior was still playing good cop to his bad cop son.

'True, it didn't go too well. But no, we're a little... how can I say this... low on resources. You need to take your share of responsibility. We heard what your minions told the press. Organised crime, drugs, turf wars.'

'So?'

'So we have an idea. Risk free, more or less. A clean, surgical hit. But we need your charm, your clout. We'll play our part, you'll play yours. No one will get hurt, no one will fire a single shot – at least, not illegally. If it comes to that, the weapons firing will be the blessed ones of the law and its enforcers. Enough risky business.'

Astroni looked at Salemme. Despite his appearance, he didn't look much older. All those years, ever since they'd taken their own paths, he'd always been able to get himself out of bad situations. He'd always survived, and he'd got rich. He'd have to trust him, one more time.

'I'm listening.'

16

Pasquale Cammello raised a hand to his forehead to shelter his eyes from the sun. He was searching the courtyard for his man, and he spotted him on the other side. In the shade. Of course.

He crossed the one place where the prisoners could finally stretch their legs: outside. The looks that came his way were respectful. Some pulled aside to let him through. When he got closer to the man he wanted to speak to, he slowed down. The Professor didn't appreciate people approaching him aggressively.

The Professor had actually taught maths at university, and was revered by colleagues and students alike. He'd been on a great career path, and then he'd become a revenge killer. He'd slaughtered the people responsible for destroying his family. People who'd avenged a wrong done to them were treated with respect in prison. Respect, by God, was still worth something.

'That,' Cammello always said, 'is a real man of honour. Prison! He should've got a medal.' He knew what De Marinis had done, of course, and he approved.

The Professor was on the other side of the yard, at peace with himself and his life sentences. He was playing chess on his own. He wasn't a misanthrope at all; people liked him and he liked them back. He helped inmates with their letter writing, translations (who knew how many languages he spoke) and he even taught maths to a few of them. Cammello had listened in a couple of times, understanding absolutely nothing but fascinated all the same. With chess, however, no one was up to his level, so the Professor played alone one day, and taught someone else the next. When he taught, he didn't want to be bothered, but when he played alone, he was open to seeing people. He had many 'students', especially among the Slavic inmates.

'*Oh oh Cammello*, was that the song? No, it was *oh oh cavallo*.'

De Marinis had a ponytail, a long salt and pepper beard and a curious sense of humour.

Cammello chuckled.

'Professor, sorry to bother you, but I need help with something.'

'Just a second.' He looked at the board, considered a move, made another and exclaimed, 'Checkmate! Okay, what can I help you with?'

'I shared a cell with Pino Petri.'

317

'A good boy, despite his past.'

'Indeed, may he rest in peace.'

'Amen. So?'

'Petri dies, the cops come in, dig around, ask questions, find nothing and leave. I'm left with a Moroccan who shanked his sister's Italian boyfriend, a Latino gang member who pummelled a taxi driver into a coma and Pelusi, a creep who dealt E outside schools.'

'Not a great selection.'

'It sucks. But one's gone missing. The creep disappeared.'

'Greener pastures?'

'No, that's the point. He still had three years to go. One day, he gets called to the talking room and never comes back. He had some personal effects. The guards come over, box them up and leave.' Cammello blew on his fingers. 'Vanished. I don't like it, but I can't figure out what's going on.'

The Professor was slowly resetting the chess board. He nodded. 'Grasser.'

'Grasser?'

'Yes. The prosecutors want something from him. They're looking for a witness.'

'That creep? A grass? Come on! He knows nothing about me.'

The Professor wagged his index finger at him, as if he were a naughty student. 'As you said, there was someone else in that cell with a past.'

Cammello's eyes widened. 'Petri! Fuck…'

'Petri had been in there for years. They knew they'd get nothing from you or the other two. They aimed for the weak link, according to your description.'

'Maybe, but I was actually close to Pino, and still knew nothing about him. So we're back to square one: what the fuck did that creep know?'

'Cammello, Cammello! What matters isn't what he knows, but what he'll say.'

'Fuck, that creep would say his mother landed on the moon just to get out.'

'Precisely.'

The Professor stood up.

'Yes, but Petri is dead, so what can he be accused of?'

'Maybe not him. But someone else may be involved, someone who's being investigated. That's how it works. If they have the smoking gun, the physical evidence, the eyewitness, that's all they need. If they don't, if they only have clues and unconnected facts, they'll come up with a theory and try to make it stick. And there's nothing better than a supergrass to lend weight to that theory. They look for one, without being obvious about it. There are several dishonest prosecutors, sure, but they usually walk this side of the law. They start talking, and if the guy gets it, and realises what they want him to say, that's all there is to it.'

Cammello slapped his forehead.

'Fuck! You're right, and I think I know who they're trying to ream. Thanks, Professor.'

He stood up and joined a group of inmates in the opposite corner of the yard. As he approached, one of them slipped him a mobile phone. They huddled round protectively while Cammello dialled.

'Look, I need you to find someone for me right away. It's urgent.'

17

Night fell early in San Fruttuoso. But in the summer, when the last ferry boat left later and private boats docked in the marina, the restaurant was always full for dinner.

Annibale helped his aunt with kitchen prep, then bussed between tables and kitchen all night. They were fully booked that night. They had help in the kitchen, a dishwasher and an extra waitress for the entire season.

When the final guest left, Annibale stayed on the terrace, going over the case and wondering what to do next. Yet in that corner of paradise, the gentle sound of the waves encouraged his more romantic thoughts, and all he could think of was Carla. Screw the age difference and everything else. He missed her the way you miss someone you love. It was pointless to try to hide it from himself. He would call her and tell her. Now.

I love you like I've never loved any other woman. I want to be with you. You can dump me when I get too old, but until then…

His train of thought was rudely interrupted by the Swiss satellite phone.

It was his lawyer friend, Cordano.

'Flavio! What's up?'

Cordano sounded rushed, as if he wanted to hang up as soon as he said what he had to.

'Annibale, I don't know if this will make sense to you, and to be frank, I don't want to know – I have to admit I find it worrying. Pasquale Cammello's lawyer called me with a message. I asked him to repeat it twice while I wrote it down.

Cop, you'd better keep an eye on your stuff. Be careful who you hang out with. To put it bluntly: watch your back. Your former friends want to fuck you over. P.S. I'm doing this for Petri – not you.

'Does that mean anything to you?'

'Maybe,' Canessa replied, his senses suddenly on the alert.

'Well, keep me posted.'

He waited for the last boat to disappear and then hurried back to the restaurant. He walked across the dark room and went upstairs to his flat. His aunt's room was at the end of the corridor. He went into his first, and quickly checked it. The weapons he'd used in via Lodovico il Moro were in the warehouse safe in Rapallo. He had only his Beretta and the Ruger, both held legally in his capacity as a former Carabiniere. He hadn't used the Beretta since the '80s, apart from training at the gun range. Luckily, he'd never fired the Ruger. He sat on the bed.

Think, Canessa, think.

What had Cammello said? His former friends… so the law, the police, Carabinieri, the magistrates. What was the angle? Was it the shooting? No: they'd already be here.

Suddenly, it hit him: the Camorra, organised crime.

He ran to his aunt's bedroom and knocked.

'Come in.'

She was reading a magazine in bed. Small, but full of energy, she had his mother's face, and also Giovanna's. When he'd told her, his aunt had welled up.

'What's wrong, Annibale?'

'This may seem like a strange question, but has anything unusual happened while I've been away? Any customers behaving oddly?'

She put the magazine down.

'Let's see… you got here last night.' She paused. 'Actually, something did happen yesterday, at lunchtime. A woman came to ask me about the bathroom because she couldn't open the door. She'd been trying for some time, she said. We went to check together, and a man in his forties came out. He'd been alone at the table and he didn't eat much but he ordered an expensive wine. I asked if he needed any help. He said he was okay, and apologised for taking so long. He had already paid, so he left right after that. Before I let the woman in, I checked the bathroom. You know, in case he'd done something… off. But everything was clean and tidy.'

Annibale thanked her with an ease he didn't actually feel.

He ran downstairs to the restaurant bathroom. There weren't many places to hide something. He went for the classic one: the toilet cistern. Feeling around, his hand touched something: a sealed plastic bag. He pulled it out: inside was another bag with white powder inside it. He went to the kitchen, took out a knife and slit the bag, spilling some of the powder.

Canessa rubbed a few grains of it on his gums.

Cocaine.

He weighed it in his hand. A good half kilo. Street value? €100,000. Prison term? Twenty years, including consorting with organised crime. If they added a murder charge, it would mean a life sentence. Well played.

So if they couldn't get him with an AK-47, they'd resort to the might of the law.

At least he'd banished his doubts, and he could call the whole mess exactly what it was: a conspiracy.

The cast was huge, and took in influential members of society, people with means and resources and people who might be hiring the Camorra at the same time they were running law enforcement.

He checked his watch and ran back upstairs. He stuffed his waterproof bag with everything he needed, including the cocaine. Then he went back to see his aunt.

'Annibale, you're scaring me. What's going on?'

'Auntie, you need to trust me. Listen: you know I'm investigating Napoleone's death. They tried to stop me by planting cocaine in the bathroom. They're trying to frame me. I need to get out of here fast.'

'But you found it…' She was stumbling over her words. 'If that man put it there, I can tell the police!'

'Even if I could prove my innocence, it would take time, and I don't have any. Go to sleep. Even if you're not tired, pretend you're asleep. They'll get here just before dawn. They'll break in, but they shouldn't cause too much damage. Stay in bed, stay calm. Act surprised, indignant. You know nothing. If they ask you about the drugs, tell them about the man in the bathroom, just like you told me. Do you remember his face? Can you help them with a portrait?'

'Of course! I may be old but I'm not blind!'

Canessa smiled. 'Good. But don't tell them anything about our conversation or the cocaine. You can let slip that I sometimes go for a night dive. Act worried. You can do it.'

She hugged him. Her eyes were blazing.

'I can, but be careful. Please, Annibale.'

Canessa reached Cala dell'Oro easily. He slipped through the town using the smaller streets and alleys, checking to ensure that no officers had been sent ahead to get him. But there weren't any. The ones on foot were probably much higher up the hill, and the ones who'd come by sea hidden behind the promontory. San Fruttuoso could only be reached by sea or by descent from Monte di Portofino. And that's how they would come, cutting off all possible exits. They were counting on the surprise element.

The town was practically empty. Voices drifted up from the beach… maybe a group of kids spending the night on the sand in sleeping bags.

Canessa was still a little shocked by the possible ramifications of the situation. He was convinced that whoever had planted the drugs would have done so in his brother's home in Reggio Emilia, too. Full circle. He thought about Sara and Giovanna: the raid, the fear, a possible arrest. But there was no way to warn them. A phone call would be intercepted and seen as a clear sign of collaboration. *They'll arrest her anyway.* This new conviction rose to the top of his list of worries. They would use his sister-in-law as leverage.

How far did this conspiracy go? And who was involved? He was nearly paralysed by his thirst for revenge. He would settle all scores, but not here, not now. For now, his sole aim was to avoid getting caught.

He reached the water. The sea was calm. He retrieved a bag from among the rocks: inside it were an oxygen tank, a suit and a small personal sub device. He'd hidden it there when the whole affair had begun in case he had to make a quick getaway. He'd covered everything with a camo tarp, and the prep had seemed excessive even to him. But old habits die hard.

He freed the device and pushed it into the water. With a silent blessing to Saint Paranoia, he secured the bag to his back and slid into the water. Quickly, soundlessly, the small sub pulled him away from shore and down into the still waters of the Ligurian Sea.

18

'Someone tipped him off.'

Guidoni was leaning against the chair in which the inscrutable Marta Bossini was sitting. Federico Astroni sat next to her. The atmosphere in Savelli's office was nasty, and not just because the windows were shut and the air conditioner switched off (Savelli hated it).

Savelli wasn't angry about Canessa's escape. He was irritated because Guidoni had come without a jacket in order to show off his *Dirty Harry* gun. Unlike these two young prosecutors, Savelli knew the escape was a positive factor in this mess. Instead of the actual allegations against him, the media would now be focusing on the fact that a former national hero was on the run, stalked by the forces of justice he'd served irreproachably before turning to crime. Savelli and Astroni could not deny, with their experience, that the actual allegations were inconsistent to say the least. There were no drugs, no weapons. Sure, they'd found a pack of cocaine during the search of his sister-in-law's house, but that only implicated his late brother, and there had been no contact between them in years. No ties, no connections.

'That means nothing. They'll have found some other way to communicate,' the two prosecutors objected. Weak. Forensics had found grains of cocaine in the San Fruttuoso restaurant, but a defence lawyer, however incompetent, would have pointed out that any public bathroom in the country would yield the same result. *Even in this very building*, Savelli thought. And then there was the aunt's statement.

Savelli was also incredibly irritated at the phone calls he'd been getting. He was used to the threats, warnings, prayers. This time, however, it wasn't the usual politicians, it was his *friends*. And they hadn't threatened him, they'd treated him like a misbehaving child.

The first to call had been the commander general of the Carabinieri. They'd grown up together, their desks side by side in primary school.

'I'm calling you with a character reference. I've worked with Canessa, and I was a young lieutenant just like him. Canessa was a legend, a warrior monk. If you think he's started dealing in middle age, you're cracked. I hope you have substantial proof, my friend.'

Then it had been Cosima Marchetti's turn; her husband, the judge, had been one of his mentors.

'Shame on you, Antonio! How can you be going after that *boy*? He's a good man and a hero. I won't believe a word said against him. Not even if I see him walk by with a bag of heroin.'

Boy? Really?

After the fifth phone call from an incredulous comrade, a terrorist victim's outraged relative or just sad old friends, he disconnected the phone.

'Are we sure about this theory?' he asked, interrupting the discussion taking place in his office.

Astroni backed him up. 'The evidence does seem a little weak, I concur. Without the drugs…'

Marta held her lover's stare.

'There are no drugs, but there is the escape. Honest people don't run away – they defend themselves. Plus, there's the fact that someone warned him.'

Savelli was forced to agree with his young colleague. 'It's true, that is suspicious. An arrest warrant makes sense. We need to find him, even if it's for his own good.' He paused before continuing with more authority. 'However, let's proceed as we should, and consider him innocent until proven guilty. That man has done the unthinkable for this country, including taking a bullet that was meant to kill him.' He threw a newspaper onto the table. 'I don't want another manhunt ending up in a public shootout. I want a memo released: he comes in alive, or he's released. Is that understood? Now, back to work.'

He closed the file and handed it to Marta Bossini. The meeting was over.

'If it wasn't one of us, who warned him?'

Chief Magistrate Calandra was furious. Without the anonymous benefactor, their prized horse would no longer be in the race. Thwarted. 'But more importantly, how did he escape the ambush?'

His man in grey stood there in front of him looking penitent, as if he were wearing a hairshirt. Calandra suspected he might have self-flagellated before coming to report.

Outside, the Rome evening was beautiful, oblivious to what was taking place. A secret war. Secret, but real.

Calandra had swooped into the offices like a fury, having been woken up in a gorgeous hotel on the coast where he'd spent the night with one of his lovers. He was raging.

He'd even taken off his jacket, and he now stood in just a shirt and his trademark red braces: an unequivocal sign that he was about to start an Inquisition.

The man in grey emerged from his melancholy to make his report.

'I take responsibility for this, your excellency. I took the day off yesterday. It won't happen again.'

'Don't be stupid. How many days off have you taken in the past year?' Calandra dismissed the apology with a wave.

'A week, ten days.'

'Exactly, so none of this self-flagellation. Everyone needs a breather once in a while. My question is: why did your stand-in not realise what was happening?'

'In all honesty, I must admit that Milan's prosecutor's office were very good. Information about the sting was scarce, and the go-ahead only came through on Friday night. As you can imagine, Friday afternoon is very quiet in the courts, especially in summer...'

'...so you're saying even our informants took a seaside break?'

Calandra would happily have had a go at anyone at this point.

The man grew increasingly uncomfortable. 'Unfortunately, we should have been able to avoid that. A careful observer would have spotted the departure of the police tactical unit for Liguria. There were signs, but my stand-in didn't notice.'

'Poor showing. Bring them in later. I'd like a word.' Calandra was simmering down. 'At least Canessa has avoided capture and if I know him as I do, he'll be furious – even more so on account of Sara's arrest. That's good! But back to the point: how did he get out?'

'We found evidence of a call from Canessa's lawyer, a...' he read his file, 'Cordano's the name. Calls went to a Swiss phone, presumably Canessa's.'

'And who warned Cordano?'

'He received a call from an untraceable number... by the police, that is.' The man smiled. 'But we know who it belongs to: the lawyer for Pasquale Cammello.'

Calandra, who'd been leaning back in his chair, snapped upright.

'Cammello helped him? Why?' Confused, he fell silent momentarily. 'Of course! Respect for Petri. Petri was looking for Canessa because he's no longer a cop. A strange ally, somewhat disturbing. But crucial. How did he find out?'

The man in grey practically curtsied. 'I don't have any proof, but I do have a theory. One of their cellmates disappeared. Cammello may have had the same hunch: he's been recruited as a supergrass.'

'And when there's a snitch, there's someone to fuck over, for better or worse. They needed this guy to confirm their theory that Petri had started dealing. Ingenious,' Calandra concluded.

There was another silence. The chief magistrate tried to imagine Canessa's whereabouts, and to anticipate his next move. The situation was bad, but the interesting thing was that there were now more possibilities.

The man in grey cleared his throat.

Calandra snapped out of his thoughts. 'Very well, if there's nothing else…'

'Actually, your excellency, there is. You'll remember you asked me to look into the Lazzarini case. Something about it was covered up, though not well enough. We found it.' He went from hangdog to mildly triumphant and handed Calandra a piece of paper.

'This is more than just *something*. Why was it kept secret at the time?' The chief magistrate was genuinely surprised.

'I found some notes. They did conduct an investigation on the down low, but they didn't find anything or anyone. So they kept quiet. It was after the Moro case, when trust in institutions was at an all-time low. It seemed like the State was unable to abolish terrorism, and the dicey activities of the Secret Service sullied public opinion of the whole system. This would've shaken the tree even more. They had no definite identification, so they said nothing.'

Calandra considered the paper, then handed it back. 'Make sure this gets to Canessa.'

The grey man staggered. 'How?'

Calandra glared at him.

'Work it out! We screwed up. We need to score a point to get back in the lead.'

19

Repetto was as restless as a benched player waiting to step into the game. But his coach was stubborn: even if he'd spotted his restlessness, he was showing no signs of letting him back on the field. His wife had forbidden him from getting involved any further, especially after Canessa had trumped all other dangerous fugitives to become Italy's Most Wanted.

But Repetto had to get away, and quickly. His wounds had more or less healed, and any lingering discomfort was nothing that a painkiller wouldn't squash. Annibale needed him, especially now. He might be risking forty years of marriage in one fell swoop, but he had to get out of that gilded prison. He looked out of a window on the first floor of the villa.

He'd already clocked the cars in front of the house. They weren't trying to hide so much as to discourage. There'd be no arrest. They weren't stupid: they knew Canessa wouldn't show up; he'd never openly involve Repetto. They were there to make a point: they had their eye on everything.

Repetto had to laugh. They didn't know him. At all. Annibale would never get caught. If he chose to disappear forever, no one would see him again. He was out there, somewhere, planning his next move. And Repetto needed to be out there with him. Helping him.

His scanned the garden, which was basically woodland. It would be easy to escape through the trees, breaking through the surveillance. But where would he go? He had no news of Canessa. Had he gone back to the loft? Unlikely. Then there was Barbara. What could he say without making her angry?

He felt a presence behind him. His wife appeared at the living-room door with an envelope.

'What's that?'

'Registered mail, from your phone provider.'

Barbara wasn't particularly beautiful, but she was confident, a strong woman in all senses.

'Why are you giving it to me?' he teased. They often played this game, but both knew who had the final word in the family.

Barbara smiled patiently. 'Because it's strange. First of all, it wasn't our usual postman, and he didn't look like any postman, really. His hands were too clean, know what I mean?'

She was the wife of a Carabiniere, after all.

Repetto looked at her. She was the best thing that had ever happened to him. He took the envelope and opened it. Inside he found another envelope addressed by hand.

Repetto started. He looked at his wife, then back at the note, signed with the name almost no one knew about.

Max.

20

Carla was reeling, but not due to the heat. Canessa's story had suddenly blown up. *Suddenly. Unexpectedly. Distressingly.* All those adverbs. And not one of them positive.

She blamed a dawn phone call from Strozzi – oddly, the same time he'd sent her to report on the double murder in via Vittor Pisani the morning after she'd slept with him. She'd learned to put that aside, but she couldn't exactly forget it. Maybe, though, things were coming full circle.

Strozzi had given her the news of the day – maybe the year – with no discernible emotion. In fact, it had actually been the news of her life.

'This morning, a police tactical unit entered the house and restaurant owned by Annibale Canessa and his aunt. He was missing. Word is that someone warned him, and he escaped the raid. He's wanted for drug dealing, criminal association and as an accessory to murder. No one knows where he is. I just wanted to let you know. Please, Carla, if you hear anything about this, anything at all… This story is becoming dangerous. I'm worried about you.'

She spent the next three hours with her eyes glued to the fan, the blades slowly rotating above her in a sort of unsuccessful hypnosis. Did Strozzi suspect her and Canessa?

She had no idea what to say or think. Of course it was all bullshit. The man she knew wasn't the one everyone else was describing. She'd skimmed the front pages of all the major news sites. Apart from a few minor publications, no one was questioning the story or attempting an alternative reading.

She'd been on that side of things more than once, but now, at the centre of the circus and knowing the person under attack, she was coming to realise how shitty that approach was. It was entirely devoid of reason. There was no attempt to dig behind the accusations.

It was all maddening! Everything was crumbling around her. The man she loved (yes, damn it, she did), the one who'd called her the night before, tired after a long day at the restaurant… He was now a fugitive from the police, the Carabinieri, even the Guardia di Finanza. She felt hurt in spite of herself. She looked around, but didn't spot anything out of the ordinary. Were they tapping her phone? Could they do that?

Where was he?

The meeting was set up for Wednesday in the Lampugnano station car park. Evening rush hour, and a man appeared in the crowd: black hair, salt-and-pepper beard, a pair of thick glasses. A bit of a limp. Someone who'd seen better days. Rossi stared for a moment before turning away. His surprise was equalled by his fear when the man opened the door and sat next to him in the Bentley.

'Rossi, really! Couldn't you have gone for a less noticeable car this time! Although… they'd never expect me to be sitting in a car like this.' It was Annibale's voice.

Rossi's jaw dropped. He couldn't get used to the transformation. The clothes, the mannerisms, tone of voice – everything belonged to a different man with a different story to Canessa's. It was an incredible disguise.

Annibale had called him in Zurich. 'You're my last asset left,' he'd told him.

'I found you a place in via del Carroccio,' Rossi said when he recovered from his surprise, 'at the junction with via De

333

Amicis. It belongs to a foreign pharmaceutical company. It's not far from the Sant'Ambrogio underground station, just like you asked.'

'Good.'

'Do you need any money?'

Canessa smiled. 'I'm good for money and weapons.' And he pointed to his feet, where he had dumped a gym bag.

The Bentley slipped into the chaotic evening traffic.

Canessa was silent, batting a single idea around in his brain.

His adversaries were always one step ahead. Whenever he got close, they made sure he fell back a square by setting a trap or blocking his path. They couldn't be that smart. Sure, they had the tools, the means, the contacts, important allies, but it was all too much.

Rossi was talking to him.

'Sorry, say again?'

'What's your priority? Dealing with the allegations, or continuing the investigation?'

Canessa looked at him, suddenly lighting up.

'Clearing the air.'

2 I

She was nervous about seeing him again. It was odd that he wanted to meet somewhere as busy as largo La Foppa at dusk. But maybe the distraction of a crowd was exactly what he was after.

To let off some steam, she'd worked out in the downstairs gym in the old newspaper building in piazza Cavour. The place was trendy now, filled with models and wannabes.

On the exercise bike, she thought back to the call that had come through to Caprile.

'Okay…' her colleague had handed her the phone, a little confused but mostly curious. The person on the other end had asked him to put Carla Trovati on without transferring the call.

'Hello?' Carla was tentative.

'Largo La Foppa, via Moscova corner, 7 p.m.'

Click. That was it.

Even though she hadn't recognised the voice, she knew it was about Annibale.

Since then, she'd been imagining their reunion. She was as nervous and excited as a teenager on her first date. The element of danger made everything stranger and more mysterious. She might be seen to be aiding and abetting a fugitive. She was, however, sure of one thing: she would tell him *I love you* the moment she saw him. She'd waited long enough.

She left the house without a bra, and now she could feel everyone's eyes on her tight-fitting sports top. After the gym, she'd headed home, intending to change quickly before her appointment. So she hadn't noticed the man behind her as she climbed the steps to the lobby. She swung around, coming face to face with a stranger.

'Follow me. Don't say a word.'

The voice. *That* voice.

'Annibale?'

His hair was black, he had a beard and he seemed bigger. She didn't recognise him. But the voice was his.

'*Shhhh!*'

He shoved her brusquely downstairs towards an emergency exit, then across an inner courtyard and through another door.

'Stop.'

Why was he treating her like this?

He looked outside, then grabbed her arm and forced her to run behind him, to the other side of the street towards the Swiss Centre skyscraper. He dragged her to a small door with a small thread running from it. He pulled on the thread and the door opened. They walked down two flights of stairs and along another putrid corridor until they came to a locked lift. Annibale pulled out a key, and turned it in the lock. The doors opened, and they whizzed to the top of the building.

Once inside the contraption, Carla couldn't hold back. 'What is going on? Why are you acting like this?'

In reply, Canessa took a pair of binoculars from the bag slung across his shoulders.

'Let me show you something.'

The lift stopped and they stepped out onto the roof.

'Stay behind me and do what I do.'

Annibale crouched over and ran behind a cube of concrete that held up an antenna. He took the binoculars and slowly leaned out. He focused for a moment and then handed them over to her.

'Right ahead, on the roof with the green tiles.'

Carla followed his instructions, but even when her eyes had adjusted to the binoculars, she couldn't see anything.

'There's nothing there.'

'Keep still. Watch for movement.'

She was exasperated, confused and hot. Here she was, wanting to tell him how much she loved him, and instead she was preparing a long list of insults.

Just then she saw what looked like a moving metal pipe… then another… Was she was imagining things? Eventually she sighted two people in balaclavas – and those 'pipes' were rifles with optical sights. Precision weapons. She spotted a third figure holding an enormous set of binoculars. She started – would she and Annibale be spotted too? But they were focused on the other side of the street. She moved back behind the antenna and handed the binoculars to Annibale. They stood facing each other for what seemed like an eternity.

'Police special forces. Snipers.' Annibale seemed distressed as he explained. 'They're monitoring the entire largo La Foppa, waiting for me to show up. Standard procedure for an armed and dangerous fugitive. Just in case the ground team needs backup.'

Carla shuddered with fear. They'd been discovered.

'But how did they know to find us there?'

Annibale shook his head. There was sadness in his voice.

'I don't think you meant to betray me. But as I always told my men during a terrorist hunt: sloppiness and distraction are forms of betrayal.'

Carla's face reddened with anger and hurt. 'How can you even think—'

'You're the only one I told. And *I* obviously didn't warn them!'

'Annibale…'

'Who did you tell?'

She rubbed her arms, which were damp from the heat, her run, the wave of emotions. She was overcome by dread.

'Giulio Strozzi. But you don't think—'

'Why did you tell him?'

'Because somehow he found out about that night we went into the archives. He told me I could lose my job and that he was worried for me. I had to promise to tell him everything. I

337

did. I trusted him and I still trust him. He's a piece of shit as a person, but he's always behaved professionally. He just wanted to protect me. He swore that everything I told him would stay between us. I reported on your investigation too, but I never told him about us, or about how I feel about you. I... I love you Annibale.'

'I love you too, but that's not what matters right now. Because of your carelessness, people have died, I'm a wanted man, and I would have been taken into custody if I'd shown up. They've always been one step ahead.'

Carla couldn't believe that Annibale held her responsible.

'Giulio can't have called the police! What does he have to do with anything? You can't possibly think he's involved with the murders of Alfridi or those killers!'

'He is, but that doesn't matter either right now. We can't waste time explaining or assembling clues. We have to focus on putting everything back in its place. We need to do the things that need doing. You know, you almost got me killed and you've put people I love in danger. But you've also given me a chance to look at all this from a different perspective. I should thank you.'

But he didn't. Annibale put the binoculars back in the bag and walked away before she could say anything. Not that it would've mattered.

Carla stood in that strangely surreal place until nightfall. When she left, she was in tears.

Repetto and Rossi were sitting in a black SUV with tinted windows in via Marina. Canessa got in front next to Rossi. He started the engine and drove off. Repetto had understood everything: Carla had somehow betrayed them. She was the mole. He also realised that now was not the time to ask. Canessa would need time to heal.

Another affair with a bad ending, another woman letting him down. He just wasn't meant to be with them. Damn it! Everything had seemed so right this time.

Rossi, however, was less expert in psychology.

'So? Was it her?'

'Yes.'

Canessa's reply was sharp, cutting.

Good sign, Repetto thought. *He's moving on.*

But Rossi was on a roll.

'Sorry, but how did you know it was her? Couldn't it have been me or Repetto?'

'Good point.' Canessa's sarcasm was biting. 'You're getting better.'

'So why did you exclude us?'

'I didn't. If I hadn't found out the truth from her, I would've moved on to you.'

In spite of it all, Rossi felt hurt. He thought he'd demonstrated his loyalty. He felt part of Team Canessa.

At the first red light, he looked at Repetto for comfort. 'He's kidding, right?'

Repetto grinned. 'Not at all.'

2 2

'It all fits.'

Canessa was stuffing his things into a bag. After three days in via del Carroccio, it was time to change locations. 'The secret of a safe house is never to let it become unsafe,' he'd tell his men during the Years of Lead.

Rossi was arranging a series of safe houses across the city, but Canessa told him he'd take care of the one night. He had something in mind but was playing it close, probably still burned from the Carla affair. He had to be alone. Typical Canessa.

Repetto, on the other hand, would be heading home. It was his pact with Canessa: he'd spend every evening at home with Barbara.

The guest flat was cold, but it was better that way. A transient abode. Modern furniture, not anonymous but not welcoming either. No decorations other than a few prints on the walls. On the coffee table, next to Canessa's bag, was the paper Repetto had received and delivered to 'Max'. Before Repetto could ask, Canessa told him it was undoubtedly a 'gift' from Calandra.

A photocopied police report. Thanks to the intuition of one of the forensics team, a few weeks after the events, detectives had worked out that the note claiming responsibility for the murder of Judge Lazzarini had been written on an electric typewriter. And not just any kind: it belonged to a batch of 250 machines with a defective R key: usually, the stem of the letter was supported by two serifs, the one on the left shorter than the other; on these machines, it was reversed. The numbered batch had been sold to Milan's courts in the summer of 1979. Which meant that Lazzarini's killer had worked within the same walls where Lazzarini himself had been serving the State. The mole who'd handed him to the Red Brigade and typed up the note was in there, and probably even knew him personally.

According to the report, however, the investigation had stopped there. It could have been anyone at all. The machines were all over the building, including in the press room, where journalists used them.

Canessa didn't think it had been someone from the press. However… a clerk, a secretary, a police officer, a judge… Why not? In any case, the fact was that whoever had sold Lazzarini came from the courts.

There was a post-it note on the police report. In elegant writing from a fountain pen it read:

This detail was never revealed. It was impossible to find an exact match, and it was considered too damaging to announce publicly in a country already disillusioned and so far from the end of terrorism.

Canessa had shared his thoughts with Repetto. 'All of the dead – Petri and my brother, right up to the attack on me – were clearly collateral damage linked to protecting someone or something connected with the Lazzarini murder. Now we have a name: Judge Federico Astroni.'

Repetto's jaw dropped, but Canessa put up a hand to stop his objection.

'I know, Astroni is a knight in shining armour in this country. But we know that Carla carelessly revealed information to Giulio Strozzi. And Strozzi is Astroni's biographer, his go-to reporter, his closest friend in the press. They've been closely linked since before the corruption inquiries. They both built their reputation during that period. He's the only one Strozzi could have told. And now we have a document that links the law courts to Lazzarini's murder. It can't be a coincidence.'

'Strozzi…'

'No, I don't think he's actually involved.'

'But the *camorristi*? The murders? Do you think Astroni coordinated all of that?' Repetto persisted in his role as devil's advocate. That was their dynamic.

Canessa closed his bag.

'No, he's clearly working with someone. Astroni himself is under surveillance, he's got bodyguards, he's very visible, and it's unlikely that he is in direct contact with killers or criminals. But he is in touch with someone who seems respectable and with whom his closeness wouldn't raise suspicions if it came out, but who still has room to operate. Someone ruthless but short-handed after we cleaned up their team. So they set up this whole charade to get rid of me. But they'll soon find the right killer to sic on me, and if I could choose, I'd rather I only had to watch my back with the police… We've got to stop them. And fast.'

Annibale took Calandra's paper, folded it and handed it to Repetto.

'Make some copies of this.'

'How are you going to proceed?' Repetto asked as they headed to the door.

'Like an inspector. I've been sort of winging it till now, relying on logic. I mean, we found a trail and I followed it. It's got us this far, but we need to work like good old-fashioned gumshoes. Starting with Petri and his buried treasure.'

They took the lift down in silence. When they reached the ground floor, Repetto checked the front door for anything out of the ordinary.

'All clear. I'll go ahead,' he told Canessa, 'but where are you off to?'

'Going for a rest, actually. I need a couple of hours' downtime. And then I need to find a way to get my sister-in-law out of custody.'

23

'It's going to rain later, maybe even storm. Good thing I'm leaving now. I'll miss most of it.'

Giannino Salemme lowered his car window and rested his hand against the door outside. He often did this, no matter the season or the weather.

They'd just turned onto the link road for Malpensa airport. Claudio was driving carefully and his father appreciated the concern. He'd needed to go on this trip for some time now, but he'd kept on postponing. He couldn't leave before dealing with the situation.

Canessa was still around, but he was a threat with an expiration date. Giannino had said as much to Claudio, who was still anxious to find a Panattoni-Rocco substitute.

'No, we need to lie low. Under the radar. Is that clear? Wait for me to get back from New York in a week. The police may have solved our problem for us by then. Canessa may get himself killed, or disappear. We might be lucky.'

Claudio pulled up to Arrivals. 'I don't think they'll catch him,' he said.

'Neither do I. We just need them to restrict his movement, keep him busy. All we need is a nil-nil score. *Go Naples!*'

He got out of the car and waved to his son, who revved away. Any other time, he would have sighed with concern, but he was too focused on meeting his companion in New York. His 'urgent business' was mostly with her. He hadn't told Claudio, but he did need some privacy, for heaven's sake.

*

Marta knew she wasn't the only person in Astroni's bed, and yet she wasn't lying naked in Guidoni's tiny attic flat in revenge. It was a necessity. Astroni had recently seemed preoccupied, and their latest encounter had been unsatisfying. A distracted, flaccid shag.

Marta wasn't naive. She knew her mentor was battling some sort of demon. So when Guidoni had invited her for a drink at a new place, she'd said yes. The alcohol loosened her up, but she had already planned on ending up in bed with him. She was curious about what he was like in bed.

He wasn't as kinky and refined as Astroni, but he was a strong and well-built lover. That was good enough.

He came back from the kitchen with two glasses of fine white wine. Who knew?!

Still in the mood, he let his hands wander over her breasts. And why not? They'd done the necessary; all they had to do now was wait for Canessa to fall into the trap.

She couldn't wait to question him. She wanted to know what had turned that hero to dust.

24

Canessa's regrets came like the tide, ebbing and flowing. Usually they were gentle, but more often he was pounded by a breaker, and that hurt. His thoughts of Carla were powerful and relentless. At that particular moment, however, it was Caterina Lazzarini who was moving on top of him, something that gave him both pleasure and comfort.

Unlike the journalist, Caterina was a talker – mostly dirty talk.

Her breasts kept rubbing against his face, and he'd grab them, squeeze them, tease them.

How had they ended up here?

When he'd left the place in via del Carroccio, he'd walked to the Sant'Agostino underground station. He'd needed some air, some time to think.

The disguise made him look older, like a retired office drudge on his way home from work. The urgency had been sudden. He was looking for a safe space to think, away from everything else. But he also wanted somewhere warm, with human company. A different kind of company from his usual two allies, something more relaxing. He needed a woman to help him tame the turmoil of his emotions for Carla. Even if he'd wanted to, he couldn't go to her.

So he'd made his way hopefully to via California and to Caterina. She might not ask him to stay – she might have guests, or be away – but she'd never report him.

The front door was closed, and no one came out this time. After ten minutes of waiting, and checking the building from several approaches, he rang the bell.

'Yes?'

'It's Annibale,' he whispered.

The door opened immediately.

She'd been waiting for him on the landing. Her fine blonde hair was gathered at the back of her neck and held there by a pencil. She was wearing a black tank top and a pair of jeans.

'Come in, stranger,' she teased, and he stepped into the flat.

'Caterina, I'm looking for somewhere to stay for a couple of days. I'm sorry to involve you in this. I'm sure you know the risk, I'm—'

She'd pressed her finger to his lips.

'You're a good man. I don't believe a word of what they're saying about you. I know you. Are you hungry?'

She made him a vegan dinner. 'It's my only condition for people who want to with me. I do have some good wine though.'

She laid the table, and set down a dish of fava beans and chicory, Apulian style, and a mixed salad. Annibale complimented her.

'Where did you learn how to cook?'

'Natural talent!' She laughed. 'I've always enjoyed it. I worked as a sous-chef during my travels in Peru.'

They sank into the sofa, Sauvignon in hand. Caterina lit a couple of large candles and the air filled with their scent.

She looked at him with her piercing green eyes.

'But now you have to tell me the truth.'

'So it was Petri who killed my dad?'

'Yes, that much I'm sure of.'

There was a moment of silence. Caterina finished her wine and put her glass down.

'But there was someone behind him, right?'

'Yes.'

Annibale paused, a little embarrassed. He wasn't sure he could ask her the question. He feared her reaction, but he went for it.

'Have you ever heard of Judge Astroni?'

Caterina smiled teasingly.

'I mean, he *is* quite famous...'

Annibale was about to speak but she stopped him with her hand. 'Come on, I'm joking! He was a good friend of my parents, way back from university. I don't remember meeting him back then. I remember you, but that was different.'

'And later?'

'I don't know. A lot of people came to see my mum. I'm sure that she did mention his name years later, though I wouldn't be able to tell you why. Some time before he rose to fame. I can ask her, if you want.'

Canessa thought things over in silence. Under the layer of apparently trivial ties – Lazzarini and Astroni had been colleagues, and before that fellow law students – there was something else.

'Please do, if it's not too much bother. And apologies in advance if it causes her any pain.'

'Don't worry, it won't.' Caterina stood up. 'What are you up to next?'

'I'm here to think and relax. But I'll be leaving tomorrow. It's better that way. I don't want you more involved than you already are.'

The voice of that strong child from years ago stopped him once again.

'I am already involved. You can stay as long as you need to. Come on, I'll help you make the bed.'

'I can sleep here...'

'The bed's much better.'

Canessa was lost in thought, as always when he woke up. He was pondering the life of a cop, the things he'd never done, things he'd told Repetto in confidence. Being a cop meant finding out all there was to know about Petri and his life, and the research he'd done with Carla and Alfridi had taken him forward quite some way. But he couldn't see the road ahead.

Having gained an important insight into Petri's pilgrimages to the cemeteries so early in the game had allowed him to see the broader outline. But now he needed to see the picture itself. The investigation that had started in the archives of the *Corriere* had raised the dust around the Lazzarini murder. But at the heart of that murder lay the motive for the more recent ones. All of these pieces, but he still hadn't been able to arrange them in any way that was fully comprehensible.

It was time to go back to square one. How had Petri lived? What had he done, other than move between home and office, prison and work? Had he made any friends? He wasn't thinking about the respect he'd earned in prison from Cammello. Did he have any interests? Did he correspond with anyone? Did he have any family to talk to? And what was the book he never let go of, the one both Cammello and Alfridi had mentioned?

That was where he had to start. But first he needed to free his sister-in-law.

He'd been focused on such thoughts when he noticed a presence in the darkness of his room. He reached instinctively for the Beretta on the bedside table.

The only light in the room came from a street lamp outside the window. And Caterina suddenly stepped out of the darkness into that light.

Naked.

Her body was slender and toned, with breasts pointing upwards and dark areolas. Blonde hair caressed her tanned skin, and a perfect golden triangle crowned her sex.

He looked up to find Caterina smiling, pleased to have caught him with his guard down.

Annibale thought of Carla and her self-righteousness when confronted with her failings. Right now, he was fragile and he needed the warmth of another person.

He took the hand Caterina held out to him, and pulled her into his bed.

Caterina was wild during sex, throwing herself into it, body and soul. She only stopped talking when her mouth was busy doing something else. And she was good, very good. Annibale wanted to tell her but he preferred to keep quiet in those moments. One question did escape him.

'How many men have you been with?'

She stopped to speak, but her hand kept busy.

'I've lost count.'

She moved her mouth back onto him, then straddled him, moving as if to music.

'Fuck me like I'm my mother!'

Canessa's clear embarrassment amused her.

She whispered a confession. 'She told me about the day when something could have happened between you, but you didn't catch her drift. Or didn't want to. Fuck me, now, like you would've fucked her.'

Annibale pushed her onto her knees and took her from behind, forcing a moan from her. He felt her orgasm build and when she cried, arching her back, her hair stuck to her back with sweat, he came inside her.

If he'd been hoping to keep his thoughts at bay and forget all those bloody deaths, in that moment, he definitely succeeded.

When he woke up – he hadn't slept for long – the sun was already high in the sky, and Caterina was no longer in bed with him. He looked around the house for her, but she'd gone out and left him a note and some breakfast.

*I hope to find you here when I get back. I'm hoping to shock my neighbour
again tonight like we did last night.*

The neighbour! Why hadn't he thought of that earlier?

25

Carla walked over to the desk of Pippo Locatelli, deputy managing editor for the news section. For at least two weeks he'd been
deputising for Strozzi who, despite all his stories of a 'troubled
marriage' to women he wanted to sleep with, was on his regular
family holiday. Every year, last two weeks of June. As soon as
schools broke up, Strozzi would take off with his wife and kids,
almost always to North America. That year it was a Canadian
coast to coast. Then in July and August, he'd send his wife to
Santa Margherita, where her parents had a big house, while he
spent his time in Milan chasing after interns and seasonal subs.

He left this morning, Carla calculated, *so he should still be on the flight.*
He wouldn't land until late, Italian time. If his bootlickers wanted
to tell him something, they wouldn't be able to until he landed.

Carla had been keeping the scoop up her sleeve for three
days. She hadn't got over the pain of Annibale's disappearance,
but at least she had something of his, and the knowledge dulled
her pain somewhat.

She grabbed the anonymous yellow file from her desk and
walked across the news room to Locatelli's desk. Strozzi's deputy
was a balding fifty-year-old, still in great shape. He sat there
reading a sports paper and looking blissful. He could never take
a moment for himself like that with his boss breathing down his
neck. The ball-buster's holidays were the time when everyone got

a breather: flexible office hours, fewer humiliations, longer breaks. The mood was good.

So finding Carla Trovati on the warpath definitely soured his mood.

'What?' he asked, annoyed.

'Can I have a moment?'

Locatelli sighed and folded his paper. He crossed his hands in resignation.

'What's up?'

'Let's go into Strozzi's office.'

His eyes widened. *What*?! The boss never locked the door in case someone needed a file, a report, a phone number during his absence – and he never kept anything compromising around – he was too smart for that. But he always warned against entering the office without a valid reason.

Locatelli was about to object but Carla had already stepped in. After a quick check to make sure all Strozzi's snitches were out, he followed her begrudgingly.

'Do you remember Canessa's aunt's story about the man who hid some drugs in the restaurant bathroom to frame Canessa? The drugs were never recovered.'

'I do. But it doesn't add up.'

'She gave the police a description of the man, but they didn't believe her either.'

Carla pulled two photos out of the file and placed them next to each other on the desk. Locatelli studied them.

'I remember this too. We reported the aunt's version – it was news, after all – but we never published the portrait because Strozzi argued that it was a red herring. So why are you showing me two copies of the same image?'

Carla smiled triumphantly. 'Because they're the same man, it's true, but they weren't taken by the same person, nor did they come from the same witness account.'

Locatelli was paying attention now. 'What do you mean?'

'The one on the left is from Canessa's aunt's witness report, while the other is from Napoleone Canessa's neighbour in Reggio Emilia.'

'Shit!'

The handful of journalists in the office looked over at Locatelli. He piped down, only just realising he'd yelled.

'How did you get the one from Reggio Emilia?'

'Canessa's lawyer, along with this.' She took out three sheets of paper stapled together. 'This is the official witness report of Cosima Maggese, the Canessas' neighbour from across the street. She saw this man entering their house one night when no one was home.'

'So…'

Carla interrupted him. 'I've been to Reggio. The woman is old, but she's very lucid and has excellent eyesight. She gave me the exact same story as her report, verbatim.'

'So why didn't she tell the police?'

Carla smiled again. 'I quote: *If they aren't smart enough to come and ask me, I'm certainly not going to go to them. But if anyone asks, I'll tell them what I know and what I saw.* Her words.'

Locatelli stared at her, transfixed. She was sly: she'd been sitting on this scoop for days now, waiting for Strozzi to piss off. The boss would've buried the story, or at least hedged it with *maybes* and *likes* and *who knows*. He had too many ties to the judges, the ones who'd given him all the juicy previews during the corruption investigations. *Fuck, fuck*. This was the perfect chance to kick Strozzi up the arse, along with his friends in high places, both inside and outside the paper. Happily, the chief editor hated Strozzi, given his close ties to the publisher and the financial and political VIPs in Milan. Strozzi was clearly out to get him, the fucker.

An opportunity like this might never come again. He wouldn't waste it. And if things went balls-up, he could blame it on this pushy babe. He stood up, handed her the papers and opened the door.

'Let's go and see the chief editor.'

26

At 6 p.m., the sun was still high in the sky. Cooler air had yet to fall on one of the darkest days for Milan's courts of law. The lobby was swarming with journalists, wolves out for blood. Anyone's. If the *Corriere* scoop had been based on unfounded rumours, they could've been sent packing, back to the office. But the story had held, and now this shapeless mass of beasts was ready to maul the magistrates. The internet was already buzzing with terrifying comments. The Association for Families of the Victims of Terrorism issued a scathing press release requesting that the inquest be fast-tracked, an inquest that had 'carelessly accused a public icon in the struggle against terrorism, a man who had helped like few others to turn the tide in a battle the State was losing'.

'Look, I've already told you about this! Never mind: I'll say it again. Whenever we're investigating someone famous, I get phone calls from politicians, lobbyists, middlemen of all sorts, people I have very little in common with. However, when we went after Canessa, it was my *friends* who started calling, the famous and the not so famous, and all claiming I was mad to let something like this happen...'

'Antonio…' Federico Astroni tried to interrupt, but Judge Savelli stopped him with a raised hand.

Canessa had damaged his heroic reputation by playing the fugitive. With the *Corriere* story, however, the media had splashed his image around to remind everyone of his previous success: Canessa with the general; Canessa in uniform talking to his team on the site of an attack; Canessa dragging handcuffed terrorists behind him; Canessa scolding officers for not having covered Lazzarini's body; Canessa leaving the hospital after being shot in via Gaeta; Canessa as remembered by ninety-year-old General Verde: 'He saved my life.'

Savelli went on. 'Now I'm getting calls from politicians. My enemies are gloating and my friends are distressed, because a new law reform is about to go to the vote. This story could change the laws on wiretapping and the statute of limitations in ways that would hamper our work. And what can I say to any of them? Nothing.'

The Bossini-Guidoni duo sat in front of Savelli's desk looking exhausted. Guidoni was haggard and perspiring while Marta, usually impeccable, looked ten years older. They'd just come back from Reggio Emilia, where they'd questioned Maggese's widow.

'How did it go with the widow?' Savelli asked.

Guidoni shook his head. 'She confirmed everything.'

With his usual cunning, Astroni attempted to poke holes in the story.

'She's of a certain age, it was nighttime, she might've—'

Guidoni interrupted. 'Look, just drop it. She's a force of nature. We tried to trap her, hoping to find out just how trustworthy she might be. We questioned her for hours. She made us coffee and offered us parmigiano and fried snacks, and then just

354

as we attempted to poke holes in her story one last time, she gets up, goes to the wall behind her and pulls down a framed photo of this guy. There was a medal on the frame. She shows us. She goes: "My maiden name is Falaschi and this is my father Zeno, deputy commander of the Garibaldi brigade, active in the Reggio Emilia area, gold medal for his action during the Resistance. The Gestapo captured him, tortured him for five days, then shot him on the main square. He said nothing. I'm his daughter in everything I do. If he resisted the Gestapo, I'm certainly not going to fall for your silly games. I said what I had to say. Now get out of my house." There's no demolishing her testimony.'

'Release Napoleone Canessa's widow tonight. Take her home to her daughter. I want her out before the main evening news – we need it shown on TV. If you get a move on, we can still make it. Let's start with damage control, then move on to the next point,' Savelli said.

Marta and Guidoni said nothing. But Astroni wouldn't let go. He'd called Strozzi at the paper only to find, to his dismay, that his journalist friend was on holiday. He felt betrayed but couldn't give up now.

'Savelli, let's think about this. Maybe it's too early to release her. Canessa did go on the run. Let's say this witness is telling the truth: why didn't he leave the drugs behind to confirm his aunt's story?'

Savelli stood up, folded up his copy of the *Corriere* and placed it inside his leather bag, a gift from his wife. He went to the coat hook and took down his jacket. He didn't understand Astroni's insistence. From the very beginning, he'd shown an almost morbid curiosity about the case. He'd always been someone who saw everyone as guilty, but his persistence in this case felt like something personal against Canessa.

'Enough, Federico. Release the woman, tell the press. Let me think about Canessa, and we'll talk about it tomorrow.'

Astroni made one last attempt: 'It's already late, protocol—'

'Track down the relevant judge, drag him away from whatever he's doing and threaten him—' he turned to Guidoni, 'with a gun to his head. I mean it literally. Call me if he refuses. I want her fucking out of there within two hours.'

Savelli's swearing, a total aberration, was heard all the way down the corridor – and it surprised him more than it did anyone else. With his hand on the door, he turned round to face the others, who hadn't moved an inch.

'Well? Are you planning on spending the night in my office? Don't you have work to do? Get on with it!'

'Thank you, Mister President, yes … No, of course… Yes, our hero… You're too kind, of course, we need to bet on the right horse… A good game, but it's not over yet. We have a couple more surprises. Too kind, Mister President, I definitely will. My regards to the wife.'

Calandra hung up and exchanged a look of triumph with the grey man.

'That was the president of the justice committee, the one who signed the reform,' he explained.

Since waking up to the news of the *Corriere* scoop, Calandra had spent most of his day answering the phone to compliments from his political contacts. He hadn't done anything, apart from realising that Canessa wouldn't be stopped by *them*. Fuck, the terrorists couldn't stop him, so how could these newcomers even try?

He was so happy that he took off his jacket again, and placed it on the sofa.

'Any news of Canessa?'

'No. He's in Milan somewhere. Last sighting was two days ago. What do you think he's planning?'

Calandra picked up his slate-blue Corneliani jacket, and tidied his braces before slipping it back on.

'My friend, he's planning his final attack. If I know him, he's already onto something. In any case, tonight we celebrate. I'm taking you out to dinner.'

The invisible man almost fainted. 'Your excellency... I... But the surveillance...'

Calandra slapped his shoulder.

'Screw the surveillance. Enough work for today. We did a good job, we deserve a break. Have you ever been to the Pergola del Cavalieri? My friend Heinz Beck runs it.'

27

Annibale sat at the large wooden table in the kitchen of Caterina's flat. She'd left that morning. He'd originally planned to be there for three days, but he'd stayed for almost two weeks. Caterina's place set his brain on fire – though who knows – it could have been the satisfaction of falling asleep beside her every night after a whirlwind of passionate sex.

The previous night, however, had been the last with that angelic creature. She'd taken him to extreme depths. No fears, no inhibitions. Her entire life was like that. After almost two hours of roller-coaster sex, they'd finally collapsed, exhausted.

'I'm off tomorrow. I'm going to see my boyfriend in London, but you can stay as long as you want. I'll leave you a set of keys.' She kissed him lightly on his lips and smiled in the dim light.

'You're a fascinating woman. I'm going to treasure these days with you for a long time to come. But I had no idea you had a partner.'

She laughed.

'Patrick's Australian. I really love him and I think I'm going to marry him. But when I meet someone like you I can't help myself. It doesn't happen that often these days.'

She rested her head on his shoulder, and he wrapped an arm around her. He could still feel her all over his skin in the cool breeze of the fan rotating above them.

'My mother told me the same thing happened to her. But it stopped once she met my dad. She may have been tempted, but she never gave in. I think that's a good compromise. What do you think? Anyone waiting for you out there?'

Annibale stroked her cheek. As if in silent agreement, they hadn't mentioned each other's personal relationships, despite talking about almost everything else. 'Yes, there is someone. She's about your age. But she did something extremely dangerous, and we've parted ways. That's why I came here. I needed a beautiful woman to distract me. It helps me think. Of course, I'm a gentleman, so I never thought...'

'Idiot.' They both laughed.

'Oh, I almost forgot.' She sat up in bed. 'I asked Mum about Astroni. She was surprised, kind of worried. She kept stalling but I insisted. When Dad died, she promised to tell me the truth, always. I've kept her to it. I got a lot out of her at the time.' She looked at him. 'Anyway, she told me she'd had a brief fling with him, just before she met my dad. But he wasn't like you.'

'What do you mean?'

'He didn't understand. When she told him it was over, he lost his mind.'

*

Astroni again.

What Canessa had turned up so far clearly showed who the main characters were in this story. But he was still missing the plot, the thread that tied everything together: facts, events and names that, as they currently stood, told him nothing. He was missing a motive, and a couple of actors – though the latter would follow.

Petri was the only one who could link things up. He would have to start from there, again. Thanks to Carla's scoop, the pressure from law enforcement had loosened. His sister-in-law had been released and had pleaded on TV: 'Annibale, turn yourself in. Together we can prove that this was all made up.'

Sweet, sensible Sara. Seeing her return home and hug her daughter (*my niece*, Canessa thought with tenderness) had made him happier than he could remember. Sara had made her appeal in good faith, and maybe at someone's suggestion. But he couldn't do as she suggested. If he turned himself in, the whole investigation would be put on hold again. And his enemies would have enough time to set another trap or cut the thread. He couldn't trust them.

He would come out of hiding only when he had proof of the conspiracy, and when he'd tied up all those loose ends.

In a double-knot.

28

'What do we know about Petri?'

He started with a question to Repetto, and ended up grabbing one of the handles on the bus that went from the Opera prison to the city centre. At 6.30 in the morning, it was packed and boiling. Number 222 started in Pieve Emanuele and reached Vigentino, the terminal for tram number 24. The tram went up towards the Duomo, but Petri had got off at Crocetta, where he made his second transfer of the morning to the number 3 service on the underground, the yellow line. Petri had taken that route every morning when he left the prison. Annibale was repeating his movements in the hope that it might throw up an answer, help him out of the current impasse. They were reconstructing Petri's life, starting with that fundamental question – which they'd ignored when they dived directly into the *Corriere della Sera* archives.

Since Annibale was keeping a low profile, Repetto had gone to visit Petri's sister on the outskirts of Turin. The marshal had ended up in the middle of a vast council estate, where his presence was immediately noted by the residents, even those with nothing to hide. *Cop.*

Repetto knew those looks. He wasn't expecting much from the visit, but he came well armed with patience. The lift was out of order, so he walked up the seven flights of stairs. He'd expected them to be filthy, but found the building as a whole surprisingly clean. Poverty and desperation were everywhere, to be sure, but he also sensed a desire to live with dignity.

Petri's sister was ten years younger than he was. She might have been a chain-smoker, but she kept herself well, despite the cloud of cigarette smoke that surrounded her.

Repetto showed his badge. It was out of date, but Simona Petri hadn't seen a cop in a while, and wouldn't have cared anyway. Repetto had neither the right nor the authority to be there questioning her, but she invited him in without protest.

'That drug affair was bullshit, excuse my French. My brother got up to all sorts, but he'd never deal drugs. Your colleagues are idiots. No offence.'

Repetto grimaced.

'Well, even if they took offence, I wouldn't care: they *are* idiots.'

Simona was warming up to him.

'I'm sorry if I seem forward, but do you have any idea what he did? Did you know anything about your brother's life? Any detail, no matter how trivial, could be useful to us.'

She poured herself some lemonade from an ice-filled jug. Repetto had already had two glasses; it was excellent. She thought about it for a while.

'Hm. Well, he called me and told me he'd discovered something about himself. That's what he said. "I discovered something about myself." And I went, "So what? What do you mean?" And he goes, "Just that". It was about a year ago. Then nothing, until a week before his death he calls me. We chat for a while. I ask him, "So, how's the discovery?" "Coming along," he says. "I'm going forward, one step at a time. I'm following the truth right now." He died seven days later.'

On his way home, he got a call from Canessa.

'You've been in Turin for a while,' he opened.

'Simona is good company, as they used to say, very welcoming. She makes excellent lemonade.'

'Hey, big guy.'

'Oh please. I got very little out of her. Take down what I tell you.'

'The truth shall set you free,' Canessa commented.

'What's that about?'

'Nobody. Everyone.'

Repetto knew these moments well, when everything stagnates and the investigation grinds to a halt. And yet the visit had confirmed something: Petri was going through some sort of turmoil and he'd wanted to share. With Canessa. And given that Canessa was neither a psychologist nor a priest, that something must've been a story. It had to be about the Lazzarini murder. Admittedly though, there was no trace of what he might have revealed. Yet Canessa was convinced that someone like Petri always had an exit plan ready, a safety exit. Insurance.

Buried treasure.

The time had come to retrace Petri's life, hour by hour, step by step. So Canessa forced a tired Rossi to drive him to Pieve Emanuele, where he took the bus Petri had taken every day until a few months earlier.

29

Giannino Salemme was dripping with sweat. The air over Malpensa was a claggy film of humidity. Only the driver was there to pick him up this time; Claudio didn't show up. They'd had a heated discussion during his last phone call from New York. Salemme senior had been euphoric: his gorgeous student lover had been particularly great, and all his worries had vanished. He'd felt good, and didn't share his son's alarm.

'Come on, be a little optimistic,' he'd murmured from across the ocean.

'Dad, it's better if I come and join you. Things here are getting seriously out of hand.'

'So what – we run away? I thought you were less flighty. You seemed so on it. I was hoping you'd grown up a bit, but here you are, trembling like a child.'

His son had shown no sign of being offended. 'Dad, even though he's still a wanted man, no one's looking for Canessa here. After those two E-FITs of Carletti – for the record, I sent him to Hungary where he's got family – no one is buying the Canessa link to drugs.'

'It doesn't matter: we got him out of the game for a while. And there's no way he'll find anything, because there's nothing to find.'

His son had been furious; he'd heard it clearly even on the phone. But he was holding back, and that was a good sign. He had grown up in some ways at least.

'So why did we set up these killings?'

'Because it's always good to prune dead branches.'

'If you say so.'

No one had ever got Giannino Salemme in a corner, and it wouldn't happen now.

He waved to the driver and handed him his luggage. He moved towards the car, mopping his brow in the morning heat.

Annibale Canessa was lying on the sofa in Rossi's safe house number three, in largo Rio de Janeiro. He was waiting for Repetto's evening debrief and thinking about Petri's commute to and from the Opera prison. He'd taken the route four times, changing his appearance each time – beard, moustache, glasses, t-shirt, a heavy jacket that made him sweat way too much – and leaving enough time between trips to confuse anyone who might've been watching. But no one was following him. Everyone on the bus was wiped out by the heat, their heads either stuck through the small windows or craning towards them to catch the slightest breeze.

Despite his freedom, Annibale hadn't found a single lead. He looked around. This third safe house seemed the most welcoming, but also the strangest. It was on the ground floor, with barred windows looking directly onto the street. Despite this small concession towards security, it was a cheerful place. There were about two dozen paintings on the walls: men and women in ponchos, clearly South American, watching over the place. The Latino atmosphere was rounded off by colourful sofas, chequered pouffes, even a strange llama tapestry. Bolivian? Peruvian? Whatever it was, Canessa liked it and he hoped to stay there a couple of extra days.

The doorbell rang. Canessa grabbed the Beretta, and leaned against the wall next to the door. 'Who is it?'

'It's me,' Repetto replied. He'd lost a lot of weight since his injury. 'Barbara doesn't know whether to curse you or thank you for helping me shift the pounds.'

They went to work. Canessa reported on his trips while Repetto took notes and drew lines. They were trying to find something, but without knowing where to look.

At one point, studying the timing of the route, Repetto muttered, almost to himself, 'I mean, he could've taken his time leaving the prison, if he had to wait in piazza Duca D'Aosta for Ragiomatica to open. Maybe the owner gave him a set of keys.'

Canessa froze in the midst of opening a beer. 'What time did his shift start?'

'Nine.'

He grabbed his notes. 'He didn't arrive at eight, and he didn't wait around. Alfridi told me something – where is it?' He rifled through his notes. 'Here: *I'd see him come out of the underground, and we'd often walk into the office together.*'

'So he didn't just wait around?'

'He did wait, but somewhere else. He'd get off somewhere earlier on the route, so we need to find out where. I'd better take a closer look. I missed something.'

'It's not easy to spot from a bus.'

'You're right!' Canessa sounded like he'd had a revelation. 'I'll walk. But from the final stop of the 24. It doesn't make sense before then.'

'It'll be dangerous to walk.'

'I'll ask Rossi to follow me in the car in case I need to make a quick escape.'

Canessa was leaning against one of the pillars outside the building, sheltering from the morning sun and looking at the church. A strange building, with a cross on its façade and an imposing steel statue of the Virgin Mary. It had been hard to see from the tram, that was for sure, as it wasn't on a main road but an inner square at the end of a street crossing corso di Porta Vigentina. The Church of the Madonna of Fatima was a modern construction in the limbo between the suburbs and city centre. He'd spotted it walking back up the road, but he went on, filing it mentally under 'irrelevant details'. He'd already walked another two hundred metres when he'd had one of his sudden hunches.

Petri's change, the mysterious small book, his search for truth, 'one step at a time', visiting the cemeteries to atone for his past. It wasn't so strange. It had happened to many before him. Prison changes your perspective, forces you to look at yourself. So simple, so banal, and because of that, hard to understand, especially in the third millennium.

If I'd gone to church with my aunt, as she's always wanted me to, I might have thought of this sooner! he told himself off as he retraced his steps.

Canessa had always considered Petri's behaviour – the candles, the flowers – as some sort of reparation, an acknowledgement of the evil he'd done and nothing more. Since his discovery of Petri's pilgrimage to the tombs, he'd taken a secular view of Petri's decision, and it left no room for any alternative explanation. He'd thought it had been a moral impulse, and that was saying something. But maybe it was an urge that came from somewhere deeper... It was a risk, but he had nothing to lose and plenty of time.

The bell rang for 7 a.m. Mass. If Petri's newfound depth was real, he would soon find out, of that he was certain. He gestured for Rossi to park the car and get a coffee – not for the coffee itself, but to avoid sitting in the car for too long and raising suspicion.

He stepped into the church and crossed himself.

30

Three days after Canessa's visit to the Church of the Madonna of Fatima, on a Friday evening, northwestern Italy and the entire Tyrrhenian coast, nearly all the way south to Naples, was hit by a storm. One had been forecast, though not at such strength. It was no summer storm, rather a full-blown monsoon, with whirlwinds that wrecked marinas, bungalows and coastal chalets and bit into produce fields.

Surprised by the sudden downpour on his way home, Giannino Salemme somehow managed not to get completely soaked, zigzagging under balconies and ledges. But it had dampened his mood, so he decided to cancel his evening with a willing young woman. The architecture student (or so she'd claimed) in the new bar where he'd stopped for happy hour had mentioned her rates with a twinkle in her eye. Rates? During their initial chat, she seemed to be hanging off his every word... The idea of paying for sex set off an alarm in him. It was easier just to cancel. Fuck her. Or rather, let some other fool do the dirty.

He called his favourite pizzeria in via Vincenzo Monti, and ordered a pizza with Gorgonzola plus a few snacks.

Claudio Salemme had been at home with two young women since earlier that afternoon. He didn't feel like working. He didn't actually feel like having fun, either. He didn't want anything. For the first time in his life, he didn't recognise himself: he was worried about his future. He'd always lived day to day, but that undertaking, the first in which he'd fought in the trenches with his father, had changed his outlook on life. At first he'd been excited, galvanised. He'd enjoyed the sense of danger and he hadn't considered the consequences. Until a week earlier, 'consequences' were an abstract concept. Not any more. He was waiting for the backlash to everything they'd set in motion by killing Pino Petri, Napoleone Canessa, and the rest. He'd never paid for anything in his life, despite his worst behaviour, from the school bullying and his disgusting attitudes towards women, to fights for the hell of it, car crashes and the first real crimes with his father. He'd never been afraid of consequences, always sure he'd come out of it just fine. He had his protector, his father, to thank.

Right now, all he wanted to do was run away, but he was even more afraid of Salemme senior. Had he been out of the picture, Claudio would already be on a plane to the Cayman Islands, where he could dip into their most sizeable offshore account.

He sat watching the two women pleasing each other: at any other time, the blonde on brunette action would have really got him going. But now he felt not a speck of desire to join in the fun.

It was Carla's shift at the *Corriere*. Since Strozzi had come back from holiday, their interaction had dwindled to nothing. Previously, his slimy nature would have led him to compliment her for the scoop, but he was furious: during his break he'd been plagued night and day with phone calls from his legal contacts, accusing him of high treason. It was enough that he had to put up with his family for two weeks, but this had screwed up everything. He'd come back two days earlier.

When he showed up at the office again, he'd nodded to Carla, and that had been it. Before, when she was on the night shift, Strozzi would find excuses to stay behind. Not any more. He left early now.

It was definitely better this way: she'd finally stopped thinking about her night with him. Now she was focused on his deceit, on how he'd repaid her professional trust. Whatever she'd told him he'd passed on to someone else. But who?

Carla dialled Annibale's number: no answer. This had been going on ever since he'd discovered her betrayal.

The rain was turning into a storm.

Federico Astroni was finishing up his indictment, the one reserved for the last politician who hadn't come crawling to him. The trial was expected to open four days from now. He wrote by hand, on the living-room table. No Friday evening company for him. He wasn't in the mood, wasn't up to dealing with human company, even less anyone's physical needs. In any case, his harem seemed to have disbanded. The wealthy ladies had disappeared, and Marta Bossini no longer even said hello. She actually looked at him in disgust, in a way that hadn't happened to him since 1992. The prosecutor was sure she was having a fling with the gym rat, Guidoni. And she held him responsible, he could tell, for pushing her onto the drug-trafficking trail, for having to hunt down Canessa and then leaving her alone to face the aftermath. She wasn't wrong. Having gone down that route and stumbled, she realised her career was now in jeopardy. The investigation had reached a dead end, and even though Canessa still eluded them, no one believed he was involved with drugs. In a matter of hours, days at most, the allegations would be dropped.

Where was the damned colonel? What was he doing? Astroni wanted to be alone and to work on that upcoming trial. He hoped for darkness to fall and a deep sleep to free him from all of this, from his thoughts and worries. But even when he managed to fall asleep, Federico Astroni always woke up tired and tense. The situation was making him jittery, just like all those years ago.

Chief Magistrate Calandra was in Sabaudia with his special lady friend, the one with the red thong (he was obsessed with lingerie and he liked to categorise his lovers according to the colour and size of their lingerie). He'd promised her a night-time swim, and they had got wet, but not from their swim.

He'd brought a hamper with a selection of treats from the best delicatessen in Rome: *foie gras*, pan brioche, chicken thighs in aspic, caviar, a few slices of Pont-L'Èvêque, his favourite cheese, a bottle of Sauternes and one of champagne. Calandra had laid towels on the beach and placed the hamper between them, and then she'd taken his hand and invited him to stroll along the beach. He'd removed his socks and shoes, rolled up his trousers. Calandra wasn't exactly a romantic, but his optimism about the Canessa situation was making him distracted and sentimental, less alert to signs of a storm. Any other time, and he would have noticed the black clouds gathering on the horizon. But how could you focus on the sky when you were hand-in-hand with such an angelic babe? They were walking along blissfully when the sky opened on them. Calandra turned back for the basket.

'We can't leave all this good food here!'

Now they sat shivering in the car as they sped back to the five-star hotel. A shame not to be able to finish that romantic moment on the beach. Calandra looked at the creature next to him, her tight dress highlighting the lack of any clothing other than the thong...

At least the night wouldn't be a total waste.

Annibale Canessa parked the car between two chestnut trees. He spotted the signs of heavy rain in the distance and changed as quickly as he could. He needed to reach his destination before the storm broke.

31

The sound of the crackling wood fire brought him unexpected joy. A raging storm, with wind blowing through trees that his grandfather had planted in the garden, now grown tall and strong, brought back memories of distant summers and of storms suddenly arriving, just like now: the children, including himself, would run into the house, their faces glued to the window on the lake, squealing in fear at the waves crashing over the boats in the dock, the trees threatening to blow away in the wind.

Milan's public prosecutor, Antonio Savelli, made for that same window. The fire had been lit by the old caretaker, whose experience told him that although it was late June, the night would be cool. It was just like old times, with the waves crashing over the dock and the trees rustling furiously. Savelli was utterly captivated by it, and he hadn't wanted to renounce his solitary weekend in the family villa on Lake Maggiore, where the gem of his fleet, the *Alessia I* awaited him.

He walked over to the comfy armchairs in front of the fireplace, deciding to stay there for a while to warm up, before heading to the kitchen for some food left by the caretaker's wife. His security detail all slept and ate in the annexe, coming over to check at regular intervals. A police car was parked in front of the main gate, too. Savelli felt safe inside these walls.

So the shock was entirely real when he sat down in his favourite of the two armchairs. He froze halfway, legs bent, his behind hovering ridiculously above the cushion.

In the other armchair, a gun casually resting on his right thigh, sat Annibale Canessa.

'Please, your honour, have a seat. Make yourself at home.'

He was struck by the former Carabiniere's wry humour. Nevertheless, he sat down.

'You're out of your mind, out there—'

'Yes, good point: and it's probably better for them to stay out there. If everyone behaves, no one gets hurt. I don't intend to cause any harm or suffering, but you need to work with me.'

Savelli nodded. After the initial shock, his mind was firing on all cylinders. If he'd come all the way here, Canessa wasn't planning on shooting anyone, but he wasn't intending to turn himself in either, or he wouldn't have the gun. What was he after?

'How did you get here?'

Canessa offered him a half smile. 'The same way I'll be leaving, but it's better if you don't know. For everyone's sake.'

'What do you want?'

'To tell you a story.'

'If you're here to give me your version of your situation, there are approp—'

Canessa interrupted him by raising his hand. 'Listen, there is no time to follow *protocol*,' he emphasised the word. 'We need to be swift. All I'm asking is one favour: listen to me.'

Savelli found his irony again. 'Do I have a choice?'

'You do. If you don't want to hear what I have to say, I'll leave, but the consequences will be distressing for everyone.'

Savelli realised from the man's expression that he had to hear him out.

'Go on, I'm listening.'

Canessa pointed to a laptop on the table between the armchairs.

'In there you'll find a DVD that explains the reasons behind Petri's murder, and everything that followed.' Canessa paused. 'But first you need to hear how I got to it.'

'Keep talking.' Savelli had always known that Canessa wasn't mad, but he was now realising that maybe what he had was actually important. They'd all underestimated him. Canessa had captured his attention.

'Four days ago, I stepped into a church in Milan, the Madonna of Fatima in Vigentino. It was 7 a.m., and first Mass was starting.

I stayed for its entirety. There weren't many of us, all women except for me and an elderly man. It can't have lasted longer than twenty, twenty-five minutes. During the service, I got the impression that the priest – in his seventies, but full of an energy that made him look younger – was staring at me. Just an impression at first. I was, shall we say, incognito. But I soon realised he was actually looking at me, almost as if he'd expected me to be there. So when Mass ended and the others left, I stayed behind. Ten minutes later, the priest walked out of the sacristy and came to sit next to me.'

'You must be Colonel Canessa.'

'Yes.'

'I was expecting you.' The priest paused. 'Giuseppe told me that if anything went wrong, sooner or later, you'd show up. *If anyone can make it here, it's Colonel Canessa.* He was right, may he rest in peace.'

Canessa listened in silence. The priest stood up. 'Please, come with me.' Annibale followed him into the sacristy. It wasn't what he expected, and it looked instead like a cross between kitchen and office. It was a wide room, full of furniture.

'Oh, by the way, I'm Don Filippo.'

They shook hands.

'Coffee?'

'Please, Father.'

They sat at the table and sipped coffee made by the priest. Annibale complimented him.

'I know, I know, it's a bit like that song, the one by De André about the *camorrista...*'

'Don Raffaé.'

373

The priest stood up again, went to a cupboard and took out a shoe box. He placed it on the table. 'That's the one. He sings that the recipe for the coffee made by the inmate was given to him by his *mammà*. That's my case too. But enough small talk. I imagine you must have questions. I mean, if you're here you already know the answer to one of them. Yes, Giuseppe,' he still called him by his first name, 'found faith. It happened in odd circumstances, as often with the paths that lead to the Lord. He was working in the prison library and one day they took him to the storage room and asked him to sort the old books, keeping any that might interest the prison's "contemporary audience", if you'll allow me the term, and those that could be repaired. Out with the rest. In that pile of books, Giuseppe found a small one, the one he started carrying around, wrapped in newspaper. It's called *A Little Goodness*.'

Another pause, before the priest continued. 'I'd never heard of it either. I wouldn't call it one of our major means of conversion. Even if I handed it to one of the oldest, most passionate of our faithful, they'd be quite baffled. But to Giuseppe, that book was the illumination on the road to Damascus. All he needed were the few words in the preface. So one day, he ends up here, with his trail of blood and desire to convert. He didn't want to repent, but I told him he must. He had to repent before God; he had no other choice. So he did, and I welcomed him in. But there was another step: he had to tell the truth, give in to human justice, render unto Caesar what belongs to Caesar. It took him a little longer to come round to that.'

Don Filippo fought to hold back his tears.

'He started coming every morning. He stayed to one side, didn't want to be recognised. All of our regulars saw him, but he never showed his face full-on. And in any case, who would remember him among our elderly visitors? Afterwards he'd stay behind with me, like you just did, to have a coffee and talk, for maybe fifteen, twenty minutes. We talked a lot, and he started confessing his sins. He told me his story. He was embarking on his path. I obviously can't tell you what he told me during confession. He was baptised and he attended his first Holy Communion, but not his Confirmation. He was going to do that at the end of June. Then one morning, he shows up with this box and asks me to keep it for him. The book is probably also in there, if it wasn't on him when he died. He told me it was a sort of insurance. *Not for me, but for the truth, Father. Please take this, as you take my words during confession and with the same sacrament. Don't hand it over to anyone, no matter what happens to me. No one – not the police, not the magistrates. No one, apart from Colonel Annibale Canessa. This is a photo of him, he's younger in the picture, but you'll recognise him.* I did, immediately, despite your disguise – but don't worry, I'm very good.' Don Filippo smiled at him. 'I was frightened. And I was right to be. Three days later, he was killed. That's all there is to it, really. The box is yours. Would you like to pray with me for Giuseppe? He did some horrific things and he was a cruel man, but he acknowledged his actions before God. And it's never too late to embrace Him.'

'I'm not good at praying, Father. I never remember the words.'

'I'll think of the words. You can join me in silence.'

Antonio Savelli was enraptured by the story. Outside, the storm had calmed, but the humidity of a house used to the heat and suddenly plunged back into cold weather was starting to creep over them.

'Can I place some more wood on the fire?' he asked. Canessa nodded. Savelli came back to the armchair.

'So where's the box? What was inside?' Savelli asked.

'The box is safe. The book was inside. It was written by another priest, Don Giulio Cantù and printed in 1907. It's old and very well thumbed. Stuffed with iconography. It's mostly prayers, but at its core, it's a rewriting of Scripture, with moral stories, sermons and explanations. The priest was right: it's not a modern tool. But it was enough to convert Petri.'

'Did he want to confess?'

Canessa smiled. 'Mostly, he wanted to ask forgiveness. I found out he'd been taking flowers and candles to the tombs of his victims. You can confirm with their families.'

'Really?' Savelli grew more surprised with every detail. 'I still don't get what his conversion has to do with his death, though.'

Canessa, his hand still on the gun, drew something out of a bag propped against the chair: papers. He handed them to Savelli.

'This is a transcription of Don Filippo's deposition, and his witness report on the contents of the box, which I opened in his presence. Besides the book, the box contained Petri's last will and confession, which he typed up and printed out, and also recorded on DVD and VHS. The VHS is the original. Petri had it converted to DVD format, and the written version is a summary.'

Savelli felt his phone buzz in his jacket. Canessa heard it too. He touched his gun and said calmly, 'Answer it.'

Savelli complied. 'Yes? Yes, everything's fine, thanks. I'm about to head up to bed. I should be able to take the boat out tomorrow. Thank you.' He hung up.

'Now what?'

Canessa turned to the laptop, opened it and typed something. 'Don't you want to know what's in Petri's will and confession? Aren't you curious? All you have to do is press ENTER.'

Savelli remained immobile for some time. He had always been an honest man, honest to the core. And discovering the truth had always been a moral imperative for him. At that moment, however, he was afraid of discovering this particular truth. Rather than setting him free, it threatened to put him in shackles.

Urged on by his conscience, however, he dismissed the thought and angrily pressed ENTER.

1979

September

(with a third-millennium introduction by Petri)

(A storage room can be seen, or a cabinet, framed by the computer webcam. There's a chair and to the left, what looks like a photocopier. Behind the chair, some wooden shelving is stacked with office paper stock, toilet and kitchen rolls; the tip of a broom handle can be seen. A man appears in front of the camera: Petri. He sits.)

My name is Giuseppe Petri. I was known as 'Pino' when I was working as a criminal. I was born in Turin, on the 6th of January 1946. My family is from Pescocostanzo in the Abruzzo. They migrated north to work in the factories like many others. I have a younger sister. My parents' two salaries meant I was able to go to school. I liked literature, but I always thought that instead of going to university, as the son of working people, I should focus on work. So I signed up for accounting, got my diploma, and was employed as accountant in a Fiat factory. From my privileged position, I saw the conditions of the manual labourers and I was drawn first to the Italian Communist Party, then to the extra-parliamentary left. In short: I journeyed all the way to terrorism. I was one of the hit squad coordinators; I planned the attacks and took part in them. I discovered I was good at two things in life: planning and shooting. I'm a killer. I murdered nine people, though I've only been sentenced for eight. The other victim was pinned on someone else, and that is who is being talked about in the video that follows. The recording was made on the 12th of September 1979, in the cellar of Bottega Rossa, a famous Primaticcio eatery at the time. The clientele was mostly left wing, though not exclusively. It was a hybrid zone, where you brushed up against all sorts of anti-statists, from the killers to the armchair theorists.

That was where we planned the murder I carried out, but which was not attributed to me. I haven't hurt anyone by not speaking up earlier since the people it was pinned on have died, including the innocent man involved. It wouldn't have made any difference. I want to make that clear. But I wouldn't have spoken, either way. The people involved in the murder, however, weren't just the actual killers. And I have now come to realise that everyone must take their share of responsibility. The video you'll see is a secret recording: the people in it didn't know I was making it. I was famous for my extreme caution. But this affair has proven me right. I needed to know who I was dealing with.

Now, if someone is watching this, and I sincerely hope it is you, Colonel Canessa, it means I'm dead. I have never been afraid of dying, but I have been afraid of not finishing what I've started. I will be entirely free in a couple of months, but it couldn't wait; the Lord showed me the way. I have never been a snitch, as I said: this is the truth. It's time it was told in full. Because what the Lord said is true: the truth shall set you free. And if I don't tell the truth, I will never be truly free. That is a fact. Don Filippo told me that it wasn't enough to tell the Lord, through him. I have to tell everyone. It is an uncomfortable, difficult, dangerous truth. I needed an honest man. I hope you understand.

And I chose you, Colonel. I've always admired you. You were as fierce as we were, but your sense of what was right was something we couldn't aspire to, no matter how hard we tried. Because you were on the right side of history, I know this now. Knowing what actually happened, you won't just keep it to yourself, you won't let it get buried. Not everyone is equal before the law: I shouted it back then and I still say it now. I have never feared the judges or man's courts. At the time, it was because I despised them and considered them slaves to power, but now I realise it's because there is no value to the justice of men. Or rather, its value is relative. I do understand that there must be rules, and someone to enforce them. I used to believe that the people were that enforcer, and that they administered this justice through me.

I was wrong, but so were you, Colonel Canessa. You served other laws, other judges.

There is only one Judge, and to Him I relinquish my spirit.

(The screen goes black before the frame changes. Petri has edited his confession before another clip. The image is clear, though visibly aged: a recording made with what was cutting edge technology at the time, but is obsolete in the third millennium. In the frame, we see what is clearly the cellar of a café or restaurant. The camera is on a shelf somewhere. In the middle of the cellar is a table, with a lightbulb hanging from the ceiling above it. There are some glasses and a bottle of wine on the table. On the walls, we see shelves of wine bottles, beer kegs, soft drinks, food. From an entrance out of frame, on the opposite side from the camera, two men walk in. Giuseppe 'Pino' Petri and Adelmo Federzoni. They look around, and then Petri sits on one of the chairs and pours himself some wine.)

FEDERZONI: You might wait.

PETRI (arrogant): For who, the two snitches we're meeting? Why do we have to meet them anyway? And why do we have to wear balaclavas? I like looking people in the eye.

FEDERZONI: Do they pay you by the question? They're not snitches. They're supporters, and we have many, even in unlikely places. You know that. And you know how crucial they are for the affirmation of our struggle.

PETRI: I don't like it. Why do we have to meet them?

(Federzoni shakes his head and hands him a balaclava.)

FEDERZONI: Pino, Pino. You're too suspicious. It's a trait that helps you to stay alive, but too much of a good thing can be bad. We have to meet them because we've decided to eliminate an investigating judge, someone who might turn out to be important. He's a potential ruthless inquisitor, someone who isn't on the front line against terrorism but is still a servant of the economic powers. And they have a name and the information we need.

(Federzoni sits down and pours himself some wine.)

PETRI (sarcastic): I thought we were supposed to wait for our 'guests'?

FEDERZONI (chuckles): I don't think they're drinkers. But remember, they're comrades. They contribute to the cause, just in another way.

PETRI: Cheers. (Looks at his watch.) One minute to go.

(Sounds of muffled knocking.)

FEDERZONI (stands up, puts on his balaclava and heads to the right, not where he came in with Petri): Put yours on.

(Petri does so. Sound of a door opening, indistinguishable voices, then Federzoni reappears with two men, also wearing balaclavas. They have on the same outfit, trousers and polo shirts in different shades of blue.)

FEDERZONI: Franco and Luca. This is Pino.

(No handshakes. The other men sit on one side of the table; Federzoni sits next to Petri.)

FEDERZONI: Okay, let's talk.

FRANCO: We have an interesting name for the brief you gave us.
  (He holds a file in his gloved hands. He places it on the table.)
PETRI: Aren't you hot with those on?

FRANCO: No, and you can never be too safe.

PETRI: Oh, I know. I'm actually fighting on the front line, unlike you.

FRANCO (wry): What is this, a political discussion or a planning meeting?

FEDERZONI: Pino, please, calm down. Don't waste time. Go on, Franco.

(Franco takes out some papers.)

FRANCO: This is all the information about the target, Rodolfo Lazzarini, investigating judge specialising in financial cases. He's not all that well known, but he's very well liked and is making a name for himself. He'll be an important judge and is already in the service of the multinational-funded imperialist state. We've highlighted two cases in which he sided with the owners rather than the workers.

FEDERZONI: Sorry, what's his name?

FRANCO: Rodolfo Lazzarini. It's all in here, address, family, routine. Whereas here…

PETRI (interrupting): Comrade, does your friend never speak? Why is he here? (He turns to Luca.)

FRANCO: Only one of us needs to explain. We conducted the research (sarcastic tone) together, but I'm the only speaker. He's here to prove his involvement. Is that okay with you?

PETRI (shrugging theatrically): It's not, but that's how it has to be (he turns to Federzoni), right comrade?

FEDERZONI (cold): It does. Franco, continue.

FRANCO: Thank you. Let's make this short. All the info is in here. And here (he takes the other paper) is the draft of a note claiming responsibility for the attack. All ready to use. You can change what you like. (Federzoni takes the paper, reads it, nods.)

FEDERZONI: That seems good to me.

PETRI: The full service.

(Federzoni stands up.)

FRANCO: Another thing.

(Petri moves his hand under the table. Franco notices but doesn't move. He smiles.)

FRANCO: You're suspicious, comrade Pino. But you can leave the gun alone. I just wanted to inform you that they've found the via Salis hideout. They're watching it. You need to vacate it.

FEDERZONI (surprised): Are you sure? I guess you are. Okay. Stay here ten minutes, then leave. I suggest one of you take the back exit, and the other go that way (he points to the door he and Petri used). You have to go past the toilets to get there. Whichever one of you goes that way, just pop inside, and pretend you were there from the start. Are we clear?

FRANCO: We're clear.

(There are no handshakes. Federzoni heads to the back exit and leaves the frame. Petri follows, walking backwards, pretending he's holding a gun. Sound of a door closing. One minute goes by in silence. Luca stands up and takes off his balaclava. It's Federico Astroni, clearly recognisable even after all this time.)

ASTRONI: Finally. I couldn't stand this any longer. Why did you drag me here?

FRANCO (also removes his balaclava. It's Giannino Salemme, several kilos thinner and with a lot more hair): Why? Because you and I are accomplices, we're on the same diving board – I jump, you jump. I've done all the dirty work so far. I even went as far as contacting these idiots, waiting for them to trust me, to consider me one of their own. I wrote the note. You wanted to stay at home, comfy and warm. But no, sir. You're in this with me.

ASTRONI: You *pretend* to be a leftist, but I never pretended. I actually believe it's possible to change the system and I believe in a more just society. I was a part of the movement and I supported some of its demands.

SALEMME (cackles): Good, now you've gone all the way, from the cultural revolution to armed conflict.

ASTRONI (sits down, puts his head in his hands): What have we done?

SALEMME (stands up, pours himself a glass of wine, then another for Astroni): We tried covering our lives, our interests, our arses.

ASTRONI (suddenly furious): You did! You and your corrupt career. You take bribes and meddle with trials. Eventually Lazzarini would have found out since he was following a fraud case that would have led him to you and your trafficking.

SALEMME (drinks, then looks at the wine still in the glass): Great stuff! These terrorists have good taste. But, my dear incorruptible colleague, you always seem to forget the part that involves *you*: you're here with me today because you also want Lazzarini out of the picture. He stole the woman of your dreams. You hate him with all your being, even more than I do.

ASTRONI (stands up and knocks the chair over): Don't you dare…

SALEMME: You're a hypocrite. You actually hate him, envy him, and it's eating you up. For me it's just business. Nothing personal, as the Godfather would say.

ASTRONI (his voice breaking): What have we done (does not sound like a question).

SALEMME: What we always do, what everyone has always done. We have conspired to remove a dangerous rival. For love and money, the most trivial and the most common reasons. (Looks at his watch.) Time to go. I'll go through the back, so I can use the toilet. I need to piss.

(They go their separate ways. All that's left in frame is the cellar, the table, the bottle, the glasses. After a few seconds, the recording ends.)

5

The Third Millennium

I

A NTONIO SAVELLI shut the laptop, his face ashen, and leaned back in the armchair. He closed his eyes. The fire had almost died out, but he couldn't move. He didn't even try stoking it, one of his favourite activities.

Canessa stood up and added some more wood. The Beretta was dangling from his finger, and he twirled it like a gunslinger. Savelli was hypnotised by the movement, and he pondered what he had just seen, the horror of that video. He felt drained, and he didn't know what to say, or above all, what to do. Something inside him had broken – his trust in people, his love for the law, his self-confidence. He knew, in that moment, that he would never be the same. And yet, he was still fighting, with every fibre of his being, against the import of that recording, against all the evidence: his right-hand man, his star pupil was nothing more than a miserable accomplice to murder. A petty man who had condemned a friend to death in order to take his wife – in his mind, one of the worst justifications for a criminal act. An act, he noted, that had not achieved its intent.

'This is meaningless. It could've been set up by anyone. We can't determine its origin, we don't know how or by whom it was recorded.' He was talking to himself more than to Canessa, without realising – or intentionally ignoring – that Petri had explicitly stated that he'd set up the camera.

Annibale, meanwhile, was playing with the poker as he put more wood on the embers. He sat down calmly. The fire crackled, the flames rose. It was cold, even though the storm had passed. The rain still pattered on the windows, but it was nowhere near as violent as earlier. It had all blown over.

'I know. It's not easy to believe. Not even after multiple viewings. It took me some time too. But the DVD hasn't been tampered with, and we have the VHS, the original source of Petri's recording. Plus, there's the priest's testimony and the original claim, which was typed on a machine from the courts. A detail that was never revealed, but has since been proven.'

Canessa was talking very casually, his voice low and without anger, as if he didn't really care whether Savelli understood and accepted what he was telling him or not. As if, for him, the whole affair was over and done with.

Savelli was about to say something, but thought better of it and kept quiet. After a few minutes, he spoke.

'What do you want?'

'What do *I* want? Actually, it's what do *you* want. I have handed you clear evidence of a conspiracy that has been going on for the past forty years. Salemme, while we're at it, was also the one who sentenced my brother to jail for no reason. Or rather, no legal reason, but with a clear motive: to stop Petri from talking to me back then. Who knows, maybe we could have avoided all these deaths.'

Savelli shook his head, still resisting. 'This is all conjecture, and the evidence has been obtained in a fraudulent manner. It could have been manipulated. We need to verify, to guarantee…'

Annibale interrupted him.

'C'mon, you've sent people to prison for much less, and without any regard for constitutional protection.'

Canessa sat studying Savelli. He had expected his reluctance. He trusted in his honesty and integrity as chief of the judiciary branch in Milan, but he also knew of his ties to Federico Astroni and could sense his turmoil. Savelli was held back by his friendship with a colleague and fear of the repercussions on Milan's courts and the magistrature in general. What Calandra had told Canessa about the conflict between the political and judicial factions now hit him. The Secret Service magistrate was a real devil, and he'd been right about this scandal, maybe even knew something about it. But it didn't make any difference. The evidence, the hard facts were there. And Canessa fully understood why Savelli might find it difficult to accept.

'You asked me what I want. I'll tell you. You see, I've never seen myself the way people have portrayed me – as a hero. I fought a dirty war – any civil war is the same. You're well aware of the methods we used back then on both sides. I've done many things I'm not proud of. But they were things that had to be done. That's it. The difference for me was never between right and wrong, moral or immoral – the lines are too blurry – but between nothingness and reality, things that are and things that aren't. Between things you shouldn't do, and things that must be done.'

Savelli was watching him, curious. 'That's a strange way of looking at the law.'

'No. It's the only way. Reality has always dictated my choices. It still does. There's a fact, a piece of evidence. At this moment in time, the fact is that this story has come to an end. Now, I'm offering you the chance to bring it to a full close using your criterion, meaning: according to the rule of law.'

'I seem to understand that you do not share that criterion, in which case...'

Canessa leaned over the table, took the DVD out of the laptop and put it in its case. He slipped the laptop into his bag, and pulled out a brown envelope. He placed the DVD in the envelope and put it on the table. He looked at Savelli.

'Everything is in here, including the VHS. Every piece of evidence. There are copies, of course, but the originals are in here.'

He picked up his bag and threw it over his shoulder.

'You still haven't told me how you came in, and how you'll be leaving.'

'It doesn't matter.'

'And you trust me with all this? I could destroy the evidence,' Savelli said, looking at the envelope and then at the fireplace, where the flames burned fiercely. 'Your copies might not be enough. Or I could rule that the evidence is insufficient, an option I'm seriously considering.'

Canessa gave him a wry smile.

'You could, true. But can you afford to?'

'What do you mean?'

'This story needs an ending, your honour, in one way or another. And if you can't end it, I will. You think you know me. You think, once a Carabiniere, always a Carabiniere, and therefore a servant of the law. It's true, I do still feel like a Carabiniere, but don't judge me according to your way of thinking. I have already shown you what I'm capable of, but I'd prefer a legitimate conclusion, in legal terms, and that, as I've already explained, is why I came to you.' He pulled a photo and some folded papers out of his jacket and placed them next to the envelope. 'It's better for you to do what has to be done. No preferential treatment, no discounts, no mercy, even if a friend is involved, a colleague. I want the total package, the one reserved for the people you hate or the powerful politicians you investigate. Handcuffs, media circus, prison. Much better than letting me have the final word, I can assure you.'

Savelli looked at the photo and the papers.

'Who's that? What does he have to do with all this?'

Canessa brought a hand to his side.

'Read the papers I've just given you. It makes for informative reading. You'll understand why it's better for me not to have the final word on the Lazzarini-Petri case.'

Savelli started reading. Two lines later, he looked up to say something, but Canessa had vanished. He ran to the window and opened it. The garden was empty, the dock abandoned. The storm had passed, the rain had stopped. There was a gentle wind, and a patch of clear sky appearing between the clouds to the east. The lake had calmed down, too. In spite of the cold night air, Savelli stood outside under the portico for at least half an hour, watching the lake.

Shortly after Savelli's return to his living room, a dark shape emerged from the water on the opposite shore of Lake Maggiore.

Stealthily, Canessa moved towards the shore, switched off his mini-sub and pulled it on land, carrying it quickly to the boot of the SsangYong SUV that Rossi had procured for the operation. He removed his wetsuit, dried off with a hair-dryer from the car and put on a dark tracksuit. After a long drink from a thermos of tea, he finally grabbed his satellite phone and called Repetto.

'So?' the marshal immediately asked.

'All said and done. Now it's up to him.'

'What if he does nothing?'

'Then we'll do what we know how to do best.'

Canessa hung up, got in the car, and headed for Milan.

Savelli made himself some toast, opened a beer, and went back to his armchair. It was past two in the morning. The silence was deafening; he couldn't hear himself think. But even if he had been able to think, it wouldn't have amounted to much. Canessa's message was clear, as was his evidence. There was little to debate. Milan's public prosecutor finished his toast and his beer, wiped his mouth with a paper napkin, picked up his mobile phone and dialled.

A sleepy voice replied.

'Yes, it's me. I apologise for the time, but I need you for a delicate matter. I'm at the lake, but I'm heading back to Milan. I'll be at the office at three. See you there.'

Savelli hung up. He'd started doing what Canessa wanted… It wasn't only Canessa who demanded it, but logic and justice. Maybe the actual end would come before dawn. With all the pain it would entail.

As Canessa said, however, it was *something that had to be done*.

2

Giannino Salemme was a heavy sleeper, with the audacity to call his 'the sleep of the just'. Even on this occasion, he came to with great difficulty. The noise that had woken him came from a great distance. Or that's what it sounded like, anyway.

The lawyer sat up in bed like a robot, his senses still dormant. No, he wasn't dreaming. Someone *was* knocking – or were they banging on the floor? Suddenly he was very much awake.

The noise stopped. He smoothed his silk pyjamas – the comfiest outfit he owned – and took a sip of water from the glass on his bedside table. He looked at the time: 5 a.m. Almost daybreak. He was still pondering the origin of the noise when his bedroom door burst open and he found himself face to face with four people and four guns.

'Police!'

'Hands over your head!'

'Quickly!'

'Hands up!'

Salemme looked at them in shock, still holding fast to his glass. They had on bulletproof vests and their badges hung round their necks. Maybe it was his glazed look or his early morning stubble, but the men gradually lowered their weapons. One went up to him and gently took the glass from his hand, setting it back down on the table. Then he invited him to stand up.

'Come with us. You're under arrest.'

The police officer pulled out a set of handcuffs and glanced at one of his colleagues. The other officer shook his head. Despite orders, they were still dealing with an old man in shock, and he might have another shock soon. They didn't want him collapsing on them.

'Please get dressed.'

Salemme took his time. He was tired, and then there was the brusque wake-up call, the drinks last night... He was trying to gather his wits, but it wasn't easy with all those police staring at him. He was being arrested, most likely because of the Petri case. Maybe Claudio had been right. He should have stayed in the States and gone somewhere else from there. But maybe they didn't have that much on him. Maybe he could still figure something out.

He finished getting dressed and walked out into the corridor with the police. He'd started thinking like Giannino Salemme again: the man who had never been put in a corner. He was just about to say something to restore his reputation when he saw his son's body on the ground by the kitchen door.

Salemme suddenly felt weak, and had to lean against the wall. There were four bullet holes in Claudio's loose white shirt, and a pool of blood was seeping from his body. The officer behind him reached out to support him, but Salemme pulled his arm away.

'You bastards! You killed him,' he said in a strangled voice.

The police officers looked at him, some with pity, some with distaste.

'He asked for it. He was the bastard.'

A man stepped forward: Silvestrin, chief of Milan's rapid response team. Salemme knew him. He'd once successfully defended a killer and let him go, ridiculing Silvestrin for the loss of all evidence against the man – a situation Salemme had orchestrated by bribing one of the clerks. Now he was savouring his revenge, Salemme thought bitterly.

Silvestrin dragged him away from the wall and pushed him towards the corridor leading to Claudio's personal entrance. 'Look.'

On the ground was a man with a hole in the middle of his forehead. Another was being moved onto a stretcher.

'That man down there was serving the State, just doing his job. He had a family. What the fuck was your imbecile of a son

394

doing with a gun? Where the hell did he think he could go? Piece of shit!'

Salemme reverted to being the old man he was underneath it all. But Silvestrin wasn't the least bit moved. He'd clocked his team's compassionate attitude, and he turned to them next.

'Don't be fooled! This man is a criminal, a venomous snake. *Cuff him now!*'

3

'It's hard to believe, but I'm glad this story has come to an end, one way or another.'

Federico Astroni had slept a couple of hours – peacefully, considering the circumstances. Before bed the previous night, he'd read an interesting essay on Robespierre, thinking that there were some interesting parallels between himself and the main protagonist during the Reign of Terror. He'd then got up at 5 a.m. to work on the forthcoming trial and to wash and shave. Quite a figure, he thought of himself, just as someone rang the doorbell. One of the Carabinieri from his security detail? He looked out of the window to the spot were his 'guardian angels' always parked. The car was there and Astroni could see a couple of people looking at a sheet of paper. What were they up to?

The doorbell's shrill sound again… He was hoping he'd just imagined it the first time. Maybe it was part of a dream he hadn't quite shaken off…

But no. It rang a third time.

'Yes?' Astroni answered.

'Federico, please let me in.'

'Antonio?'

Astroni's surprise lasted less than a second. He went to unlock his door. A few minutes, and the cranky old lift rattled its way up and stopped at his floor. Savelli stepped out, followed by Virgili, the head of the criminal investigation department. Virgili stopped at the door, holding it open for Savelli, and Astroni noticed the look the two exchanged.

'It won't be necessary,' Savelli said when Virgili made to follow them inside.

Savelli and Astroni sat across from each other in the living room. How many times had they done so on the eve of a crucial trial or an arrest that would raise a storm? After one of their many victories or rare defeats, to celebrate or simply to enjoy one another's company? Savelli liked coming here at all times of day or night – though, admittedly, he had never shown up at this hour before. He'd sit surrounded by the Milanese furniture – the wood, glass, mirrors, and rugs… That solid sense of bourgeois progress. He was from a small village in southern Italy, but he'd started coming to the house when Federico's mother was still alive. He always sat in the same armchair so he could admire the Boccioni painting, bought directly from the artist by Astroni's grandfather. Both Astroni and Savelli loved it.

Savelli looked straight at Astroni. He'd been tense and distracted in recent weeks, Savelli now remembered. But above all, he'd been obsessed with the hunt for Canessa, pushing the idea of drug-trafficking as the motive behind the entire string of deaths, from Petri to Alfridi and the Camorra killers. Astroni had also contributed to the framing.

His own resistance to Canessa suddenly crumbled. It wasn't just what he'd heard Astroni say; there was a solid logic to the route

Canessa had taken and which he too could now see as a straight line. Everything Canessa had maintained, everything he'd discovered had gained a concrete reality that could not be demolished.

'Antonio, are you there?'

Savelli snapped out of his reverie.

'*Why?*'

The question hung between them, but the answer never came. The moment Astroni started explaining, Savelli cut in.

'You lost your mind over a woman to the point that you conspired to kill your friend, a judge like you. And to defend that secret, you kept killing.'

'I never killed anyone.'

Savelli exploded. 'Stop fucking lying! Jesus Christ, all these deaths. All because of lust.'

Federico Astroni slammed his fist down on the table. There was a flurry of quick footsteps and Virgili came into the room, Beretta in hand.

Savelli stood up between him and Astroni.

'It's fine. Please return to your post.'

'But, your honour…'

'Please, I am in no danger.'

Astroni was still seated, his head drooping. The officer gone, he looked up, eyes burning.

'She wasn't the object of my *lust*. She wasn't my *desire*. She was *the love of my life*. There has never been anyone like her. Not a single woman amongst all those I've been with – and there have been many – is worth the perfect toenails of her feet. She'd paint them blue in the summer, when she wore lemon-yellow sandals and a yellow sun dress.' Astroni was drifting off into a grotesque sentimental trance which Savelli found deeply disconcerting. But

Astroni gathered himself together. 'Everything I've done since the corruption inquiries – all the shows I put on, even when they went against my personality – it was all in the hope of winning her back. But no. She called me once to compliment me, and to tell me that Rodolfo would have been proud. She was too! But not enough to come and see me in person.'

Savelli stared at him uncomprehendingly. 'You killed Rodolfo. You conspired with terrorist scum, you hired a pack of bloodthirsty killers to track down and murder a judge, a colleague, a friend. You struck deals with the Camorra, tampered with evidence, arrested innocent people, and conspired with Giannino Salemme, a corrupt magistrate and dirty lawyer guilty of countless crimes. Your hands are as filthy as his…'

Savelli ran a hand through his hair and looked outside. The sun was rising just behind the curtains. He should have been setting sail right about now, alone on the lake… Instead, here he was, drowning in the horror of betrayal, overcome by the stench of rot.

'There is no proof of my involvement in what you've just alleged. If there is, my guilt is only moral. There's nothing tangible.' Of course, there was that foreign SIM card Salemme had given him… but he had already removed it and tossed it down a drain.

Savelli looked at that man who had been his pride and joy, the son he'd always wanted. His protégé was a backstabber, a character from an Ancient Greek tragedy. But this one had none of the pathos of Aeschylus. This was a banal scene, driven by bestial instincts.

There were no further extenuating circumstances, and after the final protests, Savelli stood up. 'Virgili,' he called.

The officer ran in, this time without his gun.

Savelli moved in towards Astroni, his eyes only inches from his former protégé's. 'Moral guilt? I almost feel sorry for you, Federico. There is plenty of evidence, trust me.' He turned back to Virgili.

'Handcuffs, please.'

4

'Shoot!'

Carla Trovati rubbed her sleepy eyes. She still couldn't entirely believe the scene unfolding before her. Even the photographer had hesitated, holding his camera in his hands. He only started using it with Carla's piercing yell.

The town clock showed just past 6 a.m. The heat was already simmering, and the sun, high in the sky, would soon bring things to the boil. Last night's storm had done nothing to clear things up.

Carla had gone home at 1.45 after her long night shift, completely soaked. When she'd got in to the office, the weather seemed perfectly stable. When she'd left the *Corriere*, the worst had passed, but it was still pouring.

She'd showered and settled down on the sofa, with a book and a mug of herbal tea.

She dozed off for a few minutes until the phone woke her. It was her landline, and only two or three people had that number. One of them was Annibale. Carla picked up halfway through the second ring.

It wasn't Annibale.

'Miss Trovati, could you please open your front door?'

'Who is this?'

399

'It doesn't matter. Please open the door! We don't have much time.'

She couldn't place the voice, but it sounded kind, so she went to her door, still holding the phone. She wasn't really afraid, but she picked up a knife from the kitchen on her way.

She opened the door to find a yellow envelope taped to it. She took it down, careful not tear it. Inside were some papers and a stiff object – maybe a DVD case.

'I have it,' she said to the unknown voice.

'Good. Now listen: after we hang up, take a quick look at the contents and the summary. You don't have much time. We suggest you station yourself in front of Federico Astroni's house as soon as you can get there. You might also consider Giannino Salemme, but we recommend Astroni. Take a photographer with you. This may be story of the century.'

'Who is…'

'Good luck.'

Click.

The voice had been kindly, with a hint of an accent from the Swiss Alps.

Carla opened the envelope and started reading quickly, as instructed. As she did so, a shiver ran down her spine. Next, she watched the DVD. She was shocked rigid.

Think, Carla. And before anything else, get dressed!

She threw off her pyjamas, splashed her face with cold water and sprayed a cloud of deodorant. She slipped into a pair of jeans and a green polo shirt, then dumped all her work equipment into a bag. She'd almost left the flat when she turned around and looked at the envelope and its contents on the table. She went back and collected it all and put that in the bag too.

'I'm not fucking leaving you behind.'

On the landing, she dialled a number on her mobile.

'Tirelli? It's Carla. I know it's late – well, early. Yes, I'm a piece of shit. But listen. I have an explosive story. Get dressed and meet me in piazza del Carmine. *Im-me-di-ate-ly.*'

She watched as one of Italy's most famous magistrates, Federico Astroni – symbol of law and justice – walked out of his house in handcuffs. He'd been arrested by his friend and mentor Antonio Savelli, who now walked a few metres behind him.

But Carla wasn't thinking of the fact that she'd soon be one of Italy's most famous journalists, with TV interviews and a column with her photo and byline.

No, just as Tirelli, as excited as a monkey in mating season, was hopping back and forth across the street in order to catch the unsuspecting Astroni from every angle, Carla was thinking: *now that this story is over, there is nothing left to figure out or to be afraid of. And maybe, just maybe I'll be able to find Annibale again.*

All she could think about was how his hands felt on her skin.

5

By now, Chief Magistrate Calandra didn't even have to ask. The girl (she may have been twenty-four, but to him she was a girl) would just slip into her thong and dance by the light of the moon.

That night, however, the moon was covered by rain and heavy clouds, and she'd holed up in bed. They were in a resort in the Lazio countryside, famous for its low carbon footprint (which mattered very little to Calandra) and the quality of its food, from breakfast to dinner to midnight snacks (he cared about that a lot more). The young woman lay next to him shivering, her nipples pressed against his skin.

A good feeling. He'd fallen asleep like that, without any further action. He wasn't an old creep, just a man who enjoyed the finer things in life, and holding a frightened woman in his arms during a storm was one of them.

He was sleeping quite soundly – even his prostate was behaving that night – when he heard a voice.

'Darling…'

The girl was straddling him and looking at him kindly. She had his phone.

'Sorry, it kept ringing and I saw it said *Office* so I answered for you… I thought it might be urgent. Did I do anything wrong?'

Calandra stroked her toned butt cheek and took the BlackBerry from her. She removed her thong and looked at him with a twinkle in her eye.

'Hello,' he said. She started kissing his chest and gradually moved lower, towards his groin.

The grey man spoke from the bunker.

'They've arrested Astroni and Giannino Salemme, the lawyer, former magistrate…'

'I know him. Quite the résumé. Really? So he was the other man. That's not entirely surpris— ah!'

'Is everything okay?'

'Yes, yes… go on…' His voice went down a pitch, and his breathing was becoming heavier.

'Canessa has discovered Petri's confession and handed it over to Savelli, who arrested Astroni in person. The *Corriere* website has an exclusive gallery of the arrest, with Astroni in handcuffs.

The first comments are all about Savelli's great clean-up job. Not exactly what we were going for...'

Calandra took a long breath. 'No, but it is a result. It'll shake the tree a bit, and force some people to quieten down. With this kind of operation, complete success is hard to achieve. We can settle for that, and so will our contacts. You did well, we did well. We bet on the right horse. He may not have broken the record for speed, but he won. Now we can relax. See you on Monday.'

His speech was slurred, but he felt great. And he was about to feel even better.

6

A Saturday evening in June. It wasn't technically a celebration or a farewell party, but Annibale Canessa, Ivan Repetto and Piercarlo Rossi allowed themselves a bottle of champagne, some Pata Negra ham, and some French cheese in the safe house in largo Rio de Janeiro.

Repetto had sunk into an armchair, where he was downing glass after glass. His eyes were black and blue, as so often when he'd been part of the anti-terrorism team and they'd brought in a fugitive and closed down an investigation.

Rossi looked at him and nodded.

'You know, I'm going to miss this a little. I've had a great time with you. I can honestly say you've been the only people to shake up my life a bit, both then and now.'

'Don't be stupid,' Repetto growled, draining another glass.

Canessa had woken up in the late afternoon. He ate some breakfast and turned on the TV. All the channels were broadcasting the same images of Federico Astroni's arrest, on a loop from the *Corriere della Sera* website. He watched TV on mute for some time, then showered and waited.

Shortly after Repetto and Rossi's arrival at the safe house, Antonio Savelli's press conference had started. Canessa had listened until he heard what he needed to hear.

'…Annibale Canessa, retired lieutenant colonel of the Carabinieri, is no longer a wanted man: his arrest warrant has been recalled and he is no longer a suspect. We do, however, request his presence in our offices to record his testimony as a material witness.'

Caterina had sent him a text: *You're a man who keeps his promises, but I already knew that. If you ever need somewhere to hide, there's a bed waiting for you…* From the way she put it, he knew he wouldn't actually get much sleep in that bed – at least, not until her wedding.

He remembered Caterina with affection and erotic longing, but Canessa had already decided to call Carla when he got home. It was time to come out of hiding, to go back to his real life. He longed to resume his dawn swim, when the only sound in the San Fruttuoso bay was made by the waves. And he wanted Carla to dive in with him. He had a prickly feeling, however, that for people like him, real rest and tranquillity were not permanent. Sooner or later he would find himself caught up in an adventure like the one he'd just concluded. For the moment, though, he wouldn't ask questions or make long-term plans.

He could hear Repetto and Rossi arguing behind him. He poured some more champagne and cut himself a piece of Cantal. 'What are you two on about?'

Repetto pointed to Rossi. 'He's delirious, spouting nonsense. He just said that *the fellowship of the ring is broken*. What does that mean?'

Canessa smiled at Rossi and put his hand on his shoulder. 'It may be a little pretentious, but I get it. Ivan, did you ever read Tolkien? *The Lord of the Rings?*'

'Are you talking about those interminable fake medieval films?'

Canessa chuckled. 'Ask your grandchildren and they'll tell you all about it.'

'Okay, so who's my character?' Repetto asked.

'If I've got this right, I should be Aragorn, and you're either Sam, Frodo's devoted companion or the ugly dwarf, Gimli. What would you say, Rossi?'

'You've nailed it!'

'Fuck off!' With a smile, Repetto went off to open another bottle of champagne.

EPILOGUE

C ALANDRA LOVED SUMMER, since it meant he could finally wear his colourful linen suits and silk shirts. Most of all, it meant he could reach into the precious box containing his tailored panama hat, made for him by someone as mad as the hatter in *Alice in Wonderland* (and just as magically talented) with a shop on a small street in Tegucigalpa, the capital of Honduras.

The hat fit him perfectly, but it served many other purposes. Sometimes, it was a personal fan. Calandra belonged to a group of people who believe that August is actually less hot than June or July, but that day was testing his theory. Despite the sun umbrella, the terrace and the shade, the air was absolutely still, even on the beach. He should have come in the evening rather than midday, when he might even have needed a light cashmere jumper. Eventually he took off his jacket and draped it over the chair. He hated doing that, even in summer. But this was a special case.

Thankfully, the oppressive heat had not affected his menu choices: mussels *sauté* and Portofino-style scampi, spaghetti with seafood, and the fried fish of the day. He'd made his way through the *sauté* and the scampi and was waiting for the pasta. He saw the waitress bringing it over. Quite the show, both the dish and the waitress. The cook had been generous (he knew people here), and now the waitress was showing as much tanned skin as she could in her denim short shorts and a white tank top. Her legs were toned and muscular, and despite the apron bearing the name of the place, La Zia, he could glimpse two perfect breasts, unrestrained by a bra. It was hot today, after all, and she could definitely pull it off. Calandra arranged his large napkin over his monogrammed blue shirt. He had another in a bag on the boat, just in case.

The waitress brushed past the restaurant owner, who was coming out of the kitchen with a plate of *trofie al pesto*, complete with potatoes and green beans. When they came close, she teasingly patted his side.

Considering that Calandra was their last customer, the owner returned the favour with a light slap on her delightful behind. It would have been workplace harassment anywhere else – but in this case, you didn't want to harass the owner, Calandra thought. Anyone who'd tried to do so before had come out of it badly.

The owner reached Calandra's table.

'May I?'

Calandra bowed, flourishing his panama hat. 'Take a seat, Inspector Canessa.'

The two men ate in silence, with the occasional pleasantry on either side.

'Would you like to taste some *trofie*, your excellency?'

'This excellency happily obliges.'

When they'd finished, the waitress came to clear the table.

'Was everything to your liking?' she asked teasingly.

'It was, thank you,' Calandra replied gallantly.

She came back with the fried fish. Calandra squeezed some lemon over it.

'Care for some?'

'Thank you, but I've got enough with the *trofie.*'

When the coffee and limoncello arrived, Canessa accepted a half Toscano. 'I've only smoked them with Repetto in the past, but I'll make an exception.'

'I'd consider it an honour.'

Canessa smiled. Once the puffs of smoke had cleared, Canessa looked at Calandra.

'I wasn't expecting a visit from you. I thought you might be annoyed at me for having involved Savelli.'

Calandra waved his hand, as if to shoo away a bug. 'No, no, it was fine this way. Petri's recording clearly showed that the judiciary branch is filled with people like us, capable of betrayal and terrible deeds. Not always above the law. That was enough for my contacts. I even received a bonus, though you did all the hard work.'

'It had to be done.'

'You know, your way of thinking has always intrigued me. So out of the box, so ethical without being moralistic. We're headed for troubling times, and we need men like you who go beyond surface impressions and take a fresh look at reality.'

Canessa smiled. 'Are you offering me a job?'

'Maybe not full employment. It doesn't work like that any more. But a contract, perhaps.'

Canessa poured him some more limoncello, then topped up his own. He hadn't been expecting the offer. 'I'm reaching a certain age.'

'Ah, but this is a job you can do at any age. And you seem in good shape, to judge from the past few months.'

Canessa couldn't pretend he wasn't intrigued. He wasn't doing badly with the restaurant, and the money was good. Yet despite its tragic nature and the death of innocent people – his brother, Alfridi and Panattoni's girlfriend – the adventure had reawakened in him a taste for the only job he was really cut out to do.

'I'll think about it. I'm sure you're not expecting a reply in the middle of August.'

'Of course not.'

They sat in silence. Before long, a gentle breeze picked up and Calandra asked for the bill.

'Your excellency, please don't insult me – it's on the house.'

'Given your generosity, I wonder if you'd answer two questions for this old keeper of secrets.'

'I will if I can.'

'The first: I'm pretty sure you gave Savelli a little nudge,' Calandra narrowed his eyes like a cat's. 'I don't believe that he was very anxious to be involved, despite the evidence. What did you do?'

Canessa stood up. 'Well done.' He headed into the restaurant. After a few minutes, he came back with a photo for Calandra. It showed a tall man with thinning hair, dressed in a Carabinieri uniform.

Calandra looked at the photo in surprise. 'I know this man! What's his name again…'

'He was your colleague.'

'Yes, of course! He went by Colonel Baccini. He belonged to a different branch of the Secret Service, something a little more borderline, if you catch my drift. A leftover from the infamous classified cases.' Calandra screwed up his face, as if something had come back to him. 'Now I remember: he jumped off the roof of a loft that he'd bought with our money, along with many other things. They said his family had left him: his wife had figured everything out and was suing him for a six-figure divorce deal. Some of those close to him were extremely embarrassed by the whole ordeal. But what does he have to do with all this?'

'I gave Savelli a document containing the story. You'll have to hear it in person – if you're not in a rush.'

'Fresh air, good food, great company.' He bowed again. 'I'm all ears.'

When Canessa finished talking, Calandra was even more impressed. 'My dear Canessa, there were rumours back then about via Gaeta, but I had no idea about any of this. The story does confirm that you are an intimidating man. Savelli got your message loud and clear. If he hadn't brought the story to its conclusion the "good" way, someone would've got hurt.'

Canessa untied his apron and stood up. 'It was something that had to be done.'

'I agree.'

They shook hands.

'Please consider my offer.'

'I will. But you said you had two questions.'

'True. The second is about your beautiful waitress. What is Italy's most famous journalist doing waiting tables instead of spending her time in posh clubs, enjoying her success?'

Canessa looked around for Carla and detected movement behind the mosquito screen. He smiled: once a journalist, always a journalist. She'd listened in on everything. She was a little like him, after all. He moved closer to Calandra and whispered.

'She's making amends.'

'For what?'

'A terrible sin. I offered her atonement if she worked here for the season. And to be honest, I had something to confess myself. Less terrible, but there we are. We're looking for some balance. It's a trial period for both of us.'

'I've never had you down as a merciful man. At least, not after what you just told me.'

'Your excellency, I've committed many sins, and just like her, I've had my issues with trust. We are all in need of forgiveness.'

Calandra burst out laughing and put the panama hat back on his head.

'Amen.'

ACKNOWLEDGEMENTS

I have many people to thank, starting with those who were willing to listen to my doubts and correct my mistakes: Deputy Chief Magistrate Samuele De Lucia for his friendship; Sandro Raimondi, the Brescia assistant prosecutor, who introduced me to the justice machine; Pietro Alibani, who enlightened me about firearms; Alfio Caruso for his knowledge of organised crime. Any mistakes are mine alone. Thank you to my friends over at Rizzoli: Massimo, Sabrina, Michele and Stefano, who took care of the editing, and were excited to work with me and Annibale Canessa; I hope we haven't let them down. Thanks to Rosaria, as always, for her support. I would never have reached the end, however, had it not been for Emanuela, Cecilia, Rachele, and Giovanni, who filled the gaps with their presence. Thank you to all of you for coming this far. As Annibale would say, this was something that had to be done, and I did it.

P.S.: The novel is dedicated to Gérard de Villiers, an extraordinary, prolific and knowledgeable French writer and the first to bewitch me with his noir books when I was a teenager. I followed at least a few of his rules in my book.

ALSO AVAILABLE
IN THE WALTER PRESENTS LIBRARY